THE VISITOR

The Visitor

With illustrations by Mark Walker

MARILYNN LYNNE BERRY

SCOTFORTH BOOKS

Copyright © Marilynn Lynne Berry, 2003

Thanks to Birmingham Library Services
for the use of the photographs on pages 29 and 33

First published in 2003 on behalf of the author
by Scotforth Books,
Carnegie House,
Chatsworth Road,
Lancaster LA1 4SL,
England
Tel: +44(0)1524 840111
Fax: +44(0)1524 840222
email: info@scotforthbooks.com

All rights reserved.
Unauthorised duplication
contravenes existing laws.

British Library Cataloguing-in-Publication data
A catalogue record for this book is available from the British Library

ISBN 1,904244,31,9

Typeset by Carnegie Publishing
Printed and bound in the UK by The Alden Press, Oxford

Preface

This story is based on the life of a real person and real events. Louisa May Hirons' younger life was always a mystery, even to members of her own family. Her story starts in the early 1900s in the city of Birmingham, England, when Edward, Prince of Wales was about to ascend to the English throne as King Edward VII. This period of history was called the Edwardian era.

Without warning, in my subconscious and sometimes quite conscious moments, Louisa May Hirons' ghostly form would appear. The air around me filling with gardenia perfume and the sound of and her infectious girlish laughter were my first clues that she was coming to transport me back to her life in Edwardian England, whereupon I would become the ghost in her time!

These transportations became, over a period of five years, more frequent and unnerving experiences. After the second visitation by Louisa May, it became apparent that she wanted me to know something, pointing out clues which I invariably missed. This necessitated Louisa May having to guide me over the same part of her story again, observing the scene from a different angle, so that I would pick up the clue.

From an unsolicited contact with a clairvoyant, Louisa May communicated a message to me 'to write her story first' as at the time I was engrossed in writing children's books. This uncanny experience motivated me to redouble my efforts to complete her story.

So read on and see what you make of it.

Did these occurrences really happen, or was it all … just a dream?

*Lynne Berry would like to thank all her many friends, especially Trisha and Eddie, for their encouragement whilst writing this novel.
Lynne would especially like to thank her Father and mentor, Harry Walker, and Connie, her Mother, for their loyal support.*

Foreword

As with all the accounts in my research into after death communication, Lynne's experiences were all spontaneous and she had not actively sought communication from the beyond. As this novel portrays, sometimes, experiences convey information to the experiencer they did not previously know or could not otherwise have known but can be researched and later proven. Other examples I have studied have included the deceased locating missing money or heirlooms, or a warning to the experiencer of a previously unknown danger or imminent danger. Sometimes, events are predicted or the deceased offers reassurance about a current issue which is troubling the experiencer. Some even assist in lottery wins – indeed, Teri Bonfield took a share in a £15 million lottery prize after a dream inspired ADC!

Not predicting or locating mass fortune, what Lynne's visitations have done is provide the material to piece together bit by bit the goings on of Louisa May's colourful life which she has cleverly, thoughtfully and sensitively adapted into this most wonderful book – a book which she seemingly had no choice but to write. *The Visitor* is beautifully written outlining Louisa's communications, via dreams, to Lynne. The only unusual factor here being the length of communication and the facts given – in most instances the deceased appears in a special dream to give a last goodbye or a message of comfort. As with Lynne, the recipients did not will the communication; it is as if the deceased loved one chose to communicate within the 'dream'.

Lynne's account of Louisa May had me intrigued from the start as I am sure it will you – this really is an extraordinary story. Even more so extraordinary to me is the synchronicity which brought Lynne to me and then her writing this book as I was writing my second on this very topic – both completely unbeknownst to the other and on a more personal level, the place where Louisa May's story takes place has particular intrigue – I was brought up in Harborne and Edgbaston and attended Edgbaston High School from the age of three to eighteen. Many a day after school I would go back to friends houses, some of them large mansions in the Edgbaston vicinity – I can't help but try to wrack my memory as to whether any contained a writing bureau!

Emma Heathcote-James MA
Worcestershire, May 2003.

CHAPTER I

The Visit

How to begin my story presented some difficulty. It could be said that this story is mostly fictitious, but I can only write of my own experiences. Read on and capture the same magic that has enveloped my life for so long ...

I began to look forward to ecstatic happiness when my visitor came to me, spending time together in fun and frolic; I would know my ghostly visitor was nearby as the air around me would fill with a perfume and a sense of excitement and happiness. She would then appear, her young arms beckoning to me to join her and I had no hesitation in doing so. I felt no fear but just a longing for her visits during which I would try to question her.

'Who are you, what do you want with me? Do you want me to do something for you, or to give someone a message? What is it you want?'

My visitor would just giggle and swirl around me again and again until we both collapsed with laughter. I really did not care why she had come to me or chosen me as her earthly contact – I just longed for the happiness I felt inside myself when she visited.

Could this be just a dream – it surely must be, but it seemed so real. My visitor and I had such marvellously happy times together; we walked together through the mists of time passing friendly faces and familiar places on our frequent journeys but never stopping at any given point on the way. We always ended up at the same destination, an elegant Edwardian house with the name of Sycamore House on its plaque.

Could there be some purpose for her visitations? She was so beautiful and looking at her refined features and Edwardian clothes she lacked for nothing from the material world.

My visitor turned and smiled at me. She didn't ever speak to me, but just giggled or smiled, pointing insistently at the elegant Edwardian house we kept visiting together, pushing me forwards to go inside with her through the large oak panelled front door. We walked together into the hallway which was lavishly furnished and I observed the people inside going about their daily routines. As I looked around, to my amazement, no one seemed to notice me, but my ghostly visitor was now mortal and was being embraced by the people inside the house. She chatted endlessly to them,

The Visitor

especially to another young woman of about her own age. I tried to speak to her, but she just did not hear me or, it seemed, see me at all; it was as if I were the ghostly visitor in her time. I tried to signal to her, push her, prod her, but it was no good, for there was no recognition in her beautiful face that I was there at all. Perhaps she, my visitor, needed me to observe something, but I didn't mind, as I was enjoying my visit and the happy family atmosphere all around me in the very tasteful and comfortable surroundings.

Walking across the large hallway and peering through an open doorway into the family sitting room, I noticed that there were various family paraphernalia and silver framed family photographs carefully placed on the mantelshelf. Picking up one of the photographs, I realised, it was her, my visitor and inscribed on the photograph was: *To Mother and Father, all my love, Louisa May aged 16 years, 1908.*

I looked across the hallway at my beautiful young visitor, busily engaged with her friend, chattering feverishly and laughing loudly. I tried to attract her attention, but she was completely oblivious to me.

'It's you, isn't it? You are this, this girl, Louisa May?'

I tried to take the silver framed photograph from the mantelshelf to take it over to Louisa May, my visitor, but I was not able to lift it. So I rushed across to where she was sitting, trying to attract her attention, but it was no good, she didn't see or hear me. Louisa May just shuddered and remarked:

'Isn't it cold in here – do you feel it Jacqueline? You wouldn't think it was summer time would you?'

Louisa May went over to the lounge window and closed it firmly, with Jacqueline looking puzzled at her remark. At least I knew her name, but I was still bewildered as to why I had been chosen or, if you like, privileged to be in this beautiful family home called Sycamore House.

Suddenly the two young girls ran into the huge drawing room giggling, followed by a very serious-looking young man, somewhat older I thought – perhaps a relative? I tried communicating with them all, but it was of no use, to them I was invisible. Louisa May looked blissfully happy. This was obviously some sort of spiritual experience, something I had never believed in or thought possible but which, all the same, did seem to be happening to me! I had been chosen to document something from long ago in which Louisa May had been involved, whoever she was. Whatever it was she wanted the world or perhaps me to know, I couldn't imagine as everything looked so normal and happy inside Sycamore House. The laughter of the two girls echoed all around the large house and surely this was a very happy home.

I walked into different rooms in the house, completely undetected and it seemed that I could will myself wherever I liked; there seemed no limits. I

The Visitor

then suddenly realised that I was the ghostly visitor in Louisa May's Edwardian days.

I observed Louisa May running over to a much older woman who was seated on a heavily buttoned wine-coloured leather chair. She kissed her tenderly on her cheek; they obviously had great affection for one another.

The older woman spoke.

'Come on you two girls, play me a tune on the piano. I am sure Bertie would love to hear you play, wouldn't you Bertie?'

The older woman hugged Bertie close to her.

'Mother, don't!' Bertie showed some embarrassment especially in front of the other young woman, and he blushed awkwardly.

I thought, this must be Louisa May's mother and brother, but who is the other young woman? She looks nothing like Louisa and Bertie, with tight, curly, vibrant red hair and bright green eyes. I walked around and around them studying each person very carefully, everyone unaware of my presence. Louisa May pulled at the sleeve of the delicately framed young woman insistently dragging her towards the piano.

'Come on Jacqueline, do play, I am sure Bertie would just love to hear you play, wouldn't you dear brother?'

Louisa May gave her usual infectious giggle to everyone's amusement, prodding Bertie affectionately, which made him blush.

Observing the group, I had by now gathered that Bertie had some affection for Jacqueline. He was, there was no doubt, attracted to her and it seemed Jacqueline felt likewise, as she also blushed but started to play a Chopin Impromptu with great musical sympathy.

'Don't you just love Chopin, mother?' Louisa May hugged her mother.

Thank you Louisa May, I thought, I have all the characters in place now. Bertie the brother, the older woman her mother, but who is this Jacqueline? Perhaps a friend? Maybe Bertie's girlfriend or fiancée, but she has no rings on her fingers, so she is not engaged or married. Perhaps she is Louisa May's friend? Yes, that would be it, I thought.

Bertie moved towards the piano studying Jacqueline more closely, making it obvious to all that he had great affection for her.

'Bravo, bravo!' Mother Hirons clapped her hands. 'That was exceptional dear, you will go far in the music world, so do keep up your studies. I only wish Louisa May would do the same: you see, she lacks commitment dear, and she would be so very good if only she practiced like you Jacqueline.'

Mother Hirons gave Jacqueline a hug, looking across at her lovely daughter, but Louisa May was oblivious to her mother's comments, flicking her fingers through endless sheets of music, finding another piece for Jacqueline to play.

'Don't scold Louey mother, she does her best. When she does play it is something enchanting to listen to and it's better to have enchantment

The Visitor

occasionally than nothing at all, don't you think?'

Bertie put his arms around Louisa May who was completely engrossed in her sheet music and had not heard a word.

'How many times, dear Bertie, do I have to tell you to call Louisa May by her proper name, not this Louey business; it is so unbecoming dear.'

Mother Hirons bristled with annoyance.

'But Mother, you call me Bertie, everyone does, so what is the difference?'

Bertie sat down on the piano stool next to Jacqueline running his fingers over the ivory keys. Louisa slumped herself over the top of the piano taking the biggest ripe, red apple out of the fruit bowl, crunching into it loudly with her teeth.

'Louisa May, dear, please, have some decorum.'

Mother Hirons couldn't help but laugh at her unladylike daughter, with Bertie and Jacqueline sniggering at Louisa's total unawareness.

'Don't mind mother, Louey, you carry on munching and don't mind us.'

Bertie pinched the side of Louisa's cheek with everyone reduced to hoots of laughter as she took centre stage and continued to noisily crunch on her ripe apple, purposely annoying her beloved mother.

'Come on you three, Sarah has made some delicious teacakes for us all. Let's go through to the dining room; perhaps a few teacakes will stop Louisa May crunching on my apples.'

Everyone laughed at Mother Hirons, following her through to the dining room. High tea had been elegantly laid out on the dining table by Sarah who had worked hard in the kitchen all day baking the teacakes and other tasty food. Mother Hirons sighed.

'Ah, these teacakes, they are so delicious; who could ever improve on Sarah's cooking? Come, dears, your father will be home soon, so after we have finished our teacakes, I suggest we all get changed ready for dinner at 7 p.m. You know how your father hates to be kept waiting for his dinner?'

Mother Hirons gripped back a strand of fallen hair.

'Mother, may Jacqueline, Bertie and I go to see Lillie Lantry at the new theatre in the city? She is appearing in a few weeks' time so do you think father would allow us all to go?' Louisa May quizzed her Mother's frowning face.

'Well, what a stupid question girl. I am sure he would most definitely not let you all go, why the very idea of it! Whatever next? You know what your father is like. He has very strong views about that sort of thing and I am sure he would never listen to your reason for wanting to go so why ask the question of him in the first place dear, when you know what the answer will be?'

Mother Hirons gave one of her glares towards all the young expectant faces.

The Visitor

'But, Mother, Lillie Langtry is so very famous, anyone who is anyone will be there, won't they Jacqueline, Bertie?'

Jacqueline and Bertie nodded back to Louisa in complete agreement with everything she was saying.

'Well,' Mother Hirons sighed, 'I must admit, I have heard that the show is a wonderful one and I suppose other acts will appear on stage as well, not just that woman ... let me put it this way ... I shall talk to your father, but I can't promise anything.'

'Oh, Mother, thank you, thank you, I shall wear my new pink gown with the –'

Louisa May chattered profusely, firstly to Jacqueline, then to Bertie.

'Now, now, I only said I would ask, Louisa, don't you get thinking it is a definite outing now, you know what your father is like; such a stickler with these sort of things.'

Louisa May jumped from her seat, kissing her mother's face all over with premature gratitude. Jacqueline and Bertie giggled at her enthusiasm.

'Come on you youngsters, I can't believe it, we have eaten nearly all Sarah's delicious teacakes. Time to get ready for your father, we must look our best for dinner. The prettier we all look, the more likely your father will say "yes".'

Mother Hirons gave one of her icy stares at Louisa May, who jumped up from her dining chair, rushed into the hallway and ran up the thickly carpeted stairway two at a time as she usually did, much to her mother's annoyance at her undignified tomboy antics.

Mother Hirons shuffled out into the hallway and started to climb the steep stairs slowly as she found each step more difficult to climb, owing to her arthritis and swollen leg veins, which were becoming more and more painful.

Jacqueline was shown to the guest room, with Bertie wishing that he could follow her. There was no doubt in my mind from the tender look he gave Jacqueline that Bertie was deeply in love.

Louisa May's bedroom was lavishly furnished and equipped with a dressing room leading off the main bedroom and I observed her pulling various gowns out of her huge walk-in wardrobe and trying them against herself for colour and design; all were most elegant. I thought Louisa May a very fortunate young woman to have all those beautiful gowns.

I was still baffled, to say the least, as to why I was privy to all these events, but continued to observe Louisa May and the rest of her family: in fact, I was quite enjoying myself, as she was such a joy to watch, her likeable personality being something rare, even in those far-off days.

The young people had assembled downstairs ready for dinner but mother was still dressing upstairs and Father Hirons had not yet arrived home. It was nearly seven o'clock and Sarah, the cook and household maid, was rushing to and fro between the kitchen and dining room making sure that everything was ready and perfect for the family dinner.

'Louisa, you look so lovely, is that your new dress you were telling me about?' Jacqueline stroked Louisa's dress made of satin and lace. 'It is really exquisite, your father will love you in it I am sure. He can't refuse your request for the theatre with you looking like that.'

Jacqueline and Louisa giggled giving each other an affectionate nudge. Louisa put her arm around Jacqueline, as Jacqueline was her very best friend and she was sure, in time, that she would become her sister-in-law, which Louisa would just love.

'Well Jacqueline,' Louisa said, 'father, as you know, is father, so he can refuse me anything if he so wishes, but it does help to look a little pretty and feminine when asking a favour of him.'

The two girls laughed once more with Bertie throwing his head back also laughing at the girls' schemes directed at Father Hirons.

'Let's all go out into the hallway where I shall do my latest impression of darling Lillie. Father will be ages yet and mother ... well mother is mother and we may never see her this evening at all, as she takes so long to pin all her false curls on her head, so let's go!'

Louisa rushed downstairs into the hallway with Jacqueline and Bertie in hot pursuit.

Firmly placing on her head mother Hiron's best feathered hat which had been carefully and lovingly left on the hallstand, Louisa May picked up her father's gold-topped walking cane and the white lace runner from the hall stand and proceeded to give the performance of a lifetime with her impersonation of Lillie Langtry, the famous music hall entertainer and mistress of Edward, Prince of Wales. Louisa May had such a good sense of musical timing and pitch that she could mimic almost anyone, especially the talented Lillie.

Applauding the impersonation, Bertie and Jacqueline thought Louisa amazingly talented and their laughter brought Sarah from the kitchen to observe the spectacle.

'Be careful my darling Louisa, or should I say "Lillie", Madam will go mad if she sees yow with 'er best 'at on! Why, she only bought it last week.'

Sarah was genuinely concerned that Louisa would not get into any trouble especially with her mother, Agnes Hirons, as she was not the woman to cross and had an extremely violent temper.

'Oh, Sarah, darling Sarah, don't worry so much.'

Louisa May ran around and around Sarah in the hallway, prodding and tickling her to make her laugh.

'Be gone with yow Louisa, I worry so much for yow when yow get in these moods. Yow are so impetuous, don't let yower Mother catch yow, that's all I am saying.'

Sarah wagged her finger at Louisa and brushed the tendrils of hair lovingly from around Louisa's face.

Jacqueline looked nervously towards the top of the stairs, but Agnes was not making any grand entrances as yet. Bertie carefully took the hat from Louisa's head and placed it back carefully on the hall stand. He noticed some of the large feathers were missing from it.

'Look what you've done Louey,' Bertie remonstrated. 'Where are the rest of the feathers for God's sake?'

Bertie and Jacqueline feverishly started to search around the wooden hall floor trying to find the three, large missing feathers from mother's hat.

'Here's one of them,' said Jacqueline. 'Quick, stick it back on Louey, whilst I search for the other two, they can't be far.'

Jacqueline and Bertie were sprawled across the hall floor searching for the feathers. Louisa May giggled at them both and thought it would be most inopportune at that precise moment if father should appear.

Bertie looked up from the floor. 'Louey what are you grinning at now? It isn't funny. Mother will go mad if she notices her hat – come on, do help us find the feathers.'

'Oh Bertie don't fuss so, mother will never notice anyway if the feathers are missing, she has so many hats,' Louisa pouted. 'I have told you before Bertie, don't call me Louey, you know I hate it.'

'You call me Bertie, so why shouldn't I call you Louey? Same difference.'

Bertie jumped to his feet, handing Louisa two feathers to put back on mother's hat, which she did, pinning them anywhere and Jacqueline was sure that they were not pinned back in the right place.

Jacqueline started to laugh, so much so, that Bertie started to laugh as well with Louisa joining in.

At that moment the key went in the front door lock. Father Hirons was returning home.

'Well, you young people, what is so funny and what is going on? All this laughter, it is so refreshing to come home to so much laughter after the serious business of the day at the office.'

I noticed that Father Hirons was tall and very distinguished-looking as he handed his hat and cane to Sarah. Sarah gave Louisa May a disapproving look as she noticed Louisa had found the third feather from mother's hat and was hiding it behind her back so that her father would not see it.

Father Hirons studied himself in the hallstand mirror, tweaking his waxed moustache and precning himself. I thought him very vain, but then he was a very attractive man and I could tell a very successful one. Louisa, Bertie and Jacqueline stood motionless, Louisa still holding the large feather behind her back hardly daring to move and hoping, above all things, that Mother Hirons would not come down the stairs as she would surely see the feather and go, she was sure, quite mad.

Father looked at his giggling flock. 'Is mother upstairs changing for dinner?'

The three young people just nodded as they were sure that if they spoke just one word, they would collapse with laughter and all would be lost necessitating them to tell all about mother's hat. Father Hirons made his way up the stairs to get changed ready for dinner.

'I shall see you young people later for dinner,' he said.

'Phew, that was a close one.' Louisa wiped a bead of sweat from her forehead.

'Sarah's a good old stick you know, she didn't tell even though she saw the feather behind my back.'

Louisa May grabbed Jacqueline's arm, pulling her towards the dining room, and promptly plonked herself down at the table in readiness for the evening meal, with Bertie sitting next to his beloved Jacqueline. They were never late for any meal that Sarah had cooked. Jacqueline practically lived with the Hirons family at Sycamore House, as she was a very close friend of Louisa May's and, it seemed, much closer than that to Bertie.

Mother and Father Hirons took their places at the dining table with Sarah scurrying around the room serving each member of the family with their courses. It all looked very succulent to me and very expensive, the food obviously expertly cooked. Sarah showed a great affection for Louisa and Bertie, as when passing she would often touch their shoulders lovingly. For a change, Louisa May sat quietly at the dinner table, with only the occasional prod underneath for Jacqueline and Bertie.

The large grandfather clock chimed half past eight as the family finished off their meal. There seemed to be many huge courses of food, many more than I had ever been used to, but in those days a family dinner was an event and the food much more lavish if the family could afford it.

I wondered when Louisa May would bring up the subject of the theatre night out and Lillie Langtry; perhaps she had thought better of it as Mother Hirons and for that matter, Father Hirons didn't look in the best frame of mind.

In the short time I had come to know her I had found Louisa to be outspoken and full of fun, a lovely young woman. If only she could have seen me, I would have loved to talk to her in her own time and surroundings, but I had to be content just to observe.

'Er ...' Louisa May started to speak to her father, looking back and forth to him and then her mother.

'Er ...' she said once more as Bertie and Jacqueline tried to stifle their giggles.

Father Hirons looked up from his plate of cheese and biscuits.

The Visitor

'What is this er ... er ... business? Is this what I pay expensive tutors for, this er ...?'

Father Hirons smiled lovingly at his daughter.

'Father, could I speak to you if I may? I know that I shouldn't speak at the dinner table, but when else can I speak to you?'

Louisa May glanced nervously at each member of the family.

'Of course you can speak to me my dear, if you must and it is important; I am your father; if you cannot speak to me, to whom can you speak?'

Father Hirons dabbed his mouth with his crisp, white napkin. Mother Hirons coughed nervously for she knew what was coming next and was almost sure her husband would explode with temper at the thought of the family going to the theatre to see Lillie Langtry of all people, the very woman he hated because of her association with the dear Prince of Wales.

'Well father, we would all, that is, myself, Jacqueline, Bertie and I think, mother, er ... well ... we would all like to go to the theatre in two weeks to see, er ... well to see ... so many good and talented people with, er ...'

Louisa May blurted out Lillie Langtry's name so quickly that it was hardly recognisable to her father.

Father Hirons carefully placed his napkin back on the table.

'Well, young lady, do you imagine for one moment that I would allow a daughter of mine to be seen frequenting that sort of occasion? Why! The very idea and to see that woman with our very own Prince parading herself on the stage for all to see, the shame of it. The answer, dear child, is a definite no! Why, our dear Queen must be turning in her grave. Edward, well, he even bought that woman a house on the Isle of Wight, can you imagine that? No, the answer is no ...'

It seemed Father Hirons was adamant and Louisa May pouted her lips in disapproval, with Jacqueline looking down at her cheese and biscuits hardly daring to look at Louisa or Bertie.

Mother Hirons grunted. 'Told you so Louisa, told you!'

'But Father, anyone who is anyone will be there and I know for a fact that some royalty are going and of course, the Goldbergs will be there.'

Louisa May did her best to convince her father that it was a good idea.

'The Goldbergs, that jumped-up self-opinionated man with his social climbing wife, who thinks she is the Queen of the May.'

Mother Hirons was obviously dismayed that Mrs Goldberg, her social rival, would attend such a gathering. Abraham Hirons looked across at his beloved wife's dismay at being left out of such a special occasion, especially if Mrs Goldberg was going!

Abraham coughed.

'Well, I suppose ... well, on second thoughts, I will consider it, yes, I will consider it, if the theatre and Lillie are good enough for the Goldbergs, well ...'

The Visitor

Abraham noticed the relieved expression on Agnes' face and knew that he would have to take the whole family to the theatre, as the Goldbergs were going! Agnes would never let the matter rest until she could go and compete with Mrs Goldberg in the surroundings of a lavish theatre for she had to be seen to be the cultured and socially accepted woman that she was!

Tweaking his waxed moustache, Abraham accepted the excited hug from Louisa and thanks from Bertie and Jacqueline. It was finally settled the whole family should attend the theatre to see Lillie Lantry perform her famous songs. He couldn't help thinking to himself that the theatre night would cost him a great deal of money, not just for the tickets and of course the box seats Agnes would insist upon, but the ladies' gowns and of course, her orchid and Louisa's favourite gardenia flower to pin on her gown.

Agnes Hirons grinned to herself for she was thinking of at least two or even three shopping trips for gowns, jewellery and accessories; she must not be outshone by Mrs Goldberg.

Abraham Hirons smiled at Louisa May.

'One day, my gal, your impetuous nature will get you into serious trouble and God forbid I am around when it happens.'

Everyone laughed as they knew Louisa May would get her way with her father as she always did.

When dinner was over, Abraham retired to the sitting room to sample his favourite Havana cigar leaving Agnes asleep in her preferred chair. Louisa, Jacqueline and Bertie rushed from one bedroom to another discussing clothes, jewellery and the Lillie Langtry concert.

Louisa May paraded about her bedroom, firstly trying one gown against her petite figure then another.

'I think after all, I will have to buy a new gown, shoes and of course, jewelled hairpins, don't you think Jacqueline?'

'But Louisa, you have so many gowns, surely one of those would do?'

Jacqueline was very thrifty and thought Louisa so extravagant.

'We shall go on a wonderful shopping spree, I am sure Mother will want to go as well and you can come too, Jacqueline. Oh do come, we must choose something gorgeous, maybe pale green to complement your eyes and colouring, Jacqueline.'

Louisa waltzed around and around her bedroom with her many gowns, making Jacqueline laugh at her antics.

'We will sneak out during the interval at the theatre, Jacqueline, and see if we can find ourselves any eligible young gentlemen around the place – oh, I forgot, you are so in love with Bertie, but never mind, you can still come with me on the "hunt". We will make up all sorts of excuses to get away from mother and father and they will believe us, you'll see!'

Louisa May had everything planned in her mind and dreamed of her

The Visitor

'Prince Charming'; maybe she would find him at the theatre … who knows?

'Really Louey, is that all you ever think of, boys?'

Bertie rocked to and fro in Louisa's rocking chair.

'Anyway, I am sure Jacqueline wouldn't be the slightest bit interested in accompanying you and nor should she for we love each other, don't we darling? We don't need to impress anyone, we have each other. Such unbecoming language from my dear sister too! Where do you get these sayings from Louey, going on the "hunt"?' Bertie kissed Jacqueline on the cheek and tickled Louisa, making her shriek.

'Don't be so prudish Bertie, all you think about is Jacqueline and she you. Anyway, don't let mother or father catch you in here with us and especially kissing Jacqueline.'

Louisa May flashed her large black eyes at Bertie in defiance, piling her long hair haphazardly on top of her head with a comb slide. Even with her hair a mess, Bertie thought his sister the most incredibly beautiful girl he had ever seen, even more beautiful than his beloved Jacqueline he was ashamed to think, and couldn't imagine for one moment that Louey would ever have to look for an eligible young man.

'Well you two lovelies,' Bertie said, 'I have to go and get changed; I'll leave you to it.'

The two girls continued to examine Louisa's many gowns, fitting them closely against themselves and admiring them in the long bedroom mirror.

'Which colour do you think suits me best, that is, if I don't buy a gown, Jacqueline? You can borrow one of my gowns in you like, you are the same size as me.'

Louisa pushed a deep green velvet gown against Jacqueline.

'Do you think your parents would mind me coming to the theatre? After all I practically live at Sycamore House as it is, but I don't want to intrude on your parents' kindness any more than I should.'

Jacqueline felt a little awkward.

'Don't be so silly Jacqueline, of course neither father nor mother would mind at all. Why should they, you are practically part of our family; they wouldn't ask you otherwise.'

Louisa hugged her friend.

'Anyway, Bertie would be devastated if you didn't come with us, you know as well as I that he wants to be with you every living moment. I know he will ask you to marry him, mark my words Jacqueline.'

Louisa fell back onto her bed stretching out her arms, dangling her feet over the edge of the bed.

'Don't say things like that Louisa, Bertie won't ask me to marry him yet.'

Jacqueline blushed and giggled along with Louisa.

'Oh I think he will, he will ask you, you'll see; that is why, dear friend,

The Visitor

you must look your most ravishing on the theatre night. I am sure he will ask you then, I am sure of it.'

Louisa May jumped up from her bed, twirling Jacqueline around and around the room, just as she had done with myself on many occasions.

At last, the evening of the theatre outing had arrived: Louisa May looked beautiful and Jacqueline looked her usual neat pretty self but no way matched the exquisite beauty of Louisa May.

'No one will dare speak to us, we all look so grand and important.'

Louisa May strutted up and down the hallway admiring herself in the hallstand mirror, pulling her white satin gloves over her elbows and smoothing her dress down over her perfect figure.

'Oh, Miss Louisa, yow and Miss Jacqueline well, yow both look so grand. No young man could resist either of yow.'

Sarah had come into the hallway to wish the family a good time. She had practically brought Louisa May up from a baby, considering her just as much her child as that of Agnes and Abraham. Sarah had never married or had children of her own as circumstances had not presented themselves to her.

'Yow are my best girl, my own beautiful bab Louisa, I could almost cry with 'appiness for yow.'

Sarah took her handkerchief from her starched apron pocket to wipe away a tear from her eyes, blowing her nose loudly.

'Now Sarah, don't be a silly girl.'

Abraham put his arm around Sarah's shoulder, as he treated her like one of the family and he knew she held all the family in great affection. Sarah had been with the Hirons family for over thirty years, from a young girl in service to them, not knowing any other way of life, except to serve, cook and clean for them. Agnes Hirons was not at all maternal, but enjoyed showing off her good-looking children and boasting about their achievements, especially Bertie's. He was an accomplished and well-respected accountant in the city.

Everyone looked towards Abraham as he said,

'Dash it, I have forgotten to speak to John Garton.'

'I hope nothing is about to go wrong at this stage,' Louisa May thought. 'Surely father would not have mislaid the tickets for the theatre.' Louisa May was frustrated at her father's forgetfulness. She had spent most of the day getting ready for this wonderful occasion, so nothing must go wrong now!

Abraham sighed.

'We shall have to get young John Garton to drive us to the theatre tonight, I'm afraid Bill is still ill. I dread to think what our journey will be like, though, with young Garton driving. However, beggars can't be choosers, eh! Sarah, be a good girl run along and get John to take us to the theatre in the coach and horses. I had forgotten to mention it to him earlier.'

The Visitor

Sarah hesitated.

'Sir, I don't think John Garton is very good with the coach and 'orses, driving I mean. Do yow think yow ought to trust 'im to take yow Sir? 'E is marvellous with the 'orses, 'e loves them, but driving, don't think so Sir? Any road, I will go and ask 'im for yow.'

Sarah scurried off down the hallway to the scullery where she knew John would be.

Louisa sighed with frustration at the delay and smiled to herself at the thought of young John Garton driving the family to such an elegant affair. She hoped he would take off his garden boots first!

A few minutes later, John Garton arrived at the front of the house pulling the horses to a halt and shouting loudly,

'Ey up, my beauties.' The horses were impatient to be off.

Louisa May flounced through the front porch with the rest of the family following on behind her. Abraham made sure her cape covered her white, slender shoulders as the night air was chilly for the time of year. Swishing her newly bought blue satin and lace-trimmed gown through the grand entrance of Sycamore House, Louisa May made her way to the waiting coach. John could only gape open-mouthed at her beauty. He had never seen Miss Louisa look so sophisticated before and couldn't take his eyes from her, much to Louisa's amusement. Her eyes flirted endlessly with John's; she knew she should not flirt with servants, but it made her feel so excited and alive that any young man was looking at her admiringly. She only wished John would close his mouth!

John and Louisa had often talked in the garden whilst John worked, with her questioning him about plants and vegetables. He had always considered her a silly, giggling child, but certainly not the beautiful, sophisticated woman he was looking at now. He must not make it too obvious to the family that he was staring at her for he knew that he could never think of his young mistress in any way but a subservient one.

John was not good at driving and did not like it. Nevertheless, he would do anything for Miss Louisa, even drive a coach.

I watched the coach drive away from Sycamore House down the long, pebbled driveway, throwing up stones as it sped away out of sight. I tried to follow it to the theatre, as I felt excited at the prospect of seeing a live Edwardian theatre show from those far-off times and especially the infamous Lillie Langtry. I realised very quickly I was confined to the house and grounds of Sycamore House and I could not leave as there seemed to be a barrier all around the gardens keeping me there. Perhaps something was about to happen at the house whilst the family were away at the theatre, but there was only Sarah left clearing up and making ready for the next day and I was sure she would not be involved in anything remotely exciting or interesting.

The Visitor

I made my way to the kitchen and watched Sarah cleaning and putting away pots and pans, which all seemed pretty ordinary and normal to me.

CHAPTER II

Leaving Sycamore House

Some weeks had elapsed since my visit to Sycamore House. Not a moment had passed by without my wondering how the Hirons family had enjoyed their theatre night out. Perhaps Louisa May would have met a nice young man and made a conquest, as she did look very beautiful that night.

I hadn't any idea why I had been left watching the loyal Sarah going about her kitchen duties and then unexpectedly sent back to my own time in the late 1990s. To say I was puzzled was an understatement. Now, after all these weeks of waiting for her, my *visitor*, Louisa May Hirons to return to me, I had at last been collected, finding myself once more in the kitchen of Sycamore House, watching Sarah going about her daily routines, as if I had never left; as if a piece of history had been frozen in time waiting for my return.

It must be wintertime, I thought, as the fire grates were stacked high with logs and all the windows were firmly bolted shut. Sarah and John Garton were dressed in woollen clothes and the smell of bread baking wafted around in the air.

I hadn't seen Louisa May, Jacqueline or Bertie as I felt I was being kept in the kitchen for a reason I had yet to discover. I was, it seemed having to observe certain events, which would piece together a jigsaw of Louisa's mystery and pick up whatever clue was being handed to me, just like watching a modern-day movie.

Suddenly, I found myself standing right in front of Louisa herself. Observing her, I noticed something strangely vacant about her persona. Studying her interactions with other members of her family I realised that she was *deaf!* How and when did this happened? Was there an accident at the theatre, or somewhere else?

Something dreadful must have happened to Louisa; I followed her out of Sycamore House, not through the conventional front entrance, but out through the back of the house into the kitchen towards the back door, noticing on the way Sarah's horror-struck face. Louisa May was sobbing bitterly as her mother Agnes pushed her violently towards the kitchen door, seemingly very angry about something. Louisa turned to her mother and said,

'Mother, Oh, Mother, please don't! What are you doing to me? Mother

The Visitor

please! I love you dearly, please don't throw me out! Sarah please help me!'

Louisa May tried to reach out for Sarah throwing out her slender arms towards her, but Agnes pushed her even more violently so she could not reach Sarah, until she was outside in the yard and bolted the kitchen door firmly behind Louisa.

Sarah held each side of her face in alarm and was too dumbstruck to speak. She wanted to stop Agnes from attacking Louisa and throwing her out of the house, but felt powerless and knew she could do absolutely nothing to help her poor Louisa if she wanted to keep her job. She knew if she had intervened, her job would be gone like John Garton's.

I willed myself outside into the back yard where Louisa was standing motionless with shock.

Tears streamed down her pale face and all she could do was to call out to her mother and Sarah to let her into the house. Louisa's calls were pitiful; Sarah felt she could stand it no longer and ran towards the door to unbolt it to let her in.

'If you so much as touch that door, Sarah, it is instant dismissal for you, and you can join John Garton on the rubbish tip of life. You'll never get another position at your age, just think on that, woman, do you hear me?' Agnes bristled with temper and the frown on her forehead became even deeper. Sarah could only nod at Agnes; she understood only too clearly. It was better to have a job and some money, and perhaps in the future she could help poor Louisa financially, but she would need her job to do that.

Louisa pounded the kitchen door with her fists calling for Sarah and Agnes. The shrill of her voice became more desperate but Sarah could only stand and listen in horror, her eyes welling with tears for her beloved Louisa.

Louisa slid down the outside wall and lay crumpled on the ground, sobbing for Agnes and Sarah. I tried so hard to help her but my arms were useless as I was just a mere ghost. I could do nothing to help her.

Gradually, after wiping her tears, Louisa May mustered the strength to stand up. I noticed that she carried the crocodile bag she had bought at the store on the shopping spree I had been privileged to attend. Perhaps the clue is with that, I wondered. Should I focus on the crocodile bag? I just did not understand any of the clues I was being shown by Louisa. At least Louisa had managed to grab the bag before being attacked by Agnes.

Louisa May walked around to the front of the house very slowly, dragging her bag on the ground as she went, occasionally glancing back at the kitchen door in case Sarah opened it to let her in.

Shading each side of her face to block out any reflection, Louisa peered through the sitting room window, and saw Agnes throwing her arms about in temper and Sarah trying to comfort her. On seeing Louisa peering through the window, Agnes promptly closed the curtains to shut her out. Louisa felt

The Visitor

compelled to knock on the window, but she knew her efforts would be useless.

All I could do was to look on in confusion and horror; I couldn't imagine what could have happened to lead to this series of events, and why Louisa May had been thrown out of her own home. Where were Bertie, Jacqueline and Abraham? Surely they would have not allowed this to happen had they been home: I couldn't believe whatever Louisa had done, Abraham would allow Agnes to evict her from the family home.

I glanced down the long pebbled driveway and saw John Garton running towards Louisa May shouting her name, but of course, Louisa could hear nothing.

Louisa turned and saw John running towards her; throwing her arms about John's neck, she wept bitterly onto his strong muscular shoulder. John caringly took Louisa's crocodile bag from her, slipping his arm around her waist to lead her away from Sycamore House towards the main road to Birmingham city.

Can I go with them? I thought. Can I actually leave the grounds of the house? I hadn't been able to do it before, but I felt I must go with them for they held the clues to Louisa's mystery I was sure. It was all too upsetting and I hated to see Louisa May so distressed. John Garton seemed very happy though, and after he had kissed her passionately on the lips, I realised they were lovers.

Where was John going to take Louisa and what had happened to force Louisa and John out of the house? I knew that on previous occasions Louisa May had found John a good companion, but regarded him as a servant, which he was. Surely they were not lovers? No, I must be wrong. And why was Louisa May deaf? No doubt I would find out in time.

As John led Louisa May out onto the main road, I found myself walking alongside them. Yes, I was actually being allowed to leave the confines of Sycamore House and go along with the couple, where to I had no idea. I followed Louisa and John as they walked down the grey, cobble-stoned streets of the inner city of Birmingham into Corporation Street.

On and on they walked with Louisa looking extremely tired, until we came upon a road called Tower Street, where John led Louisa to a small, terraced house. Louisa May was helped through the battered wooden front door into a dirty hallway with the wallpaper peeling off the walls, decay and damp everywhere.

John led her up hard wooden steps to the top of the house. No luxurious carpeting on these stairs or pictures hanging on the wall.

There were no comforts or pleasures meeting her eyes here. Fumbling in his pocket for the key to the rooms, John produced a large brass key, turning it in the lock and opening the creaking door. The smell of damp and decay

The Visitor

oozed from the room. Louisa May looked all around the unwelcoming room, her eyes filled with tears at the squalor before her.

'Eah yow are, Bab,' John said in his broad Birmingham accent, gently easing Louisa towards a kitchen chair, brushing the seat with his jacket before she sat down. She hated him calling her Bab but thought it best just to smile back. She felt lucky to have a man who was willing to take care of her; after all she knew John was doing his best for her.

John took Louisa's face in his hands so that she could lip-read his words.

'No one can 'arm yow now Bab, not whilst I am 'eah. Corse' it ain't like yower been used to Bab, not like Sycamore 'Ouse, but I'll work 'ard, I'll clean it all up for yow, Bab, yow'll see. It will be better than Sycamore 'Ouse in the end.'

John did his best to comfort Louisa, pulling her close to him and smothering her with passionate kisses. Louisa May couldn't help the tears falling out of her eyes.

I realised that my worst fears for Louisa were right! John and Louisa were lovers. How can she live here in this terrible place? It is a hovel not fit for rats, let alone my dear, sweet Louisa May. She must really love John Garton to live here, but to come to this! What will become of them both?

Louisa May desperately tried not to cry or be too alarmed. She knew John was trying his best for her and had beggared himself to pay the rent for the rooms in Tower Street which would be their home for goodness knew how long.

'Come on, Bab, don't yow love me no more? Please don't cry, I can't stand it. Come over eah, look I made us up a nice, clean bed with white sheets and everything, look! I even put up curtains for us, so we can shut the dark night out. I grant yow, it an't much Bab, but we will make it 'omely Bab, yow just wait and see.

'I shall make us some cocoa. I got some from the shop today so at least we can 'ave a nice hot drink. Then young lady, yow shall go to bed, yow've 'ad enough for one day and yow look tired out; yow'll feel better in the morning.'

John felt sorry for Louisa May and the tragedy of her deafness, but loved her more because of it and knew that he would love and protect her for the rest of his life. John caringly led her to the bedroom, taking off her jacket and pulling back the bed sheets. Sitting her down on the edge of the bed, he patted the side of her face affectionately to reassure her. Louisa was very glad to take off her dress and untie her hair. Scratching her head all over, her hair fell down about her shoulders as she lay down exhausted.

In no time at all, John had returned with the cocoa, but Louisa May had fallen into a deep sleep. John leant down, kissing her forehead, and covered her tiny body with the clean, white sheets and knitted blanket. He put the cup of cocoa down on the bedside cabinet, took off his boots and clothes and quietly lay down beside his beloved, Louisa. He studied her face as she slept, marvelling at her natural beauty even in sleep.

The Next Morning

Louisa May awoke early, thinking she must have been in a terrible dream, being expelled from her home, Sycamore House, but then realising it was no dream as she turned over in bed to face her beloved John.

John slept peacefully, so she decided to get up quietly and make her way to the kitchen; there was no luxury of a bathroom or running water to wash herself. She knew she would have to fetch the water from a pump in the courtyard below behind the row of terraced houses and find a bucket from somewhere to fetch the water in. The only sink available was in the kitchen; Louisa knew she would not only have to wash herself there, but would have to carry out all other domestic duties including washing and preparing food, washing clothes and herself from one sink. John had shown her the night before where the water pump was in the courtyard. She found the bucket, dented but clean, under the kitchen sink and made her way to the courtyard. She had heard of such pumps and how very poor people had to fetch their own water but had not realised how hard it was to pump the water and carry it up a flight of stairs until she found herself in the same predicament.

Louisa returned with the water, putting the bucket down on the kitchen floor, mindful not to spill any of it. The water felt icy cold; there was not the luxury of a fire or any way of heating it.

She felt cold, hungry and worn out already and was sure she would feel even worse by the end of the day. Louisa poured some water into the kitchen sink, making sure she had left some for a precious cup of tea. When she had finished washing and dressing, she decided it was no good feeling sorry for herself and shivering with cold and fright, no one was going to help her except John, so it was a good idea to make the best of the situation. She would try and make some breakfast for John and have it ready with the kitchen table set before he woke up. Louisa had never cooked before, but remembered certain things Sarah did in the kitchen at Sycamore House, which she was determined to try.

She found one egg, a stale piece of bread and some lard. She remembered she should put the egg into boiling water to cook. Placing the battered saucepan onto gas hob and finding a taper to light the gas with, Louisa proceeded to make breakfast. There was nothing to eat for her, but she wanted John to have the very best even if it meant going without herself. Louisa decided that she would always put John's needs first before her own; she loved him so much.

The Visitor

The kitchen table was dirty, strewn with old newspapers, dirty plates and cups stained with tea; how long they had been there, Louisa didn't dare guess. Rolling up her sleeves, she decided to scrub the table clean and wash the dirty crockery. Boiling some of the precious water, Louisa found some carbolic soap and swished it around in the water until she had suds, washing the cups with her bare hands as there seemed to be no cloth or scrubbing brush. She scratched the stains off the cups and looked around for a tea towel to dry them. Of course, she might have guessed, there were no tea towels and no draining board at the sink so Louisa placed the cups on the windowsill to dry in the watery sunshine.

Taking off her lace white under-slip, Louisa carefully placed it across the scrubbed kitchen table; it looked so pretty, just like a tablecloth and would do for the moment, she thought. The cups and plates were placed on the table. Everything looked much cleaner than the night before when she had arrived. Louisa wanted the first meal she had with John to be special and decided to go outside to look for some flowers to put in the centre of the table. Looking down on the courtyard below, she noticed willowy type weeds with pretty yellow flowers and dashed downstairs to pick them. Louisa hadn't remembered the bread and egg boiling on the gas hob.

John started to stir in the bedroom. 'Bab, is that burning I can smell?

The Visitor

What yow doing?'

Louisa heard John calling as she gathered up her weeds and quickly ran up the wooden stairway back to the room. Placing the weeds across the kitchen table, she hurried to the kitchen taking the pan off the hob and turning the bread over with a fork. She was relieved it was not too burnt and the bread looked like fried bread ought to look, crisp and rather dark brown, although the egg was just starting to crack in the boiling water. She took a plate from the window sill, placing the egg and fried bread on it. The food didn't look too bad she thought.

John came into the kitchen and was amazed by Louisa's efforts at cooking him breakfast.

'Bab, what a lovely surprise, yow did this for me, how wonderful! Where did yow get that lovely table cloth from? And the plates are clean. Where did the flowers come from? Yow are a wonder, that's what yow are, Bab.' John gave Louisa a a hug. 'I'll get yow a jar or something for those lovely flowers.'

John looked around in the kitchen and found a jam jar which he filled with water, putting the weeds into it placing them in the centre of the kitchen table.

'Why, even flowers Bab, I have a wonderful woman, I certainly do.' John started to eat his breakfast, and seemed to swallow his fried bread and egg in only two mouthfuls as he was so hungry.

Louisa sat down opposite John feeling happy and pleased with herself for cooking her first breakfast.

'Eah Bab, what are yow 'aving to eat? That wasn't just for me was it? Come on, yow must eat something too.' Louisa shrugged her shoulders.

'No, I am not hungry, I just had a cup of tea, that's all I wanted John, really. Anyway, I have decided this is going to be the prettiest home ever. I'll scrub it clean as clean can be, until it shines. We shall buy some blue gingham material and I shall make pretty curtains for the kitchen and some seat pads to match them for the chairs, also some napkins and …'

'Eah, Bab, hold on.' John took Louisa's face in his hands so that she could read lip-read him.

'I've got to get a job yet Bab, but I will, don't yow worry, then yow can do all the things yow want.' John and Louisa fell into each other's arms at the thought of everything they would achieve in their new home, but John knew he would be hard-pressed to afford any of the things Louisa talked about. He would never forgive Agnes Hirons for throwing Louisa May out of Sycamore House in her pregnant condition, but he knew that was the Jewish way, especially with daughters who fell pregnant outside of marriage and especially by a gentile, namely himself!

So that's it, I thought, the mystery is solved! I had read John's mind beautifully and found that I could do this with ease now with nearly anyone.

The Visitor

So, Louisa May was pregnant by John. Of course, I had no doubt John would look after Louisa as he loved her very much, but this surely was not why I had been dragged through time to observe Louisa May, pregnant? Ah well, I thought, I shall just keep watching all the events surrounding Louisa and John and hopefully will find out what it is I am destined to know.

I looked at the happy couple, John smiling at Louisa as they held each other so tightly.

'That's the spirit Bab,' John said 'We'll show 'em all won't we, Bab? We shall 'ave to fix the day soon to be married, that is Bab, if yow will have me? We need to give our baby a proper name.'

'Of course I will marry you, John; I do so love you and want to be your wife so much.'

Louisa kissed John passionately on the lips, then jumped from his embrace and started to waltz around the room singing at the top of her voice, just as she had done many times at Sycamore House, prodding and tickling John as she glided around him. She was so very happy.

John watched Louisa dance around the room but couldn't help fretting about how he would find work to support Louisa and their coming baby and afford the ceremony of their marriage.

Jobs were very hard to come by especially if you had no references, and a lung condition which made you cough, as John had. He was handicapped before he even started to look for a job.

Louisa May had decided, if nothing else, their rooms would be clean! With John's help she would set about scrubbing the floors and furniture, what little there was of furniture, just two kitchen chairs, a table and a bed.

They both worked hard all day and well into the evening cleaning and washing with carbolic soap. Louisa May had decided that she would never again allow herself to think of her mother, father or Sycamore House! It was too painful. She would allow herself to occasionally think of Bertie and Jacqueline and of course, Sarah whom she knew would have helped her if she could.

John had managed to scrimp together some money to buy supper that night; Louisa May cooked it as best she could. John swallowed his food with great difficulty but ate it all the same. Louisa was not a good cook, but he was too hungry not to eat the meal she had prepared. Smiling across the table at his beautiful bride bride-to-be, he mouthed very carefully to her that he loved her, not daring to think too deeply about the future, or what his neighbours would think of Louisa with her education and delicate manners. He knew one thing, though; he was sure Margaret Thompson, in the rooms below, would accept Louisa. Margaret was a much older woman, wise to the world and had been a good friend to John. After all, he would eventually have to find employment and leave Louisa on her own in the rooms. John

The Visitor

once more cupped Louisa's face in his hands.

'How do yow feel, Bab,' John stroked Louisa's swelling belly.

'I am all right John, please don't worry. At least I don't have to pretend any more about my lump and I can be sick whenever I choose, without explanations. The baby inside me will be five months old, John. We shall have a birthday party for him.'

Louisa threw her head back laughing loudly at the expression on John's vacant face.

'I am sure everything will be all right, John, I know I have a son for you, and I hope he is tall, strong, fair and blue-eyed, just like you.'

The couple kissed passionately. It was obvious that they were very much in love and their surroundings paled into insignificance because of their happiness.

Ah well, I thought, now that everything seems to be all right with Louisa and John, there is no need for me to stay.

I couldn't help feeling that Louisa had made a huge mistake in living with John although she was in love with him. It was plain the couple were deeply in love, and I did hope their happiness lasted, but Louisa May had been used to so much more materially: maybe I would be proved wrong.

Louisa May turned to John,

'The only thing which would complete my happiness at this moment is that Jacqueline and Bertie could be here with us tonight and that Sarah could help me at the birth of our first child. I do so want Sarah to help me! Don't laugh, John, at my thoughts; you would really like Jacqueline and Bertie when you got to know them properly; they are not at all as you imagine you know. Bertie is not at all stuffy or snobbish, in fact, he is really funny, rather immature I always felt, playing the fool and especially in front of Jacqueline. I know you would grow to love them both very much just as I do … did.'

Louisa May sat back on the wooden kitchen chair. John fetched a pillow from the bedroom putting it at Louisa's back to support her.

'Well, Bab, the only thing I can do is to get word to them; perhaps I can get a message through somehow?' John stroked Louisa's belly. Louisa seemed agitated at that suggestion.

'How John, how would you get a message to them, you can't get near Sycamore House, besides which, mother would never allow you and would have you evicted as soon as you set foot on the driveway. Bertie and Jacqueline would be too frightened of mother's temper if she found out they had visited us here at Tower Street.'

Louisa sank into melancholy, pouting her lip.

'Bab please don't get upset, we 'ave each other at least and the baby is ours. We 'ave a roof over us heads.' John gathered Louisa into his strong arms; he was truly concerned at her mood.

'Well Bab, I think the time has come to name the day, for our wedding I mean.'

John hugged Louisa to him.

'John, it will be just wonderful, but how can I get married in white in this state? No church will marry us with me and my lump.'

'Bab, don't yow worry. Margaret Thompson can be a witness for us and I will get one of my mates for the other witness. Who says our wedding has to be in a church anyway?'

John kissed Louisa.

'I so dreamed of getting married in white with all the things that go with it, but I shall just be happy to marry you, John, wherever you decide. It is obvious I won't be able to marry in white, but I have no dress at all, except the one I have on. I would so like to look at least like a bride, that is, if we could afford a dress for me?'

'Bab, yow will have the loveliest dress ever, I shall see to that, don't yow worry. I'll go to see the Baptist minister tomorrow. He will marry us I am sure, not that I went to church much, but he knows me and the family, that is, if yow agree Bab. I know yow are Jewish, maybe yow wouldn't be allowed to marry in my church?'

'John, you are such a lovely man.'

Louisa kissed him on the cheek.

'I will marry where I choose, and I am sure your minister will advise us. I shall be only too pleased to marry in the Baptist church, I have little else left from my Jewish faith anyway. Look what happened to me: I mean, with mother who is supposed to be religious and yet cast me out. How can that be religion when a person is in trouble and someone behaves like that to their own family?'

'I agree Bab, so yow are now a fully enrolled Baptist along with our son.'

Louisa May and John married two weeks later in the local Baptist church. Margaret Thompson had given Louisa one of her gowns which just fitted her swelling figure. Margaret made up a wedding bouquet from artificial flowers taken from her old hats. No-one knew the flowers were artificial as Margaret had arranged them so perfectly in the bouquet, twirling the stems into a white doily which set the flowers off perfectly.

The ceremony at the Baptist church was short with only two witnesses and no guests. Louisa and John did not care about guests and were blissfully happy at last they were together and firmly married.

Margaret Thompson had prepared a small buffet in her rooms at Tower Street for Louisa and John. The Baptist priest, Margaret, and Josiah Freemantle, one of John's army friends from the Boer war and a witness at the couple's wedding, followed Louisa and John out of the church into a waiting

The Visitor

carriage which Josiah had paid for as a wedding gift to take the couple back to Tower Street and Margaret's waiting buffet.

I tried to leave Tower Street, as I felt perhaps this must be the end of Louisa's story as everything seemed to be at a happy conclusion. It was not solving anything staying and watching everyone eating at a wedding reception. I had no idea why I was summoned to witness these events anyway. I tried to leave but as experienced at Sycamore House, I was not being allowed to leave Tower Street.

Four Months Later

In the rooms at Tower Street Louisa May knew that it was time for the baby's arrival. She had got to know Margaret Thompson very well over the past four months and also the other neighbours who had been more than kind to her knowing she was pregnant. Everyone in the terrace block was looking forward to the arrival of John and Louisa's baby and some neighbours had even given baby clothes and knitted hand-made toys. John had busied himself making a rocking cradle for the baby out of planks of wood he found on a nearby railway embankment, painting the cradle with animals on each side. He had managed to find himself a part-time job as a street lamp lighter which kept him healthy walking around the streets as he needed fresh air for his lung condition. He had never divulged to Louisa May that he had a lung condition from the result of insanitary conditions during the Boer War as a boy soldier. He had joined the army to fight even though under age and was glad to leave his childhood home as it was so impoverished. Fighting for his country, even though he was only fifteen years old, was to him a better option, although he missed his brothers and sisters at home. One day he would tell Louisa about it all, but not yet; he had at least found a job that suited his condition and could for the moment pay for the rooms and food.

John had not expected such kindness from his neighbours and was now confident that Louisa May had been accepted into the local community. Margaret Thompson was a frequent visitor, offering her advice on babies and helping Louisa to make baby blankets out of old bits of material and wool.

Louisa May suddenly knew from the urgent regular pains in the pit of her stomach and back that the baby was at last coming. She cried quiet tears of pain that trickled down her sunken cheeks onto her glossy, black hair. The pains were now becoming more regular and she desperately tried not to cry out too loudly.

'John!' Louisa called out from the bedroom where she had gone to lie down.

Her contractions were coming every five minutes and getting worse with each painful movement. She was very frightened of giving birth and wanted so much for Sarah to be with her, and called out her name in desperation.

John rushed into the bedroom.

'What is it, Bab, is the baby coming? My God, it's coming. Don't worry Bab, I'll fetch Margaret, she'll know 'ow to 'elp yow. Won't be long Bab!'

John ran down the stairs two at a time to Margaret Thompson's rooms shouting for Margaret to come quickly.

She grabbed her shawl, placing it around her shoulders, quickly following John upstairs to Louisa's bedroom. Holding Louisa's tiny hand, Margaret reassured her.

'Now, now, don't yow worry ducks, tell me, 'ow often are the pains?'

Louisa May could only groan and cry out,

'Pain, terrible pain, oh Margaret please do something, help me.'

'Now then, John,' Margaret said, 'don't just stand there gaping, go and sterilise yower 'ands in some really hot water, then boil some water up for me! Get me some sheets off yower bed and something to wrap the bab in when it arrives. Her waters 'ave broken John, come on, lad, hurry up.'

I couldn't help feeling sorry for John, he was utterly useless, as if struck dumb by the scene in front of him.

Margaret once more shouted at him to do as she said.

Louisa's screams of pain got louder and louder – the whole of Tower Street would surely know by now she was giving birth.

The sheeting was laid under Louisa's writhing body, blood was everywhere, but no baby yet. John stroked the top of her head, wiping the beads of perspiration from her face. The agony of pushing on Margaret Thompson's instructions was almost too much for Louisa to bear.

I felt I just couldn't watch the agony of the whole affair. It was all too gruesome for me! I could never stand the sight of blood.

'This is a big baby John, must be going to be a boy!' Margaret eased the small head out of Louisa's body as Louisa gave one last scream in agony to push the baby out of her.

'Well I never, yow've got a beautiful baby daughter John, look!'

Margaret Thompson wrapped the perfect baby girl in a clean sheet, placing her at the side of Louisa May who only had the strength to smile weakly at her new-born baby.

John kissed Louisa and his new baby girl tenderly. Margaret discreetly left the couple alone and said she was going to make some tea and biscuits.

'She is so beautiful Bab, like yow. What a clever girl I've got. She is so perfect.'

John kissed the small fingers of his new baby girl and then covered his face weeping with joy. It would be the first and last time Louisa May would ever see him cry.

The Visitor

My body suddenly jerked uncontrollably and violently.

'No! Please, whatever, whoever you are, let me stay here. I don't want to leave yet. I know I found earlier events in Tower Street rather boring, but I am now enjoying myself, seeing the new baby and everything. Please, let me stay.'

But it was of no use, I was being dragged away. Louisa and John's voices faded away into the distance, leaving me in a swirling whirlwind, not knowing where I would find myself next! Would I ever see my Louisa May and John again, and would I still be privileged to witness more of Louisa May's life? Surely this was not the end of her story?

CHAPTER III

Tower Street

I was in my own home going about my daily household routines with never an hour passing without my thoughts straying to Louisa May, John and their new baby girl. I wondered what the new baby's name would be and how the family were coping in Tower Street. After such a long time had elapsed, I began to think that was the end of Louisa May's story, when late one night, once more I smelt the intoxicating gardenia perfume she always wore and my nostrils filled with the scent. I knew that she was nearby and had come back for me.

As I brushed my hair and studied my face in the bathroom mirror, my own reflection became fused with hers as my face changed back and forth firstly to Louisa's face then mine and all the time her girlish giggling echoed in my ears. I thought I was going mad. Why didn't she just come to me as she had done before, and take me with her to wherever she wanted to go? She was playing games with me and finding it extremely amusing, fitting her own face over mine and making it come and go like a clown's mask being put on and off.

I shouted out, *'Stop it, Louisa!'*

Sure enough, it stopped and so did the giggles; the atmosphere seemed very different now and I did not feel as happy about her being around me as I had done before, although I did want her there and wanted her to come back to me.

Sure enough the swirling haze in front of me cleared to reveal Louisa May, still smiling, but not the vivacious young woman I knew so well; an older woman in her mid-to late thirties; still strikingly beautiful and unmistakably Louisa May. She beckoned to me to follow her; she neither held my arms nor helped me, and I found I could follow her without any aid from her spiritual grip. I was eager to go and find out what had changed her – I knew she was older, yes, but she seemed somehow distant.

'Wait! Wait!' I cried, but she was disappearing faster than I could follow her through the mists of time, bowing her head as she glided away; I couldn't see whether she was happy or sad, in fact, I could hardly keep up with her and certainly was not by her side, but behind her. She led me past familiar places I had seen before, long ago, until we arrived on the grey, cobble-

The Visitor

stoned street we both knew so well, Tower Street. Children were playing in the street, but Louisa neither looked left nor right; she just kept her head bowed down looking at the ground.

'Let me try and help you Louisa May, please!' I said. 'What is it, what are you trying to tell me?'

Louisa May didn't answer me or look at me, as once more I had become the ghost in her time.

A young girl ran towards Louisa pulling at her dress.

'Mother, Mother,' the child said.

I looked at the child and then at Louisa

Surely this young girl was not the small baby I had left her with when I was so abruptly taken away? Then three more smaller children ran towards Louisa, all calling her mother. Surely all these children couldn't be hers? I must have been away some years and missed so much of her story.

It appeared that all the children *were* Louisa and John Garton's and poor Louisa looked worn out when I eventually had time to study her face. She opened the old, battered front door to the small terraced house in Tower Street which would lead her upstairs to her shabby rooms.

I followed her into the house and up the creaking stairs, finding the accommodation beyond comprehension, it was so dank – the poverty was unbelievable even for those far-off days – but not dirty; Louisa kept her home scrupulously clean.

On entering the rooms, I saw John and it was obvious that he had been drinking heavily as empty beer bottles were scattered all about the room and he lay lay slouched across the table, unaware of Louisa's presence. The blue gingham curtains and kitchen chair seat pads that Louisa had made when I had last visited Tower Street were faded and torn. The matching tablecloth was nowhere to be seen.

Louisa May went into her small, dingy kitchen, filling the brass kettle with water, and placing it on the gas hob then lighting a taper for the burner.

John stirred …

'So yow are 'ome Bab? At last, where yow bin, surely not scrubbing 'ouses all this time? Got any money, Bab, and what's for tea?'

John lurched across the kitchen table, belching and reaching for yet another bottle of beer. He was so drunk he could hardly sit upright.

'Here.' Louisa May threw a few pennies from her apron pocket across the kitchen table which John quickly gathered up. He wasn't too drunk to pick up every coin expertly.

The young girls I had seen outside in the street now came running into the house and were busily chattering to one another. Each of them had inherited Louisa's characteristics, her dark eyes and thick dark hair; they were surely girls to be proud of. Louisa May gave each child a tender kiss, telling them to wash their hands before tea and be quiet, so they would not disturb their father as he was very ill.

There was a great deal of pushing, shoving and giggling as the girls squabbled as to who would have the soap next at the kitchen sink.

'Girls! Girls! Show some respect for your Father, you know how ill he is, so please be quiet.'

Louisa's hands looked red and crinkled, her face pale and drawn. She worked long hours at the big houses cleaning and cooking to make a few shillings to feed the family. It was obvious John was unable to work and contributed nothing to the household as he looked so ill. Louisa explained to the girls he drank beer to obliterate the pain of his tuberculosis.

The girls all nodded; they well understood Louisa.

John tried desperately to sit upright to eat his meal.

I could see that the family were very poor and also that John had severe health problems; all these things had a profound effect on Louisa as her appearance had dramatically changed. She was more emaciated than I had ever seen her before.

'All right Gwen, I only have one pair of hands. Unless you would like to come and help me of course, and I shouldn't imagine for one moment

The Visitor

that would be very likely?'

Louisa May smiled at Gwen, and I gathered that she was the small baby I had left with Louisa and John so long ago ... so they called her Gwendolene, what a romantic name for a girl, I thought.

'Oh! Look at your father now! Come on Gwen, look at him, he has soup all in his hair. I do wish I could find help for him, he keeps falling over onto his meals all the time. Honestly, I don't know how he still keeps going, really I don't!' Louisa May put John's arms around her neck, Dora and Gwen held his waist. All three propelled him towards the sofa, but John seemed oblivious to everything happening to him.

'Mother, why don't you speak to Father about his drinking? It's getting much worse, even out of hand I'd say. Can't you get some medication from the doctor for him? Really, it is so very embarrassing.' Gwen slumped onto one of the kitchen chairs and Dora and Hilda nodded in agreement. Connie, the youngest child, played on obliviously with her new marbles on the cold linoleum floor as she thought her father to be quite a bore, especially when he had been drinking heavily.

'Gwen,' Louisa said, 'how dare you speak of your father like that. No, we can't get medication. Tablets cost money, and we don't have money, so your father has to resort to his beer for his pain. You know that and you are never to speak about your father in that way again; it is not his fault. He has been through such a lot in his life and we must all try and help him as much as we can.'

Louisa May was filled with longing for how it used to be when she had first moved to Tower Street with John. She looked around at her girls who were listening to her with wide-eyed amazement as they knew John's drinking was not only to blot out his pain but because he actually liked stout: they all knew this for a fact!

Louisa May loved all her girls and John, even though she was near to despair and had precious little money. She worked hard, cleaning other people's houses for a few pence, but she wouldn't be without her girls for the world: although Gwen was a little headstrong, Dora so sensible, Hilda so diplomatic and Connie, such a happy child that Louisa May knew she couldn't have survived the cruelty of poverty without them. She cleared the kitchen table of bottles and newspapers, cleaning it and laying it with crockery ready for the next day. Why she did it she wasn't sure, as there was precious little to eat, but Sarah at Sycamore House always did it to save time the next day and she had remembered all the routines of Sycamore with affection and carried on the traditions in Tower Street. It was no Sycamore House, that was for sure, but Louisa tried hard to set standards for her girls which she hoped they would appreciate in years to come.

I was overwhelmed seeing Louisa and John in such terrible circumstances.

The Visitor

No wonder she looked so pale and thin but what could I do to help? Nothing, for I was simply a ghost, an observer.

Suddenly there was a loud pounding at the front door which got louder and louder, in fact deafening, although Louisa May couldn't hear anything as she was profoundly deaf now. The girls heard and tugged Louisa's sleeve to alert her to the fact that someone was at the door.

Gwen, being the eldest, accompanied her to the door, opening it, to reveal a very official-looking gentleman standing before them. The man was dressed in a morning suit and top hat and carried a cane, sporting white spats on his shoes and a huge, pink carnation in his lapel. Someone very wealthy, Gwen thought.

The gentleman spoke.

'Louey, Louey, don't you recognise me, dear? Louisa it's me, Bertie, it's me!'

Bertie flung his arms about Louisa May's shoulders hugging her to him.

'Bertie! Oh, Bertie, I have longed for this day when you would find me, my dearest brother, come in, come in please. However did you find us and where is Jacqueline?'

Louisa looked over Bertie's shoulders expecting to see Jacqueline. Bertie cupped Louisa's chin in his hand positioning her eyes to read his lips.

'No, dearest one, I did not bring her, as I was not sure I would find you or how long it would take me to find you. She is well, at home, and she instructed me to tell you if I did find you, she loves you and longs to see you again.'

Bertie and Louisa kept hugging each other, with all the Garton girls now assembled in the hallway looking on with great astonishment.

'Come, come ...'

Louisa May led Bertie up the stairs to her rooms. He looked around in horror, not of course indicating any of his abhorrence at the surroundings to Louisa or her girls, who were following the couple up the stairs. Louisa chatted away endlessly as she had done years before with her girls butting in periodically and stroking Bertie's grand clothes. They had never seen anything as luxurious as the velvet coat he was wearing and kept touching the material with wonder for it felt so soft. Louisa escorted Bertie into the sitting room at Tower Street. John was still in a stupor, sprawled on the sofa looking pale and ill.

Louisa shook her head.

'Poor John, he isn't at all well, Bertie, he has been ill for such a long time.'

The girls giggled under their breath.

'Drunk you mean, mother.' Gwen couldn't help herself.

'Gwen! Really! You naughty girl! You know I have been talking to you all about your father's condition and how ill he is. Really, I can't forgive that

The Visitor

remark, Gwen. Please go to your room at once! I will not have that sort of talk.'

Gwen shrugged her shoulders, flouncing out of the room and closed the bedroom door behind her with a thud.

Louisa could bear it no longer and gathering her white apron to her face, she wept. Bertie rushed towards her to comfort her, while the girls looked on in utter amazement, as they had never seen their mother weep before.

'Girls, go outside and play please, I need to talk to your Uncle Bertie.'

Louisa May's voice was gentle, but firm.

'Must we? Oh mother, please let us stay and talk to Uncle Bertie.'

Hilda was very curious about her uncle.

'Girls, please do as you are told and don't question me.'

Louisa May pointed to the door.

'Oh, all right.' Hilda led the way, with Connie and Dora following, glancing back at their Uncle Bertie as they left who was smiling and waving at them.

When the girls had gone, Bertie sat Louisa May down opposite him at the kitchen table.

'Now then, Louey, you must tell me, what has been going on, what has gone wrong? How can I help you, for help I must? I cannot bear to see you like this in this terrible place.'

Bertie held Louisa's hands to comfort her as she proceeded to tell her story.

I had a job to keep the tears from my eyes, hardly believing what I was hearing and I could see that Bertie was very moved by his sister's circumstances.

Bertie held Louisa's chin once more so that she could read his lips.

'Come away now, Louisa, bring the girls for we have enough room at our new house for you and all the girls. Come on, now.'

Bertie stood up, ready to leave Tower Street with Louisa and her girls.

'No! no! Bertie, I can't go with you, how can I? It is so very kind and I do appreciate your offer to help us, but how could I leave my John? I love him despite everything: he is so ill, how could I leave him?'

'How could you love a drunk? Why, look at him!'

Bertie spun Louisa around to look at John still deeply unconscious. He handed her his handkerchief to wipe her eyes.

'Bertie, you just don't understand. John has an illness, he is in so much pain and we can't afford medication for him. He should be in hospital by rights, so he drinks to try and stop his pain. It is so dreadful for him Bertie, please try and understand,' Louisa sobbed.

Suddenly, John stirred.

'Who is this then? Oh, I see, it is master Herbert, the young mister Bertie himself. Burlington Bertie of Bow.'

John started to sing at the top of his voice the well-known popular song, Burlington Bertie of Bow, much to the amusement of Bertie himself.

'So, yow cum to take my Louisa from me 'ave yow? Well, I don't think so, yes, I woz not too asleep to 'eah.'

John steadied himself as he stood up to face Bertie. The punch John intended for him missed, sending John sprawling to the floor, bloodying his nose as he hit the hard floor.

'John! John!' Louisa May ran to John's side, turning him over and putting his head on her lap, wiping away the blood from his nose; but John was now out cold.

'Louey, let's get him back onto the sofa where he can sleep it off.'

With the help of Louisa, Bertie lifted John back to the sofa.

'Is he always like this, Louey?'

Bertie could not believe his sister was enduring such agony.

'No, not always, he is tender and loving and he only gets this way when he is exhausted with extreme pain from his chest and lungs, believe me Bertie, it's true!'

Louisa brushed John's fair hair out his eyes, looking back at Bertie nervously.

I wondered how Louisa May endured such an existence with John in his present state, and how she had become so very deaf? No doubt all would be revealed to me, but when?

Louisa knew that she could never leave Tower Street, or John in his present condition, although she did love Bertie and Jacqueline too.

Bertie pushed something into Louisa May's hand as he prepared to leave.

'Here, my precious, take this money; it will help you for the time being until I can decide what is the best for you, John and the girls. Here, take it and get yourself and the girls decent clothes and food on the table.' Bertie pressed a wallet full of money into Louisa May's hands.

'No, no, Bertie I just couldn't take this much money from you.'

Louisa felt embarrassed but Bertie insisted that she took the money, once more pressing the wallet into her hands.

'It is enough money to feed us for months and buy new clothes,' she thought.

Louisa May could neither laugh nor cry for she hadn't the strength any more, but was more than grateful to Bertie and hugged him passionately for his kindness.

'Jacqueline could not bear to see you like this, Louey, nor can I for that matter, so please reconsider what I have said. I shall return in about a week for your decision. You and the girls shall come and live with us. We shall get John into a hospital and get him the best attention; please think about it seriously.'

Louisa nodded to Bertie as she showed him down the wooden stairs to the front door.

'Bertie, promise me you will never tell anyone else about us here in Tower Street, not Sarah, mother, father, or anyone, promise me?'

'Dear sister, I am ashamed to say, mother and father, never speak of you and if I dare to speak your name I am quietened almost immediately, they refuse to acknowledge you exist. Very upsetting, the whole business.'

'I am not surprised. Anyway, I have made my own life now with my girls and John. I hardly think of mother and father, but of course I frequently think about you Bertie and Jacqueline and Sarah. I often wonder where you are and what is happening to you all.'

Louisa hugged him to her and gave him a gentle kiss on the cheek.

'Don't forget now, Louey.'

Bertie bade his driver to draw away from Tower Street, with Louisa May waving frantically after the coach and the girls shouting: 'Bye Uncle Bertie, bye!'

'Was that really our uncle, mother, our Uncle Bertie? Where does he live? Is it far away? I expect he lives in a very big house! Is it bigger than Buckingham Palace, mother?'

Hilda, Dora and Gwen were very inquisitive about their uncle, but Louisa offered them no explanations.

The Visitor

'Children like you should be seen and not heard. I will tell you all about him when you are older, but not now; as I said, young ladies should be seen and not heard!'

Louisa gathered her daughters around her, taking them back inside the house.

The family meal that evening was much better than usual for there was plenty to eat and drink thanks to Bertie's supplied money, although Louisa May couldn't make it look too grand as John would suspect that Bertie had given her money and that there was more money hidden away somewhere. Louisa knew John would search for it and spend it on the 'demon drink' for his pain if he could, so she was very careful not to be too extravagant, but supplied enough wholesome food for everyone.

The Next Day

'Girls!' Louisa shouted.

'I will just take baby Bert to Margaret, she said she would look after him today whilst we all get on with the housework together. At least it will give us all some peace.'

Louisa took Bert downstairs to Margaret who was more than willing to look after the toddler, as she loved all children.

I wondered when Louisa had given birth to this baby boy, but at least I knew he was very much loved as were all her children.

Louisa thanked Margaret for her help with Bert and returned to her rooms upstairs.

Once again, the front door of the small terraced house in Tower Street was being pounded just like the day before when Bertie had visited. Perhaps it was Bertie again as he had promised the girls and Louisa he would see them very soon. The girls alerted Louisa to the fact that someone was at the door and she brushed back her long hair, pinning it on top of her head neatly as she went downstairs to greet, as she thought, Bertie.

Louisa May pulled open the door excitedly, expecting Bertie to be looking back at her, but no, it was a stranger, a man, dressed in a dark suit. Outside in the street there was an open carriage waiting with two large men sitting in it.

'Mrs Garton?' the man asked.

Connie rushed forwards and stood between the man and Louisa.

'She can't hear you Mister, you will have to speak very slowly so she can read your lips.'

Connie stood by her mother, holding onto her apron, as she did not like the look of the man at all.

'Are you Mrs Garton?' the man asked once more.

The Visitor

The man glanced back at his companions, who for some reason, seemed strangely embarrassed about Louisa's deafness.

'Let me put it another way, Mrs Garton: is Mr Garton at home?'

The man took a notepad from his inside jacket pocket and held a pencil poised to write. Louisa and Connie looked puzzled. By this time, the other girls had joined them at the front door.

'Why do you ask, what do you want?'

Louisa pushed Connie behind her, shielding her, as she felt very uneasy for a moment about what the man wanted.

'Mr Garton is ill, lying down, he hasn't been well for some time.'

Louisa hesitated before she continued.

'In fact, you will have to state your business as I would hate to wake him up for no good reason.'

The man looked very official and stern.

'These all your children, Mrs Garton?'

Louisa strained to read the man's lips.

'I said, are these all your children? I had better come inside lady, better not stand here on the pavement, eh?'

The man brushed past Louisa and her girls, walking into the hallway and looking around him with disgust.

'Shall we go to your rooms Mrs Garton? I think it is best, we can talk more privately there. I've come about your children you see, there have been complaints that we have received and have to, by law, follow up. Here are my credentials for your interest.'

The man handed Louisa his papers and she read that he was from the newly formed NSPCC, a children's organisation for abused and poverty-stricken children.

'Yes, these girls are my children, and what has your organisation to do with me? I don't understand, there are no abused, orphaned or poverty-stricken children here. As you can see, my children are well cared for and happy.'

Louisa May felt panic in the pit of her stomach and the girls moved closer to her sensing something awful was about to happen to them.

Margaret Thompson from the rooms downstairs came out into the hallway to see what all the commotion was about, leaving baby Bert in the good care of her grown-up son.

'I couldn't help hearing most of the conversation Louisa. What do yow men want with her? She ain't done nothing.'

Margaret tried her best to convince the man that Louisa was a good mother to her girls, but the man did not listen and made his way up the wooden stairs to Louisa's rooms. The girls ran after him and Louisa May followed, looking bewildered and frightened. She opened her front door into the dingy rooms to reveal John in a drunken state on the sofa. The girls

The Visitor

tried to hide John by standing in front of the sofa; they did not want the man to see him so ill.

The man continued.

'We are from the newly established NSPCC, Mrs Garton. I am very sorry about this, but as Inspector I am allowed to assess each situation as I find it and it is my duty, here are my papers once more, to say, I find your dwelling not fit, especially for young children who seem malnourished and in need of special care. Therefore I serve you with this warrant and shall take them with me now until such time as you can provide a proper dwelling and proof that you can properly care for them.'

'No sir, you won't. You are not taking my daughters anywhere with you, sir.'

Louisa took the papers from him, quickly scanning over the words.

Gwen ran to Louisa's side.

'What is it, mother? What is the matter? You have gone as white as a ghost. The man can't take us from you, can he mother? Please don't let him. What about the ...'

Gwen managed to stop herself mentioning baby Bert's name. Perhaps if she did not mention him, he would be safe with Margaret and would not be taken away.

'No, no, dear of course he can't. There must be some mistake.'

Louisa shook John trying to arouse him.

'John! John! Wake up, some men are here, they are going to take the girls. John, wake up for God's sake!'

Louisa shook John once more, but no matter how she tried, John had sunk into an even deeper sleep.

'Mother! Mother! Don't let the bad man take us all!'

Connie rushed to Louisa gripping her tightly. The girls started crying and screaming. They were terrified.

'Where is Bert, Mummy; will he be taken too?'

Connie's quiet voice was not heard by the Inspector.

Louisa put her finger to her lips to instruct Connie to be quiet and not talk about baby Bert. She spoke very quietly to Connie so that the Inspector did not hear them.

'Be quiet Connie, don't mention him. If you do, the man will surely take him too.'

The Inspector did not hear Louisa or Connie as he had gone into the kitchen looking around the room and making notes.

Louisa held onto her girls tightly.

'Nothing is going to happen, darlings, to any of you, no one is going to take you away.'

Louisa's stone-faced expression met the man's eyes.

The Visitor

'Tell me sir, who has complained? By what right did they report us, for what? How dare you come here threatening us like this? I want you to leave right now.'

Louisa rose to her full height, raising her voice for the first time in front of her girls, all shaking with fright.

'There are no deprived children in this house so why are you telling me this? You are certainly not taking my girls.'

Louisa once more pushed her girls behind her small frame, trying to protect them.

'Now, now, madam, nothing will be gained by resisting us. We have the law on our side and we know your children are starving, and also that two of your girls have suffered some cruelty from your husband, so much so, one of them had to go to the hospital recently for a nose injury, isn't that true madam? It will be for their own good, until your case is assessed properly. When you can prove you and your husband can support your children properly and he is working, then maybe you will be allowed to have your children back.'

'How dare you, sir! My husband can provide properly for us and has for many years. It is just at the moment, he is very ill, isn't that right Margaret – he can't work.'

Margaret took Louisa's hands in hers.

'That's right, her husband has been very ill for weeks, he can't work that's true. Louisa works, don't yow ducks, and I look after her girls whilst she is away. I feed them as well, don't I ducks.'

Margaret said everything she could to try and convince the man.

The man moved towards the girls who all took one step back from him. Louisa pushed them further towards the wall putting herself between them and the man.

'No, Mrs Garton, nothing is to be gained by resisting us, you can visit them at the home, whenever you like; it is not a prison you know, just a stepping stone for you and your husband until you can, as I said, provide properly for them. Now come on, don't let's have a scene. I could remove them by force but that will only upset your girls more. Be sensible now.'

The man led the girls downstairs, then out of the house into the street to the waiting carriage.

Louisa once more tried in vain to wake John.

'John! John! Please, wake up!'

Louisa shook him but it was no good for he was out cold.

'Margaret, help me, please, what can I do? Where is Bertie, I shall have to get word to him. 'Oh! Margaret.'

Margaret put her arm around Louisa.

'Come on, we shall see about this, we have to stop them somehow,'

The Visitor

Margaret whispered. 'Don't worry about Baby Bert ducks, Jack will look after him. He is very sensible.'

As Louisa and Margaret rushed downstairs, Connie, the youngest of the girls, screamed as the man lifted her into the coach.

'Mother! Don't let them take us, Mother!'

Louisa shouted as the coach started to drive away.

'Don't worry darlings, it won't be for long, I shall come and get you out!'

By this time, all the neighbours were out in the street cursing the men and waving their fists, shouting at them not to take the girls away.

Louisa started to run after the coach.

'Louisa, don't run after it, you'll never catch it,' Margaret shouted.

The girls were crying and screaming for Louisa.

Louisa May ran after the coach shouting, 'Girls, I love you all.'

Louisa ran for all she was worth along the street trying to catch the coach, managing to grip a handle on the back of it. The coach dragged her with it along the street. As the coach gathered speed neighbours gasped as she fell off the back of it, crumpled and bleeding on to the cobble-stoned street.

Thankfully the girls could not see what had happened as the back window of the coach was blacked out.

Margaret and some neighbours rushed to Louisa's aid.

'Louisa, let me help yow. Yow poor dear, look at yower knees all bleeding and yower poor hands. Come on, I'll take yow back to my rooms and get yow cleaned up.'

Margaret helped Louisa to her feet; by this time, the coach had disappeared out of sight.

Margaret took Louisa to her rooms, offering her a cup of tea and some biscuits. Louisa politely refused. How could she eat or drink at a time like this. What could she do for her girls? She could get a policeman, that's what she would do, but then, these men were the law and what could a policeman do anyway? How could she get back her beloved girls? Margaret tried again to coax Louisa to drink some tea and eat some biscuits but Louisa refused, she felt too numb and sick.

'My poor Louisa, we shall get yower girls back. We will think of something, yow will see. Here, I shall fetch some warm water and clean yower knees and hands up. Yow will feel the effects tomorrow when the bruising comes out, mark my words.'

Margaret cleaned Louisa's wounds and after talking with her about her girls and what could be done, Louisa decided to go back to her rooms.

She sat at her kitchen table feeling emotionally drained, looking across to the sofa where John was still asleep, unaware of what had happened. She schemed and plotted ways to get her girls back convinced the only way to help them was to get a message to Bertie and Jacqueline, for they would know what to do and would definitely help her.

Louisa prodded and shouted at John trying to wake him but it was no use. He wouldn't wake up.

Some hours later, John began to stir and Louisa's anger had grown in the few hours she had watched him sleeping off his booze. When he did eventually wake, Louisa started to shout at him.

'It's all your fault John,' she yelled.

'All our neighbours have heard my cries of torment today about our beloved girls. They've gone, John, yes, gone! Who would have reported us to the authorities like that, who? We have done nothing wrong, only love our children. How could that be thought of as wrong? The man said our girls were starving and abused.'

John sobered up very quickly hearing Louisa's anger. He had never heard her raise her voice before and it startled him.

'What? What are yow saying?'

'John, you will never believe what has happened to our girls! I can hardly believe it myself and you, I could kill you John, you just lay there.'

Louisa dabbed her eyes with her apron and told John the whole story.

Louisa May could only wonder at herself – why didn't she go with Bertie, why she must be so stupid. None of this would have happened if she had. She remembered Bertie's words. 'Just let me know when you want to come, I shall fetch you.'

Louisa May was so tempted to do just that and rummaged in her apron pockets for the note on which she had written Bertie's address, smoothing it out so that she could read it properly. Her tears fell like raindrops onto the ink, smudging it. Bertie had married his beloved Jacqueline and bought a fine house in Solihull, seven miles' walk away from Tower Street. How would she get there?

'I can walk,' she thought, 'but it would take forever to get there.'

'Eah, Bab, don't leave us, please, Bab. I love yow, don't yow know it. It is only my pain, such terrible, nagging pain. I 'ave to drink to deaden it, please, Bab, don't leave us. I love yow.'

John hugged Louisa to him and she knew that she could not leave him but also knew that she would just have to reach Bertie to get help for her girls, whether John liked it or not. Louisa didn't answer John, so he was not sure if she would stay with him or not.

Louisa sighed, pushing John away and walked into her dank kitchen. She would make John and herself some tea and whilst doing it, she would think of how to get to Bertie. Opening the tea caddy where she had hidden some of Bertie's money she was shocked to see that there was precious little of it left, hardly enough to buy a packet of tea and certainly not enough for food, or for the tram journey. Where had the money gone? Louisa could guess.

The Visitor

John must have found it and used it for his beer money.

'John, you bastard, you absolute bastard. You have taken the money out of this tin haven't you?'

'Bab, don't be annoyed at me, I needed it, I had to, the pain was so bad, Bab, I just had no money. I found the money in the tin, I didn't think it was for anything particular, yow never said ...'

John looked pitiful and Louisa just couldn't argue with him any more.

Louisa searched John's pockets but there was no money left. She cursed and swore under her breath, deciding the best course of action was to leave right away and get Bertie's help.

John could go to his drinking friends who would console him, but for now, Louisa would leave.

John got up from the sofa, taking his coat which was hanging on a nail on the wall.

'Where are you going, John? Don't you dare to leave me, not now, John! John!'

'I'm not leaving yow, Bab. I'm going to find my girls and bring them back. Don't yow worry Bab, I'll get them back.'

'Don't be stupid John, in your state, how can you? I'm going to see Bertie – he can help us. Just stay where you are, I'll get to him somehow John.'

'Bab, eah, I've got two shillings left. Take it, I would die of pain now rather than keep my girls in any home. Eah.'

John pushed a few shillings into Louisa's hands.

'I'm going to bed Bab, I feel really bad. I feel so 'elpless, but at the same time so ill. Sorry Bab.'

'All right John. It isn't your fault. Do you need anything before I go?'

Louisa helped John to his bed and pulled the covers over his thin body. She was so worried about him. He looked as if he was dying; she should have asked Bertie for financial help to get him into a hospital.

The door to Louisa and John's rooms quietly opened.

'Louisa, are yow there ducks? Cooey, Louisa, it's only me.'

Margaret felt stupid, fancy calling out to Louisa! She was deaf and not able to hear her anyway.

Margaret tapped Louisa on the shoulder.

'Here's the bab ducks. Jack said he 'ad been really good, not a murmur.'

'Oh, Margaret, how nice of Jack to care for him. Please come in and sit down.'

'I've had to put poor John to bed, he is so ill. He has given me the few shillings he had to help me get to my brother's house but sadly it won't be enough for me to get to Solihull. We are sure my brother can help us get our girls back. I'll just put Bert to bed as well, then we can talk.'

Margaret sat down looking all around her at the deprivation that met her eyes.

The Visitor

Louisa was so glad Margaret had come for she wanted other things to keep her thoughts away from John and the girls. Margaret is just the person to do it, she thought.

'I'm afraid I have no tea or anything much to offer you, Margaret. Perhaps you would like some minted hot water with me, it is supposed to be very good for you and very refreshing? I was just going to make some.'

Louisa felt the tears welling up in her eyes, but was determined not to break down in front of Margaret.

'Deary, deary me Louisa, yow 'ave been through it today, why don't yow come to my place and have a nice cup of cocoa and something substantial to eat, eh?'

Margaret persuaded Louisa to go with her, for the thought of hot cocoa and eating was too much to refuse as she felt very weak with hunger.

'Come on, ducks, it will do yow good. Get the bab. He can sleep in Jack's room. Jack won't mind. Come on, bring 'im.'

Gathering the sleeping baby Bert from his cot, Louisa eagerly followed Margaret to her rooms downstairs.

Margaret showed Louisa into her sitting room.

'Oh, Margaret, what a beautiful room. What gorgeous furniture and pictures. It is just like Syc ...'

Louisa stopped herself in mid-sentence, as she had told no one of Sycamore House and her past, not even her girls. No one would ever know about her previous life at Sycamore House.

''Ere's Jack's room, put the bab on the bed. He can't drop off it. I can 'eah 'im cry anyway. Don't worry Louisa. Yow were saying ducks, just like where?'

Margaret busied herself in the kitchen preparing the cocoa and carefully cutting bread to make sandwiches.

'Oh, nowhere Margaret, but what a beautiful room you have.'

Margaret brought in the cocoa and sandwiches on a tray carefully placing them on a round small table near the sofa.

'Help yowerself Louisa. I shall tell yow my story. It is a long and naughty one and hope you won't be too shocked!'

Margaret made Louisa laugh and she found it easy to lip-read her as she had a large mouth and protruding teeth and her lips offered up more rounded words than most people's.

'Margaret, go on, I would be so interested and I could never think you shocking, whatever you had done in your past. Your past is private and I would never hold anything against you. You should know me better, Margaret.'

Louisa giggled.

'Well, we won't go too deeply into my story now Louisa, perhaps later, but not now as yow've got enough trouble in yower life ducks. Tell me, what has John planned to do about yower girls, how will yow ever get them back?'

'I just don't know what he intends to do Margaret, he is really too ill to do anything and will most likely have to go into either a hospital or sanatorium for his condition. I shall have to ask my brother for help with him. The only trouble is he lives so far away in Solihull, an expensive tram ride from here. So, there is nothing for it, I shall have to walk there, I can't afford the whole tram fare.'

'Ducks, yow will do nothing of the kind, yow will not walk. I'll lend yow the money. I have enough, don't need it anyway. Before you protest, I insist and I shall tell yow how I came about my possessions and how I have money stashed away. It wasn't my husband who helped me, oh no; he left, he did, long ago, left me with my little Jack to bring up on my own. We never went hungry though, not once because do yow know what I had to do to survive?'

Louisa shook her head and said,

'No, I have no idea, do tell me Margaret.'

Margaret drew Louisa close to her to lip-read, so that she would not mistake what she was about to tell her …

CHAPTER IV

Lady of the Night

Louisa May giggled at Margaret's stories about her earlier life as she made them sound so funny; both ladies enjoyed telling their own life stories to one another. Louisa May gave Margaret the occasional friendly prod as she did when she really liked someone. Margaret's story unfolded slowly with Louisa concentrating in utter amazement.

'When he was only seven years old, that's my Jack, my Syd left us.'

Margaret continued …

'I never heard from him again from that day to this. Good riddance if yow ask me! I would never have him back now, not even if he begged me, Louisa.'

'How terrible, Margaret, you and Jack must have really suffered, left alone like that!'

'Yes ducks, we did and if it wasn't for, well yow know, we would have starved.'

Margaret's face flushed, her eyes narrowed as she continued with her story. She told how she had grown to hate her husband Sydney and that she had not thought of him from that day to this.

'Well ducks, I hardly dare tell yow what I 'ad to do next, yow would never believe it, but I did it to keep body and soul together. Look at what I got now, these rooms, my lovely furniture, pictures and a little money put by. If I hadn't done it, ducks, I would never 'ave survived. My Jack and me, well, we were so 'appy in the end and never missed Syd after a while.'

Louisa felt very sorry for Margaret and hugged her to comfort her, reassuring her that if nothing else, she had a friend.

Louisa smiled and said, 'Margaret, you know, I would never think badly of you whatever you did. I am your friend and will stand by you through thick and thin. You have always been there for me in my hour of need.'

'Thank yow ducks, yow are so sweet and kind, yow don't deserve what has 'appened. All that yow suffered, unbelievable, yow are still smiling and kind.'

Margaret touched the hand of Louisa in friendship.

Both women chatted well into the night, laughing and enjoying each other's company. Margaret told Louisa how she had spent all the savings she had accumulated whilst married to Syd to keep her Jack, until in the end the savings were gone and they were both starving.

'Yow see, Louisa, no one knew where Syd was and I had searched all over for him, so there was nothing for it yow see, for me with no breeding or qualifications like yowerself, so I had to be a "lady of the night". There, now I've really shocked yow, haven't I?'

'No! No! You haven't at all, in fact Margaret I think you so very brave to do such a thing. It must have taken a lot of courage to come to a decision like that. No, really, I admire you tremendously.'

Louisa once more hugged Margaret.

Margaret continued, forming her lips around every word she uttered so that Louisa would be able to lip-read.

'I tried all the big houses for cleaning work, no good yow see, I 'ad a bab, no one to care for 'im during the daytime, whilst I worked. So off I went to all the pubs getting friendly with the so-called "girls", observing how they worked. Yow see, I just learned their chat up lines, it wasn't too 'ard. Very soon I started to get my own clients and left the bab at night with my neighbours. Of course, I couldn't tell the neighbours what I was really working as, I told them I was working behind the bar in the pub. Thankfully, they never found out what I really did for a job, only that I paid them well. So, 'ence the things around yow here. I found the best place for the punters and the big money was the Minstrel pub in Digbeth.'

Louisa May was fascinated by Margaret's story, and asked her to carry on.

'Well, after a few months, I began to look like the other "ladies of the night". I had beautiful gowns, nice jewellery, got myself some nice 'ouse 'old things and furniture from the money I earned, but most of all, Jack and me were never going to starve again. Then I managed put some money in the bank for a rainy day. The looks I got from the men cashiers at the bank. Yow would 'owl with laughter Louisa, some of them were my bloody clients from the Minstrel.'

Margaret laughed out loud as she thought it highly amusing.

'So what happened next Margaret?'

Louisa May was very interested in all that Margaret was saying.

'Well,' said Margaret, 'in the end of course, my looks started to go, getting older and rounder yow see. I 'ad banked enough money to keep Jack and me, so I knew I could still live in Tower Street without worrying too much. So I decided enough is enough and just stopped doing it, just like that! Funnily enough, no one from the Minstrel pub recognises me now when I go over there, I must look very different from them days. Let's 'ave another cuppa shall we Louisa? I 'aven't enjoyed myself so much in years as I 'ave tonight talking to yow. Yower poor thing, fancy, not being able to 'ear, but yow can understand all right, can't yow?'

The Visitor

Louisa nodded that she could understand.

'Yow must come again, Louisa and I'll tell yow some more of my stories, yow would really laugh at some of them.'

'I would love to hear more, Margaret, but I had better get back for John. I have imposed on your kindness for long enough. Bert hasn't stirred at all. We must have been talking for hours.'

Louisa felt saddened as she spoke of John.

'The doctor says that John may have to go into a sanatorium for his tuberculosis condition; it is getting much worse and the doctor thinks he may have to be away for months. I just feel at my wits' end at the thought and with the girls gone. John is so ill; did you realise, Margaret, he contracted his condition in the Boer war? He was only fifteen years old and lied about his age to get into the army. He said he felt guilty that all the other men were going to fight for Queen and country and he was left at home. Can you imagine that, being so brave and so young? The army didn't even question him; I have no doubt they knew he was underage, but the army were desperate for fighting men of any description. John was so brave, I can't believe he is suffering as a consequence. He wasn't going to tell me you know, Margaret, about his tuberculosis, but he is so ill, he had no alternative. So as you know, he has taken to drink to help his pain.'

Louisa's eyes filled with tears.

'There, there, ducks, don't take on so. Yow do 'ave to go and see your brother, I think that is the only alternative; 'e's the one with all the money to 'elp yow get John into the sanatorium and get the girls back. The few shillings I can afford and yower few shillings, ain't gonna be enough to get yow to Solihull. But we will find a way ducks, mark my words; we will.'

Margaret put her arms around Louisa's shoulders and drew her face around to hers so that she read her lips.

'Everything is meant to be, I am a great believer in fate. Yow are meant to suffer before things will get better. Yow will see, they will get better. Louisa ducks, I know I shouldn't suggest this, but, er ... yower girls ... well, I was thinking.'

Margaret looked a little embarrassed at her suggestion, as she knew Louisa was from an educated background and would hardly consider becoming a "lady of the night" but she knew she was desperate for money and to get her beloved girls back from the orphanage. It seemed the only thing open for her to earn large amounts of cash quickly. Margaret was convinced it would be the salvation for Louisa and her girls, especially if John had to go away into a sanatorium.

'Oh Margaret, how funny.' Louisa laughed heartily. 'Me, a "lady of the night?" Ha, ha, that's silly – I just couldn't imagine it. Me! I wouldn't know where to begin, or how to seduce a man!'

The Visitor

Louisa kept laughing about Margaret's suggestion.

'Well ducks, it would be a thought. Why not? You are still very beautiful Louisa, you could attract a man from fifty paces without doing anything at all. With a little powder and paint, which makes a girl what she ain't, well, there's no telling what yow could earn. Anyway, John may be in the sanatorium soon anyway, poor devil. Yow wouldn't 'ave the girls to think about, not meaning to sound cruel about them, and I would love to 'ave the bab, whilst my Jack is at work. It would give me something to think about, I would love to 'ave 'im. Yow could give it a try, make some money. What will be the 'arm?'

Margaret waited for Louisa to nod. Eventually, she did! Yes she would become a "lady of the night". After all, what was the harm?

Margaret took Louisa's arm pulling her through to her elaborately decorated bedroom.

'See ducks, this is what yow get if yow work hard like me at being sociable.'

Margaret and Louisa fell onto the bed in fits of laughter. Being with Margaret reminded Louisa of her far-off days at Sycamore House with Jacqueline. Margaret opened her wardrobe doors to reveal many beautiful gowns in all styles and colours, taking them out one by one, pressing them against Louisa's body for size.

''Ere is a beautiful dress Louisa, it cost the earth, only from the best shops in the city for me in them days. Just the colour for yow ducks; isn't it gorgeous? Blue is definitely yower colour. I wouldn't have thought so with those black eyes and black hair, but it is definitely yow.'

Louisa studied herself in Margaret's long dressing mirror, pushing the blue velvet dress against her tiny body and tossing her head back in admiration of the reflection of herself looking back.

'Pile yower hair up on the top of yower 'ead, like this, Louisa.'

Margaret swept up Louisa's thick long black hair on top of her head which defined her delicate features and high cheekbones.

'Louisa ducks, yow are so beautiful, yow don't give yower self credit for it. Why yow could get any man up there at the Minstrel, they will go mad for a woman of quality with looks like yow. Yow will make an absolute fortune! Yow should really consider the possibility of working up there. Who would ever know about it? I would never tell. John would never find out if yow were clever about it. I'll teach yow how to chat and talk to the gents. Yow will learn quick, I know it. And please don't worry about the bab, I shall tek good care of 'im.'

Louisa once more studied herself in Margaret's long mirror: she knew what Margaret was saying would be more than a possibility. Yes, she still looked beautiful and with the right clothes and her hair styled, could become a "lady of the night".

The Visitor

'Margaret, I am really nervous about doing this. I know nothing of men and worldly things, well … er … I know you said you would teach me to seduce them, but what if they got, well … over zealous, how would I cope with it? I just don't know about it, although I am very tempted.'

'Eah, I'll put some of me paste diamonds around yower neck with that dress. Don't give it another thought Louisa, yow will soon learn and soon know 'ow to cope with men. I 'ad to learn, bedding them is the easy part, nothing to that, but yow 'ave to be careful who yow pick. Yow will soon learn who to trust. Yow will soon get yower "regulars".'

Thoughts of Sycamore House flooded back into Louisa's mind, but she must not think of it now, she must just think of earning enough money to save her girls. Yes, she would earn a lot of money she was sure. She would take Margaret's advice on how to be a "lady of the night" and would do it gladly for the sake of her girls and John.

Margaret helped Louisa out of her gown.

'After all Louisa, our beloved Prince of Wales and Lillie … well, if she ain't doing the same as yow are thinking of doing? It's the oldest profession in the world and one which will pay extremely well. Let's face it Louisa, yow need the money. If it's good enough for her and our King, it's good enough for yow.'

Margaret threw her head back and laughed loudly. Louisa laughed too as she knew Margaret was right, but hardly dared to imagine what the next few weeks would bring for her. She wondered when Bertie would come back to see her. It had been over two weeks since he visited and maybe he could save her and the girls. Then she would not have to resort to being a 'lady of the night'. But what if he didn't come? What if he had thought better of it? Surely not; he did love her and would come back, she was sure.

During the next few days, Louisa frequented Margaret's rooms, learning her trade well; she was an excellent pupil.

A few days later

John had become acutely ill and the doctor strongly advised that he should go to the sanatorium he recommended in the country.

Leaving baby Bert with Margaret, Louisa accompanied John on his journey to the sanatorium and could hardly come to terms with the fact he would be confined for a few months at least. She consoled herself with the fact that if she could earn large amounts from her liaisons at the Minstrel pub whilst he was gone; perhaps she could surprise him with the return of the girls from the money she had earned when he got back from his convalescence, but how could she explain all the money she had made? She wouldn't think of that now, the important thing was to get John better and to help him on

The Visitor

his journey to the sanatorium. John looked dreadfully ill and was hardly able to stifle his uncontrollable cough; he hadn't had a drink in two hours, and the pain was telling on his ashen face.

'It won't be long now John, we shall soon be there. Have another sweet, it will help you with the cough.'

The other passengers in the train carriage looked annoyed at John, frowning at his incessant cough.

The train journey seemed to take such a long time and Louisa's thoughts welled in her mind over and over as to how she would repay Margaret for the train fare and when would Bertie come to rescue the family.

'If only I could hear,' she thought.

All she could think of was being a 'lady of the night'. Would people guess she was a prostitute by just looking at her? She could tell them by just looking! Oh my God, was she doing the right thing? It had to be the right thing. She was only doing it for John and her girls' sake! Anyway, who would want a deaf woman to work for them? No one wants a deaf woman however well qualified. Why do people think deaf people are mentally backward, she wondered.'

'Penny for them, Bab.'

John took Louisa's hand in his. 'Yow are so deep in thought Louisa.'

John slouched forward gripping his chest. 'This bloody pain, I can't stand it no more, I need a drink!'

'Here's the station John, come on, we can get off now, you will soon feel better in the fresh air. We'll get a coach ride to the sanatorium. There must be some coaches to hire around here somewhere.'

Louisa helped John off the train. He leaned against her for support as he felt so weak and ill. She could hardly take the weight of him and passers-by just looked on in disgust, thinking John was drunk.

'Look, over there John, there is a coach. We can hire it to take us to the sanatorium, it can't be far from the station.'

Louisa hailed the coach, helping John into it.

The sanatorium was a huge rambling stone-built building with rolling lawns in front of it leading down to the road. It must have been a spectacular house at one time, Louisa thought.

The coach stopped outside the front entrance of the sanatorium. Louisa helped John get down from the coach, supporting him as they went through the entrance into the grand hall.

'Don't worry John, everything is going to be all right now, you will be well looked after. You never know, they may cure you forever, you may never get this awful cough again, nor pain and certainly no blood. Take care darling, I shall try and come and see you again. Don't worry about me John, I shall get a job somewhere, Margaret Thompson says she knows of a few

The Visitor

cleaning jobs going, although I lost the one at the big house.'

Louisa kissed John's lips tenderly.

'I do worry about yow Bab; what will yow do without any money, without me?'

'What everyone else has to do John, survive, and I shall, but I don't want you to worry about me, the girls or anything. Just concentrate on getting well. I need you well.'

Once more Louisa kissed John's lips, handing his small case of clothes and belongings to a nurse who seemed to appear from nowhere.

'Mr and Mrs Garton, would you come this way please.'

'I was leaving because of the train timetables. Let's see, the time now is quarter past three, the next train is quarter past four, but if the consultation only takes a few minutes, I will go with you John to see the consultant and get you settled. I shall possibly be able to get a coach back to the station?'

The nurse nodded and said,

'Yes, there is a coach every ten minutes from here to the station. You should be all right to connect with your train. If you like I can let you know when the next coach comes in. It should take twenty minutes with the consultant, that is all.'

Louisa thanked the nurse.

The nurse took Louisa and John into a small office.

'The consultant will be here in just a moment; he will give you details on how long Mr Garton is likely to be here and will answer any of your questions.'

Louisa and John sat down, smiling at each other. John started to cough.

'There, there, John.'

Louisa patted John's back.

A tall, middle aged man in a white coat came through the door, closing it and sitting behind the desk, smiling at Louisa and John.

'Please, don't get up, do remain seated. I am Mr Reynolds, the consultant here.' Mr Reynolds shook Louisa's hand and then John's.

'Now then Mr Garton, you have been experiencing some serious problems?'

'Yes sir,' John said.

Louisa studied hard the lips of Mr Reynolds.

'Let me explain to you both what the prognosis is on your illness, your treatment and hopefully, your recovery Mr Garton.'

'Please sir, would yow mind speaking a little slower, my wife is deaf yow see, but she can lip-read very well. Yow will have to go a bit slower for her.'

John started to cough once more, taking out his handkerchief to catch the spots of blood which dropped from his mouth.

'Here, Mr Garton, have a glass of water. Take deep breaths, put your head back for a while, try not to panic. Panic brings on an attack quicker than anything else.'

Mr Reynolds got up from his chair bringing the glass of water to John and feeling his forehead.

'Are you all right Mr Garton?'

'Yes sir, please, yow carry on.'

'The letter from your own doctor says you have had this condition for months and it has steadily got worse. Well, I can see, without a real examination, you have acute tuberculosis and this has to be treated immediately. The ideal situation would be to send you to Switzerland for a year or so, that would help immensely but, in your circumstances, would be out of the question.'

John and Louisa nodded, laughing at the suggestion. It was completely beyond their financial capabilities to even think of sending John to Switzerland.

'The other option you have Mr Garton is … I don't know if you would agree to something which is not altogether tested and proved.'

'What is that then Doctor? I will do anything to get rid of this terrible cough. It drives me mad and I just can't stand it any more. I'm worn out.' John once more started to cough uncontrollably.

Mr Reynolds continued.

'You see, although in its experimental stage, we are carrying out the occasional operation using a new drug, but not yet thoroughly tested, called anaesthetic. This means a lengthy operation of course as the anaesthetic puts you into a deep sleep and you, the patient will know nothing of the pain of the surgery. I have to add, it is not completely proven and tested, although our beloved King underwent his surgery with the new drug anaesthetic only months ago. He survived to tell the tale. You understand we are using the drug on seriously ill people, to test it mainly. This is completely voluntary on your part and if you agree, you will of course have to sign papers to say that if anything goes wrong we are not to blame and you agreed to the usage of the drug. You understand Mr Garton, if anything did go wrong during the operation, we are not liable but apart from that you would not experience any pain. There is no guarantee at all, but your damaged lung must be removed. You will surely die anyway if it is not. Take some time to discuss it with your wife if you like, but I can assure you in your case it is your only option.'

Mr Reynolds looked back and forth from Louisa to John, John looking down at the floor seemingly toying with the idea of the operation.

'All right Mr Reynolds, I'll need time to discuss it with my wife.'

Louisa stood up putting her arms around John's shoulders for support.

'Oh John, you are so brave. My dearest. I shall do my best to come and see you soon.'

Mr Reynolds helped John to his feet.

The Visitor

'Well, in your place Mr Garton, I would do the same, you need to think about it. We are using you as our guinea pig, but without the operation, be assured, you would surely die. With the operation you have a good chance of recovery. I have to advise you both the cost of the operation is two hundred pounds. The drug is extremely expensive to buy so unfortunately we have to pass on that cost to our patients. However, I shall leave you both to consider the matter and will return shortly.'

Mr Reynolds shook John and Louisa's hands.

'Thank you doctor.'

John squeezed Louisa's hand.

'John,' Louisa said, 'you must have the operation. I will get the money from somewhere. I shall go to Bertie, he said he would help us financially if ever we needed him. I know he will help us. I know you don't want me to ask him John, but really, it is our only option. You do have to have this operation, there is no doubt in my mind.'

'Bab, I feel so helpless, and so inadequate. I 'ave brought yow nothing but pain and worry, please forgive me, Bab?'

John buried his head in Louisa's chest.

'You shall have the operation John. I'll shall see Bertie as soon as possible. I know he will help. Anyway the job I am going to get through Margaret will also help. I have five pounds Margaret gave us in case we are asked for a deposit. If it's any more John, I don't know what we shall do.'

'Bab, oh my beautiful Bab.'

John kissed Louisa on the lips.

'Come on now Bab, yow 'ave to stop crying.'

John wiped away Louisa's tears.

Mr Reynolds returned.

'Well, have you reached your decision Mr Garton?'

'Yes sir, I 'ave. I will 'ave the operation.'

'Good man; I have to ask, though, for a five pounds deposit and then the rest of the money when the operation is completed. We shall send word to your wife when this will be. Your operation will be scheduled in say, three days' time. In the meantime you will rest in the ward.'

Louisa hugged John, thanking Mr Reynolds for his time.

'Don't worry John, everything will be all right. I'll get the money.'

Louisa stood in the hallway for a while watching John being taken down a long corridor to the ward and blew a kiss to him as he disappeared out of sight. So many thoughts were whirling around in her head.

The Visitor

Two Days Later

Louisa had spent her days with Margaret carefully learning her 'new trade' while young baby Bert slept in Jack's room.

'Most women go into the work well ducks, but I can tell yow are so frightened. Don't be, as it becomes quite pleasurable after a while. Yow will be all right!'

'But Margaret, what about little Bert; who will look after him?'

'That is a minor detail ducks,' Margaret said. 'I will look after 'im. If I can't, well, Jack is in from six o'clock of an evening. He would love to play with 'im and look after 'im. The first night at the Minstrel, I will go with yow, while Jack looks after Bert, mark my words, he will be no trouble to us. If yow are not back 'til late one night, the bab will stay over with us and I will bring 'im up to yow in the morning. Don't worry about it ducks.'

Margaret kept laughing loudly but Louisa was very nervous at the prospect of working at night at the Minstrel. The women had chosen a Friday night to go to the pub as Margaret had assured Louisa that it was the best night for acquiring money from any man as it was 'pay day' and the men had money in their pockets.

The night had arrived. Jack played with Bert on the sitting room floor in Margaret's rooms.

'Yow mek sure Jack, the bab gets 'is supper at seven o'clock. Keep 'im up to eat it, then he will sleep till the morning. Yow come and fetch me from the Minstrel if anything is wrong. Understand lad?'

'Yes Mam, don't worry.'

Jack played with Bert and his toys and cared for him like his own brother.

Margaret had dressed Louisa carefully, powdering her face and spraying her with exotic perfumes, making her cough and choke. She smelled exquisite, but a little over-perfumed she thought!

'Come on, ducks, ready, don't be nervous now.'

Margaret took Louisa May's arm, leading her out into the dark night. If she had not been holding her arm, Louisa felt sure she would have fainted with shock at what she was about to do. Whom would she meet? What would he be like, or they? Oh, my goodness, she thought, what have I done? But Louisa knew there was no room now for sentiment or nerves, for she had to get her girls back and pay for John's treatment at the sanatorium.

After walking for about thirty minutes, the women arrived at the Minstrel pub. Louisa May's heart sank and she was sure she would be sick. The other girls will surely guess I am new and not experienced like them, she thought. The other 'ladies of the night' were standing against the Minstrel pub's walls, with their painted faces and common dress, glaring at Louisa and Margaret.

The Visitor

Louisa looked every inch a lady in comparison, but the others knew what she was there for, to find a client, just like the other girls.

Margaret led Louisa through the pub doorway and sat her down at a round wooden table near the bar. Louisa's hands became hot and sweaty with nerves and her legs started to tremble, even though she was sitting down. Her thoughts strayed to Bertie – he could help me now and why hasn't he replied to my letter.

Margaret guided Louisa's face towards her so that she could lip-read, mouthing her words carefully for Louisa's eyes to study.

'We need this drink of gin, ducks, give us some Dutch courage; drink up, Louisa, drink yower gin, yow'll feel much better then.'

John's face kept flooding into Louisa's mind, then far-off days at Sycamore House and her girls each took their turn. She was sure she would die, but knew she would have to find her strength from somewhere to do this work, if only for her girls' sake. The pub was filled with dense pipe smoke, loud voices and bawdy women. There was a man playing the piano in the corner of the room, not that Louisa could hear any of it. Louisa knew from watching the pianist's technique that he had been taught well and what a comedown it must be for him to be actually reduced to playing in the Minstrel pub.

Margaret drew Louisa's face around to meet hers.

'Come on, Louisa, smile, try and look wordly and happy. Yow want to trap a man, not drive him away. Stop worrying about the bab, he is all right with our Jack. Concentrate, Louisa.'

Margaret laughed, trying to reassure her as she signalled the barman to bring over two more gins. Louisa dared not study any face too closely, in case the 'face' came over to her, but wasn't that what she was there for? She gathered all her inner strength, starting to smile widely at all the men in the room and laughed loudly with Margaret.

In the corner of the room, a middle-aged gentleman unbeknown to Louisa had been watching her and trying to attract her attention. Margaret noticed him, nudging Louisa to smile back at him and encourage him.

'Go on, give him a bigger smile than that Louisa.'

Louisa looked back at the gentleman who was extremely well dressed and looked every inch a 'gentleman'. What was a man like that doing in the Minstrel pub? Louisa felt stupid for questioning what he was doing there for she knew very well that he was looking for a lady to accommodate him. The gentleman came over to where the two ladies were sitting.

'Ladies,' he said. 'May I join you? What are you drinking; may I buy your drinks?'

Margaret nodded.

'Yes sir, two gins if yow please. Thank yow. Yow will 'ave to speak very slowly and clearly for my friend Louisa. She is deaf yow know. Only lip-reads.'

The Visitor

Margaret gave Louisa a reassuring smile.

'How sad,' the genteman said, tapping Louisa's arm to gain her attention.

'Would you mind very much if I sit here next to you?' the gentleman asked.

Louisa just smiled and nodded and the well-dressed gentleman brought his chair as close to Louisa as he could. The drinks arrived and Louisa went into her carefully rehearsed routine, flirting outrageously with the gentleman until it was obvious that he would ask her for trade.

Margaret got up from the table.

'Well, Louisa, yow know yower way back so I shall see yow later and don't be too late will yow, ducks?'

Margaret winked at Louisa, who looked visibly worried about Margaret leaving her, but knew the plan and knew that she was going to depart eventually leaving her to her trade.

The middle-aged gentleman smiled at Louisa.

'My dear,' he said, gaining Louisa's attention. 'How much do you charge? I will pay the going rate. Why, you are a prize indeed, such a beauty, rare around here. Where are you from? I have never seen you here before.'

Louisa just smiled and nodded, hardly understanding what the gentleman was saying, although she gathered she would be leaving with him before very long to do her 'job'. She felt he had a kindly face and he was elegant and, dare she hope, a real gentleman. She was sure she would be quite safe with him and was glad in a way that he had picked her, as compared to the other men in the pub he was surely the best of the bunch! The gentleman's bushy moustache obscured his lips and Louisa found it very difficult to grasp everything he was saying.

'You don't have to be afraid of me, you know.'

The gentleman seemed kind, realising Louisa was not like the other girls at the Minstrel and was not used to the work she was forced into.

'I am not afraid of you sir, not at all and am well used to my work. What would make you think otherwise? Please don't assume that I am some sort of novice. I know what I am doing.'

Louisa had to make the gentleman believe that she was used to her trade although the pit of her stomach didn't agree.

'Do you have rooms or somewhere we can go to sir?'

The gentleman looked amazed as he felt he had misjudged this delicate creature beside him, for perhaps she was well used to her work. The gentleman got up from his chair taking Louisa's arm and leading her out of the pub. The punters shouted and jeered abuse at Louisa but she heard none of it. Turning Louisa's face to his, the gentleman seemed genuinely concerned for her trying to put her at her ease.

'Don't take any notice of those awful people, they know nothing of life.

The Visitor

Come on, my dear, this way. I shall take you to my house, it is not far away and we won't be disturbed.'

Louisa tried not to look frightened, as the man gripped her arm tightly, leading her to his waiting carriage.

The carriage had gone quite a few miles as buildings and roads flashed by and Louisa nervously looked out of the windows, trying to recognise any part of the city they were speeding through.

'Don't be alarmed my dear, I am not going to hurt you, I only want some affection, that's all. You see, my wife died some years back and well, I just need company more than anything.'

The gentleman drew Louisa's face around to his to continue the conversation.

'You see, my wife died some years back now and well, I just need the company of a lady from time to time. The only comfort I can get is from you "ladies of the night" but you, my dear, you are different, you took my eye straight away. You are so beautiful and I detect some education in that voice. Why are you doing this? Surely a lady of your stature need not resort to prostitution?'

The gentleman fired question after question at Louisa but she gave nothing away, just smiling and nodding back. Louisa looked into the man's face, studying his lips, reading all his questions. She thought, he could have been very handsome in his day. He was a man in his fifties, his face reddened and well weathered, freckled and deeply lined. He had very bright, blue eyes and sandy red hair with a matching moustache. Louisa was not at all afraid of him, as he seemed to genuinely care for her. Perhaps he did just want her company and it wouldn't be too terrible being with him for an evening after all?

He smiled at her as he took her small hand in his, caressing it with kisses, as the carriage came to a halt outside a very large, expensive-looking Edwardian-built house.

'Here we are.'

The gentleman helped Louisa from the carriage, his manners impeccable. Louisa felt quite the lady once more. She did not dare to think of John or the girls, but just kept her mind on what she was about to do. The carriage moved away, leaving Louisa and the gentleman standing outside the three-storey house.

The front door opened and a maid welcomed Louisa and her master inside the house. The maid took his cape, top hat and cane and Louisa's shawl, carefully placing them on the hallstand. The house was so reminiscent of Sycamore House with the lavish carpeting, furniture and ornate decoration. Louisa realised that this was a gentleman and a very wealthy one at that!

Louisa turned to the gentleman, who was now leading her up the ornate staircase towards the bedrooms.

The Visitor

'Sir, can I ask your name?'

Louisa looked into the gentle face of the man taking her to her first experience of prostitution. 'I can't kept calling you, sir, can I, especially if I am lucky enough to meet with you again?'

Louisa felt herself very forward and very uninhibited. She felt sure that she would benefit greatly from this gentleman financially and that was her objective.

'I think not my dear, it is better you do not know my name then nothing can harm you and you can't get into any sort of trouble because of knowing it. I am a well-respected gentleman in the area and it is better that you don't know about me. However, I realise you have to call me something, so I tell you what my dear, call me John.'

Louisa nervously smiled, how could she call him John?

'No, not John,' she said. 'That is not exotic enough for you sir. How about Frederick. That is a wonderfully distinguished sort of a name.'

They both laughed.

'Frederick it shall be then.'

As they reached the bedroom door Louisa once more felt the pangs of fright at the pit of her stomach.

'You can undress here and get into bed Louisa. I shall be with you in a few moments. Help yourself to any of the adornments around, perfume, whatever.'

The gentleman left the room leaving Louisa feeling very sick with fright.

Well, this is the moment, this is it. What will it be like? Louisa had never been unfaithful or even thought about being unfaithful to John! She did not love this gentleman and had always vowed that she would love a man before sleeping with him. How can I do this? She knew very well how; she must, she had to – what other alternative was open to her?

Her innermost fears and thoughts flooded into her mind as she took off all her clothes, glancing around the lavishly equipped bedroom, hardly daring to study anything too closely. Undoing her hair and carefully placing her hair slides on the bedside cabinet she climbed into the huge double bed, pulling the cream, silk sheets over her chest, but noticing the embroidered crests of E.B. on the edge of the sheet and pillowcase.

'Who was E.B.? She would try and find out! She would ask Margaret. Perhaps Margaret had come across these initials before, perhaps she would know who E.B. was?

The curtains at the window were slightly open, casting a stream of light over some parts of the room.

Frederick is being a long time, she thought, but the longer the better. The bedroom door eventually opened letting in more light, casting shadows across the bedroom from the landing light.

The Visitor

Frederick came towards the bed, the silk sheets drew back slowly and he slid into bed beside Louisa's tiny body. Frederick drew closer to Louisa putting his arms around her perfect body and caressing every part of her silken skin. Louisa didn't feel that she could object and started to enjoy his stroking and tenderness. After a short time, it was obvious that Frederick was not going to make physical love to Louisa for he just kissed her, sometimes fully on the lips, sometimes on her body. They lay together for what seemed hours to Louisa, but nothing physical took place.

Eventually Louisa turned to Frederick, looking puzzled and feeling just a little relieved, but at the same time, rejected. She was bewildered by her own thoughts. Is there something wrong with me physically? He is paying for the privilege so why isn't he taking advantage? Louisa was extremely puzzled.

Eventually Frederick spoke, drawing Louisa's face around to meet his as he said:

'I am sorry, my dear, but I don't want physical lovemaking. It isn't anything you have done, nothing to do with you personally, but I cannot, you see, well … I was desperately in love with my late wife and no one, ever, will replace her, but I just occasionally need to feel a woman's form next to me at night when I miss her the most and I am alone; do you see?'

Louisa nodded tenderly, stroking Frederick's face, kissing him gently on his lips.

'Yes I do see, please, you don't have to explain or apologise to me Frederick. It is my job to keep you company and you are paying for the privilege. I, too, have a similar situation to your own and I …'

Louisa managed to stop herself from saying any more. She trusted Frederick and felt she could confide in him about her girls, John and everything in her life, but she remembered Margaret's words, to never disclose anything to anyone however trustworthy they seemed. Louisa decided not to talk any more about herself.

'You don't need to know about me and I am very sorry about your dear wife. She must have been a wonderful person?'

'Yes, she was, a very dear lady.'

Frederick took Louisa in his arms crying bitterly at the loss of his wife.

'Please Frederick, don't cry so. Let's go downstairs and have some wine. It will make you feel much better.'

Louisa got out of bed and started to dress, handing Frederick his dressing gown.

'You are certainly a very special lady Louisa. If you agree, I would like to see you again. Perhaps we can dine out somewhere?'

'Thank you, I would very much like that Frederick.'

'You know, I think Frederick quite suits me, I am getting used to being

The Visitor

called that. It is very clever of you Louisa to invent such a good name for me.'

As they finished dressing, both started to laugh.

Frederick escorted Louisa downstairs into the library, taking her to one of the three sofas in the room.

'What a beautiful room Frederick, so tasteful and comfortable.'

'Do you take red or white wine Louisa?'

'Oh thank you, red will suit me well.'

Frederick handed Louisa a glass of wine and with it nine pounds.

'Frederick! Thank you so much, but nine pounds? This is too much, I only charge five shillings!'

'Nonsense Louisa, please take it. I have never enjoyed an evening so much for a long time and you are well worth the money. In fact every time I see you, you shall have nine pounds.'

'Thank you so much, it is so kind.'

Louisa sipped her red wine feeling very comfortable in her surroundings and especially with Frederick.

'Well, my dear, we have to get you back before it gets too late. I shall have my coachman take you to the Minstrel pub; I hope this is all right for you? My coachman can take you anywhere you wish.'

'That will do nicely Frederick, thank you so much.'

Frederick lit a candle, carefully placing it in the glass-domed table lamp. He escorted Louisa downstairs into the hallway. Kissing her forehead and her hand he made an appointment with her for the following Friday evening.

'Let me get your cape. Unfortunately all my staff seem to have retired to bed, the hour is late. Come, I'll take you to the coach. My coachman is always on hand.'

Frederick caringly draped Louisa's cape around her shoulders and led her outside to the coach bidding his coachman to take her back to the Minstrel pub.

Louisa smiled to herself, resting her head back on the heavily quilted velvet seating in the coach.

'Nine pounds, nine whole pounds. Margaret will never believe me when I tell her.'

Every week for six weeks Louisa visited Frederick at his home, giving him the feminine company he needed. The Minstrel pub was their meeting place and she was returned there after each liaison. Frederick never asked anything else of her or she of him, but it was apparent that he was very fond of her, showing her great tenderness. Frederick lavished her with gifts, money, jewellery and even on one occasion took her to another city, buying her the most elegant gown, which she kept hidden in Margaret's wardrobe in Tower Street.

The Visitor

Margaret was highly delighted with Louisa's progress with Frederick and was proud that she had taught her the 'trade' so well. The two women discussed the night's work, laughing and talking well into the early hours of Saturday morning. Friday nights soon came around. One particular Friday night, Louisa decided to wear the gown Frederick had bought her as she thought they may go out somewhere to another city.

'I shall see you much later Margaret, that is, if you want to stay up and hear all about it?'

'Stay up, of course I shall Louisa, can't wait to hear where you are going tonight.'

Louisa hugged Margaret as she prepared to leave to meet Frederick.

'Louisa, yow look so beautiful, just look at the clothes yow are acquiring. Why, I can't imagine what J ...' Margaret stopped herself in mid-sentence.

'Sorry ducks, I didn't mean that, I know it's so hard for yow.'

'That's all right Margaret, don't worry, you and I realise I am doing this just for the money. I think of John and the girls all the time. It is just for them I am doing it. Don't fret Margaret, you haven't offended me in any way. Oh, I nearly forgot, how much do I owe you still? I must have nearly paid you back by now? John should be back from the sanatorium in about three weeks. He has made wonderful progress and looks a different man, not like he used to. He no longer needs a drink. I feel so pleased with myself as I nearly have the money to pay the sanatorium fees. I don't have to go to Bertie begging and am so pleased I can be independent from my earnings. I can't thank you enough Margaret. My meetings with Frederick are going to have to stop shortly and it will be so difficult to explain to him. I rather think he has fallen in love with me Margaret. He is such a sweet man but I have to tell him after next week we can't meet again.'

Louisa hugged her friend, kissing her on her cheek as she left her rooms in Tower Street to meet Frederick.

The evening with Frederick was much the same as any other. The caresses and kisses Louisa had come to enjoy. She was escorted out of the house in the early hours of the morning to the waiting coach outside, to be taken back to the Minstrel pub; she could make her way home from there. The coach could never take her to Tower Street as no one there must ever find out about her liaisons at the Minstrel.

Frederick had given her his usual nine pounds fee. The coach drew away from the large Victorian house. Louisa kissed the money.

'This will be the last payment to Margaret and the whole payment for the sanatorium. I am so relieved.'

She smiled to herself. 'John will be home soon, I shall have paid the sanatorium, paid Margaret back, and I even have a small amount of money towards getting my girls out of that place. To get the rest of the money will be difficult; I shall possibly have to see Frederick perhaps just one more time and then ask Bertie for the rest of the money for the girls. I just can't understand why Bertie hasn't contacted me. With the money I have I could afford to go to Bertie's and be taken there in style. I f I break into my money though, I will be unable to pay Margaret and the Sanatorium.

CHAPTER V

The Escape

Louisa had spent another pleasant night with Frederick. She had been wined and dined. Once more Frederick had shown her out to the waiting coach to take her back to the Minstrel pub. It was midnight and very cold. The carriage stopped outside the Minstrel and the driver helped Louisa down from the carriage onto the cobbled street.

'Er ... Miss ... before yow go?'

The coachman held Louisa's arm and didn't realise she was deaf. Louisa turned around her eye flashing in temper at the coachman.

'Let go of my arm! How dare you touch me, your master will have something to say about this! If you don't let go, there will be trouble.'

Louisa tried to break free from the coachman's grip, but he was a large man with strong hands and a grip to match. She felt his fingernails digging into her flesh through her clothes.

'Miss,' the coachman said.

'I've been meaning to speak with yow – yow are one of them ain't yow? Well, I think I deserve a bit of affection myself don't yow? What do yow want with an old bloke like the master, he can't give yow what I can.'

The coachman started to pull Louisa away from the coach and down the side entry of the Minstrel pub towards the back of the pub where there was waste ground covered with debris and weeds.

'Take your hands off me, how dare you!' Louisa cried.

The coachman did not answer, but continued to pull Louisa down the side entry of the Minstrel pub.

Louisa was terrified, and fought bravely with the coachman who threw her to the ground like a rag doll. Her screams were unheard as the noise from the pub was louder than ever it seemed and no one could hear Louisa's desperate screams for help.

'Now yow can give me some of yower pleasure, lady.'

The coachman laughed loudly as Louisa fought and struggled against his brute strength. He smelled of beer and sweat, which made her feel sick. She could feel the material of her beautiful, new dress, being ripped and her underwear being dragged from her body as she desperately fought. Wriggling, biting and fighting for all she was worth, Louisa stretched out her arm, grappling amongst the weeds and found a large brick that she brought down onto the coachman's head with all her strength. Screaming in pain and falling backwards, he slumped back bleeding profusely, but now everything had gone quiet and he did not move at all.

'Oh, my God, I've killed him.' Louisa struggled to her feet.

Louisa could only stare down at the motionless body of the coachman, blood gushing down his face from his wound and a small trickle of blood was running down his chin from his mouth. He was surely dead. Louisa gathered herself together trying to cover up the torn sleeve on her dress and pulling down her layers of skirts. She cautiously made her way out of the side entry of the pub, occasionally glancing back at the coachman's motionless body. The Minstrel was very busy, none of the girls were outside as it was so cold so Louisa was sure no one had witnessed her attempted rape. Gingerly glancing back at the lifeless body, she began to run for all she was worth. The coach and the four horses were still tied up to the railings as she rushed passed them and out of sight of the Minstrel pub.

It seemed a long way back to Tower Street; Louisa stopped halfway to gather her breath, her heart pounding in fear. She felt sick and weak; what had she done?

'I've murdered someone,' she thought 'Now to add to my crimes, I am a murderess, but I had no choice, it was him or me. I had to hit him to save myself. But who will believe a deaf prostitute?'

Louisa felt she must keep calm, she must tell Margaret as soon as she got home, she would know what to do. Her mind drifted back to Sycamore House and how she had been seduced by Peter Dupont and now again by this animal of a man.

What was it about herself which made men want to do this, she wondered? Her thoughts raced to baby Bert. Poor baby, what a mother you have in me.

Louisa was too frightened to cry; all she wanted to do was to wash the stench of the coachman off her body and eradicate him from her mind forever.

'I must not even think of him, not even admit I have seen him.'

She was sure Margaret would agree with her.

'She will know what to do.'

Reaching Tower Street, Louisa opened the front door leading into the hallway, and breathed a sigh of relief. She banged on Margaret's door to let her in.

'Margaret, quickly, open the door! Margaret! It's me, Louisa, quick, open the door!'

'I'm coming.'

Margaret opened the door, and Louisa slumped down at her feet, dirty

The Visitor

and bleeding, with her dress torn to shreds.

'Oh my God, what on earth has happened to yow Louisa?'

Margaret sat down on the floor, cradling Louisa's head on her lap.

'Did Frederick do this to yow? Well, I never did, I'll sort 'im out that's for sure Louisa duck!'

Margaret got Louisa to her feet and helped her onto a sofa to lie down.

'I'll get some warm water to bathe yower wounds. Don't cry Louisa, we'll sort it out.'

'How is Bert? I will have surely woken him and Jack. What sort of mother am I, Margaret? Oh Margaret!'

Margaret bathed Louisa's face and hands which were cut and bleeding, while Louisa sobbed out the story of the terrible attack on her by the coachman.

'Yow are a caring and good mother Louisa. Stop panicking ducks. The bab is sleeping, so is our Jack. Yow won't 'ave woken them. Ducks, are yower sure the bloke is dead, I mean, was 'e breathing when you left 'im?'

Margaret continued to bathe Louisa's cuts and bruises.

'No I am not sure, but I had to hit him Margaret, I just had to.'

'I know yow did ducks, don't yow worry. No one will ever find out about it, I shall go and make enquiries myself, discreet like, to see if the bloke is still lying there. We shall get 'im moved if 'e is and no one will be any the wiser. We 'ave means, yow know, ducks. I've got some very good friends up at the Minstrel, don't yow fret. Yow stay 'eah for a while and yow will feel better in a few hours.'

Louisa hugged Margaret and was glad to be shown to a clean bed to sleep in and forget the fears of that night.

The Next Morning

'Come on, ducks, wakey wakey, it's a beautiful day, not like yesterday. Let's put 'orrible days behind us and 'ave a nice cuppa and some toast. Jack 'as taken the bab out in 'is pram for some fresh air. The bab 'as 'ad his breakfast.'

Margaret drew back the curtains to let in the sunlight.

'Margaret, what shall I do, Margaret?'

Louisa was still in deep shock and was amazed that she could have slept at all that night.

'Look, ducks, I'm off after breakfast up to the Minstrel to see some friends, don't yow worry about nothing, I told yow. Stay 'eah till I get back. Be a couple of hours I would think.'

Margaret hugged Louisa, brushing back her long hair.

'Thank you Margaret, what would I have done without you?'

Louisa got out of bed and got herself dressed.

The Visitor

After breakfast, Margaret put on her best hat and bid her goodbye.

'Told yow ducks, don't yow fret now. I shall be back soon. Make yowerself some tea if you like. Jack and the bab should be back 'ome soon.'

Margaret closed the door behind her, leaving Louisa sitting on the sofa reading old newspapers Margaret had kept.

Louisa May decided to busy herself by making Margaret's lunch and tidying her rooms. She found polish and dusters and cleaned the rooms, then started to prepare lunch. Margaret had been gone three or four hours and it was well past lunch-time. Where can she be and what if the coachman is dead, Louisa wondered and Margaret has been arrested by the police for knowing the murderess – me! Panic was setting into Louisa's stomach, but she did not feel guilty of the crime: after all, she had only been defending herself, but who would believe her?

'Jack, Bert! Thank you very much Jack for taking care of Bert. He is a handful. You are so kind.'

Louisa picked Bert up from his pram and cuddled him.

'No trouble Louisa, my pleasure. Tell Mam I am going out to see me mate. I will be back at teatime.'

Jack said goodbye and closed the front door.

A few hours later Margaret returned smiling and hugging Louisa who had rushed to greet her, leaving young Bert playing with his toys on the floor.

'Well, ducks, didn't I tell yow, the coachman is all right, 'e was only knocked out and 'it 'is 'ead on the wall after too many beers, so the publican said, but we know better, don't we ducks?'

Margaret and Louisa danced around the sitting room with joy. Louisa hardly noticed her painful bruises she was so relieved at the news.

'I'll tell you one thing, Margaret,' Louisa said.

'What's that then ducks?'

'I shall never see E.B., I mean Frederick ever again and shall never go to the Minstrel pub or ever see anyone connected with my late night encounters. Not that Frederick wasn't a nice man, he knew nothing of the attack I am sure, but I can never put myself in such a dangerous situation with anyone again, for my girls' sake if nothing else.'

Louisa was adamant that she would never again be a 'lady of the night'.

'Ducks, don't yow be too sure of that, at least yow know what to do and 'ow to go about things now, don't yow? It was just unfortunate, the attack, I never 'ad nothing like that ever 'appen to me, so don't be too sure yow will never 'ave to resort to nightly liaisons again ducks. I 'ope for your sake yow don't though.'

Louisa flung her arms around Margaret's neck.

'You are my dearest friend, if there is anything I can ever do for you now or in the future Margaret, you must tell me. If it's in my power I will do anything for you.'

Louisa spent the rest of the day with her friend and stayed for a late meal helping with the dishes afterwards.

'Well, Margaret, I had better go back to my own rooms and get them tidied up before John comes home. I would like the place to look welcoming and homely. Of course I won't have much time now to do it, if I am to meet him at the station. I am so looking forward to him coming home and perhaps we can think of our girls now and get them back home.'

Louisa gathered up her shawl, and Bert's toys from the floor. Picking up Bert she thanked Margaret again.

'Perhaps I shall see yow tomorrow Louisa?'

Margaret opened her front door to let Louisa out.

'Yes, you surely will see me tomorrow.'

CHAPTER VI

The Orphanage

Once more I found myself transported away from Tower Street. I was observing Louisa May's girls inside the orphanage. Why I had been spirited away, I was not sure, but realised I had to document this episode of the Garton saga as well as all the other happenings. So, all I could do was to watch and try to understand what it was Louisa May needed me to find out: Louisa's story seems so disjointed, but I can only record what I was being shown. Perhaps it was all to do with the Orphanage and the four Garton girls being taken there? It was very strange but here goes! The story unfolds …

None of Louisa's girls cried as the carriage drew to a halt at the front of the huge stone building. In the doorway stood a middle-aged woman in a dark blue long dress and white starched apron, obviously the matron. She beckoned the girls to get out of the carriage and follow her into the building.

'Come along, girls, we can't keep Mrs Foster waiting any longer. We have been expecting you; now then, there is no need to be frightened.'

Matron ushered the girls along a grey, cold corridor; Gwen, Dora, Hilda and Connie followed cautiously, not daring to speak to one another. They were led along several more cold corridors with high windows and dirty net curtains haphazardly draped across the stained glass to meet Mrs Foster, the proprietor of the orphanage.

A dark, oak panelled door, with an inscribed nameplate, 'Mrs Foster, Principal,' met their eyes as the girls approached the room. Dora gave a reassuring smile to all her frightened sisters and swirls of great apprehension churned their stomachs as the door opened and they were led into the room to meet Mrs Foster.

A log fire blazed in the open grate and the room seemed warm and cosy so perhaps it wouldn't be too bad after all, the girls thought. Seated behind the inlaid leather desk was a very thin, hollow-cheeked woman, whom the girls could only presume was Mrs Foster. The woman wrote feverishly, without looking up at the girls, or even acknowledging their presence.

Connie was impatient as always being the youngest of the sisters and started to fidget, looking down at her old, worn shoes which needed a clean and her dirty, white socks. She was sure Mrs Foster would not notice the

The Visitor

fact that she hadn't had time to clean her shoes.

After what seemed such a long time to the girls, Mrs Foster stood up, clapping her hands together with a resounding slap.

'Well, let me see now, you must be the Garton girls. Stand up straight girls, shoulders back and pay attention to me when I am speaking to you.'

Pulling Connie's shoulders back, Mrs Foster continued.

'We do not look at one's feet, we look straight at the person who is talking, namely me!'

Mrs Foster prodded Connie again, panicking her into looking up and paying attention.

'All children must know their place here; we are to teach our children manners, decorum and above all, how to keep themselves clean and tidy.'

The girls nodded to make sure that Mrs Foster understood they knew what she meant. Was this lady real? Connie thought, looking most disapprovingly at Mrs Foster. Already the girls resented her but Gwen, Dora and Hilda knew that they would not be wholly co-operative and wished that they were back in Tower Street with their dear mother.

Connie was too young to understand such things, or what was happening to her. Gwen, Dora and Hilda knew they must protect their sister from this woman, as they were sure she was an educated bully.

'Please, Miss, my mummy says I am a good girl and ...'

Connie did not seem at all afraid of Mrs Foster. Dora nudged her, trying to make her realise that she must be quiet and only speak when spoken to, but she was too young to understand the meaning of the nudge.

'How dare you interrupt me, girl? Be quiet and speak only when I give you permission to speak! How dare you be so rude!'

Mrs Foster's red, angry face glowered down at Connie's small figure, looming over her like the devil. Connie took two steps back from Mrs Foster's glowing, bad tempered face, just uttering a quiet:

'Yes Miss.'

'I should think so. Now then, matron will show you Garton girls to your dormitory and give you your duties for the day. We have no lazy people here, you start work immediately, girls.'

Matron ushered the girls out of Mrs Foster's office and they were glad to leave, to say the least. The girls were led down the long, dark corridor and up three flights of stairs to their dormitory, which was equally as cold and unwelcoming, with huge barred windows as in the hallway and the rest of the building.

It was clear that there would be no happy times here; the girls could only think of their mother at home in Tower Street and all their friends they had left behind. When would they ever see mother or father again? Gwen didn't care if she never saw father again as he had become so violent because of his ill health: though she hoped the sanatorium would cure him, though she doubted it. She did care for mother though and longed for the day when they would be reunited.

The four new arrivals were shown to the dormitory. The other children kept their distance and treated the Garton girls with great suspicion, but the girls didn't care for they had each other and were sure they would not be parted from one another whilst at the orphanage.

'This is a wonderful place, we actually have our very own beds, I can't believe it!'

Connie ran around the dormitory from one bed to another, jumping on and off all the surrounding beds much to the delight of the other children. She was so excited about having her very own bed as she had never been used to it at home, having to share a double bed with all her sisters.

'Are we on holiday, Gwen, when do we see the sea?'

Connie rushed to Gwen and the rest of her sisters, questioning them all.

'Don't be so silly, Connie, we are not on holiday as you well know and we won't see the sea.'

Gwen sat down on her own bed swinging her legs to and fro. Connie's face dropped.

'Oh, so why are we here? Where is mummy?'

Gwen ruffled Connie's black, curly hair.

'Dear Connie, I don't know why we are here, but we shall go home very soon and we have to make the best of it until mother can come and fetch us.'

Gwen started to unpack her meagre belongings from her bag. She hadn't the luxury of a suitcase and neither had her sisters. Dora, Hilda and Connie gathered around Gwen's bed.

'Oh, dear, poor Connie, I am sorry, I didn't mean to snap at you.'

Gwen hugged Connie close to her with Dora and Hilda sitting on the bed beside their sisters. Dora looked around her at the dark, dim room and the small beds with just one blanket per bed; the windows were tightly shut and barred; the glass was so dirty that hardly any daylight shone through.

'What a place,' she thought, 'more like a prison than a children's home. What will become of us all in this awful place?' She looked across at Connie who was busily making friends with some children who were actually willing to play with her. She was very outgoing, but always liked to win at any game and sulked bitterly if she lost.

'Right, girls, off you go, get yourselves washed ready for lunch. You know what Mrs Foster is like if you keep her waiting and you are not ready for mealtimes.'

Matron ushered all the other girls into the bathroom and showed the Garton girls where the wash basins were, giving them each a clean towel,

The Visitor

flannel and some carbolic soap. After everyone had washed themselves, the children were marched down the stairs to the dining room.

The dining room was sparsely furnished with a large wooden table and chairs in the centre of the room. Each child took their place behind a chair and waited for Mrs Foster to make her grand entrance at the head of the table. The wait for her seemed an eternity as the Garton girls were very hungry. Connie felt her stomach growl with pangs of hunger, which made all the other children giggle just as Mrs Foster entered the room. Connie and her sisters found it difficult to keep still as they had been standing for so long waiting for Mrs Foster. They were impatient to start their meal.

'Who is Grace?' Connie asked loudly.

All the children sniggered at Connie's remark.

Clapping her hands together, Mrs Foster proclaimed:

'Children, manners, manners, quiet please!'

Connie copied the other children, putting her hands together for prayers before the meal. She kept an eye open firmly fixed on Mrs Foster, as she didn't trust her at all!

After grace, Mrs Foster said:

'Be seated, you may all commence eating.'

She pointed to the piles of bread, butter, scones, jam and cakes which had been brought to the table by three waitresses, dressed in black and white uniforms, all wearing white moll caps. The Garton girls were fascinated by all the proceedings. Hot tea or cocoa was served, and the girls were so hungry that they had no time to bother with the manners Louisa had so carefully taught them. Dora thought their mother would be so upset by their lack of manners but they didn't care. Connie was delighted with every morsel of food.

'Better than the usual bread and dripping at home. I love these funny buttered cake things, don't you Gwen?'

All the other children giggled at Connie, who was quite unaware of the 'no talking at the dining table' rule introduced so strictly by Mrs Foster some weeks before. Mrs Foster was angry with Connie and stood up at the top of the table, clapping her hands to gain the attention of the children.

'That girl there, yes, you, you. Connie Garton. Stand up! As you are a new girl here and to all intents and purposes a bit of a dimwit, I will not cane you this time for speaking at the table. Talking at mealtimes is not allowed, have you got that girl, do you understand?'

Mrs Foster emphasised the *not*, making Connie jump out of her skin with fright as she looked at her in horror. Not even father had ever talked to her like that, or caned her, although he was sometimes very fierce.

'The cane! The cane! You will certainly not cane my sister Mrs Foster, not for any reason. You will not dare to.'

The Visitor

Gwen's face reddened with temper as she started to get up from her seat to move towards Mrs Foster.

'My sister is only five years old and she doesn't understand your so-called "rules" and neither do the rest of us, as they have not exactly been explained to us!'

'Sit down, Gwen,' Dora whispered. 'Be sensible, don't annoy her please!'

Dora tugged at Gwen's sleeve to try and make her sister sit down. She was always the sensible sister but it was clear, even to herself, that Gwen was determined to confront Mrs Foster, as she now hated her and looked upon her as a tyrant as did the other sisters. Dora was worried for Gwen and the consequences of her outbursts, but she knew her sister was not afraid of Mrs Foster. Hilda was also brave, but decided that enough people were fighting, so carried on enjoying her scone and butter, at least for the time being.

Mrs Foster ordered Gwen out of the room to stand alone in the cold corridor outside, as a punishment for speaking out; so of course, Gwen would be unable to finish her meal.

'But, Mrs Foster, I haven't finished my tea yet and I am very hungry,' Gwen said.

Hilda quietly stood up and looked Mrs Foster straight in the eye.

'Let my sister finish her meal, please, and let us be civil about all this. She can then face any punishment you care to dish out to her, Mrs Foster.'

She carried on eating her scone and after Hilda's statement, Dora gave a hearty: 'Hear! Hear!'

All the children started to clap their hands together, waiting for the next round in the verbal fight.

Mrs Foster's face reddened with temper; she cursed Gwen and Hilda and told them that they would forego any supper. All the other unfortunate children became very quiet, carrying on with their meal, but giving the occasional sympathetic glance towards Hilda, Connie and Dora.

It seemed like hours that Gwen had been standing alone in the cold corridor waiting for the children to finish their meal. Matron's long petticoats could be heard some distance away swishing on the stone floors of the corridor. Coming across Gwen standing alone in the corridor, matron asked her what had happened so soon after her arrival at the orphanage.

She had a kindly face and was genuinely concerned for the child, promising her some food later though she was not to tell Mrs Foster. Gwen nodded and smiled back.

'Don't worry yourself, my dear, her bark is worse than her bite; she'll not cane Connie or anyone, she would not dare. Why, these days, the inspectors would be down on her like a ton of bricks before you knew it, so don't you worry yourself.'

The Visitor

She tried to reassure Gwen, but the girl was not convinced that matron was right.

'Just you stay there until Mrs Foster comes out. If you don't then there will be *real* trouble. So stay put, there's a good girl.'

Matron gave Gwen a wink. 'Keep your pecker up ducks, it is not all bad here.'

Gwen could hardly raise a smile as matron bustled off to carry out the rest of her duties. She thought to herself, 'We must all stick together and I shall devise a plan of escape from this place, that's what I'll do: yes, we shall all escape.' Leaning against the wall, Gwen gazed out through the barred window, watching the trees swaying in the autumn breeze. Perhaps in some way it *was* better than home. No, she must not think that, ever. She did miss mother terribly, but hardly ever thought of father. He didn't mean to hit me and he didn't know his own strength, she thought. I suppose I was being very naughty at the time. At least here no one will take my beloved books from me and throw them on the fire like father did. Here I will be able to read unhindered.

Gwen consoled herself with the knowledge that perhaps things would get better.

At last, the meal was over. Mrs Foster excused the children from the table and they all rushed out into the corridor to find their heroine, Gwen, who was sitting on the cold, stone floor pressing her back into the wall. All the children thought she was very courageous and admired her tremendously for standing up to Mrs Foster's bullying. No one had ever dared to retaliate before the Garton girls arrived.

Connie flung her arms about Gwen's neck.

'Everything is all right now, Gwen. I should think you are starving, ain't you? I pinched some bread and butter, look, it's in me pocket!'

Connie handed her a soggy piece of bread and butter, making all the other children laugh, as it was really very soggy indeed.

Gwen was so hungry that it didn't matter and gobbled down the bread and butter hardly dropping a single crumb.

'Connie, you are so very sweet to think about me, thank you for the bread and butter darling. Remember though, mother has always taught us to speak properly. You do not say "pinch" or "me" pocket, or "ain't", now do you?'

Gwen hugged Connie who giggled and wriggled as she started to tickle her.

Suddenly the girls became aware of a presence: it was Mrs Foster. All the other children had suddenly vanished, leaving the Garton girls alone. They jumped to their feet.

'Right, you four girls, you have some horrible, yes really horrible, domestic chores to do. I have sorted out the worst of jobs for you four. As I explained, every child pulls their weight here and works hard and that goes for you four also.'

The four girls could only utter: 'Yes, Miss.'

'Gwen Garton, you will polish all the staircases and all the furniture in the whole place, until you can see your face in it. Believe me, I shall make sure you can see your face. If you make a bad job of it and I can't see my reflection, you will do it all again.'

Gwen could only utter: 'Yes, Miss.'

'Now, Dora Garton.' Mrs Foster folded her arms and tapped her long, bony fingers on her forearm.

'What can I find for you? Ah, yes, your job will be to stiff-brush all the hall and stairway carpeting and when you have done that, you will clean out all the toilets in the dormitory and of course all the sinks.'

Dora was horrified but could only mutter: 'Yes, Miss.'

'Hilda, it will be your job to scrub all the dining furniture, properly mind you, and the floors in the kitchen.'

'Yes, Miss.'

The girls passed disapproving glances between them they were sure each job would be very hard work and take them hours.

'Ah, yes, I nearly forgot about little miss cheeky! Yes, the very thing for you, Connie: you will polish all the door knobs and handles which, as you can see, are brass and need a lot of hard buffing. You will notice that there are literally hundreds of door knobs in the place and they must all shine like new. Do you understand Connie?'

'Yes, Miss.'

Mrs Foster grinned a very self-satisfied grin as she looked into each girl's terrified face. It was obvious to all that Mrs Foster enjoyed her work and giving out her demands to all the children, watching them work hard. Every child had a job to do, which usually took hours of work.

Dora held Gwen's arm, as she knew she was about to lose her temper with Mrs Foster once more, but this time Dora was sure Mrs Foster would beat Gwen, from the thunderous look on her thin face. Gwen could no longer contain herself.

'We *won't* do it, we are not your slaves, Mrs Foster, and you wait until our mother hears of all this and how we are being treated. You'll see, you'll be sorry then.'

Gwen had such spirit, but realised she had overstepped the mark with Mrs Foster and she had gone too far this time. Mrs Foster raised herself to her full height and made towards Gwen who took a step back from the tall, domineering, angry figure lurching at her. The Garton girls formed a defensive circle around Gwen standing very close to her in case Mrs Foster felt inclined to lash out. Fortunately for Gwen, she did not, but she did put Gwen on

The Visitor

yet another detention, standing against the cold corridor wall without food or drink for a whole day. Gwen would never give up and felt the situation would, without doubt, escalate. She would *not* be bullied, nor would she allow her sisters to be, either.

The three sisters tried to pass signals to Gwen as they went about their household duties, but it seemed that Mrs Foster was ever-watchful of them.

Time for bed soon arrived and the four girls, exhausted, were shown to their beds. They knew they had to escape from the orphanage, as they could not endure another week with Mrs Foster.

Gwen had plenty of time to devise a plan of escape and ordered her sisters to meet her in the bathroom at nine o'clock sharp that night, where they would plan their means of escape.

The time on the large clock in the dormitory seemed to stand still at eight thirty for hours.

The girls grew increasingly impatient watching the other children fall asleep in their beds.

Nine o'clock at last. The Garton girls quietly crept towards the bathroom.

I followed the girls in my ghostly form; of course, no one could see or hear me, although I felt at one time that perhaps Connie noticed I was there, but then again, maybe not! I was the ghost in their time and privy, it seemed, to Louisa May's story and even that of her girls. But where was my Louisa and John and why hadn't they come for their girls? I knew John was ill in the sanatorium but even so, surely Louisa would have come to get her girls? Very strange: perhaps there was yet another problem for the Garton family back in Tower Street that I didn't know about.

I wondered how the girls were going to escape from the orphanage, and where would they go? They couldn't go home to Louisa as they would surely be discovered and taken away again back to the orphanage by the NSPCC Inspectors.

I listened to the plan of escape Gwen had devised. It sounded very good and just as I was getting engrossed, a great force once more was swirling me around and around until Gwen's voice started to fade away from me. I was so angry, I wanted to stay with the girls and listen to their plan of escape. For God's sake! Where was I being taken to now? I really did want to stay with the Garton girls but their voices and the orphanage were fading away from me. Please, don't take me away now, whoever or whatever force you are.

Was this Louisa's doing? I couldn't sense her around me as I usually did, or smell her delicate perfume. It couldn't be her forcing me away, so what or who was swirling me around and dragging me off?

The foggy mists and swirling eventually stopped. My head was still spinning around. I gathered myself together and found that I was back at the family

The Visitor

home in Tower Street. It was a lovely, sunny day. I stood up and brushed down my clothes and looked up to the first floor level of the house where Louisa and John had their rooms. I couldn't hear or see anything out of the ordinary, so why was I back here? I decided to think my way into the house and to Louisa and John's rooms to see if they were in.

CHAPTER VII

Hospitalisation

I had spirited myself back into the rooms of Louisa May and John Garton. Louisa's story as I observed it was disjointed to say the least, as I was finding out!

John had at last come out of his drunken state.

'What the 'ell as been going on 'eah then? Where are me girls? Get up off the floor woman, stop blubbering, Bab, and tell me what yow are crying for?'

John could hardly stand up straight; he was swaying to and fro, the worse for drink to deaden the dreadful pain in his chest. Louisa sobbed bitterly, hardly coherent through her crying, but proceeded to tell the story of the inspector from the NSPCC and how the girls had been taken away to the orphanage.

Ah! I'm back at this part of Louisa's story am I? I wondered when John would sober up. I looked at their faces, waiting for him to take some sort of action to get his girls back from the orphanage; I only wished Louisa May could sense my presence as it would be of some comfort to her I was sure, knowing that I was near and sympathizing with her. I had to be content with the order in which Louisa May collected me to record her story, however disjointed. So I decided to sit myself down on the family sofa, might as well make myself comfortable. It seemed so strange that each time Louisa collected me to witness family events, she could neither see nor hear me. But when Louisa visited my times, she *could* see and hear me. I wondered to myself what she must have thought of my modern world of computers, telephones and cars. Was she even aware of all these things? Ah well, here I was, so I had better make the best of it all. Let's see what John had to say for himself about his girls. He had finally focussed on what had happened to his girls now he had come home from the sanatorium. John was still ill and unfortunately needing his occasional alcoholic medicine.

'Me girls, me babs. Why, that's impossible – how, why?'

John was completely bewildered and shocked that such a thing could have happened without him knowing of it or hearing the commotion in his own home.

Louisa May sobbed as she explained what had happened.

The Visitor

'Our beautiful daughters, John. We have failed them, their own parents, we have, we failed them! Thank God Bert was with Margaret Thompson when the Inspectors came. Of course, I didn't say I had another child, we couldn't let him be taken as well John. The organization is called the NSPCC or something. It is a new organization to help, so they say, deprived children and they said that our girls, yes, *our* girls were – well, starving and ill treated! Can you imagine that?'

Louisa could no longer bear the pain of telling John the story so she decided that her only course of action was to make her way to Bertie and Jacqueline for they would know what to do, and she was sure the little money she had saved from her night visits to the Minstrel would be of little help. She couldn't visit her gentleman, her E.B., now that John was back home from the sanatorium for how could she get out and be missing for hours on end? Anyway, how would she explain to John where she had been, whom she was seeing and worst of all, where her money was coming from? John must never know anything of her visits to the Minstrel and E.B.

John swayed to and fro for he was still a long way from being completely sober, but was trying to comprehend the shocking news about his daughters.

'John, I can't bear it, just get the girls back!'

Crying bitterly, Louisa May refused to let John comfort her and blamed him for everything that had happened.

'The Inspector from the NSPCC took the girls mainly because of you, John. I was prepared to forgive you a lot because of your tuberculosis pain and your condition, but now, well now I shall hate you forever, ill or not ill. My poor girls!'

Louisa sobbed uncontrollably and John couldn't answer her accusations against him for he knew they were true; he hardly dared to look her way as he knew she would not let him hold her close as he used to.

How could I help? I found myself emotionally drained on behalf of both Louisa and John, but mostly Louisa. I must help, but how? Looking around the sitting room, there on the table was Bertie's address scribbled on a small piece of paper. If only I could blow it hard enough, perhaps it might flutter around and Louisa would see it. That would re-establish the thought in her head to go to her brother for help. I blew as hard as I could, my cheeks like balloons. Suddenly, yes the piece of paper moved and fluttered gently off the table floating down to Louisa's feet like a feather.

Louisa picked up the piece of paper, smiling at it, realizing it was Bertie's new address and put it into her apron pocket.

Yes! Yes! I did it, she had the piece of paper. The thought would dawn on her soon she must go to Bertie and Jacqueline for help. I willed the thought more and more into her mind that she should go to Bertie.

John rose to his feet.

The Visitor

'No one, takes me girls, no one! Anyroad, what dow yow mean Bab, suffering? Our girls never suffered, neither were they ever hungry. What a cheek!'

John poured himself yet another stout knowing in his heart that the Inspector was right. He would have to blot that thought out of his mind with the drink. He was obviously not about to do anything at all for his girls, not that he didn't want to, but he felt too ill to care about anything.

I tried to console Louisa by blowing warm air from my ghostly mouth into the room to make it at least a little warmer for her, but it didn't seem to work as she was still shivering. She looked pale and ill, her beautiful black eyes now tired and listless, but her facial bone structure was still as beautiful. If she were in my time, cosmetics would cover her fine lines and she would still be able to turn men's heads with her beauty.

I couldn't help wondering where Bertie was and why he hadn't come to help Louisa as he said he would.

Suddenly, Louisa May gasped and fell to the cold floor in a dead faint, with John rushing to her side.

'Bab, oh, me sweet, Bab! What 'ave I done to yow? Come on, Bab, don't play games, wake up, come on, Bab, say somert to me!'

Louisa was unconscious and, it seemed, very ill. It was plain to anyone, even to John in his drunken state, who shouted and bellowed for Margaret downstairs to come and help.

'Margaret heard John's screams for help, rushing up the stairs to John and Louisa's rooms to see him cradling Louisa in his arms.

'Come on, John, help me to get her on to a bed! She looks so ill, that's plain, what 'appened to her! How did she get like this, John?'

Margaret helped him carry her to bed.

'I dunno what 'appened! She just collapsed. She ain't been eating too well lately and with the girls being taken, it's all too much I think.' John stroked Louisa's pale face.

'I dunno what to do Margaret, tell me what to do? She looks so poorly.'

John looked worriedly down at his lifeless Louisa who was hardly taking a breath as she lay unconscious on the bed. Margaret covered her with a thick blanket.

'Got to keep her warm first, John, get some heat in this place, it's so cold. How can yow stand it cold like this? Yow will have to fetch the doctor, John, there's nothing for it, she is really bad. Go on, lad, hurry up!'

'What do yow think it is Margaret, not another bab is it? I can't afford a doctor Margaret, what the bloody 'ell am I to do?'

It was all too much for John to bear.

'Dunno what is wrong John, she looks bad.'

Margaret rubbed Louisa's face and hands for they were so cold.

The Visitor

'Could be anything John, not eating, a bab, she just looks white and half starved to me. How could yow let her get like this John? I know yow are bad yowerself, but surely yow noticed her getting in this state didn't yow, even though yower bad?'

John started to cry like a small boy.

'It's all my fault ain't it Margaret? If I wasn't ill myself and 'adn't 'ad to go away to the sanatorium.'

John buried his face in his strong hands.

'Now lad, come on, it's no one's fault, just a fact of life around 'eah. Every one of us is poor, but God forbid if yow get ill. What can anyone do about illness? Nothing!'

Margaret hugged John close to her.

'The fact remains duck, we 'ave to get the doctor to 'er and yow will 'ave to go while I stay with her.'

Margaret pushed John towards the door, handing him his coat and flat cap.

'Eah, a few shillings. This will pay for the doctor. Now don't protest, I insist. One of us 'as to do something for her.'

An hour later, John returned with the doctor who quickly opened his medical bag, taking out medical instruments with which he examined Louisa May. There was no change in her condition, she was still unconscious, so not aware of the doctor's presence or his examination of her. The doctor finished his examination without delay.

He looked first at Margaret, then John.

'Well, Mr Garton,' the doctor said, 'your wife is to say the least extremely ill, as you both so rightly had realized. You were quite right to fetch me.'

'What is it doctor, what she got?'

John took Louisa's stone-cold hands and rubbed them, trying to warm them up.

The doctor continued:

'Your wife is dangerously ill, Mr Garton, and we need to transport her to hospital immediately, so I shall need your help to carry her to my carriage outside. Because of the urgency of her condition and the fact that you are willing to pay, I shall get her hospitalized right away.'

The doctor signalled to John to wrap Louisa in a blanket ready to take her downstairs and outside to his waiting carriage then he looked at his pocket watch.

'If we set off now, Mr Garton, we can be at the hospital in half an hour, the quicker the better. By the way, Mr Garton, you need to do something about that nasty cough. You may like to see me later when your wife is sorted out.'

'Thank you doctor, I 'ave tuberculosis, well I did 'ave. Just come back

The Visitor

from being treated at the sanatorium but I still 'ave the cough. Don't think I will ever get rid of it.'

'Can you manage to carry your wife downstairs in that case? Shall I help you with her?'

'I can manage 'er doctor, she is so light. She 'ardly weighs anything.'

John gathered Louisa up in his arms, Margaret helping to cover her with a blanket.

'Can yow tell us what is wrong doctor?'

Margaret quizzed the doctor, who was packing his instruments away in his bag.

'Mrs Garton has, if I am not mistaken, suffered a severe stroke; such a great pity in a woman so young. So the quicker we can get her to hospital the better her chances of survival will be. If she stays in her present state, she won't know anything much of the journey, which will be better for her sake. Come on, now, let's get a move on. If you, dear lady, can pack her a nightdress and whatever she needs?'

Margaret nodded.

'It will be all right John, yow will see. The hospital will take good care of 'er. Why, if it ain't yow, it's now 'er.'

Margaret tried to make light of the situation but John looked pale and worried for his beloved Louisa. He lifted Louisa up; she was still unconscious, resembling a rag doll as she was so light to carry . John followed the doctor and Margaret downstairs and out to the waiting carriage. Neighbours had gathered outside to watch the proceedings and wished John well as he gently laid Louisa down. John sat beside her resting her head on his lap and holding her lifeless hand in his. The doctor ordered his driver to drive on.

'We must get this lady and her husband to the hospital as quickly as we can, but try not to bump her around too much as she is gravely ill.'

The doctor felt Louisa's forehead once more and touched John's shoulder to reassure him that everything would be all right.

'Bye, John, let me know if she is all right and if there is anything you need. I will look after Bert and yower place, don't worry.'

Margaret waved goodbye wishing she could have gone to the hospital with her dear friend and she wondered if she would ever see her again.

Some Weeks Later

Bertie and Jacqueline had made frequent visits to Louisa and John's rooms in Tower Street, but on each occasion, they got no reply from their thunderous knocking at the door. Margaret decided she was not opening her door to strangers, especially rich strangers, whom she felt could only be trouble, not realizing that the strangers were her beloved friend's relations!

The Visitor

The neighbours also treated Bertie and Jacqueline with suspicion and would not help them to locate Louisa, so they were completely unaware that Louisa was in hospital and so very ill.

The hospital doctors all agreed that Louisa was at last making a slow recovery from her stroke. John had hardly left her bedside and was told that if she did recover enough to leave the hospital, she would surely be left with a paralysed right side, the effects of the stroke. Margaret had been a frequent visitor to the hospital to see Louisa and looked forward to her visits. She knew it made Louisa feel a lot better as she had started to laugh at her jokes.

The nurse brought Louisa a hand mirror and comb for her hair.

'There yow are ducks, yow can comb yower hair now. Yow are looking much brighter. Perhaps yow will be allowed a cup of tea today?'

Louisa smiled at Margaret and looked at her reflection which shocked her. An old, grey haired woman was looking back at her. The once beautiful, thick, black hair was now limp and grey and her smooth, pale skin lined and dry. She ran her slender long fingers over her face, muttering to herself.

'A lady of the night, eh? Not any more.'

John was sure she must be in some sort of delirium.

'What are yow saying, Bab?'

'Oh, nothing, just thinking aloud!'

Louisa smiled at John, stroking the side of his face, and smiled at Margaret. She was feeling quite a lot better and the paralysis to her right side didn't seem too bad at all. At least she could speak and move her arms. She wasn't sure about her leg yet and would have to put the strength of that to the test when out of bed for the first time later on. All she could think about now were her girls in that dreadful orphanage and how she could get them out. It was all they could speak about when John and Margaret visited.

On Louisa's behalf, John and Margaret wrote letters to the girls and John was managing to stay away from his stout, but for how long, he didn't dare think! The pain was worse without it.

Margaret had cleaned Louisa and John's rooms, making new seat covers for their kitchen chairs and new curtains at the windows ready for Louisa's return home. That was the least she could do as she adored her friend and wanted to help as much as she could, if only in a small way.

The shock of Louisa's illness had made John try even harder to give up the dreaded stout but he was finding it so difficult as his chest gave him so much pain and there was no treatment. The doctors at the sanatorium said he would always have pain and would have to try and live with it.

Several more weeks passed and Louisa was discharged from hospital. John collected her, showering her with kisses and helping her to walk to the nearest tram to get home. Louisa loved riding on trams and was thrilled that he had

The Visitor

acquired some money to take her.

'Have you heard from Bertie, John? It is so very strange that Bertie hasn't been to Tower Street or to the hospital. I wonder why; he said he would call in a week's time last time he paid us a visit.'

Louisa was puzzled and knew that she would have to make the journey to Solihull to see Bertie and Jacqueline as soon as she was able and her health would let her. She would have to ask for Bertie's help, financially, she knew that.

'No, not a word. It's best, Bab, to forget them all at Sycamore House as they are no good to us now.'

John squeezed Louisa's hand, knowing that she missed her brother terribly.

Over the next few weeks, Louisa rested as much as she could gaining more and more strength as each day passed. She knew she would need a great deal of strength to walk the seven miles to Bertie's house in Solihull. She doubted that she would be able to afford the tram fare and felt that she couldn't encroach on Margaret Thompson's financial kindness any more, even though she was a good friend. Louisa had closely guarded her piece of crumped paper with Bertie's address on it. She would choose her day carefully to make the journey to Solihull to ask his help to free her girls from the orphanage. Louisa knew that John would not be best pleased if she were to ask her brother for financial help. John was proud and wanted to free his girls himself but Louisa knew this would possibly never happen, as where would he obtain the vast amount of money needed? John's newly acquired part-time job would not supply it.

John, at last, left for work.

I watched Louisa May take her best hat from years gone by out of its box, securing it firmly on her head with a huge hat pin. She placed her knitted shawl around her small, bony shoulders and clutching her once very fashionable and expensive crocodile skin bag, she closed the door to her rooms and made her way downstairs to the street outside.

The day was bright, although quite cold for the time of year. The cold made her leg ache so the only comfort from the pain was to drag it clumsily over the cobbles of Tower Street and beyond. Her stroke had left its mark.

What would Jacqueline and Bertie think of her now? She had grey hair and deep lines on her face and limped badly on her right leg.

'Fiddle-de-dee,' she thought, 'I don't care about my physical state, all I want is to see my beloved Bertie again and of course Jacqueline, and get my girls out of that terrible place. John will not miss me, he won't be home for hours yet. In fact, if needs be, I can take a tram part of the way with the few pennies I have in my purse'. She was sure that once she was at Bertie's house he would help her and would then drive her back home to Tower Street.

The Visitor

She took the tram part of the way and walked the last two miles towards Solihull.

She found herself in a fashionable Solihull street with newly built, three-storey houses, some resembling Sycamore House in design, but on a much smaller scale. Louisa looked at her crumpled piece of paper with Bertie's address on it.

'Ah! this must be it. Number forty three.'

Louisa climbed the five steps to the ornately carved, oak front door. A mixture of great excitement and apprehension churned around inside her stomach. She didn't know why, as she knew Bertie and Jacqueline would be more than pleased to see her, but very shocked, that she had made the journey to them alone. Louisa pulled the long, brass chain which loudly rang inside the house.

A freckle-faced, red haired young maid opened the door.

'Servants and trades people around the back if yow please. What do yow mean ringing our master's front doorbell like that? Well I never did. Cheek!'

The door was promptly shut in Louisa's face, so she pulled the long doorbell chain again.

The young maid answered the door again.

'What 'ave I just told yow? Around the back. Don't yow 'ear well or somert?'

Little did the maid realize that Louisa was deaf.

She tried to explain to the maid that the master was her brother!

'Yower brother, ha, don't make me laugh! What with yower clothes and bedraggled state, never, yow must think I am stupid!'

Louisa understood the maid's lips and started to get angry as the door was promptly shut.

She couldn't believe it and decided to walk around to the back of the house to the servant's quarters. She knocked on the back door with all her might but no one came so she pulled the bell cord but still no one came. Trying the door handle was no good either, the door was locked. It was obvious to her no one from the servant's quarters was going to let her into the house. Leaning against the back wall, she began to wonder if she had made all the effort of travelling to Solihull for nothing! John was right, nobody wanted to know her now.

Well, there was nothing for it, she would just have to go back home and leave Bertie and Jacqueline a note. She was sure that if they had known she was there at their house, they would have had no hesitation in seeing her.

Bertie called out to his maid from the library.

'Who was that at the door Molly?'

'If yow please sir, just some old stupid woman. Think she was looking for work 'eah sir. She didn't actually say that. I told 'er in no uncertain terms

The Visitor

to go away. Servants around the back sir. But yow wouldn't believe it, the cheeky cow came around the back and kept knocking at the door and pulling the bell. I told 'er, we 'ave no jobs, but she kept ringing the bell. I think she was deaf or something sir. She seemed a bit simple if yow ask me and she was dressed in terrible old fashioned clothes. It made me laugh it did.'

Molly gathered up the afternoon tea cups, placing them on a silver tray to take away to the kitchen. Bertie casually walked over to the sitting room window and looked out onto the front garden and driveway. His eyes saw a small, thin woman dragging her right leg badly. Studying her more closely he said:

'Molly, come quickly girl, is that the woman who came to the house?'

'Yes sir, that's 'er, funny ain't she?'

Molly shrugged her shoulders.

'Quickly, Molly, run after her, I know that woman. Fetch her back here immediately. Show her in here when you catch up with her. Quickly now girl, run.'

Bertie pushed Molly out of the sitting room into the hallway, opening the front door for her.

'Yow want me to run after 'er sir.'

'Go on Molly, just do it.'

Bertie stood in the doorway watching Molly running quickly, holding onto her white moll cap in case it blew away and shouting,

'Miss, stop miss, the master wants to see yow.'

Molly's cries fell on Louisa's deaf ears.

Touching Louisa's arm, Molly leaned over to catch her breath, with Louisa May looking puzzled at the changed attitude of the maid towards her.

'The master wants yow to come back to the 'ouse to see him. Goodness knows why I'm sure.'

Louisa had read Molly's lips perfectly and followed her back to the large house.

Bertie had rushed upstairs to where Jacqueline was brushing her hair in the bedroom.

'Jacqueline, you will never guess, I think Louisa is here. Come quickly. Our prayers have been answered Jacqueline. If it is her, where has she been all his time?'

Bertie took Jacqueline's hand, pulling her down to the hallway. As Louisa entered with Molly, they hesitated for they couldn't believe the transformation in Louisa from a beautiful, young woman, to the wretch who stood before them. Jacqueline rushed to Louisa hugging her close to her with Bertie following and they all embraced.

Molly could only stare – she couldn't understand who this wretched woman was, certainly not from her mistress and master's circle of friends, she was sure.

The Visitor

Jacqueline led Louisa into the sitting room, ordering tea and cakes to be brought immediately. Louisa was persuaded to tell her long agonizing story about the girls and how she had been admitted to hospital. That was why Bertie couldn't find her or hear the girls playing when he had called at Tower Street. The amazed couple listened in horror to the story of her walk to find them.

The door of the sitting room opened; Molly set the tea, cakes and biscuits down on the polished, mahogany coffee table, handing a cup of tea to Louisa.

There was a three-tiered cake stand with her favourite chocolate éclair cakes on it so Louisa took one without hesitation. She hadn't tasted chocolate éclair cakes for years.

'Oh Jacqueline, this is so wonderful, seeing you and Bertie again and these cakes, they are delicious.'

In no time at all, the cakes were gone. Louisa was so hungry, she had forgotten her manners and had eaten the lot!

'Have a biscuit Louisa. We didn't realize you were that hungry. You must stay to lunch, please do.'

Bertie handed Louisa the plate of biscuits.

'You must never go back to Tower Street Louisa, never to that hovel. We have decided, haven't we Jacqueline?'

Bertie squeezed Jacqueline's hand and she could only nod to Bertie, as she was too overcome with emotion after listening to Louisa's story. She could not believe that she was the same person she had known all those years before.

Louisa became agitated. She would like to accept Bertie's invitation to stay forever at the house, but how could she leave her beloved John, who after all was trying so desperately to give up drink and work hard for herself, the girls, and tiny Bert? Never! she thought.

Bertie asked Louisa once more.

'Louisa, please come home to us. You can bring the girls and John, we should be so delighted to have you all live with us here.'

Bertie hated John now because of Louisa's condition and state of health, but knew she would not come to Solihull without her beloved John.

'You could stay here in the house, with Jacqueline and me ... well, you will have to know eventually. There is no other way but to tell you straight out Louisa. Jacqueline and I are emigrating to Montreal, Canada.'

Louisa gasped! 'Montreal! Emigrating!'

'You see darling, we loved the place so much when we were on our honeymoon and after many years of working at my business interests, which have done so very well, I decided to open an office in Montreal. So it will mean I shall have to go to get things started over there and of course,

The Visitor

Jacqueline will be coming too.'

Louisa May nodded and smiled.

'Of course Bertie, I am very pleased for you both. Indeed, looking around your home you do seem to have done extremely well. I am so pleased for you.'

She was really devastated. How could Bertie and Jacqueline leave her now?

Bertie continued:

'I have decided to open an office overseas because in my particular type of business, that is the way to go and Montreal is expanding business-wise, more so than Birmingham or London. Great opportunities there not to be missed.'

Louisa's voice trembled.

'But Bertie it is so far away, the other side of the world. Oh, Jacqueline!'

Louisa took out her handkerchief and dabbed her eyes. She couldn't bear to think of Jacqueline and Bertie going away so soon when she had only just found them again.

'Drink your tea dear and have another biscuit. Please do.'

Bertie handed the plate of biscuits once more to Louisa but she refused, as she could not eat now, knowing the news.

'Very well, if you have made up your mind not to live in our house whilst we are away Louisa, let us help you in some other way. I am very well able to provide for you and the family you know.'

Bertie put his arms about Louisa's shoulders, leading her into the library.

'Look, Louey, look at this writing bureau. Beautiful, isn't it? Have you ever seen anything so exquisite? A wedding gift from mother and father. It is also magic, not like any other bureau. I shall show you why.'

Bertie stood Louisa in front of the bureau and she looked at it, but it looked like any other writing bureau to her.

'I can't see anything different about this bureau Bertie. To me it looks like any other.'

'Not like any other bureau Louisa, that is where you are completely wrong! This bureau is one of a kind.'

Bertie proceeded to demonstrate the bureau's secret. Turning the small, gold key anticlockwise three times, to Louisa's amazement a small drawer from the back of the bureau flew open.

'What do you think of that Louey?'

Bertie stood back from the bureau knowing that he had impressed his sister.

'Why, that is unbelievable Bertie. No-one would guess there was a drawer at all and would never find it unless shown how to operate it. That is truly amazing.'

'I have a plan for you dear Louey,' Bertie said. 'A plan that will help you through all your troubles whilst Jacqueline and I are away.'

The Visitor

Louisa looked puzzled.

'A plan Bertie?'

'I shall give you this writing bureau to look after for me, dear sister, until we return from Montreal. You now know the secret of the bureau which only *you* must know. To the onlooker the secret drawer is not apparent.'

Bertie handed a tiny, gold key to Louisa May.

'You are giving it to me? Oh, Bertie it is just beautiful, I shall always treasure it.'

Louisa studied the small, gold key.

'Keep the gold key very safe Louisa, perhaps around your neck. Here, have Jacqueline's gold chain and put the key on it.'

Bertie unclasped the chain around Jacqueline's neck, putting the small, gold key on to it and fastening it around Louisa's neck.

'There, the chain is fastened and the key secure.'

Bertie kissed Louisa's cheek and then kissed Jacqueline.

'Dear sister, you have to learn how to operate the secret drawer and this is why I am telling you about it. Not only am I going to put a large amount of money in it for your future security but I shall leave bonds to my company in England and jewellery. Whenever you are worried or financially embarrassed you just need to open the secret drawer and your troubles will be over.'

Louisa hugged Bertie in gratitude.

'Promise me Louey, that you will keep all these things safe. Never take them out of the secret drawer unless you are really compelled to do so.'

Bertie made Louisa promise.

'Now we have to teach you how to operate the secret drawer. Take the key from around your neck and let's see if you can remember what I did to open the drawer.'

Louisa took the key from around her neck and proceeded to operate the secret drawer.

The drawer did not open!

'Bertie, it's not working!'

Louisa handed Bertie the small, gold, key.

'Do it again Louey, it does work. You must remember to turn the key anticlockwise three times.'

Louisa turned the key again.

'It worked! It worked!'

Jacqueline and Bertie congratulated Louisa.

'Now young lady, that is enough of that. We need to know that you are safe and the bureau was the only way I could think of to help you. We shall have to arrange for you to be taken home in a while along with the bureau. Meanwhile, I shall think of a plan to get your girls back. Never fear, Louey, Jacqueline and I will be seeing you very soon and if you need us, send word

The Visitor

or even come in person. After all you can afford a cab now! Oh, by the way, where is young Bert? He is such a handful, he must be toddling now.'

'Yes, he is a handful, especially now he has found he has legs and feet. He can certainly run! Bert is with Margaret, Margaret Thompson, you remember, the woman who lives downstairs from me. She is a real friend. Thank goodness she was looking after Bert when the Inspectors came to take the girls away. Of course, I did not admit I had any other children and Margaret kept him well hidden. It was especially fortunate that day, Margaret's grown up son was visiting, so he looked after Bert whilst I dealt with the Inspectors. I was only thankful none of the girls asked where Bert was. That would have been the end for me if the Inspectors had taken him too. I think Dora was sensible enough not to mention Bert, explaining to Connie, Hilda and Gwen what the consequences would be if they talked about him. I am so thankful for Dora sometimes. She is so very sensible.'

Bertie chuckled.

'I have decided,' Bertie said. 'I shall find you and your family a fitting house somewhere out of the city before we leave for Montreal. That's the least we can do for you Louey. As you know, I have many business contacts who can help and believe me, many of them owe me favours.'

Bertie strutted to and fro lighting a huge cigar as he went, thinking deeply, so reminiscent of Father Hirons, Louisa thought.

'Jacqueline, Bertie, I really do have to go. John will be home soon and I need to do all sorts of things before he gets in. I am so thankful we have been reunited and so grateful for all your kindness.'

'Don't be silly Louey.'

Jacqueline took Louisa into her arms.

'Bertie and I are your family; if you can't come to us, who can you turn to? We are only too relieved that you are alive and well.'

Louisa made her way to the hallway, pinning her best hat to her head and wrapping her shawl around her shoulders. She kept touching her gold neck chain making sure that the small, gold key was still attached to it. Bertie hugged his sister.

'Come on, I shall get my driver to take you home, Louey. He can put the bureau in the back of the carriage.'

I was so relieved for at last, Louisa May had found her brother and Jacqueline. I was unable to move once more, pinned to the spot in Bertie's house and only watching through the sitting room window as Louisa was driven away from the house, waving goodbye to Jacqueline and Bertie. I was so angry as I wanted to go with her in the carriage. Why was I being held prisoner here in Bertie's house?

'Come here my dear. Dear, dear, husband of mine.'

Jacqueline kissed Bertie full on the lips.

The Visitor

'You are the kindest, most generous man in the world and I dearly love you.'

Jacqueline once more kissed Bertie's lips.

'Thank you my dear, I love you too.'

Jacqueline and Bertie embraced and after they again kissed passionately, Bertie said:

'Well, what an earth are we to do about Louey? She looks so frail and ill. To think that my Louisa was once so very beautiful and the toast of the town.'

Jacqueline shrugged her shoulders.

'We have done everything possible to help her Bertie. She won't take up our offer to come and live here, so, my darling, you did the only thing possible for her, to make her financially secure as best you can. Don't fret so, you will find things will work out for her. I know you will find a suitable house for them all; after all, you do have many contacts, dear, so please don't worry any more.'

Bertie jumped to his feet.

'Yes, that's it! Saul Levy. He owes me a favour and so much money.'

'Who is Saul Levy dear?'

Jacqueline warmed her hands in front of the open coal fire.

'He is the most successful house builder in Birmingham. He has some houses being built in a new part of the city called Hall Green. I am sure we could get a house for Louisa, John and the girls out of him.'

I listened to both Bertie and Jacqueline and they seemed convinced that they could help Louisa and her family via Saul Levy. I dearly hoped so, for I felt that Louisa had to get out of those damp rooms in Tower Street very soon as she and John were becoming ill, and goodness knows what effect all this would have on their girls and young Bert.

Jacqueline and Bertie's voices were suddenly fading away from me.

'Not again!'

I found myself being dragged away once more, swirling into the foggy mists of time as I was thrust towards the ornate ceiling in Bertie's house and catapulted outside onto the roof! My ghostly form was being sucked upwards and upwards until I eventually found myself standing in front of the forbidding, grey walls of the orphanage once more. I couldn't see the Garton girls anywhere.

CHAPTER VIII

The Homecoming

I looked through the orphanage windows and could see the Garton girls, Gwen, Dora, Hilda and Connie, going about their daily cleaning duties as given to them by Mrs Foster. The girls looked pale and unhappy and I wished that I could communicate with them to let them know that their Mother and Uncle Bertie were going to help them to get out of the orphanage. But it was no use, try as I may, I couldn't give them any sign or communication. I was a mere ghost.

Thinking myself inside the orphanage, I found that I was standing next to Connie who was desperately trying to reach the brass door knobs to clean them but finding them too high for her to reach. The dusters were scattered all around her feet and the Brasso cleaning tin precariously placed nearby.

'How can I give the girls a sign, that their mother and father and Bert are well, and their Uncle Bertie will be coming to help them?' I thought.

Connie suddenly started to cry.

'I wish mother would come for us, I wonder if she ever will?'

Connie wiped her eyes with the back of her hand trying to stop her tears.

'Connie! How can you say such a thing?' said Gwen, 'Of course mother will come for us, she loves us all, you know that. There must be a good reason for her not coming for us, she always has visited us until a few weeks ago. Perhaps she is unwell, or perhaps Bert is poorly or she has managed to find a job. Yes that's it, she will have found a job, and is working all the time to get some money for us all.' Gwen hugged Connie close to her, stroking her bedraggled hair. 'We have received her letters haven't we, we all know she will come for us soon.' All the sisters smiled weakly at each other.

How could I make the girls understand? Yes, someone will be coming to help you very soon. Could I do something, give them a sign, something they would believe in, something to cheer them up? I concentrated with all my might on the dusters and the polish on the floor.

'Move! Move!'

Try as I might, nothing happened. Perhaps I could blow on the dusters and polish. Nothing! I sat on the first step of the stairs, next to Gwen and I just didn't know how I could give them a sign. I tried one more time.

The Visitor

'Move! Move!' This time I concentrated extremely hard on the dusters and polish.

'Look girls, Dora, Hilda, Connie, look! The polish and dusters, they are moving completely unaided, on their own. Can you believe that? Amazing!'

The Garton girls could only stare at the polish and dusters moving of their own accord. The girls could not believe their eyes and the spectacle brought the other children running to watch also.

'How is this happening? There is no wind, what is it?'

Hilda tried to pick up the dusters running after them, but I made them move just as she got close enough to pick on up, so she couldn't catch any of them. In fact, I laughed watching Hilda trying to catch them.

Dora took Gwen and Connie's hands in hers.

'Don't you realise, this is a sign, I am sure of it. It's a sign from mother, it just has to be. I feel it in my bones that everything is going to be all right!'

All the sisters hugged each other, knowing that it *was* a sign from their mother.

'I did it! I did it!'

I danced around the hallway with joy. Of course, no one knew I was there, or could see me, but I had managed to communicate with the Garton girls through my ghostly form so they now knew that they were not alone. Gwen was still a little sceptical about the gust of wind being able to blow dusters around and that it could be a sign from her mother, but she wanted to believe it was a sign and was prepared to go along with her sister's beliefs.

Well, I did try and I couldn't think of anything else I could do to convince the Garton girls that everything was going to be all right. I followed the girls watching them work and listened to their endless chatter. Their plan of escape had obviously failed and I wondered when their Uncle Bertie would come for them. I hoped he wouldn't be too long for the girls looked decidedly pale to me.

Gwen resumed her position on the first step of the stairs, heaving a great sigh, and said:

'I wonder if the baby has come yet, Dora? Probably that is the reason mother hasn't come for us?'

'Oh, I shouldn't think so, not yet Gwen,' Dora said. 'Mother has some time to go yet, at least on my reckoning.'

Dora carried on helping Connie finish polishing the brass door knobs.

Baby! What baby? Had I missed something else here? I continued to listen and follow the girls around.

'No, we would have heard by now if the baby had come, surely? Someone would have got word to us.'

Gwen wiped her forehead with her arm and stood up, pulling her long

The Visitor

hair into an elastic band, making a rather splendid ponytail.

'Has Mrs Foster gone out yet?'

Connie ran to the window to make sure Mrs Foster had actually left the building.

'Well, that's that! I am *not* polishing any more today.'

Connie threw her dusters down with relief.

'I am sick of polishing door knobs and when I grow up, I shall never polish anything again, ever!'

She sat on the first step of the stairs giving a sigh of relief.

'I feel like a prisoner here and I hate it! Do you know what I feel like doing Gwen, Dora, Hilda?'

Gwen and her sisters shook their heads.

'No, what do you feel like doing, little sister?'

Gwen was hoping that Connie was not going to make a nuisance of herself by singing.'

Connie continued:

'I feel like doing something really exciting, like putting on a show for the other children and of course me being top of the bill. I shall sing! We shall have a concert. Mrs Foster will never know about it, she is out and matron won't tell.'

'Oh, for goodness sake, you aren't going to do your Lillie Langtry impressions again Connie, are you? What a bore, she has been dead for I don't know how many years. Anyway, the children here won't know who she is, or rather was.'

Hilda was quite bored and gave an open-mouthed yawn.

'Anyway, you had better be careful for should Mrs Foster catch you there will be real trouble.'

Connie pouted her lip.

'Mrs Foster! Ah! she won't catch me, I am far too clever for her. I shall put a look-out on the front door, don't you worry, Hilda. She won't catch us.'

The sisters all laughed but were slightly nervous about the whole idea.

'Anyway, I shall do a rehearsal right now. Here goes!'

Connie stood up and started to give her rendition of one of Lillie's songs. The other children gathered around her and clapped her with great approval. Connie was truly talented and could sing very well. As she sang she gathered up the hall runner, wrapping it around her shoulders and arranging it around herself to resemble Lillie's gown.

'Oh!' Connie stopped singing. 'I need a parasol, it wouldn't be Lillie if I didn't have one!'

Connie looked everywhere and decided that she would search for a substitute in Mrs Foster's office, much to the astonishment of the other

The Visitor

children at her bravery in doing this.

'No, Connie, what if Mrs Foster should come back? Don't take her umbrella please, she will go absolutely mad. It looks nothing like a parasol to me anyway! Not like Lillie's, please don't Connie.'

Gwen tried to stop Connie but without success for the umbrella was the perfect substitute. There was just one thing more, Connie had to have a posh hat like Lillie's. There was just the thing hanging on the coat stand – Mrs Foster's hat!

Gwen, Hilda and Dora were just a little uneasy about all Connie's props, especially from Mrs Foster's office, but they were sure their sister's concert would be well over and everything put back in its place before Mrs Foster returned.

All the children were assembled ready for Connie's concert.

Dora cleared her throat.

'Quiet! Quiet, everyone please. Ladies and gentlemen, we present for your entertainment this evening the famous, the alluring, the sensational, the talented Miss er ... Miss Lillie Langtry.'

Dora bowed, walking slowly backwards towards the stairs to sit with some of the other children as she pointed in the direction of Mrs Foster's office. Suddenly, the office door flew open and Connie swept out displaying Mrs Foster's hat with a feather quill pen stuck into the top of it, the carpet, which made a beautiful gown and of course, Mrs Foster's umbrella, which did look just like the parasol Lillie used. All the children clapped madly as she started her performance and sounded just like Lillie Langtry herself.

Everyone was transfixed by Connie's talent.

I was pretty impressed myself, sitting back with all the other children on the stairs, enjoying the show. So much so, that neither me nor the lookout posted at the front door had noticed Mrs Foster's carriage drawing up outside.

Connie was still strutting up and down, singing at the top of her voice, blissfully unaware of Mrs Foster's folded arms and tapping foot of impatience on the stone hall floor, or in fact, of the other children becoming strangely quiet. All the sisters were much too concerned watching Connie to notice Mrs Foster. As Connie turned around and strutted back towards her audience, she became aware of Mrs Foster's angry face!

'What on earth is going on here?'

Connie immediately stopped her performance, with Gwen, Dora and Hilda running to her side to support her.

'That girl there! Yes, you, Connie Garton.'

Mrs Foster glared angrily at Connie and came closer to her peering down at her hat with the feather quill pen stuck in it, the hall runner strewn about her shoulders and her very own umbrella fully out and rolling about on the floor. Connie could only gape quivering with fright in front of the forbidding, woman.

The Visitor

'Take that hat off your head, put the carpet runner back where it belongs immediately! Now!'

Mrs Foster's voice echoed around the hallway like a lion's roar. The Garton girls ran to put things back in their rightful place. Dragging Connie by her ear, Mrs Foster pulled her into her study.

'Ouch!' Connie screamed. 'You are hurting my ear, leave me alone!'

'Hurting! I'll make you hurt, girl. Get in there!'

Mrs Foster flung Connie half way across her study.

Gwen, Hilda and Dora rushed into the study after Connie and Mrs. Foster.

'Leave her alone Mrs Foster,' Gwen shouted. 'We were only having a bit of fun, really that is all it was.'

The other Garton girls nodded in agreement.

'Fun! Fun! You are not here to have fun! Innocent was it? We shall see about that.'

Pushing Connie towards her large desk, Mrs Foster bent her over the edge and grabbed her cane with a metal top to inflict the severest pain.

'I told you girls what would happen if you disobeyed the house rules and you have surely done that today. So now, Connie Garton, you must pay the penalty!'

Mrs Foster, wielding the metal-topped cane above her head, brought it down onto Connie's back with a mighty blow, causing her to scream out in pain and faint.

'No! No! Mrs Foster, please!'

Gwen grabbed Mrs Foster's arm, battling to control the cane so that she could not inflict any more pain on Connie. Dora and Hilda joined in, grappling with Mrs Foster to seize the cane.

Matron, hearing the noise coming from the study and Connie's screams, rushed into the study.

'Mrs Foster! Girls! What an earth is going on in here? Mrs Foster, what do you think you are doing to this poor child? Why, you might have broken her back. She is so small.'

Matron's face was red with temper as Mrs Foster gathered her senses and slumped into a nearby chair.

'You have no idea Matron what I came back to, why these girls, they ...'

Gwen interrupted Mrs Foster in mid-sentence.

'Connie was giving us a concert and singing, that is all. Mrs Foster attacked her with this cane. Look at my poor sister, she is barely breathing. We have to get a doctor matron, really we do.'

'I have never before seen such a scene and I can only say Mrs Foster, I am ashamed and amazed at you stooping to these levels of cruelty.'

Mrs Foster retaliated.

'These girls are not only disobedient, but they are thieves. Yes, thieves.'

The Visitor

Everyone gasped.

'We are not thieves. We have stolen nothing, and never would. How dare you call us such things.'

Gwen helped Connie to her feet.

Matron looked on in horror.

'Thieves, why, what have they stolen? I just don't believe that Mrs Foster. Mischief-makers yes, but certainly not thieves. Why I have come to know these girls and am convinced they would never take anything.'

Mrs Foster stood up.

'Don't you dare interrupt me Matron. Connie Garton *was* stealing, why she took my umbrella, my hat and the hall runner carpet. She needs to be taught a lesson, in fact, I shall get a policeman. By golly I'll make sure all these girls are arrested and have a criminal record.'

Mrs Foster proceeded to leave her study to send for a policeman.

On reaching the door, Matron strategically placed herself between the door and Mrs Foster.

'Now, let us all calm down. There is no need for the law, Mrs Foster. I am sure the girls meant no harm and am sure they will apologise, won't you girls?'

All the girls nodded.

Mrs Foster stepped aside and walked towards her desk.

Matron ushered the girls out of the study.

'Come on girls, out you go! I'll deal with Mrs Foster. Go and get on with your duties and I shall see you all later. Connie, you go up to your bed and I shall look at your back later.'

Matron pushed the girls out of the study, closing the door firmly behind them.

The Garton girls pressed their ears against the study door trying to hear what Matron was saying to Mrs Foster. They could hear raised, muffled voices, but couldn't decipher what exactly was being said. Connie decided not to try and listen any more and retire to bed as Matron had requested as her back was very painful.

'Isn't Matron brave, I would think Mrs Foster will kill her, wouldn't you Hilda?'

Gwen, Hilda and Dora made an arm seat for Connie to sit on and took her upstairs to the dormitory.

'Let's have a look at your back Connie.'

Gwen helped Connie off with her dress and undergarments.

All the girls gasped.

'You are going to have terrible bruising there Connie. I expect it is very painful for you.' Gwen rubbed some oil into the wound.

'Ouch! That hurt me Gwen.'

The Visitor

Connie flinched at every stroke of Gwen's fingers over her wound.

'Come on Connie, get your nightdress on and get into bed. Rest is the only cure for your back.'

Gwen tucked Connie into bed. Dora and Hilda bent down and kissed her forehead.

'Get some rest now Connie. We shall be back later when it is dinner time.'

Matron and Mrs Foster were still arguing about the Garton girls when the maid knocked on the study door.

'Well, what is it, girl?'

Mrs Foster growled in disapproval at the maid's interruption.

'If you please madam, there is a posh gent in the hallway saying he wants to see you right away! He seems very important.'

Mrs Foster threw her pen across the desk in temper, making the maid jump with fright.

'A posh gent, girl! How many times do I have to tell you? Get the name! Get the name!'

Mrs Foster was annoyed and brushed past the maid nearly knocking her over as she made her way into the hallway to meet the 'posh gent'.

Her eyes saw a very distinguished gentleman, obviously wealthy, who tipped his top hat as she came towards him. His top hat, walking cane and white leather gloves were taken by the maid and placed on the hall table.

Mrs Foster thought he must be some titled person, or someone very important from the NSPCC.

'Ah, madam, you must be Mrs Foster?' the gentleman said.

'Yes I am, and whom might you be sir? State your business with me.'

'Can we go somewhere a little more private than standing in the hallway. Do you mind, Mrs Foster. The matter I have come about is somewhat delicate.'

Mrs Foster beckoned the gentleman to follow her.

'Please, come in here sir, the library is very private. We shall not be disturbed here. Please be seated. What is this delicate business you have come to see me about, sir?'

The posh gent of course, I knew, it was Bertie Hirons. Thank goodness he had come for the girls. I listened carefully to what Bertie had to say to Mrs Foster, who was scowling back at him, looking very unpleasant indeed.

Bertie had taken an instant dislike to Mrs Foster.

'I shall come straight to the point, Mrs Foster. I realise that you are an extremely busy woman.'

Bertie took some papers from inside his jacket pocket.

'I have certain papers here, all legitimate and lawful as you will observe.'

Bertie handed all the papers to Mrs Foster who studied them very carefully.

'The point is madam, I have the authority to collect four girls who are

The Visitor

in your care to be released to me forthwith.'

Bertie pointed out the legalities on the paperwork to Mrs Foster.

'As these unfortunate girls' mother is unwell and unable to come in person their release into my custody has been arranged by the NSPCC as you will observe, so I have come to collect them. My automobile is outside waiting to take them away, so if you would be so kind as to arrange for them to be brought to me now.'

Bertie stood up lighting his huge cigar, without permission to smoke from Mrs Foster.

Mrs Foster, realising Bertie had come for the Garton girls, could not wait to send for them and get them out of her establishment. She hated them. Never had she known such girls who had actually had the audacity to question her rules and on so many occasions.

'So!' said Mrs Foster. 'You are their uncle are you? What trouble the girls have all been, especially Connie. Make no mistake, sir, I am well rid of them!'

Bertie continued to puff on his cigar and said:

'And, if I may say so madam, they of you!'

'Like uncle, like nieces,' said Mrs Foster as she flounced out of the room.

Bertie chuckled to himself.

Matron and the maid were in the study, still reeling from Mrs Foster's earlier rantings.

Mrs Foster thrust open the door, with Matron and the maid nervously looking at her bad-tempered expression.

'Get all the Garton girls now! Bring them here,' she said. 'Their uncle is here to collect them and good riddance if you ask me! Go on then! Get them! Don't stand gawping at me Matron.'

Mrs Foster clapped her hands at Matron and the maid spurring them both into action.

Matron gathered all the Garton girls together.

'Girls, good news for you. You will never guess what?' She smiled and giggled.

'Your uncle Bertie has come for you to take you away from here. Isn't that wonderful?'

All the girls cheered. They could not believe what Matron was saying to them.

Matron continued …

'Your uncle is waiting for you all in the library.'

The Garton girls jumped up and down with joy, laughing and hugging Matron and each other.

'I told you, Connie! I told you! We had a sign the other day. Isn't it just wonderful! Is our mother with my uncle Bertie, Matron?'

The Visitor

Gwen looked enquiringly at Matron.

'No, ducks, afraid not. Something about her being poorly, nothing too serious though.'

Matron helped the girls to gather their few pitiful belongings together, leading them all downstairs towards the library. The Garton sisters talked and giggled all the way down the spiral staircase to the library.

Connie turned to Gwen and Hilda, Dora following on behind them.

'I told you, the moving dusters were a sign from mother.'

All the sisters nodded in agreement.

Before they arrived at the library, Mrs Foster met them in the hallway. They no longer cared what Mrs Foster said or did for they knew she could not harm them any more. Mrs Foster stood before the sisters as they all looked at her with unashamed contempt.

'Well, girls,' she said, 'It's your lucky day it seems. Shoulders back! Straighten up when I am talking to you.'

The girls purposely slouched their shoulders to annoy Mrs Foster and she was more than irritated by them.

'It seems, girls, that you have an uncle who has come to take you home and good riddance to bad rubbish is what I say!'

Mrs Foster ushered the girls into the library and they took no persuading to run to see their beloved Uncle Bertie.

Bertie hugged each niece in turn.

'Girls! How wonderful to see you all. Your knight has arrived and your coach awaits you in the driveway outside. So, let us all go!'

Bertie held out his arms for Gwen, Hilda and Dora to put their hands on his forearms. Connie had already disappeared out of the library and had made her way to the front door making sure to kiss Matron and the maid as she left. Mrs Foster gave her usual scowl of disapproval and said nothing as the Garton sisters and Bertie left the orphanage.

The girls did not care where Uncle Bertie might be taking them, just as long as they were escaping from the orphanage; of course, they all hoped it would be home. Never again did they ever want to speak of the place, Mrs Foster or anything to do with it. Bertie escorted them to the waiting automobile outside and Mrs Foster, Matron and all the other children watched them from the windows as they drove away.

As the autmobile drew away, Gwen turned to Bertie and said,

'How is mother and of course, father, and Bert? Why didn't they come for us? I mean … well … we are all so glad *you* came for us?'

All the girls fired question after question at Bertie, who couldn't hear any of their questions properly as they were all so very excited and chattering all at once.

'Hold it right there, girls! Just let's take one question at a time from one of you shall we? Now then, you first Gwen.'

Bertie sat back in the comfortable leather automobile seat and awaited all the girls' questions, pointing his finger at each inquisitive face to commence talking, but one at a time.

'Well, in answer to all your questions, your mother is very well, the baby is nearly due and she was far too tired to make the journey today, although of course, she dearly wanted to come. As for your father, well ... he has been unwell again, but despite his illness, he has managed to acquire another job, but still has to go for his check-ups at the sanatorium periodically. His lung is still quite bad and causing him pain, but nevertheless, he has managed to carry on and is trying very hard to stop drinking. He is so looking forward to seeing you all but had to work today.'

All the girls cheered, with Bertie stroking each small, excited face as they giggled with delight. As the journey home was a long one, Gwen decided that it was an opportune time to tell her uncle about Mrs Foster's cruelty, especially towards Connie.

'We were not the only children Mrs Foster caned or intimidated, Uncle Bertie. She is the most dreadful woman, you have no idea how terrible it was for us all. She actually caned poor Connie, she actually did and hurt her back dreadfully.'

Connie nodded her head in agreement with what Gwen said with all the sisters confirming their sister's story.

'Right! That is enough.'

Bertie commanded his driver to turn the automobile around and head back towards the orphanage.

'What are you doing Uncle? Surely we are not to go back to that dreadful place? What have I said to annoy you, Uncle?'

'Sweet child, nothing, you are certainly not going to set foot in that place again, but I am. I have a few choice words to say to Mrs Foster. She shall not get away with caning a child I know, or for that matter, any other child in her so-called care.'

The sisters all cheered for at last, they knew Mrs Foster was to get her just deserts. They didn't ever want to go back to the orphanage, they had vowed that, but wanted to see Mrs Foster punished. They sat quietly in the automobile whilst Uncle Bertie rang the orphanage doorbell. They wished they could go inside with Bertie to listen to what he had to say to her, but they had vowed never to set foot in that dreadful place.

The maid opened the door.

'Oh! It's you again sir! Please come in.'

She offered to take Bertie's hat and cane, but he declined.

'Yes, it surely is me and I would like to see Mrs Foster for a moment, if you please.'

The Visitor

The maid once more directed Bertie to the library, asking him to take a seat. The children working around the house nudged each other and knew something special was about to happen that they would more than enjoy!

Mrs Foster flounced into the library.

'Ah! Mrs Foster,' Bertie said, as he stood up.

'Please don't close the door Mrs Foster. I won't take up too much of your valuable time. Anyway, I think there are people here who will want to hear what I am about to say to you.'

Bertie took a large cigar from his inside jacket pocket making Mrs Foster wait to hear what he was going to say to her, much to her frustration. He billowed smoke all around the room and spoke as loudly as he could so that all the children working nearby would hear.

'Mrs Foster,' Bertie said. 'Do you imagine madam, for one single minute, that I would have come here to collect my nieces ill-prepared and naïve about what has been going on here for the past goodness knows how many years regarding your cruelty to the children here and my nieces in your so-called care?'

Mrs Foster took two steps back from Bertie in amazement as he puffed away at his cigar, blowing smoke everywhere and making her cough.

'Why sir, I don't know what you mean? Cruelty! What cruelty? You should not take notice of hysterical stupid young girls sir. They are all prone to great exaggeration and worse at their age.'

Mrs Foster sat down and nervously tapped her long bony fingers on the polished table top.

Bertie continued:

'Well, Mrs Foster! I think you do know what I mean! I think you know very well and so, because of your cruelty towards my nieces and God knows how many other children here, I am without a doubt reporting you to the authorities. As a member of the board, I shall certainly draw attention to the fact that children here have been ill-treated. I shall request that you are removed, dismissed, whatever you care to call it, but make no mistake, you shall never be in charge of children ever again. Do not imagine madam I am without influence and that I could not do such a thing. Believe me, I can.'

Bertie stood up, tapping his cigar ash into a priceless porcelain vase, much to Mrs Foster's astonishment. He slammed the library door behind him as he left.

The children all ran after Bertie cheering and slapping him on the back.

'Bravo!' they all shouted.

The Garton girls were impatient to know what exactly Uncle Bertie had said to Mrs Foster.

'What happened, Uncle, whatever did you say to her?'

The Visitor

All the girls questioned Bertie.

'When I have calmed down a bit girls I shall tell you, but let's get out of here as quickly as we can, eh? Driver, more speed. You have lots of surprises when you get home. Your mother has bought you all new beds, sheets and blankets. Now what do you all think of that? There is a feast awaiting us all better than you have ever dreamed of.'

Bertie threw back his head laughing loudly and he just hoped that Louisa May had managed to buy everything he had asked for and prepare the meal for the girls in time for their homecoming.

Hilda threw her arms about her uncle's neck.

'Uncle, how wonderful! Have we suddenly died and gone to heaven or something?'

Bertie laughed.

'No my dear, but let's say a little "windfall" has come your mother's way.'

Bertie laughed heartily once more.

The girls couldn't help thinking that it was all just a dream as their mother had always made their clothes and bed linen from old bits of rag she bought from the rag and bone man who called at Tower Street every week. They just could not believe what their uncle was telling them; actually new sheets and new beds! Unbelievable!

Bertie studied each of his nieces and they all had the look of Louisa about them, but none as beautiful as she had been at their ages.

'Now then girls, we have a way to go yet. Does anyone know a song we can all sing to pass the journey home?'

Bertie looked from face to face.

'I know one.'

Connie stood up in the back of the automobile.

'Oh, no!' Gwen said. 'Uncle you have started something now!'

Gwen started to laugh.

'Why, if you ask Connie to sing, she'll never stop! She got into so much trouble at the orphanage doing her song impersonations, didn't you Connie?'

All the sisters laughed, but Bertie felt a little sorry for Connie.

'Go ahead Connie, if you want to sing so be it.'

Bertie put his head back on the leather seat of the automobile and listened to her singing all her favourite songs. Everyone joined in and as the automobile passed pedestrians in the street, people clapped as the car drove by hearing all the girls singing!

The Visitor

Back at the House in Tower Street, Aston, Birmingham

Louisa May had prepared an absolute feast for the girls return, with Margaret Thompson's help. Margaret had gone back to her rooms to rest and suggested Louisa did the same until her girls arrived. They had both found Bert more than stressful, but thankfully, he was now tucked up in bed for his afternoon's sleep.

Louisa sat on the window seat overlooking the street below for she wanted a good all-round view of the street so she would catch the first sight of the girls coming home. She fingered the neck chain with the small, gold key at the end of it, the one Bertie and Jacqueline had given her as she waited for her girls. She wondered what time John would be home. He knew Bertie was fetching the girls from the orphanage.

Louisa felt very tired and quite lonely just waiting. Her baby's kicks inside her were making her feel quite faint so she decided to rest her head against the window pane. Looking out of the window down at the cobbled street below, there was still no sign of Bertie's automobile. Perhaps he had met trouble at the orphanage and couldn't get the girls after all? Oh, no! Please, no! she thought. She sat on her padded window seat, the cold glass of the window pane giving some relief to her headache.

I was just waiting around and was also excited at the prospect of the girls coming home. I looked into Louisa's face studying her exquisite features. She was still very beautiful although completely grey-haired now. She looked so small and vulnerable and much too tiny to be pregnant! I felt that I always wanted to be with her; the love I felt was passionate. Never, since I had come to know her, had she ever given up on anything, despite what life had thrown at her. She was always 'the optimist' and determined, which I greatly admired in her character. I sighed. Like Louisa, I was getting bored and tired waiting for the girls and watching Louisa sitting on her window seat falling into a deep sleep which she had been so determined not to do, I felt like joining her. I decided to keep myself awake so I walked around the room, looking at photographs of Louisa and her girls, Bert and John when suddenly, the room lit up all around me as if in bright sunlight! Shadows started to bounce about the room, forming themselves into girl-like silhouettes, skipping from one wall to another and off the ceiling. My eyes followed the shadows around the room but they were far too quick for me to determine what or where they were coming from, who they were, and what they meant. Louisa hadn't stirred at all and was still fast asleep as the shadows pranced about more quickly. With them had come the perfume of gardenias, which I recognised so well as the perfume of Louisa, but she was asleep in front of me! The sound of girlish laughter then followed and the perfume I knew so well and I actually became afraid as I recognised both anomalies.

The Visitor

The shadows in the room got larger and moved more furiously around the walls until I was gripped by an all-too familiar hand. The shadows had now grouped together to form one, large shadow and as the hand of the shadow gripped me tighter and tighter drawing me to it, I realised that it was that of the younger Louisa May Hirons.

The shadow faded away and left the ghostly figure of Louisa May giggling and pulling at my sleeve. She was once more dressed in her elegant Edwardian clothes as when I had first known her. How could this be? It seemed there were, two Louisas now, the older version sitting on her window seat asleep waiting for her girls, the younger ghostly version in front of me! I just couldn't believe my eyes. Both versions of Louisa May were in the same room with me.

I kept glancing back at the older version of Louisa May, still peacefully sleeping, but the younger Louisa did not seem to notice or recognise her older self at all. I shouted out! I don't know why, as her ghost visiting me before never seemed to hear me and I knew my older version of Louisa on the window seat was so deaf, she would never hear me.

'Stop! Stop! Who are you?'

That was a stupid remark, after all I knew who she was. All I could do was to try and keep calm. That was a joke for I felt the beads of perspiration trickling down my face. I thought to myself, 'How can a ghost perspire? How could there be one ghost, leading another ghost anywhere?' I just didn't understand any of it.

The younger Louisa May tugged and tugged at my sleeve as she had done on so many previous occasions. I knew she wanted me to go with her. She swirled me around and around, giggling, and pointing towards the older Louisa's neck chain with the small gold key on it. I did not see what the significance was so I didn't take much notice. She kept pointing at the chain and laughing loudly.

'So you can see yourself can you, your older version?'

The younger version Louisa just laughed and laughed still swirling me around and around.

It was becoming plain to me that I must leave Tower Street with the younger version Louisa for she was so insistent, swirling me higher and higher towards the ceiling of the room, until we were eventually outside and above the house in Tower Street looking down on the cobbles below. I found myself once more being transported through the foggy mists of time.

'Please, don't take me now. I want to wait here with the older Louisa to see her girls come home. Please, let me stay here.'

My protests made no difference: I was still transported away and found myself at Sycamore House again witnessing the day-to-day routines of the family inside. Believe it or not, the younger Louisa just, as I had first found her all those times before, about sixteen years old and very, very beautiful, was inside the house. She could neither see me nor hear me and it was as if none of her future life had yet happened!

Obviously, I hadn't been clever enough to pick up the clue Louisa May wanted me to find, so she had brought me back again to that particular time in her life where I could find it and document her story more thoroughly. Perhaps I would manage to find the clue this time? I just didn't understand but there she was, as bold as you like, in her expensive gowns with Bertie and Jacqueline not yet married, Louisa's parents and Sarah.

CHAPTER IX

Romance

Louisa May fiddled with her long, white, satin gloves, making sure that her elbows were not visible; to her, it seemed to matter a great deal that young ladies did *not* show their elbows in public! Bertie, Jacqueline and Louisa giggled and chatted about who would come to their special evening while Louisa preened herself in front of the long hall mirror.

A stern, woman's voice called out from one of the rooms leading off the hallway.

'Come in here, you three! Stop chattering and laughing so much, you know it gives me a headache, and we have lots more to do you know. Louisa darling go and make yourself useful instead of admiring yourself in the mirror all the time. Welcome our guests as they arrive, there's a good girl.'

The voice was that of Agnes Hirons, Louisa's mother, who was nervously flapping about in her usual way.

I realised some important event was about to happen at the house, as the servants Sarah the cook-cum-housekeeper and even John Garton, the gardener and stableman had been seconded to help. They worked hard, arranging the food on the huge dining table and moving furniture around to accommodate the expected volume of guests.

Sarah grunted.

'Come on, John, get a move on lad, please; move the sideboard more to the wall for me.'

John was not really concentrating on Sarah, as he hadn't taken his eyes away from Louisa, who hadn't noticed the longing gaze he was giving her as she was far too busy chattering.

Agnes Hirons sighed.

'Goodness knows where the orchestra has got to. Shush. Every time we have this trouble with them, they are always late! And this, such a great occasion for our family!'

Agnes shrugged her shoulders in disbelief that the orchestra could be late yet again.

I wondered what this great event was. It all seemed very grand for all the Hiron's family were dressed in their finest clothes, especially Louisa May, who looked radiant.

The Visitor

'Now, mother, don't you fret so. You know how it gives you the vapours! Everything will be all right, you will see. The orchestra will be here in plenty of time.'

Louisa hugged her mother and rushed out of the room into the hallway to the long hall window overlooking the driveway, to watch for the first signs of guests arriving. She wanted to be the first to signal anyone's arrival and was very excited.

'Louisa, dear, see if my hairpieces are still secure will you?'

Agnes bent her head towards Louisa who was much too busy looking down the long drive way through the window to bother with her mother's false curls. She spoke impatiently.

'Yes, yes, mother you look splendid. Don't you always? Don't worry so, your curls won't drop off, I secured them well.'

Louisa was visibly vexed by her mother's vanity.

John chuckled, trying to stifle his laughter at Mrs Hiron's pinned on false curls, but hurried away down the hallway with Sarah to help with food preparations in the kitchen. He was doubling up today, not only gardener and coachman, but cooking help as well! It was 'all hands on deck' as Sarah knew she would not cope alone in the kitchen today of all days.

Grand carriages and some automobiles started to arrive outside Sycamore House.

I became a little more enthusiastic about being back at the house at this stage, because of the party. I meandered down the long hallway to the front door, where Louisa May was excitedly jumping up and down. I couldn't help wondering what it was all about and getting a little excited myself.

'Oh, doesn't everyone look wonderful? The men are so handsome and the ladies, well! Look at the beautiful gowns! Oh, mother, do come and look! Jacqueline and Bertie, come, look!'

Louisa May took Bertie's hand dragging him across to the window.

'Do look, Bertie.'

'Dear, sweet, Louey, we should not be seen peering through the window as our guests arrive. You must be genteel and a composed young lady. Come, little sister, Jacqueline. I will escort you both to the sitting room. Everyone will be announced to us in the proper manner by Sarah, or John. We shall look every inch the "grand family".'

Bertie took Louisa and Jacqueline by the arm, leading them to the sitting room. Agnes Hirons was already waiting, still preening her false curls and straightening her gown ready to receive the first of the guests.

Sarah knocked on the sitting room door and announced the orchestra's arrival first. Agnes nearly had a fit.

'Oh my God! Not now! Just when all the guests are arriving. Sarah dear, be a darling and show the musicians into the dining room. Show them where

The Visitor

Sycamore House

they are to sit and hurry now, don't let any of our guests see them!'

Agnes once more sat herself down composing herself. The guests were shown into the dining room and offered a glass of sherry by John Garton who was dressed as a butler, much to Louisa's amusement. He looked most uncomfortable and he felt it!

Louisa giggled, as she had never seen John dressed up before, especially not in a butler's uniform. She thought him, strangely, quite handsome and nudged him in his back as she passed by. She loved to flirt with him. She felt she could, he was only a mere servant. John swung around wondering who had prodded him. He caught the impish grin on Louisa's face as she passed and tried not to laugh out loud. If he did, that would be the end of his job! He knew he loved Louisa more than he could ever endure, but he must suppress his feelings for her. After all she was the master's daughter and he, a servant. What could he ever give her? No, he mustn't think any more about it for they were friends and that was how it had to be.

He enjoyed Louisa's visits to the garden to see him even though she played with his affections, and he did enjoy their deep talks about life; but there was no future for him with her in any other way. He would, he was sure, die for her if required to do so and protect her to his last breath. She was life itself to him and he was glad he worked at the great house so that at least he could see her every day. How he wished they could be alone in the garden at this very minute, instead of in the stuffy surroundings of the

The Visitor

party. He knew Louisa adored parties and dressing up in her grand gowns. She did look gorgeous and John was sure that she did not think of him in any other way but as a friend and servant.

Sarah prodded John.

'Come on, lad, what are yow dolly-daydreaming about now? More people arriving, so come on, get 'em a drink, lad!'

'Oh, yeah, er … sorry, Sarah.'

John made his way past Louisa May who was now deeply engrossed in conversation with Jacqueline and another young lady.

At least there is no competition, male-wise, John thought, as he scanned the room.

Sarah directed a young man dressed in military uniform and his aunt towards John Garton. John offered the silver tray of drinks and the young man took one handing it to his aunt, but declined himself.

'Thank you, sonny.'

The young man's eyes scanned the room and John took an instant dislike to him and hoped Louisa did not meet him. He was far too handsome by half. John proceeded to go around the room, half-attentive on what he was doing and half-watching every move Louisa May made.

Suddenly, Abraham Hirons banged on the table with the end of his knife to alert everyone's attention.

'As you are all very aware, we are here this evening to celebrate two things. First, we are here to raise our glass to our new king and long may he reign.'

Everyone raised their glasses saying:

'Long live the king, long live Edward.'

'And secondly, to once more raise our glasses to my son, Bertie and his beautiful Jacqueline, who have become engaged this very day to be married. Ah, yes, I had nearly forgotton. You are all invited to the wedding which shall be on the ninth of September. Of course, you will all receive official invitations.'

Everyone cheered, raising their glasses to Bertie and Jacqueline, with Louisa rushing towards them congratulating them and hugging the couple close to her.

'Oh, Jacqueline, I told you so, didn't I tell you he would propose? I am so very happy for you both.'

Bertie threw his head back and gave one of his resounding belly laughs, twirling his little sister around and around.

'Well, Louey, it's your turn next! You had better find yourself someone soon. No more sitting at home or talking to servants in the garden for you!'

Bertie laughed out loud once more with Louisa pouting her lip in disapproval of his loud voice. Anyway, what was wrong with talking to servants in the garden, especially if you liked them? Louisa looked towards John, who was visibly hurt by Bertie's remarks. She wished she could comfort him; she hated to see him embarrassed and hurt. She knew she could not do anything about Bertie's remarks, and could not talk to John, not in company.

Louisa May was genuinely happy for her brother and her best friend, Jacqueline, but slightly bored by the whole evening's proceedings. There were no eligible young men for her, just mother, father's and Bertie's stuffy friends and of course, the family. Perhaps she would be left 'on the shelf' and become an old maid! That would be a fate worse than death! Would she ever find her Prince Charming? Of course, there would be someone, somewhere for her, how could any young man resist her tonight? Sarah said she looked more beautiful than she had ever seen her. Louisa fiddled with the ends of her long hair, something she always did when bored or agitated.

'Fiddle-de-dee,' she thought, 'I don't care anyway. I will enjoy the food tonight, if nothing else. I shall be the perfect English lady and make mother and father really proud of me tonight.' She spread out the layers of her fan and wondered how many names, if any, would be written on them for her dances. Who would be her first conquest? In fact, there were no names written on her fan yet!

Louisa carefully studied every face in the room, each face busily stuffing its mouth with tempting morsels of food Sarah had so carefully prepared. The room sounds like the 'monkey house' at the zoo, Louisa thought. A wide smile spread across her face as the more she studied the faces of the guests, the more she tried to imagine what type of animal at the zoo they were most like. Agnes's voice became more and more shrill, talking to her guests above the expert playing of the orchestra.

Louisa imagined Agnes as a hyena and perhaps father a wise, old owl, bespectacled and just listening to mother's shrill demands and nodding occasionally in agreement. He was too timid of her to do otherwise! The carefully spread fan was placed across Louisa's face so no one would suspect her of laughing at them. Louisa had imagined all sorts of things about her guests and was becoming quite bored with the whole affair. Perhaps she would sneak outside away from the party to the garden and talk to John if he could get away. Maybe John wouldn't be able to leave as he was so busy helping Sarah.

What shall I do now? Louisa thought. How shall I keep myself from drowning in complete boredom?

Once more, the noisy room was hushed by the loud banging on the dining room table.

'Attention, everyone!'

Abraham Hirons gained everyone's attention in the room and Louisa yawned widely, behind her fan of course!

The Visitor

'We are all here as you know and as I have said once before this evening, to congratulate our two young people here and also to toast our new king, but there is one more thing I would like to bring your attention to!'

Everyone gasped and looked at each other in amazement as to what it could be.

'Come here, son, come and join me.'

Abraham signalled Bertie to his side. Bertie blushed with embarrassment.

Louisa started to pay more attention to events.

'I know my son Bertie here would be very embarrassed at me telling you this and I know that he would not have said anything about it. But I am proud of my only son and I am going to say it whether he feels embarrassed or not. I would like you all to raise your glasses once more to my son, Herbert, as he has now become a full partner in a business in the city, as of today! So please, everyone, raise your glasses to his success.'

Everyone cheered and raised their glasses including Louisa, who had no idea that Bertie had been so very clever. Bertie gave Jacqueline a kiss, much to everyone's amazement, and Louisa wished that she had a young man who would kiss her. Her thoughts spun into romantic notions, thinking Jacqueline the luckiest of women. Abraham Hirons once more raised his voice.

'Everyone, your attention again please! Just one more time I promise.'

All the guests laughed.

'There is, as you know, food in the dining room and also dancing. There is a marquee outside in the garden and yet more food in there.'

Everyone laughed again.

'So please, do help yourselves and enjoy this beautifully hot summer evening.'

The guests clapped, congratulating Bertie and Jacqueline on their way out to the garden. The evening had become warm and humid, with Louisa fanning herself and thinking she might go outside for some food in the marquee. The orchestra started to play and some couples took to the dance floor to waltz. The dancing all looked very refined as Louisa made her way towards the door leading out to the garden. She hadn't noticed the handsome army officer watching her very closely. There was suddenly a click of heels, a bowed head and a manly voice asking Louisa if she would care to waltz.

'I do hope you are not booked for this dance. Should I write my name on your fan? Should I reserve my place?'

The young man's bright blue eyes twinkled at Louisa's shocked expression and he smiled widely, displaying perfect white teeth. Louisa May could only gape back at the officer for she had never seen any man so handsome before. She couldn't speak and seemed as though struck dumb. Surely, this *was* her Prince Charming here at last! Of course she would say yes to his invitation to dance.

The Visitor

Louisa was caringly escorted to the centre of the dance floor by the young man. He took her gently in his arms, holding her tiny, white gloved hand in his and expertly guided her around the dance floor to the romantic swaying of the waltz. The young man spoke.

'Do you have a name? For that matter, do you speak?'

He laughed loudly at Louisa's shyness, cupping her chin with his hand and promptly closing her gaping mouth.

Louisa May flashed her ebony eyes at him saying:

'Yes, I do of course have a name. It's Louisa! Louisa May Hirons and this is my home, sir. You know my parents I take it, Agnes and Abraham Hirons? Look! There they are talking to Mrs Pizer.'

'Ah, yes, I don't know them well of course; I was told that I met them when I was very young, but I can't really remember them.'

The young man smiled back at Louisa, gazing into her eyes. He had never seen such beautiful eyes and could not stop looking at her whilst they danced. She hated being stared at, but didn't seem to mind the young man's attention.

Louisa said:

'It seems that my parents have been cornered by the most boring Mrs Pizer and my brother, Bertie, and Jacqueline have joined them, look!'

Louisa pointed to her family whilst dancing, but the young man did not look, he on had eyes for Louisa drawing her hand back to his and placing it on his chest. When the orchestra stopped playing, the young man still held her close to him as if still dancing.

'Please don't go, may I have the next dance? I mean ... are you engaged with anyone else or ... er ... have you anyone listed on your fan for more dances?'

The young man looked self-conscious.

'No one!' Louisa said. 'Yes, I shall be delighted to dance with you.' She started to giggle, with the young man returning her smiles. 'You must think me very rude, sir. I don't even know your name. How are you distantly related to my family?'

Louisa started to fan her flushed face for she was quite sure that she was madly in love with her young man already! The young man once more took her in his arms as the orchestra started to play.

'My name, Louisa, is Peter, Peter Dupont. I am here visiting my aunt, as you quite rightly say, the boring Mrs Pizer.'

Peter chuckled and Louisa lowered her eyes in shame at her earlier comments about Mrs Pizer.

'Oh, my goodness, how terrible of me! What must you think of me? I had no idea she was your aunt.'

Peter threw back his head and roared with laughter.

'Don't you worry Louisa, my dear, there is no offence taken for you are

The Visitor

right, she is boring, but adorable in a funny way. I am visiting her as I am on leave from the military academy in Camberley. I shall have to resume my duties on Monday so I am not here for long!'

During the evening, the couple danced every dance. Louisa could not believe that such a man as Peter was finding her interesting and was actually speaking to her for any length of time. She was always starved of company of her own age and only had Jacqueline as her friend and now she was to be married and possibly whisked away to some distant place. Peter was certainly a prince among men. There was no one else in the room to compare with him or for that matter, anyone in the whole of England to match his good looks and charm, she thought.

'I have a suggestion, Louisa! I hope you won't be shocked.' The young man took Louisa's hand.

'Shall we make our way to the marquee, that is, if you would like me to accompany you there?'

Louisa nodded. Peter took her arm and lead her towards the marquee. As they walked, he took quick glances at her when she was not looking.

'Louisa, I hope you don't think me too bold, but I thought, well, if you wanted to, we could write to one another. What do you think?'

Louisa's heart leapt. Little did Peter know but she was already in love with him so of course she would write.

'Yes, I would like that very much.'

Louisa blushed once more as Peter was having a profound effect on her. Could she actually have fallen in love with him at such an early stage? How could she feel this way so quickly about a man she had just met?

'Well, Louisa May, who are you keeping to yourself here? Introduce me to this young man.'

Agnes extended her hand to Peter, who promptly turned it over from a shake of the hand, to a kiss on top of it, clicking his heels as he did so. This sent Agnes into twittering coyness, fingering her false curls and giggling, much to Louisa's annoyance. Louisa found her most annoying when she behaved so stupidly.

'Peter, this is my mother, as you already know. This is my father and you already know Jacqueline and Bertie, my brother.'

Louisa politely introduced her family to Peter Dupont.

'I am honoured to meet you all.'

Peter once more clicked his heels together, bowing his head to the gentlemen and kissing the ladies' hands, then offering Jacqueline and Bertie his congratulations for their engagement.

He coughed nervously.

'Mr and Mrs Hirons, could I speak with you? Whilst I am here at your very kind invitation, I wondered if I could ask your permission to write to

The Visitor

Louisa and perhaps call on her from time to time. We believe we are to become very good friends.'

Peter smiled awkwardly in Louisa's direction, she lowering her eyes in coyness at his suggestion. Louisa's heart raced as never before. He said we will become very good friends, she thought. Abraham and Agnes smiled at one another and then back at Peter.

'Of course, why not. You may visit and we should have no objections at all.'

Abraham patted Peter on the back, pushing him towards Louisa as he did so.

'Here, Peter, take Louisa down to the marquee as there is plenty of food there and if I know my daughter, she is always hungry. Needs no encouragement, especially with the strawberries and cream!'

Agnes and Abraham laughed as Peter led Louisa towards the marquee, which was crowded with people putting food onto plates from the buffet table. Sarah and the other servants stood behind long tables ready to serve any manner of meats and rich foods.

'Well, Louisa, it looks as if we shall have to wait a while in the queue. We can always listen to the lady pianist. She is doing her very best I am sure.'

Peter tried not to laugh out loud, as Louisa's wide grin met his eyes. The lady pianist was, to say the least, bad, but doing her very best to play pieces from Gilbert and Sullivan, without much success, for most of her playing was unrecognisable. Louisa leaned over to Peter and whispered in his ear.

'Shush, Peter, we shouldn't talk about her for she is a dear friend of Mother's and insisted on helping her. Mother couldn't refuse her, although we didn't really want her to play. I am sure Mr Gilbert and Mr Sullivan would not be amused!'

Louisa once more drew her fan across her face to hide her grins but the more she tried to control her laughter, the more hysterical she became, especially with Peter chuckling. The giggling became uncontrollable, with both Louisa and Peter now laughing out loud. The lady pianist was oblivious to it all, engrossed in her playing. Everyone in the queue looked back at Louisa and Peter angrily but even the glares could not stop their laughter. At last the queue got smaller and the lady pianist decided to join it for some food and stopped playing, much to everyone's relief.

Louisa and Peter found themselves at the buffet table full of succulent dishes. He served her with some salad to go with her chicken and a huge bowl of strawberries and cream, which were Louisa's absolute favourite. Expertly placing their plates of food on a tray, Peter lifted it up and picked his way through the crowds of people to two spare places that happened to be near his aunt, Miriam Pizer, who was already sitting at a table. Quick as

The Visitor

a flash, Peter pulled out a chair for Louisa to sit on, carefully brushing off particles of food and dust with his serviette before she sat down.

'Thank you, Peter,' she said.

Peter introduced his aunt Miriam to Lousa, leaning across the table and kissing his aunt's forehead.

'Be gone with you, lad.' Aunt Miriam was embarrassed by Peter's kiss. 'Don't do that, you know you can always get around me with your charm. He has this charm you know Louisa, you shall have to be very careful of him. Who could refuse those bright blue eyes anything?'

Miriam Pizer chuckled then waded through her huge dish of strawberries and cream, cramming as many strawberries as she possibly could into her large mouth at one time, until the sides of her cheeks bulged out. Louisa May thought that she looked like a 'chipmunk' and her cheeks would surely explode as they expanded so much. After devouring all the strawberries, Miriam commented:

'Louisa, my dear, it was so charming of your dear mother and father to invite Peter today. After all they haven't seen him since he was a baby. You know, dear, you are very like your dear mother was when she was your age. Those big, dark eyes and high cheekbones; yes, just like her, dear.'

Miriam continued to gobble yet more strawberries. Peter, it was plain, was not really listening to his aunt but continually gazed at Louisa and she at him! It was so obvious that Peter was besotted with Louisa and she had fallen madly in love with him.

Later That Night

It was two o'clock in the morning. Sarah and John, the servants, were still clearing away the party plates in the marquee and the main house. The Hirons family were bidding farewell to the last of their guests. The engagement party and celebrations of the coronation had been a success, everyone agreed. Louisa, Bertie and Jacqueline had enjoyed the evening immensely.

'I shall not say "goodbye" Louisa, but shall look forward to our next meeting very soon. I have spent a wonderful evening.'

Peter clicked his heels and kissed Louisa's hand, but more passionately this time. She wished it was her lips he kissed and not her hand and knew that he felt the same way. Looking first at her mother and then the rest of her family, who were in agreement with Peter's intended visit to Syacmore House, Louisa said her goodbye to Peter and his aunt Miriam.

'Thank you all most sincerely for the most delightful evening.'

Peter was given his cane and military hat and escorted to the front door by Sarah.

As he went through the doorway when no one was looking, he turned and

The Visitor

blew a kiss to Louisa May who promptly blew one back. He mouthed to Louisa, 'Be back soon! I think I am in love with you' and helping his aunt Miriam into his newly acquired automobile, he waved goodbye to Louisa, who watched him leave, standing at the hallway window.

Sarah gave Louisa a wink of approval as she passed her and Bertie ruffled her hair.

'Come on, Louey, he'll be back soon. You have been really smitten haven't you little sister? Let's go and have a nightcap.'

Bertie led Louisa into the dining room where Jacqueline and Agnes were sitting down, watching the orchestra pack away their instruments. He leaned back in a comfortable chair.

'Phew, I am so very tired. I expect you ladies are tired too?'

Bertie took Jacqueline's hand, kissing it gently.

'Oh, stop it you two! Honestly, billing and cooing! Aren't you going to retire to bed yet?'

Louisa fiddled with her hair as Bertie retorted:

'Look who's talking the biggest "biller and cooer" of them all!'

Bertie and Jacqueline started laughing.

'What was his name, Louey, our long-lost cousin, Peter what? Why, you couldn't take your eyes off him Louey, so don't tell us that we "bill and coo" too much!'

Bertie jumped from his chair and started to chase and tickle Louisa making her scream for him to stop.

'Children, children please!' Agnes bristled past Louisa and Bertie. 'Please have a little more decorum. I can't stand you shrieking like that Louisa, please be quiet, it goes right through my poor head!'

Louisa and Bertie stopped immediately for they could see that Agnes was in no mood to be crossed. Louisa and Bertie could not stop giggling for they couldn't take their eyes off Agnes's false curls, which had slid down to the ends of her hair and looked like spiders holding onto a web! The musicians in the orchestra hardly dared to smile, although Louisa knew that they wanted to. Agnes Hirons sat down exhausted.

'Shush! What an evening! We shall all be so tired in the morning, so I am off to my bed. I think you children should do the same, especially you, Louisa. You are not used to such late hours.'

Agnes put her arms about Louisa's shoulders.

'But, mother, how could I possibly sleep ever again? Wasn't Peter just devine?'

Louisa May sighed and started to waltz around the room with a pretend partner.

'Shush, such goings on! Such a daughter I have!' Agnes started to shuffle off towards the stairs.

The Visitor

'I suppose he was quite charming, considering ...'
Louisa stopped waltzing and said:
'Considering what, mother?'
Louisa chased after Agnes.
'Considering he is related, but not on my side of the family you understand.'

Agnes dragged herself up the stairs one by one. Louisa followed, questioning Agnes all the way up to the top of the stairs.

'He's the son of your father's distant cousins who got himself into terrible debt. A disgrace to the family he was. In the end he went and shot himself, he owed so much money, it seemed to everyone. Young Peter was sent away to live with his aunt who virtually brought him up. Sissie, his mother, died when he was very young, so you see, we tended to keep away from that side of the family. Such a disgrace.'

'Mother, that is terrible. Poor Peter, he must have been devastated by his father's death.'

'You must not gossip about it Louisa, we tend to keep these sort of things hidden. You mustn't let Peter know that I have told you about it.'

'Oh, I won't. Thank you for telling me mother.'

Louisa skipped down the stairs to rejoin Jacqueline and Bertie.

'What's mother been saying to you Louisa? Full of anti for Peter I suppose?'
Bertie picked up the newspaper to read.

'Do you know, with all the excitement today, I haven't even read the newspaper.'

The Next Day

'Wakey, wakey, rise and shine! It's a beautiful sunny day out there and really hot. I've laid out yower new white dress, miss Louisa and yower new undergarments. Come on, I'll put yower 'air up for yow. Yow are going to the city today with madam and the master, or did yow forget?'

Sarah drew back the bedroom curtains, letting the sunlight stream onto Louisa's face.

'I'll fetch yow some toast and a boiled egg, if yow like. Yow won't 'ave time to go down to the dining room now. It's well after nine o'clock and the master will be furious with yow if yow don't 'urry yowerself.'

Sarah bustled around the bedroom hanging up Louisa's clothes in the adjoining dressing room.

'Oh, Sarah, I am so very, very happy. Did you see me last night dancing with Peter, so handsome, and oh, so charming? Wasn't he just adorable?'

'Yes, Louisa, I saw yow. Yes, I suppose he was adorable, but yow be careful miss Louisa, none of me business, but yow like me own flesh and blood. Yow know I love yow don't yow? Like me own, yow are and I wouldn't want to see yow 'urt by any man.'

Louisa threw herself back onto her bed, looking up at the ceiling.

'Hurt? Me? I know Peter would never hurt me, not Peter. I am sure he is madly in love with me. He's actually coming soon to Sycamore House to see me especially and even asked mother and father's permission to do so. What do you think about that Sarah?'

Louisa hugged one of her pillows and wished it was Peter.

'Ah, yes, Bab, I can believe that, but come along now, get yowerself ready. Yower mother will go mad if you ain't down those stairs in two minutes!'

Sarah brushed Louisa's hair into her band and poured hot water into her washing bowl set on the washstand. Jacqueline had stayed the night at the Hirons' house and was already dressed, having eaten her breakfast with Agnes and Abraham, but as usual, no sign of Bertie or Louisa! She knocked on Louisa's bedroom door and looked into the room.

'Are you getting dressed, Louisa? We are all waiting for you! Your father is going mad downstairs.'

Sarah laughed.

'I told yow miss, didn't I tell yow?'

Louisa started to wash herself.

'Well, he will just have to go completely mad for all I care. I can only think about Peter.'

Jacqueline sighed.

'For goodness sake, Louey, I shall wait for you downstairs, hurry up!'

Agnes was sorting out the plans for the shopping day ahead.

'Where is that daughter of mine? Really this is too bad.'

Agnes went into the hall and put on the largest feathered hat she could find, securing it with huge hat pins ornately set with glistening stones.

'I did so want to get into the city before the main shops got too busy. I need to see about a wedding gift for you, my dear.'

Agnes patted Jacqueline's hand.

'Mrs Hirons, you shouldn't, really. You have already given Bertie and myself enough.'

'Rubbish,' Agnes said. 'We shall choose something today, something gorgeous. I just feel like spending money!'

Agnes dabbed her face with her handkerchief.

'My, it is so hot,' she said.

'Oh, do you, my dear? You want to spend all my money.' Abraham was not too thrilled.

'I hope not too much money as I have to see about one of those contraptions young Peter arrived in last night. I shall be some time in the city, so you ladies, for a change, can be as long as you like shopping.'

Agnes turned to Abraham.

The Visitor

'You don't mean, you can't mean, you are actually going to buy an automobile? How wonderful! Oh, I can tell that Mrs Goldberg. Won't she be jealous! How exquisitely delightful, she will have something to be envious of me about.'

Agmes gave a contented smile. She had always hated Mrs Goldberg and her wealth and wanted to prove that the Hirons family were equally as wealthy.

'At last, Louisa, now come along. We are already late!'

Agnes bustled Louisa and Jacqueline outside.

'Late? Mother! For what?'

Louisa pouted her lip.

'I don't suppose we shall see our son until well after lunchtime and we are back home. He sleeps so much these days so I think there must be something very wrong with him. You shall have to watch that, Jacqueline, when you are married.'

Agnes was clearly annoyed with Bertie. Abraham helped the three ladies into the waiting carriage, John Garton making sure the doors were securely shut and winking at Louisa. She smiled at him but he did not dare to smile back as Agnes was watching him closely.

Louisa knew that she must never speak to John in front of her parents, although she did on so many secret occasions in the garden, for they would surely not approve. Perhaps she would go later that evening to talk to John when he tidied up the garden before retiring for the night and tell him about Peter. She was sure he would be more than interested for he was always interested in anything she had to say. Louisa felt that John Garton was, after Jacqueline, her very best friend.

On the way to the city, the garlands and streamers were still hanging in the streets from the coronation celebrations for Edward, Prince of Wales now King Edward and Louisa thought it looked like fairyland. The two young girls giggled and chatted all the way to the city, watching John trying to manoeuvre the horses and carriage, knocking kerbs and missing pedestrians only by inches. It was a very large carriage to handle, but John did his job well. Louisa had never really noticed him before, only feeling that he was nice and kind to talk to and finding him easy to be with. He is surely, for his class of person, quite handsome, she thought, when he is clean! When she talked to him in the garden, he was always so very dirty. She had never noticed before how fair his hair was, nor how blue his eyes. He was not at all dark and Jewish-looking like Peter, in fact, a real contrast. Louisa could never understand why father had employed John as he was a gentile and looked it, but she liked him all the same.

'John, do you have to whip the horses so, please, don't!'

One of the horses cried out with pain.

The Visitor

'I won't, Miss, if yow say so, but it makes the 'orses go faster see and master has to get to the city quick. Anyway, I wouldn't 'urt 'em deliberate. They are me mates and I wouldn't 'urt a mate.'

John took a quick glance back at Louisa's concerned face and thought he had never seen a woman so beautiful in all his days.

Jacqueline and Louisa couldn't help giggling at John's strong Birmingham accent but Abraham scolded them for their insensitivity towards him. John didn't seem to notice for anything Louisa said or did was all right by him.

The carriage arrived in Corporation Street in the middle of the city at Agnes's favourite department store. Each lady was carefully helped from the carriage by John, who made sure Louisa was the last to alight as he wanted to help her much more than anyone else and held on to her the longest. Abraham showed his ladies into the store.

'Now, ladies, don't spend all my money at once!'

Abraham laughed as he went back to the carriage to be driven to the automobile centre. Agnes smoothed down her fox fur stole, which wasn't really needed at all, as the weather was hot and humid. She looked around the store to see if anyone was watching her and if they were impressed. Louisa smiled to herself.

The Commissionaire offered his assistance to the ladies.

'We shall go and look at the hats, handbags and matching shoes. Jacqueline, Louisa ... come!'

Agnes led the way like a captain leading her troops into battle and Louisa pulled at Jacqueline's sleeve to follow her. Agnes walked over to the millinery counter and tried on all manner of hats.

'Oh, do look, mother!'

Louisa shrieked across the shop floor to Agnes who was still trying on all the hats.

'Louisa dear, please don't shout. Come over to speak to me dear, but do not shout!'

'Mother, isn't this bag just wonderful, look! There are matching shoes. Can I please have them, I would so love them?'

Agnes nodded and was smothered with kisses from Louisa. The crocodile leather shoes were a perfect match for the bag. The store saleslady wrapped up the bag and the shoes whilst Louisa and Jacqueline went over to help Agnes to decide which of the ostentatious hats she would choose. The sales assistant positioned the hand mirror so that she could see herself from every angle.

'It's only nine guineas, madam, a snip.'

Everyone agreed it was a beautiful hat, large and a bit flamboyant, but beautifully made. The feathers were a little large, but Louisa and Jacqueline said that Agnes could do the hat justice!

The Visitor

'Right, girls! Now that's settled. I shall have the hat, but I need Jacqueline to come with me to the furniture department. No arguments please, Jacqueline. I know you say I have bought you and Bertie enough wedding presents, but I insist.'

Agnes led the way with the two girls following dutifully behind her.

I couldn't help wondering why I was witnessing all these events. I felt fed up and totally confused, as I couldn't find any clues to any mystery surrounding Louisa or her family. Anyway, I decided I had no option but to follow my three ladies around the store and just observe them.

A shop assistant was very quick to notice Agnes looking at various items of furniture and came over to assist to where she was admiring a writing bureau.

'Madam, if I might say so, you are looking at the most exquisite of pieces of furniture.'

The shop assistant proceeded to show Agnes and Jacqueline the unique writing bureau. Louisa was quite bored and sat herself down on numerous chairs deciding which was the most comfortable, whilst Agnes and Jacqueline looked at the bureau.

'Oh, Agnes, you can't possibly think of buying us this bureau. It is so very expensive, we couldn't possibly accept this.'

Jacqueline was clearly embarrassed.

'Rubbish, it is expensive, I agree, but you pay for what you get. This is the best so you and Bertie shall have it, I insist.'

No one could dissuade Agnes for she was determined to buy the bureau for Bertie and Jacqueline and asked the sales assistant to deliver it.

The shop assistant cleared his throat.

'Well, madam, I have to agree, it is exquisite; however, I have just realised and I must sincerely apologise; it is reserved. I am very sorry. We can obtain another bureau very similar to this one for you madam, however, delivery will take several months. I must apologize, I didn't see the "reserved" ticket on this piece. It is a very expensive item and the lady who has reserved it is an extremely wealthy woman. You can see my predicament. I would love to sell you the bureau but sadly, it is not available.'

Agnes immediately flew into a rage.

'Expensive! How dare you! How dare you assume that my family could not afford such a bureau? Who has reserved it? Tell me her name! I shall pay double for it. Why leave a piece of furniture on display if it is spoken for already? Get me the manager!'

The shop assistant nervously hurried away to fetch the manager.

'Mother, really, do you have to make such a scene about a stupid bureau of all things.'

Louisa sighed.

The Visitor

'Really, Mrs Hirons, we don't expect you to go to such lengths, really we don't. You have already bought us a house and many fine pieces of furniture. Please, don't put yourself to this expense for us.'

Jacqueline hugged Agnes.

'Rubbish! That stupid shop assistant tried to tell me we can't afford such things. Well, I shall show him.'

Agnes bristled with temper.

'I am sure he didn't mean it mother.'

Louisa once more walked around all the furniture sitting first in one chair, then another.

The manager arrived.

'Mrs Hirons. How very charming you look today. I am so pleased to see you again. You seem to be experiencing a little trouble here. How can I help you?'

'You can first get rid of that stupid assistant who seems to think I can't have this bureau here because someone else has put a reserved ticket on it. What rubbish! I want it and I shall have it.'

Agnes threw her fur wrap around her neck with temper.

The manager smiled and said,

'Of course you shall have it Mrs Hirons. Of course. Such regular and respected customers as yourself and Mr Hirons to our store, how could we possibly refuse? We can get another bureau for the other lady. This bureau is particularly unique. I shall show you why.'

The manager proceeded to show Agnes and Jacqueline the bureau.

'You will see Mrs Hirons, the bureau comes with a small gold key, for well … there is …' the manager whispered to Agnes.

'There is a *secret* drawer. To the naked eye, not apparent. I shall show you how to operate it. Watch closely.'

The two ladies watched intently.

I felt thoroughly bored by the whole day. What was I supposed to think about a bureau? Surely there was just no significance in any of this! To my way of thinking, the Hirons' wealth was vulgar and boring and I still could not understand why Louisa had brought me back to this particular time in her life. I tried to give her a signal like pushing something over in the store, or making a gust of wind from nowhere, but nothing worked.

'Come on, girls, we shall go to the tea rooms and have a nice cup of tea and some of those delicious cakes. I am exhausted!'

Agnes led the way to the tea room at the top of the store. She picked a table right in the centre so that everyone could admire her, especially if any of her so-called friends were eating there.

'Mother! Look! Mrs Goldberg and Jennifer are over there, but don't look now. They are looking our way!'

The Visitor

Louisa nudged Jacqueline and both girls started to giggle at Agnes's expression of pure hatred at the Goldbergs.

'They can't take their eyes off us, mother, so please don't look at them.'

Louisa could hardly stifle her giggling as Agnes did, immediately look and smile, stroking her fur stole and summoning one of the waitresses to hang it up saying very loudly, so that the Goldbergs could hear of course:

'Be extremely careful of my fur dear, be sure and take good care of it as it was very expensive. I wouldn't like to tell you how much it cost my dear husband.'

The waitress was careful with the fur and placed it on a coat hanger. Jacqueline felt very uncomfortable with Agnes's boastfulness and social climbing.

Agnes patted Jacqueline's hand.

'It's a good idea to order the most expensive cream cakes, dear. The Goldbergs will realise that we are people of substance if we do, girls. Always order too much, rather than too little, girls.'

'Mother, please, what does it all matter? The Goldbergs probably won't even notice what we order,' Louisa said.

Some time had passed, the cakes had been devoured. Louisa May especially enjoyed the chocolate éclairs, her favourites.

'Well, girls, we have to leave soon. Father will no doubt have purchased his new automobile by now.'

Agnes once more talked more loudly than she needed to, so that Mrs Goldberg would be sure to hear.

'Mother, Mrs Goldberg is coming over to our table.'

Louisa May lowered her eyes as she was sure that if she caught Jacqueline's gaze they would surely fall into hysterical laughter at the stupidity of her mother. Mrs Goldberg hesitated at Agnes's table.

'Agnes dear. How very nice to see you again.' Mrs Goldberg nodded with Agnes smiling back.

'Your Louisa gets more beautiful by the day doesn't she? So slender, so dainty.'

Agnes smiled weakly.

'I wonder who she takes after? Not you Agnes, I can't see a likeness at all.'

'Really,' Agnes said.

'You are probably wondering where Abraham is? Well, he has gone to buy one of those expensive new contraptions, an automobile. He left us ladies here to buy whatever we liked and of course, we have, haven't we girls? Such a generous man.'

Agnes sipped her tea and the girls nodded.

Mrs Goldberg was visibly jealous.

The Visitor

'Yes, he is always the gentleman and generous too. Don't often find that in a man. My husband is the same. I, too can buy anything I like. We haven't started to shop yet. I shall tell my husband about the automobile. I am sure he will want one in time. Well Agnes, very nice to have met you again. You too, Louisa, Jacqueline.'

Mrs Goldberg couldn't wait to get away from Agnes, ushering her daughter out of the restaurant.

'That showed her, didn't you think, girls? They must be so very jealous of us. She will tell anyone who is anyone about the automobile and we shall be the talk of the city.'

Agnes chuckled and helped herself to yet another cream cake.

'Mother! Why do you have to try to impress every single person we meet? It isn't at all necessary you know. I am sure Mrs Goldberg would be very nice if you tried to get to know her properly. No one really cares if we have money or not. People can see you are a wealthy woman so you certainly don't need to impress them or prove it.'

Louisa May squeezed Agnes's hand.

'Yes, of course dear, you are right. They can see I am a wealthy woman can't they? I am a most fortunate one and thank you, my dear, for bringing me down to earth. I can always rely on you to do that!'

Agnes got up from the table and Jacqueline and Louisa looked at each other. Louisa knew she had annoyed her mother, but she had only said what was the truth. The waitress handed Agnes her fur stole and helped to put it around her shoulders.

CHAPTER X

Deaf

I followed the ladies out of the tea rooms, but was so terribly bored by all the events that I had witnessed over the past few weeks and couldn't understand why Louisa wanted me with her at all these family functions. Maybe there was a reason for it, or maybe I had to witness all these outings and family parties because clues were being left for me. What clues? Where? I just hadn't any notion as to what the mystery was.

Louisa May and Jacqueline were chattering in their usual way, laughing and prodding each other every time a lady or young girl like themselves left the department store. Agnes gave them both disapproving looks, straightening her own hair and false pieces as she occasionally picked up her reflection in the revolving glass doors.

I looked from face to face; first at the girls who were busily discussing the latest fashion trends and young men and then at Agnes, who watched for Abraham coming through the revolving store door. I studied the store counters with the beautifully displayed goods and even the assistants busily going about their business, but could find no clue as to why Louisa May wanted me there.

Some Days Later

I found myself transported back to Sycamore House, listening to the conversations of Sarah and John Garton, the servants of the household, and learning from them that Peter Dupont had been a frequent visitor. There was obviously a romance budding between Louisa May and Peter. I was totally and utterly confused and wished that Louisa would let me understand her story in a more orderly way, instead of collecting me so disjointedly. She obviously was not deaf in this part of her story, so how did she become deaf? Perhaps now I would be privileged to find out? But what was I supposed to find out at Sycamore House? I was still the ghost in Louisa May's time and knew she could neither see nor hear me, so I would just have to go along with documenting her story. I knew I couldn't leave of my own free will. I was trapped, until she made it clear to me what it was she needed me to know. Could this really be happening to me and could I explain this

The Visitor

story to my family and friends? More to the point, would they believe it?

I sat down on a kitchen chair and watched Sarah expertly decorate a huge chocolate cake and prepare all manner of sandwiches, jellies and blancmanges. Sarah was the ultimate cook and I thought how artistic and clever she was. In my time, I was sure she would have written a cookery book or even appeared on the television presenting a cookery show.

'I'll shut the window John, getting a bit chilly in 'eah. I keep feeling these chills these days, don't know where they are coming from all the time. Perhaps I am sickening for somert?'

Sarah closed the kitchen window. She seemed the coldest when near me. Strange, I thought.

'I'll go and get the feed in now for the 'orses, be back for me tea about six, Sarah.'

John took his cap and jacket from the nail he had hammered into the kitchen wall for everyone to hang up their coats and patted Sarah's bottom as he usually did when leaving.

'Less of that, lad, just watch it yow!'

Sarah chuckled to herself as she started to wash up all the cooking implements in the white enamel sink.

'I could do with some 'elp around 'eah, that's for sure.'

Sarah wiped her forehead with her arm.

I sat myself down on the kitchen chair again, totally bored by all these events, and couldn't help thinking about the older Louisa May I had left in Tower Street, sitting on the window seat waiting for her girls to return home from the orphanage. Why was I brought here at this stage of Louisa's story? I did so want to be at Tower Street when the girls arrived home with Bertie. Ah well! Perhaps there would be something relevant in her story here at Sycamore House.

Sarah and the whole household were excitedly waiting for Peter Dupont's next visit. He was a very personable young man and everyone in the household had taken to him immediately. Louisa looked forward to every minute she spent with Peter and couldn't wait for him to arrive.

Ah, that's what the chocolate cake's for, for Peter's visit, I thought. I just wish I could stick my finger into its creamy chocolate, but my ghostly finger would be no good at all. Anyway, I had learned that in my ghostly state, I couldn't eat or drink, not that I felt hungry anyway!

Louisa had no doubt that Peter would make a fine and gallant officer in His Majesty's army, but should she dare imagine for one moment at this early stage of their romance, that he would also make a caring and devoted husband as she would a wife? Jacqueline was sure it wouldn't be too long before Peter Dupont proposed to Louisa May, judging from the number of visits he was making to Sycamore House.

The Visitor

'Father, may I have a party for my birthday present please? Father, oh, please? I have so many gowns I really don't wear any more and would love to show one of them off at a party. Please, father.' Louisa May flashed her heavy lidded, ebony eyes in anticipation of her father's reply and swept the tendrils of long, thick black hair back from her face. How could anyone refuse her request, especially Abraham?

'Well, dear, as you look so delightfully beautiful today, why not. Of course you may.'

Abraham put his arms around Louisa's shoulders and she jumped up and down clapping her hands in delight at the prospect of a birthday party at Sycamore House just for her.

'There is a but, Louisa,' said Abraham, pointing his long, bony finger at her.

'We shall draw up a guest list of your friends my dear and leave all the arrangements to your mother, for she is so very good at this sort of thing.'

'Oh father, must we? You know what she is like, she will invite all her friends and not mine, you know that, so please allow Jacqueline and me to do it, oh, please father.'

Louisa begged her father.

Abraham grunted; he knew Louisa was right about Agnes.

'Do you want this party or not? You know it is out of the question for you and Jacqueline to arrange such things and yes, I do know what your mother is like. Either she does it, or we don't have a party at all!'

Louisa pouted her lips sulkily.

'Come on now, it won't be that bad, darling, mother will do it so very expertly and the food at all our family parties has always been excellent, hasn't it?'

Abraham hugged his daughter who nodded in agreement. Yes, it was true, mother was a good organiser, but Louisa did so want to compile the guest list herself. She sat down in one of the heavily buttoned leather chairs and I could see that she was not pleased. I sat next to her and noticed the beautiful perfume she was wearing smelling like gardenias. It was all too familiar to me, as each time Louisa May came to fetch me from my modern world, I noticed the smell of gardenia and knew that she was near.

Louisa sat still pouting her lips in a sulk and swinging her legs to and fro.

'Don't do that dear, it is so unladylike, and stop pouting. Whatever is wrong with you, girl?'

Agnes rearranged the flowers in the vase on the small, round table, as she always did that so well and Sarah, in Agnes's estimation, could never arrange flowers properly!

'Anyone would think this was some sort of disaster.'

Agnes glared at her daughter. Abraham briefly explained about Louisa's birthday party sending Agnes into twittering delight that she would be arranging such an event.

'At least,' Louisa thought, 'I am to have a party and shall see my beloved Peter again. Surely mother will not overlook an invitation for him, as he is an absolutely essential guest and especially on my birthday? I must run upstairs and tell Bertie the news; no doubt he will be still asleep. He is always sleeping!'

Louisa ran up the steep staircase in her usual two-at-a-time manner, calling for Bertie.

'Bertie, Bertie.' Louisa knocked loudly on Bertie's bedroom door. 'Bertie, can I come in?'

Before he could even answer, she had flung open the bedroom door, throwing herself onto Bertie's bed and taking his sleepy head in her two small hands. Bertie was still fast asleep. Louisa decided her news was of the utmost importance, so he must be woken up.

'For God's sake, Louey! Is there an earthquake or a robbery? Louey can't a fellow sleep? Get off! I am so tired.'

Bertie pulled the blankets over his head and turned over.

'But, Bertie, you will never guess, you have to wake up so I can tell you properly.'

Louisa ran around to the other side of the bed so that she could look into Bertie's face.

'Bertie, you will never guess. I am to have a birthday party, can you imagine that? All our friends are to be invited, there will be dancing and wonderful food.'

She proceeded to waltz around Bertie's bedroom with her imaginary dancing partner, singing at the top of her voice. Moving to the bedroom window and throwing open the curtains, Louisa started her usual incessant chatter about what she would wear to the party, who would be invited and when the dancing would start.

'We shall invite Alice and David Franklin, they are very funny to be with, when they have had a few glasses of wine that is, and ...'

'Louey, please!'

Bertie turned away from the streaming sunlight coming in through the window.

'Ah, yes, Alice: you were very keen on her once, Bertie, if I remember rightly weren't you? Don't dare deny it, I remember it vividly. Ha, ha, yes I do, Bertie, you can't escape me!'

Louisa threw herself once more onto Bertie's bed and started to tickle him.

'Right, that's it! I am wide awake now so you have succeeded in waking me up. Will I never know peace in my own lifetime and in my own bedroom?'

The Visitor

Bertie looked into the face of his excited sister.

'Come here, my little sister, I am sorry, let me give you a big hug. I didn't mean to shout at you. Of course I am excited for you, it will be wonderful and I suppose you will see your Mr Peter Dupont. I am sure mother will do you proud, Louey, she always does you know.'

'I shall go and tell John about my party, perhaps Sarah can save him some cake and sandwiches. We haven't talked for ages and he will be thrilled for me, I know he will.'

Louisa straightened her hair whilst looking in the mirror.

'I would be very careful if I were you, Louey. Don't let mother catch you patronising the servants. You know her views on that sort of thing. I know you consider John Garton a friend, but now that you are older, you should try to detach yourself a little from him, it isn't a healthy situation.'

Bertie kissed his sister's forehead as she rushed out of the room and sat astride the banister, sliding down to the bottom with ease.

'Be careful, Louey!' Bertie cried. 'Young ladies should not do that as it is not becoming.'

Bertie despaired of Louisa sometimes. She was certainly not the lady his Jacqueline was, although she was only a year younger.

Louisa made her way out to the garden, where John was planting out ready for the autumn.

'What are you planting now, John?'

Louisa crunched an apple she had taken from a bowl of fruit in the sitting room on her way through to the garden.

'Oh, it's yow miss Louisa; I'm planting some pretty chrysanths ready for the autumn. Madam always like 'em to put in 'er vases in the 'ouse. They 'ave such pretty colours, yow know, golds, reds, yellas.'

'John, you are so clever, I wish I knew about flowers and what needed planting and when. They will be lovely I am sure, but I've come to tell you about my party!'

'Yower party, miss, when is that then? Yow ain't getting married are yow?'

John's heart sank for he hoped Louisa would never find a young man. He felt such jealousy towards Peter Dupont, but could never let it be known to Louisa, or to anyone.

'Married, no, don't be silly John. No, the party is for my birthday, my mother is arranging everything. John, I am so excited. I shall ask Sarah to save you some cakes and jellies if you like, won't that be fun?'

Louisa skipped around the plants.

'Oh, yeah, miss, real fun!' John said, sarcastically.

The Visitor

Some Weeks Later

Agnes had organised Louisa May's birthday party expertly, leaving nothing to chance. It was the night of the party and everyone in the Hirons household was getting ready for the evening ahead with Sarah scurrying around for all she was worth in the kitchen. Sarah wanted to make Louisa's birthday special for she adored her and treated her as if she were her own child. Sarah gave Louisa love and understanding which was far more than her own mother ever did as Agnes was a social climber and only displayed affection towards Louisa for the outside world to see. There was certainly no motherly love shown towards Louisa by Agnes. Louisa was just another of her ornaments to be displayed at social events.

The Night of Louisa May's Seventeenth Birthday Party

It would be a very grand affair, with all the 'right people' in attendance, including Peter Dupont!

'Louisa, Louisa! Where is that girl?'

Agnes was becoming more and more agitated.

'Don't fret so Agnes, you always look so charming and I am sure tonight will be no exception to the rule.'

Abraham was securing the top button on his white dress shirt.

'I can't get these confounded false curls right and Louisa always make them look so natural somehow. Where can she be?'

Agnes prodded and pinned her false curls but they just would not stay in place.

'Yes, mother?' Louisa called out from her bedroom.

'Louisa, will you come in here please. I can't get these wretched curls to stay put! Shush, what shall I do with them? I am despairing.'

Louisa had finished dressing and quickly ran into her mother's dressing room, picking up the large hairgrips to secure the hairpieces on her head.

'Ah, that's better, you certainly know how to make your mother look her usual beautiful self, Louey. The curls are just perfect now.' Agnes patted her artificial curls with satisfaction.

'Let me look at my lovely daughter: well, such beauty, such elegance, almost as beautiful as her mother.'

Abraham swung Louisa around and around the dressing room, with Agnes glaring at them.

Chattering incessantly, Louisa walked out onto the landing, peering over the banister.

'Mother, father, I think I can hear carriages arriving! Oh, I am so very excited, I shall run down and tell Sarah to start opening the door to the guests.'

The Visitor

Louisa was so thrilled, she decided not to walk down the stairs for she hardly ever did anyway. She would slide astride the banister as it would be a much quicker way to get downstairs. After all, no one had actually arrived yet, so nobody would see her do it.

Agnes swished out onto the landing ready to walk downstairs. She felt very grand indeed with Abraham dutifully following behind her ready to greet their first guests.

'Shush, look at our refined, beautiful daughter, just look at her cascading backwards down the banisters! Whatever next? I hope none of our guests see that, Abraham. Isn't she just terrible? Whatever shall we do with her? Whatever is her generation coming to?'

Abraham grinned.

'We shall do nothing, mother, just wait for her to mature like most young women.' He dearly loved Louisa's impetuous nature.

Suddenly, there was a loud, piercing scream followed by a resounding thud! Louisa had landed at the bottom of the huge staircase, severely knocking her head on the highly polished wooden hall floor.

I rushed to her side. Was she dead? She was motionless! No of course she wasn't dead for I knew the rest of her story. She had given birth to all her daughters, so how could she be dead! She looked dead though!

I tried to shake her, to wake her up, but my ghostly form wouldn't allow me to do anything to help her. I watched the horror-struck faces of Agnes, Abraham and Bertie who were running down the stairs to reach her. Sarah came running into the hall after hearing the thud and screaming.

'My bab is dead, she is, she is dead!'

Agnes glanced at the front door to see if any of the guests were arriving.

'Sarah, stand at the door, make our apologies to any guests, tell them what's happened and say we are sorry, but the party is cancelled. Do it Sarah!'

Agnes cradled her daughter in her arms as blood from Louisa's head wound trickled onto her pale green dress.

Abraham felt her pulse and lifted up her lifeless body, carrying her back upstairs to her room.

Bertie followed, full of explanations as to how the accident could have happened and not believing his lovely sister could actually be dead. Abraham lay Louisa on her bed and the bleeding from her head was worse, covering the bed linen with a bright red stain.

'Bertie, pass me that towel. I'll put it at the back of her head and try to stop the bleeding. Go and fetch the doctor, quickly man. She has a pulse! She is not dead yet! I think whatever has happened is serious so go quickly man.'

Abraham carefully placed the towel behind Louisa's head, stroking her

The Visitor

face as he did so, but there was no movement, she lay pale and lifeless.

Bertie ran through to the kitchen to get John Garton to drive him for the doctor.

'John, John, there you are.'

'Why, Master Bertie! What's wrong? Yow look as if yow seen a ghost!'

John wiped his hands on the kitchen towel.

Ha, ha, I thought that was funny. Here I am, you all might see a ghost, me! I wished they all could see me, I thought. I can tell them that everything will be all right with Louisa. I did not know whether to go, if I was allowed to, with Bertie and John, or stay with Louisa May, but I decided to stay.

John, you will have to drive me and quickly, to fetch the doctor for Louisa. I'll help you with the horses.'

John and Bertie ran into the courtyard, coupling the horses to the buggy, with Bertie explaining to John what had happened to Louisa. John's heart sank, and all he could think was not my beautiful Louisa, no not 'er. John could hardly speak with shock let alone couple the horses, in fact he could hardly move at all. All he wanted to do was to rush to Louisa's sick bed and tell her how desperately he loved her before it was too late, but there was no way he could and it would never be allowed anyway. Somehow, he managed to couple the horses to the buggy and rallied them as never before, speeding down the long, winding driveway passing all the guests arriving for the party and wondering why Bertie Hirons was rushing in the opposite direction. Sarah was busily giving the Hirons' apologies to the guests arriving, but young Peter had not arrived as yet. She dreaded him coming for how could she tell him what had happened? He would be so upset.

Bertie and John were back with the doctor in no time at all. Bertie showed the doctor where he could wash his hands, with John hovering in the background. No one had noticed John's worried face as he tried to catch a glimpse of his beloved Louisa through the bedroom doorway. Agnes would have thrown a fit of temper if she had noticed him standing on her luxurious landing carpet wearing his Wellington boots. She was far too busy with Louisa to notice John.

Peter Dupont had arrived and Sarah told him the news.

'Can I see her? Is there anything I can do, Sarah?'

Peter gave his military cap to Sarah as he made his way upstairs towards Louisa's bedroom. John stood on the landing, holding his cap, his head bowed. He really feared for Louisa.

'Yow can't go in there Mr Peter, sir, the doctor is with 'er now, yow best wait 'eah.'

John stepped forward and blocked Peter's entry to the bedroom.

'How dare you, a mere servant telling me what I can and can't do.'

Peter was astounded that John had had the audacity to stop him.

The Visitor

'Ah, young Peter.' Abraham stepped onto the landing.

'Peter, we have to wait out here for the moment whilst the doctor is examining Louisa. Perhaps you would care to come downstairs and have a drink in the library with me as there is nothing us men can do? John, you had better go back to your duties and we will let you and Sarah know how Louisa is progressing.'

Abraham escorted Peter and John down the stairs, all three men reluctant to be far away from Louisa.

'How did it happen, Mr Hirons? Whatever was she doing?'

Peter quizzed Abraham who explained what his impish daughter had been doing. Peter began to laugh. 'I should not laugh sir, but it is so like her. Poor Louisa.'

'Whisky, Peter?'

'Thank you kindly Mr Hirons.'

Abraham handed Peter his drink.

Sarah had given the news of the cancelled party to the last of the guests and made her way upstairs to enquire after Louisa. As she got closer to the bedroom, Agnes's cries became shriller, but Sarah knew that she was always very dramatic and her cries sounded shallow and insincere.

'Come on madam, I am sure it is not as bad as we all think.' Sarah put her arms around Agnes.

Bertie sat on the edge of Louisa's bed holding her small, dainty hand, whilst the doctor once more washed his hands in the adjoining dressing room. Sarah also sat down on the bed and looked across at the worried face of Bertie who was still stroking his sister's hand.

'It will be all right Mr Bertie you will see.'

Sarah leaned towards Louisa's face and whispered into her ears.

'Come along Louisa. Come on my own little princess. Peter is here downstairs, longing to see you. He is so disappointed about your party as well and very upset that you have had this accident. Please Louisa, open yower eyes for me.'

Sarah tapped the side of Louisa May's face, but there was no reaction from her, not even a flicker of an eyelid. She took her into her arms cradling her close and stroking her face.

'Ah, doctor.'

Agnes got up from the bedroom chair. Sarah and Bertie both waited for the doctor's findings on Louisa's condition.

'Doctor, why is she not opening her eyes and responding to us, what is wrong with her?'

Bertie was visibly distressed.

'Well, I think it is best that we leave her alone for a few hours. I have given her a sedative and she will sleep for hours yet. When she wakes, I

The Visitor

would be pleased if you would send for me straight away. I have to confirm my suspicions and I would like, if possible, the family to gather somewhere where I can talk to you all about Louisa.'

The doctor picked up his leather bag and made his way down the stairs to the hallway with Sarah showing everyone into the sitting room. When everyone had assembled, the doctor gave his diagnosis.

'It is very early days yet and I would like to make further examinations of Louisa at varying stages but her condition may not be as bad as we think. Really, I should not give you a diagnosis at this stage, but I think it only fair to prepare you all in case – well, just in case there is a problem.'

'A problem, doctor, what sort of problem?'

Abraham drew Agnes to his side.

'Sometimes, a severe bang to the head such as Louisa has sustained, can result temporarily or in some very rare cases, permanently, in impairment and that is why I am saying I need to see Louisa over a period of time, even when she is fully recovered. Her accident could cause, and may I emphasise the could, either blindness or deafness. She has a concussion anyway which will take her time to recover from. At this stage, I don't know if she has cracked her skull but we need to keep her quiet and warm for the time being. I will, of course, arrange for her to see a consultant when she is up and about. She has sustained a great shock to her system.'

Everyone in the room gasped.

'Not Louey, please, no!'

Bertie buried his head in his hands.

'Now then everyone, I did say, possibly, neither of these things may happen; Louisa may fully recover and nothing of this nature happen at all, but I am warning you all in case either one, or maybe both, should happen. At least you are all prepared for the worst.'

The doctor bid his farewells, saying he would call back when Louisa woke. Everyone in the room felt stunned with shock, not knowing what to think or how to react to the situation.

'Begging yower pardon madam.'

Sarah coughed.

'Well, what is it?'

Agnes was clearly irritated.

'I saw someone once, back from the Boer war he was, he 'ad a bang on the 'ead out there in Africa. Well, he was all right, just deaf in one ear, but he was all right!'

Peter put his whisky glass down on the small, polished coach table and said,

'I had better go, Mr Hirons, Mrs Hirons, I have to get back tonight anyway and we don't know when Louisa will awake. I would be pleased if

The Visitor

you could write to me or my aunt and let me know how things are progressing?'

Peter shook Abraham and Bertie's hands, kissing Agnes's hand, saying 'goodbye' and from the kitchen window, John watched him drive away.

I would never 'ave left Louisa if I were courting 'er, he thought, never!

Tears trickled down Agnes's face. She couldn't help it. The party arrangements were ruined! What would all her friends think of the Hirons family now, especially the Goldbergs? She did so want to show off the newly installed electricity in the house and it would be months before another party could be arranged!

Sarah decided to make the family their supper; they could have the party food so it would not be wasted. Bertie made his way back to Louisa's bedroom, where Louisa was still motionless and pale. Abraham and Agnes had stayed in Louisa's bedroom for some time, just watching her. Jacqueline had brushed her friend's hair, trying to get the dried blood out of it.

'Her beautiful hair, Bertie. Louey would go mad if she could see it now.'

'Don't worry about that, pet, she can't see herself anyway.'

Bertie smiled at his caring Jacqueline.

'It's the least I can do for my dear Louey.'

Jacqueline continued to brush Louisa's hair, her face quite motionless.

Hours had now passed by and Louisa still had not stirred out of her unconsciousness.

Sarah had asked if she could sit with Louisa most of the night in case she stirred.

'Well, I don't think Louisa will awake tonight,' Bertie said. 'I think I shall call it a day.'

At that moment, Louisa opened her eyes, much to everyone's delight and said:

'Bertie, Jacqueline, what happened to me, why am I in bed feeling so awful with this ghastly headache? Have the guests arrived yet for the party?'

She sat up in her bed. 'Ouch, my head, did I bang it or something? It is so very painful and there is blood on my pillow.'

Louisa felt her head. It really did hurt and felt very swollen. She looked from Bertie to Jacqueline and then to Sarah, Abraham and Agnes. She screamed out loudly in shock! Jacqueline hugged her close as Sarah and Bertie held her hands.

'I can see your lips moving, but I can't hear anything! I can't hear any of you speaking!'

The doctor's fears had been confirmed. Louisa was deaf, whether temporarily or permanently no one yet knew.

At least I now knew how Louisa May had become deaf, but surely this was not the end of her story? She must want me to know more. I moved around her bedroom, admiring her clothes and jewellery and came across

The Visitor

the gardenia perfume in a most expensive looking bottle. I tried to spray it around Louisa's bedroom, but I just couldn't lift it or make it move, in my ghostly form. I wondered if Louisa realised I was there with her? I doubted it. Louisa May still continued to scream uncontrollably about her deafness.

Bertie had sent John Garton for the doctor once more. Everyone tried to comfort Louisa but she was heartbroken for she could hear nothing! Thoughts raced through her mind. Would she always be deaf? What would life hold for me now? Worst of all, what would Peter Dupont think of her now? Would he ever ask her to marry him if her deafness was permanent?

Some weeks passed and Louisa was still deaf, but managing to understand most people by lip-reading. Peter visited Sycamore House less frequently but often sent her flowers and cards.

Four Months Later

Bertie and Jacqueline were arranging their wedding and Agnes frequented city shops for expensive dresses and hats to wear on the big day.

Louisa was finding John Garton a great comfort, often visiting the garden to talk to him, although with difficulty. She had to really study John's lips as he spoke to her. Every day he grew to love her more and wished he could declare his feelings, but he knew it would not be allowed as she was not even supposed to be talking to him. They would both be in terrible trouble if the madam or the master knew Louisa was spending so much time with John.

CHAPTER XI

The Wedding Day of Jacqueline and Bertie

Jacqueline looked every inch the beautiful blushing bride wearing an elegant, long, white wedding dress and carrying her bouquet of pink and yellow roses, which co-ordinated with her matching headdress. Her vibrant red hair blended perfectly with all her accessories.

Louisa May had never seen such a beautiful bride and hoped that one day, she would look as radiant, especially if she married Peter. She had a gown of pale pink lace, the same colour pink as the small pink roses in Jacqueline's headdress and bouquet. Her beauty outshone that of the bride, but no one noticed as Jacqueline, the bride, was the centre of attention.

Louisa's spirits had returned and she was extremely happy for her brother and her best friend. She wished it could have been Peter and herself. She cursed her deafness every second, but she had learned to lip-read very well and could even do so from across a room. Louisa only wished that she could hear Peter for he had such a depth to his educated voice. He still visited her at Sycamore House, but not as often as she would have liked.

The wedding group positioned themselves for the photographs outside Sycamore House before all the guests went inside to celebrate. Louisa gave the camera her biggest smile, as she felt so happy for her brother and her friend and that Peter was standing so tall and handsome beside her. As the camera flashed, Louisa slipped her hand into Peter's but there was no usual squeeze of love from him.

After the photograph session, everyone stood around on the driveway, talking and laughing, some guests going inside the house to celebrate. Agnes Hirons had excelled herself, insisting that the bride's family should let her arrange all the feasting after the ceremony, which delighted Jacqueline's parents for Sycamore House was so much larger than theirs and could entertain more people. There were over three hundred guests.

Sarah tapped Louisa on the shoulder.

'Yow look beautiful, Bab.'

Cupping her face in her hands she said,

'Yow are me own little princess Louisa.'

The Visitor

Louisa was pleased as Peter stood closer holding her hand.

'It'll be yow and Peter next, yow mark me words, Bab.'

Sarah chuckled as she handed more drinks to the waiting guests.

'Peter, what's the matter, you look so uneasy?'

Louisa looked into Peter's large sapphire blue eyes.

'Nothing, sweetheart, it was just Sarah being so presumptuous. You know what she is like.'

Peter guided Louisa into the house, where the orchestra players were in their places and dancing had begun.

All the guests applauded as Bertie bowed to his bride and led her to the centre of the dance floor. The newlyweds looked the picture of happiness and Louisa wished so hard that she would be the next bride with Peter. Peter excused himself from Louisa to ask Agnes and several other ladies for duty dances, leaving her sitting quite alone and feeling lonely. She wished he had not left her, but she understood that he was only doing his duty. Peter hardly glanced Louisa's way for quite some time.

He must love me, Louisa thought. If not, he wouldn't have come all this way today to attend the wedding, would he? He is being the gallant officer and gentleman, pleasant, charming and good looking.

Louisa wondered if Peter was embarrassed being with her because of her deafness, especially when with his friends and she began to feel depressed. Would I be an embarrassment to Peter if I married him, like I am to mother? she thought. I shall probably become an old maid and live with mother and father into my old age. What a terrible thought! Oh, no! I couldn't, I must marry Peter. I am being too melodramatic, Peter does love me, I am sure of it.

Louisa sipped her glass of champagne and was deep in thought, not noticing John Garton peering through the French windows from the patio looking at Louisa sitting alone. John couldn't bear to see her alone and wished that he could go inside and ask her to dance. He would never leave her and would dance with her all night. How could Peter have left her alone for so long? He knew he never would have done.

John's dreaming was suddenly interrupted.

'John, lad. Where an earth 'ave yow been? I've been looking for yow everywhere. What an earth are yow doing out 'eah? Don't let the master catch you spying on the party, he would 'ave yower guts for garters he would! It's no good 'ankering after her lad, for she will never look at yow and besides, what could yow do for her, or give her, lad? Now come on, come back inside, come and 'elp me. Tek yower mind off her, lad.'

Sarah persuaded John to help her in the kitchen.

Louisa noticed Jacqueline's parents standing nearby and wandered over to them as they watched their beloved daughter being danced away by her

The Visitor

adoring Bertie. Louisa tried to make polite conversation but it was difficult and embarrassing as she desperately tried to lip-read Jacqueline's father's lips. His waxed moustache hung over his top lip and she could not see his lips well enough to read them. Making their excuses, Jacqueline's parents moved away from Louisa to the dance floor, leaving her alone once more and still watching Peter dance, with yet another young cousin. He did manage to wink at her though when passing by with his dance partner.

Louisa glanced around the room at all the guests. She could hear none of the music, but realised the orchestra must be wonderful, as after each dance had finished, everyone clapped for such a long time. It all seemed very strange to her watching people's lips moving and the orchestra playing, but with no sound! Walking out to the hallway, she looked out of the window onto the front pebbled driveway and noticed how many newly invented automobiles there were, instead of carriages. Even Peter had arrived in one and it all seemed very grand.

'Louisa! Louisa!'

John tried to make her hear from the end of the hallway as he had noticed her on her own.

He realised how stupid he was after a while, as his cries fell on her deaf ears. He just could not get used to the fact that she was deaf. He dared to walk along the hallway towards her, making sure that none of her family would see him, especially Agnes, as he had his muddy Wellington boots on. On reaching Louisa, he tapped her on her shoulder.

'Oh, John, it's you. What are you doing in here? Don't let mother catch you, she will be so angry. Please be careful, John. What's the matter?'

Louisa quizzed his face. Cupping her face gently in his hands, John said:

'I noticed yow were all alone and wondered, as we are such good friends, if yow were all right? Do yow want to go out to the garden and talk with me for a while?'

'Oh, John, you are so very sweet, such a good friend to me. But how can I when I am supposed to be in here with all our guests? I can't suddenly disappear and anyway, Peter is here and he would not take too kindly to me talking to you, let alone walking in the garden with you. You know we are practically engaged don't you, John? It wouldn't be the done thing but thank you for thinking about me anyway. You are so kind to me, John and a true friend.'

John felt anger and frustration inside himself: why was she so possessed with this Peter fellow, who appeared not to care if she was left sitting alone? Once more he cupped Louisa's face in his powerful hands, but held her face so gently.

'All right, miss, I know my place, but if yow should change yower mind ...'

John cautiously made his way down the hallway, occasionally looking back at Louisa who was smiling at him. He stopped before the library doorway to check that no one was watching him and then quietly slipped back to the kitchen to help Sarah.

Peter had at last asked Louisa for a dance and she began to feel much happier now.

'Well, my dear,' he said, 'how are you feeling?' Peter formed his words very carefully for Louisa to lip-read. 'Let me look at you, Louisa; you look just so beautiful, in fact, more so than ever.'

Louisa searched his face to try to understand what he meant but noticed his blue eyes were not the same as before; they did not shine down with love at her now and they did not 'glaze over' in love as they had done before. Surely she must be misinterpreting his eyes, surely she must be wrong? He surely must still love her?

At the end of the dance, Peter cupped Louisa's face in his hands, mouthing the words very carefully to her that he did love her then kissed her gently on the lips. The reaction from the rest of the guests was of dismay, as no one ever displayed their emotions and certainly not in public, but the scene was soon forgotten as Peter led Louisa away into the garden.

Louisa suddenly felt more content. Surely Peter does love me after all, surely he does or he would not have taken such a liberty in front of everyone, she thought.

I was becoming very bored again by everything and the hour was late. I still hadn't picked up any clues and couldn't think that there were any. Perhaps this was just a 'wild goose chase'?

I decided to follow Louisa and Peter out into the garden for there was no point in me hanging around inside the house listening to all the inane conversations. But then again, I didn't want to intrude on the lovers.

Jacqueline and Bertie were preparing to leave for their honeymoon in Montreal and had gone to change their clothes and pack for their trip. Agnes and Abraham were certainly enjoying the evening dancing and talking to their family and friends.

The night was so humid that I wondered how elegant women in those times could stand the layers of long clothing. It must have been very uncomfortable for them.

Peter once more cupped Louisa's face in his hands so that she could lip-read.

'It is such a large garden, Louisa, let's walk farther down away from the house where we can be alone.'

Louisa's favourite place was the large summerhouse, right at the end of the huge garden, to which she led Peter. She felt so romantic and was sure that once inside the summerhouse, they could kiss each other as much as they liked for no one could see them from the house.

The Visitor

Once inside, the couple sat down on the rattan sofa. Peter put his arms around Louisa and gently turned her face towards his own, placing his lips on hers with a kiss that was gentle and warm. She responded to his kisses without giving a thought to anyone else. Peter pulled her closer, but this time his kisses became much harder and more urgent than before. Louisa could hardly breathe and felt uneasy and a little frightened. She tried to push Peter away as he was hurting her, but he was far too strong for her small frame and once more pulled her closer to him. The moonlight was particularly bright, lighting up Peter's bright blue eyes. Louisa managed at last to push Peter away.

'Peter, we really should go back into the house now, for mother and father will be wondering where we have got to.'

But Peter grabbed Louisa, kissing her once more with urgent passion so hard that she thought she would break in two. He pulled the hairpins out of her hair, sending it cascading downwards onto her shoulders.

'There, that's better, Louisa, I always liked you with your hair about your shoulders.'

Peter started to unbutton Louisa's dress, still holding her close so that she could not move or struggle.

'Peter, stop! No, Peter! I love you, but we must wait, you know we must!'

Louisa desperately started to struggle to free herself from him for she did so want to be a virgin on her wedding night and did not want to be taken advantage of now, even though she desperately loved Peter. She would do anything for him, but not this, not now.

'Peter!' Louisa's scream were shrill, but the door to the summerhouse was firmly closed and no one could hear her cries. Peter delved deeper and deeper into her clothing and she felt weak and helpless to stop his advances.

Louisa sobbed as she struggled to break free, managing to push the summerhouse door open. Peter once more grabbed her, throwing her to the ground and thrusting himself on top of her. All the way through Peter's lovemaking she suffered great pain with every thrust of his body. How can he do this before we are married? Louisa wondered. She felt degraded and dirty. The pain of his lovemaking was unbearable and not as she had dreamed about, and the weight of his body on hers crushed feeble cries out of her. She managed to let out a cry so piercing that even Peter stopped momentarily.

John was busying himself just outside the kitchen door, brushing down the pathway and considering going to bed down the horses for the night. He thought he heard a scream, but he must be mistaken. Perhaps it was a cat or a fox somewhere, he thought.

'Sarah! Just going down to the stables to tend the 'orses. Back in a minute!' John made his way towards the stables.

Meanwhile in the summerhouse, Louisa was sobbing bitterly. Peter had helped her up from the floor back onto the rattan sofa. Throwing his head back he let out a loud laugh and bringing Louisa's face to meet his, he said:

'You silly, little thing, no one will ever know what we did. You know I have been very careful.'

He took Louisa's hands, pulling her up towards him and once more kissed her lips passionately. She could feel his passion surging for her once more and cried out,

'Peter, stop! Please, stop!'

Her cries became more urgent. Surely he was not about to rape her again.

'No! Peter!' Louisa began to cry out loudly.

John was fastening the bolts on the stable doors. He heard Louisa's cries and swirling around, wondered where they were coming from. Scanning the garden he realised that they were coming from the summerhouse so he raced with all speed, flinging open the door, revealing Peter pushing Louisa to the floor once more.

John grabbed Peter's rumpled shirt, whirling him around to face him, punching him a full-fisted blow on the jaw and knocking him to the ground. Peter fell next to Louisa who had covered her face with her hands in horror.

'Please, stop! John, Peter!'

Louisa's pleas went unheeded as the men fought on, rolling out of the summerhouse locked together in mortal combat. John hated Peter and fought him with all the strength he had, even to the death, he thought. Louisa had fainted. She felt so ill and dirty she just wanted to die! Peter was the first to jump to his feet.

'Come on then, man, let's see what you're made of. Not much by the look of you.'

Peter held his fists in front of his face. He had been expertly trained in the art of self defence and knew that John stood little chance against him. John kept glancing around Peter's gyrating body to see if Louisa was standing but she was not. The bastard, I'll kill 'im, he thought. John lurched forwards towards Peter, but his punch missed and Peter thrust a resounding blow to John's head, sending him reeling to the ground, knocked out.

John lay quiet and still. His head felt as if one of his beloved horses had trampled all over it. He could hear muffled talking around him, but was powerless to get to his feet. Peter had managed to clean himself up and dab the blood from his lip. He made his way back to the house, leaving Louisa in the summerhouse and John lying semi-conscious on the ground.

Sobbing bitterly, Louisa managed to drag herself out of the summerhouse, buttoning up her dress as she slowly walked towards the house. Was that John? It was! Poor John. For God's sake, what had Peter done to him? Louisa rushed to his side as quickly as she could in her state and knelt down beside him.

The Visitor

'John, talk to me, look at me!'

Louisa rested John's bruised head in her lap. John could have got up, for he felt a little stronger and he was not badly hurt, but he decided to play on his injury so that he could be close to Louisa just once.

'John! Please! Oh, my God!' Louisa started to weep.

Sitting upright, John took her hands in his.

'It's all right Bab. Thank yow for caring for me. That Peter Dupont, if he's 'urt yow, Bab, I'll, I'll ...'

Louisa helped John to his feet.

'No, John, please never ever tell anyone what has happened here tonight and I mean, anyone! Not even Sarah! Sarah and you are my dearest friends, but you must never say, promise me, John!'

Louisa held John's arm so tightly and looked so frightened that John promised. He would have promised her anything.

'But look at yow, Bab, yow are all untidy and dirty. 'Ow are yow goin' back in the 'ouse looking as yow do? Eah, come into the stables, I 'ave a mirror in there, yow can tidy yowerself up.'

John led Louisa to the stables. How he longed to take her in his arms and make love to her, but he mustn't even think of it. He watched her smooth down her dress and brush the dirt from her skirt, then pile her long hair back on the top of her head; she once again became perfect, the real young lady. But what of Peter Dupont? Would he report the fight? He wouldn't dare. And had he actually raped Miss Louisa? How could John ask that question of Louisa? No, he must not, he must be as good a friend as he could to her.

'There, John, how do I look now?'

'Perfect Miss, like an angel.'

John lowered his eyes and blushed to the roots of his blond hair. Louisa giggled and quickly left the stable, thanking him very much for his help. She felt degraded and wanted to soak herself in a hot bath for hours, but knew she could not. She wanted to wash away her guilt and Peter's from her body.

'I must regain some composure and not dwell on what has happened. Peter, oh, Peter! How could you have done this to me? But I must not dwell on it. Yes, show Peter you are angry with him, but don't dwell on it. Why didn't Peter wait for me? Can't understand him dashing off like that. He is supposed to love me, so he says. Peter certainly had better marry me now. I shall have to confide in Jacqueline though, she will help me. Oh, my God, what if I get, what if I am ...? No, Peter said he had been more than careful so no, I am sure I can't be ...'

All manner of thoughts rushed through Louisa's head as she made her way back to rejoin the wedding party in the house.

The Visitor

Agnes caught Louisa's attention as she walked into the sitting room.

'Louisa! Where on earth have you been? We have been looking for you. Even Peter has been looking for you, and so have Bertie and Jacqueline. Well, it is really too bad of you dear. Jaqueline and Bertie have gone off now as they had to be at Southampton by midnight to catch their boat. They really did want to see you before they left. Really, you are too bad.'

Agnes scowled at Louisa, then rejoined her friends and continued talking. The orchestra were still playing and people still dancing. Peter was nowhere to be seen, not that Louisa particularly wanted to find him just yet, especially after what had happened. Helping herself to sandwiches left over from the buffet, she found herself a comfortable chair and sat down. Ah, there he is. Peter is in the hallway, talking to yet another cousin, she thought. But in no way am I going to make the first move towards him. He will have to come to me, she decided. Devouring three, whole sandwiches and sipping her wine, Louisa's eyes once more met with the black, shiny boots and army uniform. Peter stood before her, so handsome and charming, grinning widely.

'Are you all right, Louisa? What can I say?'

Louisa had lip-read very well.

'What can you say? Sorry, for a start. Don't dare to touch me Peter.'

Louisa flushed with temper.

'Thank God you are all right. All I can say is sorry, my dearest. I am very sorry. I love you so much, my emotions got the better of me, I just couldn't stop myself. Come on darling, don't dwell on it. Let's dance.'

Peter led Louisa to the dance floor but she felt weak and not ready to dance. As they held each other to the sounds of the Strauss waltz, tears started to trickle down her face as she remembered the passionate attack Peter had made on her. How could Peter appear so calm and collected after what had happened? His lip doesn't look too bad, although just slightly swollen, but no one would notice; in fact, Louisa thought, who would know anything from just looking at us both? We are both so composed. The waltz finished and Peter escorted Louisa back to her seat. Lifting up her face to meet his, Peter said:

'Louisa, I have to go now but I shall call again soon, if you still want me to that is, say in a few weeks' time.'

Peter kissed Louisa's dainty hand, clicking his heels and bidding her goodbye. She didn't get up, but watched him make his farewells to her parents, who obviously liked him very much. He showed no remorse for what had happened and did not even glance back at her as he left.

Louisa made her way to the hallway and watched Peter leave. From the window she saw him get into his automobile and watched it vanish out of sight. Louisa did wonder to herself if she would in fact, ever see him again after what had happened.

The Visitor

As her ghostly visitor, I knew she would never see Peter Dupont again, but not for the reasons she thought. He wouldn't be able to see her again, even if he had wanted to. But the story would unfold later. I wandered around the guests, listening to their small talk and stopping at Agnes and Abraham as I was interested in their conversations about the coronation of Edward VII. Surely then this must be 1902? How interesting, for at least I was learning what the ordinary people thought of their new king and world affairs and found this part of Louisa's story quite fascinating. A bit dramatic, but thought-provoking. I couldn't help feeling sorry for Louisa; she was so lovely and so very lonely, confined to a world of quiet solitude. She hadn't deserved the abuse she had received from Peter and obviously was not aware that John Garton loved her either.

Fiddle-de-dee, Louisa thought, I shall just have to wait until Jacqueline and Bertie get back from Montreal to tell them about Peter. They will be so shocked, but I know they will understand. Louisa couldn't help wondering if she had imagined Peter's raping her and the fight he had with John. Poor John, how gallant he was, how brave, he was such a gentleman even though just a mere servant, trying to save my honour. God! I *was* raped, wasn't I!

Fingering the ends of her hair, all Louisa could think of was the rape and how Peter had abused her. The thought went over and over in her mind. Nevertheless she still loved him, but why? She didn't know. I shall really have to try and put what happened out of my mind as I shall go insane if I don't, she thought. Yes, I have decided to enjoy the shopping trip tomorrow with mother and shall buy all my favourite perfumes. I shall try to forget what Peter did to me.

The Next Day

Agnes and Louisa were good companions on their shopping day out and spent vast amounts of money indulging themselves with lots of womanly things; clothes, jewellery, perfume and of course, the afternoon tea and cakes. Later that day at Sycamore House:

'Mother I think I shall go and lie down for a few minutes. I am feeling rather tired.'

Agnes nodded in agreement with Louisa.

'I shall do the same. It was a bit too much all that shopping today. Shush, my poor feet, how they ache!'

'I wonder if Jacqueline and Bertie think of us much on their way to Montreal? I expect they are having a wonderful time.'

Louisa did not wait to read Agnes's lips and climbed the stairs to go to her room.

Eight weeks had passed and the Hirons family had received three telegrams

The Visitor

from the happy couple in Montreal.

How exciting, Louisa thought. I would love to go there some day myself. Better get myself dressed for dinner. Wish I didn't feel so tired all the time, these awful headaches and this nausea feeling. I wish it would go away. Perhaps these feelings are something to do with my accident, my ears. I must make an appointment to see the doctor.

When dressed, Louisa flounced downstairs to the dining room but she wasn't at all tempted by any of the food that Sarah had so caringly prepared. They were all Louisa's favourites, but nothing whet her appetite. It always seemed too empty and dull without Bertie and Jacqueline for they were both so full of fun. Louisa felt so bored by all the pomp her parents insisted upon at every meal.

Agnes found it very frustrating trying to hold a conversation with Louisa as she was so deaf and her attention had to be gained first before any conversation. Abraham usually smiled kindly at Louisa, but communicated very little with her.

After the meal, of which Louisa ate very little, Agnes was escorted to the sitting room to drink her favourite brandy and read the daily newspapers.

'Ah, I think I shall just close my eyes for a while, if no one objects.'

Agnes leaned her head back on her favourite chair, grunting and falling asleep, occasionally bellowing out a loud snore, much to Abraham's disapproval. He puffed on his large, Havana cigar, shaking out the newspaper as he read. The flames of the open fire licked at the logs and coal nuggets as Louisa gazed into it, imagining the faces of her favourite people and trying to make a picture of Peter from the flames. Peter hadn't visited Sycamore House or contacted Louisa for weeks since their encounter in the summerhouse, and she felt that he might have abandoned her.

There was a knock at the lounge door. Sarah entered the room and coughed politely.

'Excuse me, sir, there is a gentleman here to see yow and well, madam and Miss Louisa also.'

'A gentleman?' Abraham shot around in his chair. 'From where, who?'

Sarah handed him the gentleman's card.

'A solicitor, is it? Well, we had better see him then.'

'Who is it, father?'

Louisa gathered someone had come to see them and thought it might be Peter!

'I've shown the gentleman to the study, sir, hope that is all right?'

Sarah shuffled along in front of Abraham, opened the study door and introduced her master, Louisa and Agnes to the waiting gentleman. Louisa and Agnes took a seat, but the gentleman preferred to stand and then he spoke.

The Visitor

'Thank you for seeing me today. I shall come straight to the point. I am very sorry to disturb you and to be the bearer of terribly sad news.'

The gentleman shuffled around on the spot making it evident that he found it difficult to be the conveyor of the bad news to the Hirons family.

Agnes shrieked:

'No! Not our Bertie and Jacqueline? For God's sake, no!'

Louisa May rushed to her mother's side and both women hugged each other in fear of what the news could be.

'No, Mrs Hirons. No, I can say with some relief that it is not bad news about your close family, but rather distant family, and it concerns mostly, well … Miss Louisa.'

Louisa had read the gentleman's lips well and gasped in alarm at what the news could be. The gentleman wiped his brow with his handkerchief and was clearly distressed. Abraham put his arm around Louisa's shoulders.

'The news concerns my daughter? How does anything concern her, sir?'

Abraham drew Louisa close to him and everyone was puzzled at what this grave news could be.

'I'll try to come straight to the point, which is the only way, I feel. My company, Levy and Soper, solicitors, has received word this morning of this grave news and I felt it my duty to come in person to deliver it to you, me being the Levy of the partnership.' Mr Levy had everyone's full attention and he once more wiped the perspiration from his forehead. 'I will continue, sir, madam, miss. There was the most terrible accident in London, actually on Sunday afternoon in Hyde Park. I'm afraid, miss, that Mr Peter Dupont was killed outright in his automobile along with his aunt, a Mrs Miriam Pizer, terrible business, terrible!' Mr Levy lowered his head and sat down. 'It seems that a horse reared up in front of Mr Dupont's vehicle as he tried to swerve to miss it, but subsequently hit a tree. The automobile burst into flames. Mr Dupont was pronounced dead at the scene and his aunt died later from her injuries in hospital. Terrible!'

Louisa froze with shock .

'No! No! Impossible. Peter and I, we … Peter, oh, my dear, dear, Peter!' Louisa cried out and Abraham took her in his arms to try to comfort her.

Louisa had lip-read Mr Levy well, understanding every word.

Crying hysterically she buried her face in her father's chest.

'No! No! It can't be true. Tell me it isn't true.'

'Oh dear, I am so very sorry for you all. What a terrible business.'

Mr Levy was still very distressed and made his way to the door. 'I had better go, Mr and Mrs Hirons. Oh, I nearly forgot. I was asked to pass on to Miss Louisa this small box.'

Mr Levy handed a small blue box to Louisa May who took it from him with a 'thank you,' holding it close to her heart, but not daring to open it.

The Visitor

She had an idea what it could be and knew she would not be able to endure the pain and emotion of looking at an engagement ring after her news. Agnes took the small box from her and made her sit down in a comfortable chair.

'I'll look after the box for a while, until you are feeling a bit better dear. You jut sit there for a moment.'

It was the first real understanding that Agnes had ever shown Louisa.

'Won't you stay for some tea Mr Levy? It was extremely kind of you to come in person to bring such distressing news. It can't have been easy for you. Thank you. Poor Miriam and Peter. Shush. What a shock for us all!'

Agnes sat herself down in a chair, fanning her face with her handkerchief as Louisa ran out of the room, snatching her small box still unopened, and fled up the stairs as fast as she could, flinging herself onto her bed weeping bitterly for Peter.

Abraham explained:

'You see, Mr Levy, Louisa and Peter were betrothed. What a disaster, I just can't believe it!'

'I am sorry, sir, very sorry indeed. But if you don't mind, I think it inappropriate to stay and take tea. Thank you for your kindness but I had best go, sir.'

Mr Levy was shown to the door by Sarah, who gathered that something terrible had happened.

'Can I 'elp with anything, sir?'

Sarah's face was filled with concern for she could hear Louisa sobbing and crying out for her Peter from upstairs.

'No, Sarah, thank you. There is nothing, absolutely nothing, anyone can do. I will explain to you later when I have calmed the two ladies.'

'Very well, sir.'

Abraham slowly walked upstairs to his beloved daughter's room. Lifting up her chin so that she could lip-read and wiping away her tears, he spoke.

'Well, it's a funeral now, darling. I am so dreadfully sorry, my dear, dreadfully sorry. Do you feel like opening the box to see what Peter left for you? He would want you to I am sure. Shall I open it for you dear?'

Abraham reached for Louisa's small box as she could only nod. She did so want to see what was inside, but felt that her heart would surely break when she discovered what it was, as Peter wasn't there to share her moment. Abraham opened the tiny box and inside was a beautiful, three-stoned, sapphire and diamond engagement ring.

They both gasped.

'My dear, how beautiful it is.'

Abraham took Louisa's tiny hand and put the ring on her finger. The emotion was almost too much to bear for Louisa, but she knew she would always wear it with love and pride. Abraham stroked Louisa's face, but she

The Visitor

didn't look up and kept looking at Peter's ring with tear-filled eyes.

'You stay here, dear, and Sarah will bring your meal up to your room later. The ring is so beautiful and befitting, my daughter. I am so sorry, darling.'

Abraham hugged Louisa to him trying his best to comfort her, but there was no way that he could. He left her still sobbing bitterly as she took comfort in her lover's ring, kissing every stone and uttering Peter's name out loud.

Abraham rejoined Agnes in the study.

'She is terribly upset as you can imagine and the box from Peter, well, it contained the most beautiful of rings I have ever seen, Agnes. Of course, it made matters worse giving it to Louisa, but what else could I have done, for she had to have it sometime. Better now than later, I thought. What a shocking business!'

Agnes nodded in agreement.

'Fancy, a beautiful ring! Something Louisa can keep forever. It may serve her well in the future.'

Abraham looked shocked at Agnes. How could she say such a thing at this awful time?

'Agnes, really! Can you only think of money at this sad time, dear?'

Abraham tutted, as she replied:

'Well dear, what else has she? Who will have her now in her state? Peter was really the only one who looked at her and was prepared to take her on, with her deafness and everything. I am sorry to sound so callous, darling, but these are the facts! Who will look at a deaf woman? At least she has the ring as an investment!'

Abraham just nodded.

'Yes, dear, if you say so.'

Sarah hesitated outside the study door in case she was needed and overheard everything Agnes and Abraham had said. 'The bitch,' she thought. 'Me poor bab upset and poor old Peter. I must go to me bab and comfort her.'

Sarah knocked on Louisa's bedroom door. That is silly, she thought. She can't hear me. So she gently opened the bedroom door. Louisa was sitting with her back to her, looking out of her window into the garden below and Sarah noticed that she had Peter Dupont's ring on her finger. Putting her arms around Louisa Sarah cuddled and comforted her as best she could, as she knew nothing that she could say would relieve Louisa's suffering.

Lifting Louisa's face around to meet hers, Sarah said:

'Yow must carry on, Miss, it will be terrible 'ard without 'im but I know Peter wouldn't like to think of yow distressing yowerself like this, now would he? Yow'll never get over it, Bab, but yow will feel a bit stronger as each day goes by, yow mark me words.'

The Visitor

Sarah cradled Louisa like a baby, as she bitterly sobbed for her Peter.

'Come on now, Bab, we shall go downstairs. Peter would want yow to carry on and if he is watching yow from up there in 'Eaven, yow will only make 'im feel upset. Yow wouldn't want that, now would yow, Bab?'

'No, I wouldn't. You are right of course, as always, Sarah.'

Sarah helped Louisa downstairs and sat her down near the coal fire in the lounge.

'I shall get yow and the mistress and master a nice cuppa and some of me teacakes I cooked yesterday. Yow would like that wouldn't yow?'

Louisa could not face the prospect of eating or drinking anything and felt as though she would probably never take another morsel of food again, but just nodded in appreciation of Sarah's kindness. Sarah had always been like a real mother to her whom she turned to in times of trouble or worry, so why did she feel that she could not confide in her about the night of the rape? She mustn't think of that now and must put it behind her and forget about it. She felt she just couldn't cope and her fingers closed around Peter's ring as she thought of their night of passion together in the summerhouse. Peter was dead! All Louisa had left of him was his beautiful ring which she looked at constantly. The sapphires sparkled like Peter's eyes. The blue stones would always remind her of his eyes and the white of the diamonds, his teeth. He had had such white teeth. Yes, she would always be in love with Peter until the day she died.

Some weeks had passed by and Agnes, Abraham and Louisa had attended the joint funerals of Peter Dupont and his aunt Miriam. The ordeal was all too much for Louisa and on arrival home, it had made her ill. Jacqueline and Bertie were still on their honeymoon and knew nothing of the disaster. Agnes and Abraham had thought it best not to telegraph them and spoil it all with the bad news.

Sarah busied herself around the house and in the kitchen, trying desperately to cheer Louisa up each time she saw her. She had hung out lines of washing, there seemed to be so much washing these days and John Garton sat at the scrubbed, pine kitchen table, taking out his clay pipe to have a smoke.

'God, where all this washing comes from, John, I shall never know. Wish the mistress would find someone to 'elp me soon as it is all getting beyond me.'

Sarah brushed back her grey hair and started to fold some of the washing into neat piles.

John tapped his clay pipe on the side of the open fire grate.

'I knew somert were about to 'appen, Sarah, I told yow didn't I?'

'Don't you dare to smoke in my nice, clean kitchen, John.'

Sarah snatched the clay pipe out of John's hands.

'Eah, Sarah, don't be so 'orrible, it's me only pleasure in life, me pipe.'

The Visitor

John tried to snatch back his pipe, but Sarah had dropped it into her apron pocket.

'What do yow mean John, somert was going to 'appen?'

Sarah looked across at John's mischievous blue eyes and his shock of blond hair.

'Well, that Mr Peter, he was all too "ponzey" by 'alf he was. They way he went after Miss Louisa, turning her 'ead like that. I know things about 'im, Sarah, which would make yower 'air curl.'

'Don't be stupid, John, don't yow ever speak about Miss Louisa like that or for that matter, speak ill of the dead. Why, if the mistress or master 'eard yow, yow would be sacked for that.'

Later That Day in the Kitchen at Sycamore House

John started to wash his hands in the kitchen sink.

'Yow will never guess what, Sarah, I 'ave been asked to take Miss Louisa to the doctors. Would yow believe it? Just at the time when I am busiest, cutting back, planting out.' John finished washing the mud from his hands.

'I thought yow would be pleased to tek 'er. What's the matter with yow?'

Sarah hooted with laughter.

'I'll just couple up the 'orses and drive around to the front. While I'm gone Sarah, do us a favour and dry me boots off in front of the fire will yow?'

John took his peaked cap from the nail on the wall, placing it firmly on his head. He coupled the horses to the buggy outside after saying his goodbyes to Sarah. She waved to him, throwing open the kitchen window and yelling, 'Tek care, lad, nice bit of pie for yow when yow gets back.'

John climbed into the buggy, steadying the horses.

'Oh, Sarah,' he shouted, 'I nearly forgot, yow know that bloke, what's 'is name, the one yower keen on?'

John laughed at the top of his voice, holding back the rearing horses.

'What bloke? I've no blokes, don't yow be so cheeky.' Sarah coloured up and felt very self conscious, something that she had never allowed herself to be in front of John.

'Yow know, the one with the black 'air, the one down Summers Row, yow know ...'

Sarah knew very well, but did not want the world to know and especially not John Garton. She knew she would be teased for ever more if he thought she was really keen on a man.

'Oh, 'im! I know the one yow mean! No! Not keen on 'im. Just playing John! Just playing with 'im!'

John chuckled for all he was worth for he knew he was embarrassing Sarah

The Visitor

and he liked to make her blush.

'He said he is keen on yow and wants to walk out with yow, Sarah, on yower day off.'

John laughed out loud.

'Don't be stupid, John. Stop teasing me. Any road, when do I ever get a day off from 'eah?'

Sarah tried to dismiss her real feelings of elated joy at the news. Secretly she certainly would be more than willing to walk out with her newly acquired man friend, any time!

John tipped his peak cap at her.

'I'll see yow later Sarah.'

John drove the horses and buggy to the front of the house and patiently waited for his Miss Louisa to come out. He waited and waited but no Miss Louisa came. Jumping down from the buggy, he secured the horses to the brass hook near the front door and walked back to the kitchen to ask if Sarah knew where Miss Louisa was and how long she would be. Sarah was still folding up washing in neat piles, ready to be ironed.

'Ah! There yow are, lad. I was just coming to tell yow. Miss Louisa will be another half an hour yet, so yow might as well 'ave a cuppa while yow are waiting.'

John took no persuading to have some tea as he knew some sort of cooking delight such as a home-made teacake or sponge cake would go with it.

Sarah poured the tea.

'So, John, what did yow mean earlier? Yow know, when yow said, yow could tell me a thing or two about Peter Dupont, eh?'

Sarah started to cut into a huge Victoria sandwich cake and John licked his lips in anticipation. Sarah knew he would be more inclined to tell her his secret, if she tempted him with tea and cake!

'I really wanted yow to know Sarah, about the wedding night when Master Bertie married, when I 'urt me 'ead and you bathed it for me. Do yow remember when I 'urt me 'ead?'

Sarah nodded and poured out his tea, handing him her delicious cake on a plate.

'Oh, yes, I remember, go on John.'

'Well ... I swore to Miss Louisa that I would never tell a living soul, on the Bible I swore.'

John proceeded to eat his cake and drink his tea, pouring it into his saucer and drinking it from there. Sarah always hated him doing that, but was so anxious to know about what happened, that she thought it best not to reprimand him, as he might not tell her.

'Well, I am half dead John, so yow wouldn't be telling a living soul, would yow? Yow would be telling me!'

The Visitor

John laughed at Sarah's wit and then continued ...

'Well ... it was the night of the wedding, I was putting me garden tools away and securing the 'orses, when I 'eard this noise. A cry, well, more like a squeal. Didn't know where it was coming from, so I walked down the garden a bit and eventually realised it was coming from the summer 'ouse.'

'Yes, yes, lad, 'urry up, I ain't got all day yow know.'

Sarah became agitated at the slow way John was telling her the story.

'Any road,' John continued, 'as I got closer to the summer 'ouse the door opened and I saw the bastard, Dupont, cross me soul Sarah, 'onest I did abusing Miss Louisa!'

Sarah put her hands to the sides of her face with shock.

'Go on! What did yow do then, lad?'

'I punched Dupont's 'ead in, that's what I done! But he punched me back, that's when yow saw me and bathed me 'ead. I did promise Miss Louisa I would never tell, but as yow say, Sarah, someone else loyal to 'er should know what 'appened.'

John told the whole story of Louisa May's rape and the ensuing fight between himself and Peter.

'Yow did the right thing, lad, telling me, that would explain a lot of things!'

Sarah took John's plate and cup and saucer to the sink. I wonder, she thought. She was thoughtful as she had her suspicions that Louisa could be pregnant by Peter Dupont. With all her fainting fits and sickness lately, that would explain it, she thought.

'Yower right, John, we should not speak of this again and we know nothing, should the mistress or master ever question us about it.'

John nodded in agreement as Sarah brushed back his thick, wavy, blond hair and handed him his cap, opening the door for him as she pushed another piece of cake into his hands.

''urry now John, as Miss Louisa will be nearly ready I should think.'

Louisa was waiting inside the porch at the front of the house. John rushed to her aid to help her into the buggy, carefully placing the tartan blanket over her knees, although the day was not cold. The horses were restless and wanted to be off. John found it difficult to steady them as they had become impatient waiting on the front driveway. He giddy-upped the horses, making clicking noises with his tongue as they drove away from Sycamore House.

John knew he could not make conversation with Louisa, as she could not read his lips, so he would have to wait to talk to her when they arrived at the doctor's house and he could face her. Then she would be able to read his lips, not that she would discuss anything about the dreadful night with him anyway, he was sure of that. John knew it was hopeless and he should try and control his emotions for her for they could never be together; they were so different, worlds apart both culturally and intellectually. The only

The Visitor

thing they had in common was their age; what could he give her that she hadn't got? Only love, which she had never had from either her family or men!

On reaching the doctor's house, John jumped from the buggy, helping Louisa May down to the ground. She is so small, light as a feather, child-like, John thought. Her perfume filled the air around her which left him feeling that he would surely faint with love for her. Louisa looked neither left nor right and gave John no room to talk to her at all, but just gave a weak smile as she made her way to the front door. John knew that he would be waiting for some time, so he took out his clay pipe and leaned against the buggy. It would probably be his only chance to have a smoke for the rest of the day. He certainly had a busy evening too at Sycamore House and could hardly spare time to take Miss Louisa to the doctor's.

Inside the doctor's house, Louisa was asked to wait in the sitting room. Eventually she was called into the doctor's surgery where the doctor examined her carefully.

'Well, young lady, your deafness is still profound, so perhaps we need to make another appointment with the specialist to see if things will improve.'

Pulling her face around to meet his, the doctor once more repeated his sentence, but shouting.

'Your deafness hasn't improved has it? I shall make another appointment for you to see the specialist, whom I think can give us some more up to date information on your condition. We must keep hopeful.'

Louisa just nodded back at the doctor, who proceeded to write out an address of the specialist for her.

'Doctor, I came not only about my ears, but there is, er … there is something else. Oh, doctor, I am so ashamed and very frightened!'

Louisa started to cry and the doctor swung to face Louisa at once, lifting her chin so that her tear-filled eyes could read his lips.

'Now, now, my dear. Don't fret so. It can't be so bad, whatever you are frightened of. You have been through a great deal lately, what with young Peter Dupont dying like that. Terrible, just terrible.'

The doctor reached into his medicine cabinet for a suitable tonic.

'No! No, doctor. You don't understand. I think, well, I think I could be pregnant!'

With this, the doctor spun his chair around to face Louisa.

'Pregnant, you say? My dear girl, whatever makes you think a thing like that?'

'But, doctor, Peter and I, we were very much in love, and …'

'Oh, I see, the inevitable happened, did it? My poor child. Well, I can only confirm your fears by an examination. You had better get undressed, Louisa, down to your undergarments please and lie on the sofa so I can examine you.'

The Visitor

Louisa lay on the cold leather sofa. The doctor proceeded with his examination, asking her questions about her symptoms.

'Get dressed please, Louisa,' the doctor said.

'Well, doctor, am I? Am I pregnant?'

Louisa proceeded to do up the buttons on her dress.

'Yes, I fear it is highly likely that you are, Louisa. Now, I don't have to tell you how serious this matter is, especially concerning your family. You know what I mean?'

Louisa just nodded.

'The only thing I can suggest to help you is for me to delay my diagnosis for a few weeks to give you time to come to terms with your condition and telling your parents. You *must tell them*, Louisa. They will know soon enough anyway but I can cover for you for the moment, which I am more than prepared to do, but after the two weeks are up, you will be showing signs and we can't get away with it any longer. For now though, you are not too swollen, that's good. I shall say you have a stomach ailment. Is that all right for you, my dear?'

Louisa nodded.

'Thank you, doctor, it will give me time to think of what I am to say to mother and father, and by that time my brother Bertie will be back from his honeymoon. He will know what to do about it all.'

Louisa thought it best not to divulge to the doctor the fact that Peter had raped her. She couldn't even bear to think of it herself. The doctor looked at his pocket watch.

'I will show you out, Louisa, but what I can't understand is why you encouraged this young man, for you knew what the end consequence would be? Why, Louisa? I have been your family doctor all your life and thought I knew you. But it is done now and I can only help you as much as I can.'

The doctor opened the front door to let Louisa out.

'Thank you doctor, thank you so much. You have been more than kind.'

Louisa made her way back to John and the buggy.

Louisa's heart sang at the thought of her coming baby for she would at least have something of Peter's. She was secretly overjoyed but at the same time terrified of telling her parents about her pregnancy. She knew her mother especially would never understand.

John jumped down from the buggy and put out his pipe when he saw Louisa coming.

'Everything all right Miss Louisa?'

John noticed Louisa had a worried expression on her face.

'I am perfectly all right.'

John helped Louisa into the buggy.

She felt sick and ill and dreaded the thought of confronting her parents with her news. How would she tell them? For the time being, I shall say I have a germ in my stomach, she thought. That is what the doctor said I was to say, but I hate deceiving father for he is such a good man and does not deserve a deceitful daughter. What of mother? Louisa dreaded to think! When she finds out, she will have one of her regular, faked heart attacks! But then again, after all, the rape was not my fault, Louisa thought. If the fault lies with anyone, it is with Peter! He forced himself upon me, but who will believe me anyway, now that he is dead?

All the way back to Sycamore House, Louisa was glad she could not talk to John for she just wanted to be alone and quiet with her thoughts. How could she keep her secret for two whole weeks until the doctor's visit and would her stomach start to swell out before then? She felt so sick all the time, so it wouldn't be easy to hide her pregnancy. Sarah is bound to notice; in fact, I think she already suspects, Louisa thought.

Later that Afternoon in the Kitchen at Sycamore House

'I'll go into the garden now Sarah and finish off me weeding before I turn in.'

John put on his Wellington boots, opened the kitchen door and picked up his garden hoe, which was leaning on the back kitchen wall outside.

'Oh, goodness, yow gave me a real turn, gal. Who might yow be? Who are yow looking for?'

John shouted for Sarah to come and deal with the frightened young girl who was standing on the kitchen doorstep.

'What is it now, John? Stop shouting.'

Sarah scurried into the kitchen; she always seemed to be in a hurry and flapping about something or other.

The young girl spoke.

'If yow please, sir, ma'am, I'm the new help, the new kitchen maid yower master asked for. Sorry I'm a bit late, but I only just knew I 'ad to come 'eah and I couldn't find the 'ouse.'

The young girl seemed timid and awkward. John and Sarah knew she was very nervous.

John grinned.

'Well, the 'ouse is big enough ain't it. Couldn't find the 'ouse. Well I never!'

John and Sarah laughed and laughed.

'Tek no notice of 'im young'un, he's so cheeky. What's yower name?'

Sarah sat the young girl down on one of the kitchen chairs. 'Yow must be exhausted coming 'eah this late. Why it's nearly seven thirty now.'

'Me name is Mavis, miss. I'm fourteen years old and worked at one of the big 'ouses on Calthorpe Road before I come 'eah.'

The Visitor

'Well, Mavis,' Sarah said, 'better late than never. Two things yow 'ave to know. Don't call John sir 'cause 'e ain't. Call 'im, John and me, Sarah.'

The young girl gave a wide grin for she knew she would be very happy here.

'I bet yower parched Mavis. Let's 'ave a nice cuppa, yow look as if yow could do with one. Eah, 'ave some of me 'ome-made biscuits.'

Sarah handed Mavis a cup of tea and a plate of biscuits, which she devoured in a matter of seconds.

'No work for yow tonight young'un, I'll show yow to yower room at the top of the 'ouse. It ain't much. Yow will be glad of it after a day's work 'eah. I shall get yow up at five sharp, so be sure yow are washed and scrubbed clean in case the mistress sees yow. She cannot abide dirtiness of any sort yow know!'

Mavis followed Sarah to her room at the top of the house.

'Another thing, Mavis, yow can 'ave some breakfast down eah in the kitchen before yow start yower work and then 'elp me with the mistress and master's breakfast. The master leaves the 'ouse first around eight thirty for business in the city, then the others get up for theirs.'

'Others?'

Mavis looked puzzled.

'Don't be nervous, Mavis, we won't eat yow. The others; Miss Louisa's seventeen years old, Master Bertie and 'is new wife, Miss Jacqueline, when they get back from their honeymoon in Montreal. They won't be with us long as they are 'aving an 'ouse built in Solihull village. The master is our main concern, Mavis, for 'e's the one what pays yower wages, so we tek really good care of 'im.' Mavis chuckled to herself.

'The madam and Miss Louisa get up around eight to eight thirty and it will be yower job, Mavis, to see to Miss Louisa. Yow make sure she 'as everything she needs and be a good girl for 'er.'

Patting the bed and pulling back the covers, Sarah said:

'Yow will be comfy in 'eah. I shall bring yow some of me home-made teacakes for supper in a while, they are the master's favourites. He loves 'is teacakes. Look! From this window yow can see the full view of the garden right down to the summer'ouse.'

When Sarah had left the room, Mavis jumped up and down on her bed admiring her surroundings. She had never been in such luxury, her own bed, her own room, even pictures on the walls and wallpaper. At her last employment she had to share a bed with another maid and there were certainly no pictures on the walls, or wallpaper.

Abraham met Sarah coming down the stairs from Mavis's room.

'Ah, Sarah! There you are! Have you seen Louisa May anywhere, not that I am worried about her or need her for anything? She saw the doctor earlier today and I just wanted to know how she got on.'

'No, sir, I 'aven't. Oh, by the way, sir, the new kitchen maid, Mavis, 'as arrived. A bit late, but I've put her at the top of the 'ouse, sir, in the attic room. Is that all right?'

'Yes, perfectly, Sarah. Terrible room that, but no doubt she will be as comfortable there as anywhere else in the servants' quarters. Thank you, Sarah.'

Sarah hurried back to the kitchen to prepare supper and sat in front of the huge kitchen range fire, toasting teacakes that she had attached to a long, brass-handled fork, holding them over the flames of the fire. The evening was cool for the time of year, giving everyone more of an appetite, everyone that is, except Louisa May who seemed to have completely lost hers.

John was busily gardening at the top end of the garden, near the summerhouse where the vegetable patches and rose gardens were, and was starting to feel hungry for his supper. John lit a fire to burn the garden rubbish when he became aware of quiet sobbing nearby. He looked around, but could see no one and realised the sobbing was coming from inside the summerhouse. He stood outside for a moment wondering what he should do. Peering through the window he saw Miss Louisa, cradling her face in her hands and sobbing bitterly. John wasn't sure whether to go in and comfort her, or to just leave her alone and tell Sarah that she was crying. 'Women!' he thought. They are always crying and usually about nothing. Louisa's cries were so pathetic, no one could have resisted helping her, certainly not John.

As John opened the creaking summerhouse door, Louisa looked up, startled that anyone should have discovered her.

'Oh, John it's you! I thought it was my father looking for me.'

Louisa started to cry once more.

'Miss, please don't cry, nothing can be that bad, can it?'

Realising that she could not hear him, John moved closer to her so that she could read his lips.

'Whatever is wrong, Miss, can I help yow, Bab. Please don't cry any more. I can't stand to see yow cry.'

John sat down beside Louisa although he knew he shouldn't, but he couldn't help himself. She looked even lovelier, if that were possible, when her eyes were full of tears; how could he resist her. John hardly knew whether to put his strong arms around her to comfort her, or to fetch Sarah, who would not thank him for disturbing her when making the supper. Or should he just carry on trying to comfort Louisa? He decided to put his arms around her.

'There, there, Miss, don't cry so. Would yow like to tell me about it? Perhaps I can 'elp? Yow never know?'

'Oh, John, you are always so very kind to me and such a good friend, but I fear everyone will know my problem soon enough; whatever shall I do? I have no one left at home in whom I can confide, only Sarah and of course, er … you. Jacqueline and Bertie are away and I definitely cannot tell my parents, at least not yet. Oh, John, I am so alone.'

'No yower not, Miss! Yow can tell me and Sarah if yow like. I promise, cross me 'eart, I shall never tell, I didn't before did I?'

John brushed Louisa's black hair away from her wet eyes.

'Look what yow are doing to yower pretty face, making it all red and yower eyes all puffy. 'Eah, dry yower tears.'

John handed Louisa a grubby handkerchief with which she wiped away her tears and blew her nose. He persuaded her to go back into the house with him to confide in Sarah. John put his arm around Louisa's shoulders and gently walked her to the kitchen where Sarah had finished making the last of her teacakes.

'Sarah!'

John's voice was calm but assertive. Sarah had never heard him speak like this before, with such authority. Sarah spun around from her fireside seat.

'My goodness, what 'ave we 'eah? What is wrong with Miss Louisa? John? Yow know the 'ouse rules; no one from upstairs should be in 'eah.'

'Sarah, oh Sarah!'

Louisa flung her arms around Sarah clinging to her as if she was her own mother. Sarah had been more of a mother to Louisa in the past than Agnes ever had and Louisa knew she would know what to do to help her. John tried to explain how he had come across Louisa crying and brought her back to the kitchen to see Sarah.

'All right! All right! Let's sit Miss Louisa down 'eah, put the kettle on, John. We'll mek some tea. It is always a good comforter, tea.' Sarah caringly smoothed Louisa's hair and smiled at her. 'Stop whispering, John, Louisa can't 'eah yow, ducks.' Sarah frowned at John as he tried to whisper to her that he was sure Louisa had received bad news!

'Oh, yes, I forgot she is deaf! She seemed to understand me in the summer house.'

Sarah looked surprised.

'In the summerhouse? What 'ave yow been doing with her in the summerhouse, John?'

'Nothing, Sarah, as I said, just listening to 'er crying. I'll fetch 'er a cushion to lean back on. She looks all in to me.'

John rushed around the kitchen looking for a suitable cushion. Finding one, he carefully placed it behind Louisa's back, pulling up a chair alongside her and sitting down.

'John, you are too kind to me, thank you.'

Louisa started to tell her story about Peter Dupont and the night in the summerhouse at Jacqueline and Bertie's wedding and how it had all resulted

The Visitor

in her now finding herself pregnant with Peter's baby. Sarah and John showed real compassion towards Louisa, hugging her to them both, with all three in tears.

'Oh, my God! My beautiful girl. What misery for yow. Of course, yow must tell yower parents, it ain't yower fault.'

Sarah was adamant that Louisa would have to tell her parents for that was the only way.

John took Louisa's hand in his.

'No. Sarah, wait! She must not tell, not yet. I agree with Miss Louisa, I think she should wait a couple of weeks if she can possibly 'ide the fact that she is pregnant till then. Wait till Master Bertie gets back. It would be easier for 'er to tell when Master Bertie is there to 'elp 'er. Why, the mistress will go potty when she knows and Miss Louisa needs the 'elp of Master Bertie. We can't expect 'er to tell on 'er own.'

'John, be quiet! Can't yow see yow are frightening 'er?'

Sarah pushed John away and put her arms around Louisa, whose large black eyes were once more filling with tears. John was gutted at the news of Louisa's pregnancy, as if an arrow had pierced his heart. There would be absolutely no hope at all for him now, as Louisa carried another man's child. She would more than likely be married off quickly to the first available man of means when the news broke. Her parents would pay handsomely for someone to marry her to hide any disgrace attached to the family.

'I knew I should 'ave killed that Peter Dupont.'

John kicked the kitchen wall in a temper.

'John! Now then!' Sarah said 'That's no way to talk. Why, the poor girl 'as enough to contend with, without yow talking like that! Thank God she weren't looking at yow, lad, when yow said that! Now, lad, let's 'ave a drink. Shouldn't encourage us to drink, but under the circumstances, we need to all steady our nerves.'

John poured out three glasses of sherry, handing the first to Louisa, then one to Sarah and gulping his own drink down in one swallow. After all, at that moment, he needed it much more than anyone for he was the one who was deeply hurt and shocked.

Louisa sipped her sherry gently; it did make her feel a little better, knowing that Sarah and John sympathized with her and would keep her secret.

Sarah knew the situation would be bad from now on for Louisa May at Sycamore House. Agnes, she was sure, would fly into one of her rages when she found out about Louisa, and even worse, might throw her daughter out of the house altogether. Oh, no! Surely she would not do that? Sarah thought.

Louisa started to sob once more.

'Oh, Sarah, John! Who will want a deaf woman with a bastard child? Who in their right mind, go on, tell me?'

The Visitor

Louisa looked for answers from Sarah and John. Caringly, John took her hand across the clean, kitchen table and focused on her face so that she could read his lips.

'Bab, if I were a rich gent, I would want yow. Why yow are the most beautiful of creatures, a diamond shining brighter than any other. Any man would want yow by his side.'

John flushed with embarrassment when he saw Sarah glaring at him for what he had just said, although he had meant every word.

'John, I know you are only trying to be kind to me and I appreciate it, but tell me, how could I marry anyone other than my beloved Peter, who is dead? John, you are only a servant here and even that would be too good for me when my parents find out! Anyway, it would be far too ridiculous even to consider, for how can I marry anyone, even you?'

John laughed off what Louisa had said and pretended that it was all a joke to make Louisa laugh and feel better. Louisa certainly did not realise how much she had wounded him.

Lifting her chin up to view her face, Sarah said:

'I think yow 'ad better find yower father, Louisa. He did ask me to find yow earlier and yow had better 'ave a good story as to where yow have been all this time.'

Louisa nodded and left the kitchen, thanking Sarah and John for their kindness and understanding. When Sarah was sure she had gone:

'God forbid, John! What an earth were yow thinking of, talking to the Miss like that? Fancy, yow telling 'er yow loved 'er! Ha, well I never did! Whatever next?'

Sarah bustled away to the open range fire to toast yet more teacakes. She had completely forgotten about Mavis with all the commotion.

'I hope young Mavis 'asn't gone off to sleep, thinking I 'ave forgotten 'er?'

John slumped onto one of the kitchen chairs.

'Well a man can but try Sarah, I adore 'er, Sarah, yow might as well know it. I always 'ave and always will. She can mock me, 'urt me, I shall never stop loving 'er.'

Sarah felt sympathy for John.

'I know yow do lad! I know yow love 'er! It's written in yower big, blue eyes, but think careful on it, lad, and never mention it again for goodness sake. It can't lead anywhere; she will never think of yow in that way. If they 'ear yow talking like that upstairs, yow will definitely get the push from 'eah.'

John nodded.

'I know that, I know. But if needs be, if it required it, I would die for 'er Sarah, that is 'ow much I love 'er.'

'My God, yow 'ave got it bad lad.'

John knew he could hardly support himself, let alone a wife and a baby!

The Visitor

He wouldn't ever be able to get a well-paid job and would always have to work outside in the open air, owing to his lung condition.

CHAPTER XII

Forbidden Fruits

Louisa sat at the breakfast table staring at the oatcake, toast and salt beef set before her. She couldn't eat it. Sooner or later she knew that Agnes and Abraham would notice that she was pregnant.

Abraham studied his mail whist eating his salt beef sandwich glancing over periodically at his pale Louisa.

'Come on, dear girl,' said Abraham, 'please eat something or else you will waste away; you look so peaky these days. A hearty breakfast will make all the difference Louisa, come on now try and eat something, all this moping around won't help and I am sure Peter wouldn't have wanted you to be so sad for so long dear.'

'Yes Father, I am sure he wouldn't.' Louisa bit her lip.

If only Father knew, she thought. It wasn't only the loss of Peter which was bothering her. Abraham did his best to coax Louisa to eat, but she felt so sick even the smallest bite of anything would send her scurrying to the bathroom. Louis's stomach swayed with emotion when she thought of her dear Peter and the coming baby inside her. She missed Peter so desperately even though he had been so cruel to her. She couldn't understand herself really, how she could be so in love with him even when dead, after what had happened in the summerhouse. Her deafness was so frustrating; if only she could hear. Louisa found people tapping her shoulder to get her attention so humiliating.

I felt very sorry for Louisa and found that I could, in fact, read her mind and everyone else's. I wished I had this ability in my own time for it would be such an advantage. But I still felt powerless to help her or do anything at all for her in my ghostly form.

'If you don't mind, mother, father, I think I will go outside into the garden and get some fresh air, perhaps a walk around will make me feel better.'

Louisa got up from the dining table, bending forwards to hide the slight lump starting to appear in her stomach.

'I'll come with you, Louisa, we can't have you fainting again alone out there, now can we?'

Abraham started to get up from the table. Agnes gave an irritated sigh, and feeling that her husband pampered Louisa too much, said:

The Visitor

'I am sure, darling, Louisa can manage quite well on her own, stay here with me. Anyway I want to talk to you, dear.'

'No! Father really, it is quite all right, I am not about to faint, really I'm not. You stay here with mother, it isn't at all necessary. Look! There is Mavis, our new maid in the garden hanging out the washing. I'll go and talk to her, so I shall be all right.'

Louisa made for the door.

'It is not for young ladies to familiarize themselves with household servants Louisa.'

Agnes shifted about in her seat, showing some annoyance at Louisa's suggestion and the fact that she was sure her daughter hadn't read her lips and hadn't understood a word.

The early morning air felt so good on Louisa's delicate skin as she walked around the garden; the flowers John had planted were blooming beautifully and looked particularly radiant as the sun shone on each petal, seemingly lighting the head of each flower as she walked by. She was sure God was looking down on her, helping her to look at life and nature and showing her a different world and outlook. As she passed each bed of flowers, Louisa gently brushed the heads of them with her long fingers. The nausea seemed to be getting worse, especially this morning and each mealtime more of a trauma for her to hide her pregnancy from her parents.

'Good morning Miss Louisa.'

Mavis curtsied.

'Good morning, Mavis. I am so pleased to see you.' Louisa giggled. 'You really don't have to curtsey to me you know, I am not royalty. Please, I should like to be friends; don't hold me in any great esteem. We are about the same age aren't we, Mavis?'

Louisa watched Mavis hang the last white shirt on the line.

'I don't know Miss. I am fourteen, how old are you then?'

Mavis picked up the washing basket, placing it on her hip.

'Oh, you are a mere child in comparison, Mavis, for I am seventeen years old.'

'Oh! So yow will be getting married soon and leaving won't yow? All my sisters were married long before seventeen and moved out of the 'ouse.'

'Well, I would have been married Mavis, I was engaged, but unfortunately, my fiancé was killed some time ago now, so I don't have any other suitors. It looks as if I shall be at home for a while yet.'

'Oh, Miss, I am sorry, I 'ad no idea, I wouldn't 'ave said nothing if I'd 'ave known he died.'

'Don't you worry Mavis. I am coming to terms with his death now and am only glad I had the chance of knowing him.'

Mavis was visibly embarrassed.

The Visitor

'Mavis! Mavis!'

Sarah's voice carried from the kitchen.

'Oh, God, I shall be in trouble now! Talking! I 'ave to go Miss, it was very nice talking to yow. I 'ope we can talk again soon.'

Mavis started to run down the crazy paving pathway towards the kitchen.

'Where 'ave yow been, girl? We 'ave so much work to do yet, now come on, get on with it.'

Louisa stood in the doorway of the kitchen watching Sarah who was busy making dough for bread.

'Hello, Bab, yow looking a bit peaky to me, come into the kitchen, 'ave a nice cuppa with us.'

Sarah put her arms around Louisa.

'No, thank you Sarah, it is so kind, but I am supposed to be walking around the garden to get some fresh air. Mother would be annoyed if I were not getting the air.'

'All right, Bab, perhaps see yow later then?'

Louisa walked farther into the garden, passed the apple and plum tree orchards, towards the summerhouse. John Garton was busily weeding and didn't notice Louisa watching him intently.

'Oh, Miss Louisa, yow startled me. What are yow doing down 'eah? Yow looking a bit pale to me, but still like a bright diamond all the same.' John flushed as he spoke to Louisa for she always had an effect on him. She always found John so funny. Mother and father had never allowed her to mix with anyone other than the very élite, she had never found anyone funny like John. She did enjoy the real, city people more than anyone else if they were all like Sarah, John and Mavis, but mother had always made sure she only met chosen people, who seemed to her very boring.

'What are you planting now, John? How knowledgeable you are about plants and flowers. I have to say the garden does look particularly pretty. Perhaps one day you will teach me, John, for I would love to know more about flowers and when to plant them.'

John's heart skipped a beat for she, his Louisa, was asking for his help, so could he dare to believe that she would actually like to be in his company, even though it was just to learn about flowers? He faced her so that she could lip-read. Even though deaf, Louisa knew that John spoke differently from family and friends and remembered that he had a broad, city accent before her accident and couldn't help giggling to herself as she made sense of his lips.

'Well, Bab, these ain't flowers, these are veg for yower table, yow eat them. Plant 'em early I say, get a good crop then.'

John looked very dirty, soil covered his trousers and hands and seemed to be all over his face too. Louisa thought to herself, if he were cleaned up,

The Visitor

he would be half a handsome fellow with his bright blue eyes and blond hair. As he was talking away to her about his plants and vegetables, she felt a sudden, acute pain in her stomach, almost unbearable so that it took her breath away. She tried desperately to read John's lips as he spoke and to take deep breaths. It was probably the baby kicking again. She must try and overcome the pain but it was getting much worse, she could hardly bear it and fell to the ground clutching her stomach in agony.

Rushing towards her, John cradled her in his arms.

'Bab! Whatever is wrong? Is it the …?'

John dreaded to think that it was anything to do with the baby, but as he looked down at her dress, there were small spots of blood filtering through the delicate, white cotton.

'There, there, Bab, is the pain still bad, shall I fetch yower parents?'

John held Louisa's hand. She looked pale and very ill and he hardly knew what to do but could not possibly leave her like this.

'No! no! John, please, don't get my parents. As we said, they must not know yet, not yet, fetch Sarah please, fetch her. Take me into the summerhouse, quickly, John!'

Louisa had fainted. John picked her up with ease as she was so light and small and carried her into the summerhouse, laying her on the rattan sofa.

'It'll be all right, Bab, I'll go for Sarah now. She will know 'ow to 'elp yow, Bab. Don't yow worry!'

John was beside himself with worry. Rushing out from the summerhouse he saw Sarah fetching in some washing.

'Sarah! Come quick!'

John could hardly speak for lack of breath.

'John, whatever is wrong with yow, yow look as if yow seen a ghost. Yow shouldn't run like that lad.' Sarah knew by the expression on John's face that something was very wrong.

Mavis immediately stopped her washing in the kitchen at the dolly tub, hearing the commotion outside, but didn't need any excuse to stop work for she hated wash days.

'What's going on, is John all right?'

Mavis stood in the kitchen doorway leaning against the wall and Sarah glared at her.

'How many times do I 'ave to tell yow, girl, get on with the washing, we are so busy today, no time for yow chatting and standing there.'

Mavis slouched away, and walked very slowly towards her dolly tub, not wanting to miss a single part of the commotion.

'Sarah, it's Miss Louisa, come quick. I think she's gonna, yow know!'

Sarah and John rushed along the crazy paving path towards the summer house.

The Visitor

'Don't be so silly, John. I am sure it is just a false alarm, sure of it. She's probably just fainted. Pregnant women do a lot of that yow know.'

Sarah hurried to the summerhouse and John flung open the door to reveal Louisa lying on the sofa but now covered in blood.

'Oh my God!'

Sarah rushed to her lifting up her dress to examine her.

'We 'ad better fetch 'er parents, Sarah, don't yow think?'

John once more cradled Louisa's head in his strong, tanned hands.

'No! Don't be stupid, John. Do exactly what I tell yow and we must stay very calm. Louisa is losing 'er bab, sure of it, it's obvious. We shall need big towels, sheets and some hot water. Go on, yow fetch them and I'll tend to 'er. Oh, I nearly forgot, bring a bucket as well!'

John wasted no time and fled back to the kitchen where he opened every cupboard looking for towels, sheets and a bucket.

'What's up John, what are yow looking for? Can I 'elp yow?'

Mavis stopped her washing once more for she would love to help with anything as long as it wasn't washing!

'Be quiet Mavis. Get on with yower work. Nothing to do with yow, just keep yower nose out of it.'

'All right John, keep yower 'air on. I am only trying to 'elp.'

Mavis slouched back to her washing but when John left with all the towels, sheets and a bucket, she wasted no time in rushing to the kitchen window to see if she could see anything 'unusual,' but she couldn't. No doubt time would reveal the secret.

Sarah had made Louisa as comfortable as she could. She was losing her beloved Peter's baby but she felt too ill to care and just wanted the whole affair to be over.

Sarah was thankful that John had been so quick in getting back to the summerhouse with the required items.

'Here lad, give us the sheets and the bucket quick, lad.'

Sarah wrapped the sheets around Louisa's body and they quickly soaked up the blood. John thought he would surely faint at the sight of his Louisa's blood, but knew he had to be strong to help her. It was clear that she had lost her baby and a lot of blood and he was, although it seemed cruel, glad.

'Do yow think we should go and fetch the doctor Sarah? She seems so bad and she has lost so much blood.'

'Don't be stupid lad, no doctors, we shall manage. Just keep doing what I tell yow, then we will be all right and so will she. I 'ave seen many women like this in my life, she'll be all right.'

John followed Sarah's instructions, watching Louisa May closely as he feared for her very life.

'John, fetch me the bucket, lad, quick!'

The Visitor

Sarah pushed John away from the sight of a very tiny, perfectly formed, but dead baby, being put into the bucket.

'Give us those leftover sheets, John.'

Sarah pointed to the sheets not yet used and wrapped them around Louisa. She was still in a dead faint, which Sarah was thankful for as she didn't want her screaming out. The whole operation was over in less than ten minutes. Louisa had lost her beloved baby!

'We shall 'ave to get 'er cleaned up, John and that sofa. Just look at all the mess and blood, she will be ill for days after this. Don't know how she'll explain 'erself, but we'll think of something to say. For God's sake, look at me dress. I shall 'ave to change this as well. Come on, John lad, 'elp me with the bab, get 'er dress off and the sheets, get this sofa cleaned up. Try and get the blood off as best yow can.'

John picked Louisa up. She looked so frail and ill as he carefully laid her on the tiled floor of the summerhouse. He started to scrub the sofa; the blood was coming off easily as it was fresh and not dried. Tears trickled down his face as he occasionally glanced at at his sleeping Louisa who was unaware of her pitiful loss.

Sarah moved the bucket away with the dead baby inside it; they would find a burial place later when Louisa felt a bit better, perhaps later that night. John can dig a grave and bury the baby when everyone else in the house was asleep and no one will be any the wiser, she thought.

'Poor child, such a tender age. What the girl 'as been through already in 'er young life is beyond belief. John, I shall 'ave to leave yow to clean up the rest of the mess and 'er, I will go in the 'ouse now and find 'er a clean dress to wear. I'll bring back some fresh water to get 'er cleaned up. Start getting 'er clothes off ready and put 'er bloody dress to one side.'

'Me, Sarah? I can't do that, why it wouldn't be right!'

John felt reluctant to clean Louisa up for although he loved her and would do anything for her, what if she came around and screamed out, especially in a state of undress? How could he look on the body of his Louisa, although he wanted to?

Sarah smiled at John and said:

'Yow love 'er don't yow? Well do it then.'

John nodded.

Sarah scurried off towards the kitchen to change her dress and find Louisa May another dress to wear. John was left looking down at his bloodstained mistress who was quietly groaning in pain.

"Eah, come on, Bab.'

John took Louisa into his arms and unbuttoned her clothes, gently starting to take them off over her head. Her undergarments were ruined. The only thing for them will be to burn them, he thought.

The Visitor

He took off her liberty bodice and her undergarments, marvelling at her soft, white, skin and beautifully formed body. How could he stand this torture, seeing her like this, but not able to express his love for her? He could hardly bear it, but knew he must do his duty by her and help her in her hour of need.

Sarah was soon back with Louisa's clean dress.

''Eah, John, help me get this dress on 'er.'

John and Sarah dressed her as if a baby, pushing her arms through her undergarments and then her dress.

'Button up the back of the dress, John, whilst I put her 'air back up on top. Tell yow what, think it's a good idea yow stay with her a bit, say twenty minutes or so. No one will miss 'er, then I'll bring some tea down 'eah for her and some biscuits. It will 'elp her to come round a bit. Think it best to burn 'er things, they are so badly stained, we would never get the blood off them.'

John agreed with Sarah and spread some sheeting over the wet sofa for Louisa to lie on.

'All right then, John, I'll leave 'er to yow, pet, whilst I get sorted out.'

Sarah closed the summerhouse door and made for the kitchen, leaving John and Louisa alone.

John sat next to Louisa, cradling her to his chest, as she began to come around, groaning.

'There, there, Bab, how do yow feel now? We've been through a lot together ain't we?'

Louisa looked up into John's face and realised what had happened to her. Tears started to trickle down her cheeks but he gently brushed them away.

'There, Bab, it is a terrible thing what 'appened, but yow will be all right now, Bab. Yow are with good friends. Sarah's been 'eah as well 'elping yow. Yower been out cold for about half an hour. Do yow remember when yow fell down in the garden? We were talking, yow must have fainted with the pain and well, we just 'ad to 'elp yow, Bab. No one knows nothing. Sarah has gone to fetch some tea and biscuits. Yow will feel better after yow 'ave 'ad a drink and something to eat.'

'Oh, John, what would I have done without you and Sarah? My dearest friends. I feel so drained, so awful, I feel I shall never walk again, my legs have gone to jelly. I don't think I could even stand up. My parents are bound to notice something is wrong, as I have been missing for ages.'

Louisa didn't want to leave John's side, she felt so protected when with him. He brought her beautiful face around to meet his so that she could lip-read. He dearly wanted to kiss her passionately, but this was not the time or place so decided to tell her funny stories to try and cheer her up.

'Do yow remember, Bab, when yow fell off that log when yow were playing about in the garden? Yow was only about fifteen and yow sprained yower ankle.'

Louisa smiled and nodded.

'I 'ad just started at the 'ouse and was ordered by yower mother to carry yow up two flights of stairs. She 'ad a fit, 'er shouting at me to tek off me boots on 'er best carpets. She didn't care about yow, Bab, that yow was 'urt and in pain, no, only about 'er carpets. Did she want me to drop yow on the spot, whilst I took of my wellies? Well, I laughed to meself, I did.'

Louisa had read John's lips perfectly and started to giggle.

'She is a demon, isn't she John? Only concerned about her carpets, furniture and ornaments. I sometimes think I am classed along with those objects as she only takes me out with her to show me off to people.' She giggled again.

'That is better, Bab.'

John wiped away a stray tear from Louisa's cheek, tenderly kissing it.

John talked incessantly, trying to hide his real feelings for her and the fact that he had actually dared to kiss the cheek of his beloved Louisa.

It was the first time in months that Louisa had laughed heartily and she started to feel much better for it.

'John, what would I have done without you and Sarah? I feel so ashamed and yet so grateful to you both for your help. I shall never forget you. I love you both dearly.'

Louisa held John's strong hand and kissed it gently, brushing her soft lips over the rough-textured, tanned surface. John looked down at her, amazed that she had actually kissed him.

'Bab, I, er ...'

'What's the matter John?'

Louisa looked inquisitively into John's blue eyes.

'How can I tell yow, Bab?'

John decided that it was now or never and even if he lost her forever, he would have to tell her how he felt about her, that he loved her and always had, and wanted to be with her, always. Yes, he would tell her now! His face reddened with shyness and he could hardly look at her. Louisa studied John's lips closely. She knew he was fond of her and ran her fingers over his lips with John kissing each one as they passed. His face moved closer to hers, kissing first her forehead, then her small nose, each beautiful eye and lastly down to her soft lips. The kiss was gentle, but passionate and Louisa's heart leapt with excitement as never before. How could she be doing this when she felt so ill? How could she allow this to happen? She should have respect for Peter's memory and her baby. What about her baby inside her? She didn't understand herself, only that she wanted John's kisses to go on and on.

John suddenly drew away from Louisa, gently stroking her face as he did so.

The Visitor

'Sarah's coming so we have to behave, Bab.'

'How are things now, John? How is my best girl doing? Yow look a lot better, yower colour is back.'

Sarah bent down looking into Louisa's face. 'Yow will have to be careful, Bab, and wash yowerself thoroughly like, down there, when yow get back to yower room. Yow understand what I am saying?'

Louisa nodded.

'Thank you so much for helping me Sarah.'

Louisa hugged Sarah.

'Now, Bab, it's what anyone would 'ave done. Yow tek care. John and me will 'elp yow back to the 'ouse. Try and get to bed early as yow will need a few hours sleep before we meet later tonight. I thought about midnight if yow feel up to it? If not, John and me will see to the baby. Yow know what I am meaning?'

Sarah helped to steady Louisa for she had difficulty in standing and wobbled from side to side with weakness.

'There that's yow sorted out, Louisa. Yow look a lot better. 'Eah, 'ave another drink of the tea, and eat yower biscuit. Make yow feel stronger.'

John winked at Louisa, making her blush.

Louisa spoke quietly but forcefully.

'Before we go back to the house, Sarah, John er ... what happened to me? Did I faint?'

Sarah and John looked at each other hardly knowing what to say to her. Surely Louisa realised that she had miscarried her baby? Surely she was not that naïve?

'Don't yow fret now.'

Sarah tried to calm Louisa.

'Yower bab, well, he is quite safe now, he is with the Lord Jesus. We shall give 'im a proper burial, just us three. Yow will see, Bab, don't get upset. John and me, well, we thought we would dig a grave and yow can choose the place. Perhaps at the back of the summerhouse eh? I've been thinking whilst back at the 'ouse, we could all meet, say, at midnight tonight, that is if yow feel yow can Louisa and yow want it like that. But the sooner we get the poor thing properly buried, the better.' Sarah folded her arms and waited for Louisa's reply.

Louisa's body stiffened.

'Are you telling me that my baby is dead? Well, are you?'

The looks exchanged between Sarah and John confirmed to Louisa this was so.

'He is dead, my own, dearest, precious baby, dead!' Louisa screamed out in disbelief. 'No! No! My baby, I don't believe it. Peter's baby!' Louisa moaned and cried hysterically.

The Visitor

John's heart broke to think that Louisa still held Peter Dupont dear to her heart.

'Now, Miss, calm yowerself. Yes,' Sarah said, 'yower baby is dead. Louisa yow 'ave to pull yowerself together. At this rate, yower parents will surely 'ear the commotion out 'eah. Yower baby is in a better place now, honestly, believe me.'

John looked to Sarah to comfort Louisa.

Louisa could only stare ahead in complete disbelief that she could have lost her baby and not even realised what had happened! At least no explanations would be necessary now but she would have nothing of Peter left.

She reproached herself for kissing John Garton, how could she? Louisa looked firstly at John, then at Sarah, both reassuringly smiling at her.

'What good friends, how selfish I am,' she said.

Sarah put her arms around Louisa.

'There, Bab, yow will feel better about things in time, yow will see. Everything 'appens for the best yow know, although it seems cruel at the time. The Lord Jesus wanted yower bab, no doubt for somert special up there. He will be 'appy now he is with the Lord.'

John nodded in agreement, holding Louisa's arm to steady her.

'Oh, Sarah, John!'

Louisa understood that she must be brave and strong and go back to the house as if nothing had happened. All three agreed to meet later that night, depending on Louisa's condition, to give the infant a proper burial behind the summerhouse.

Walking back to the house, Louisa's thoughts embraced her dead Peter. How can I ever go on without him, will he know I have lost his baby? Can he see me? Perhaps it was meant to be. I don't know or understand my feelings, how could I have let John Garton, of all people, kiss me so sweetly? Her feelings were so mixed, she hardly knew what to think any more.

Mavis had neatly placed all the clean washing in a wicker basket ready to be pegged out on the line. She noticed how pale and ill Louisa looked as she walked into the kitchen with John and Sarah, but hardly dared pass any comment and obediently took yet more washing out to peg on the line.

Sarah closed the kitchen door so that Mavis would not hear any of their conversation from the garden.

'Now, Mavis is outside and we can talk – try to be strong Louisa, for yower own sake.'

Sarah's eyes met Louisa's, both women realising that if the master or mistress got any wind of what had happened, Sarah and John would surely be dismissed and perhaps Louisa thrown out of the house. Agnes was so volatile and everyone knew she would not think twice about sacking loyal

The Visitor

servants, and Abraham would have absolutely no say in the matter as Agnes ruled the house hold with a firm hand.

The events of the day would be their own secret, between the three of them.

Later that Evening

Agnes sat in the drawing room reading one of her many books.

'Oh, there you are, my dear, your father and I were looking for you. Where have you been all this time? Not talking to the servants again I hope? The fresh air doesn't seem to have done much good for you, you still look very pale to me, doesn't she father? That's funny,' Agnes said.

'What is funny, mother?'

Louisa couldn't help looking guilty.

'I could have sworn you had your white dress on today! Just shows! Shush! Your poor old mother is getting very forgetful in her old age. Can't remember what my own daughter is wearing! Still, I've always liked you in pink, dear, very becoming. I must see that doctor about my veins too, they are so troublesome these days.'

Agnes rubbed her legs and she was obviously in discomfort, but Louisa's mind wandered to her small baby lying alone somewhere waiting for his mother. How could she ever, ever get over the past few hours? Mother's vein problem seemed so trivial compared to her own, dear baby's life.

'I think I shall go and lie down Mother, I feel a little tired,' Louisa said.

'Tired, tired? Not again! You are always tired these days. I don't know what is wrong with you. You are certainly no fun to be with. You don't want to go shopping with me and are always having to lie down. I think we have to pay another visit to the doctor for you girl. Do you know what I think you are; just lazy, just bone idle.' Agnes flicked another page over in her book.

'If only mother knew,' Louisa thought as she as she passed by her mother and out into the hallway to climb the stairs to go to her bedroom.

Later that night, at around eleven-thirty, Louisa had found the strength to raise herself from her bed and creep quietly down to the kitchen where she knew Sarah and John would be waiting for her. She crept by her mother and father's bedroom and could hear Agnes snoring loudly. She stepped over the creaking floorboards and cautiously made her way down the stairs to the hallway below and then the kitchen.

'Sarah! John!' she whispered.

Everything was in darkness and very quiet.

"Eah, Bab.'

John came out of the shadows and lit a candle that had been cemented

The Visitor

in wax onto a saucer.

'Are yow all right, Bab? Don't know where Sarah has got to, probably still asleep.'

John took hold of Louisa's arm, quietly leading her to the back kitchen door and unbolting the top and bottom quietly and expertly.

'It seems to me, John Garton, that you have done this sort of thing before?' Louisa frowned.

'Not me, miss! Not me!'

John gently squeezed Louisa's arm.

'Ah, 'eah she is.'

John guided Louisa and Sarah out of the kitchen. Sarah had her hair tightly bound in rag curlers and wrapped her long, pink dressing gown around her. Due to the lateness of the hour, Sarah had decided to get ready for bed before she went outside to attend the burial. Louisa was still in her daytime clothes which Sarah and John had dressed her in earlier. John quietly locked the kitchen door behind them.

The night air was warm with a soft summer breeze swaying the trees in the orchard as the three passed by. John took a spade from his garden shed and started to dig out the rose bush that was hidden from the house behind the summerhouse. Louisa cried out and buried her head into Sarah's shoulder.

'Now then, Bab, let's all try and be as strong as we can.'

Sarah caressed Louisa, trying to comfort her as best she could.

'The hole is dug now!'

John stood awkwardly by the small hole in the ground, waiting for Sarah to say something or at least collect the bucket which held the dead baby's body. He felt so much pain for his dearest Louisa, whom he thought was being extremely brave.

Sarah fetched the bucket with the small infant inside and gathered the tiny frame up, wrapping it securely in her own shawl, then handing the bundle to Louisa. She held it for a few seconds and wept over the body, kissing what she thought was the head of her baby through the shawl and then handing it to John, who carefully and caringly placed the bundle at the bottom of the hole. Louisa's eyes filled with tears, but she knew she must be strong and try not to cry out.

Sarah took out a small Bible from her dressing gown pocket. Everyone bowed their heads.

'Lord Jesus,' she said, 'Yow took from Louisa and Peter their baby, no doubt for a good reason. Please Lord, tek good care of 'im. Thank yow Lord.'

Everyone made the sign of the cross. Louisa blew a kiss to her lost infant and tugged a rose from the bush, dropping it into the grave. John wasted no time in pushing the soil over the infant and planting the rose bush on

The Visitor

the top of the grave. Louisa could only stare with shock and wished she still had her baby and had held on to him for just a few more minutes.

John smoothed the soil around the rose bush. The grave was totally undetectable now with the rose bush on top of it. Louisa was sure she would come every day to pray and talk to her baby for she loved him dearly, even though he had had no chance of life.

Sarah put her arm around Louisa's waist.

'Well, bab, that is that! Come on back to the 'ouse and get to bed for yow must rest after yower ordeal.'

Sarah stretched out her hand to John.

'Thank you lad, you were wonderful.'

Floating around the garden, I felt drained with all this emotion. Could I possibly bear to see any more of this poor girl's story? Whatever would become of her now? I followed Louisa May back to her room and watched her get into bed as if in a trance and fall fast asleep with exhaustion. The day's events were enough for the strongest of women; surely nothing more could happen to her?

When would I be going back to Tower Street? What of the older Louisa May left with her girls? What, or when would I discover the clue? I was so bemused.

Four Days Later at Sycamore House

The doctor had been called to Louisa as she had been very ill, with a fever, which was worrying everyone. Sarah was very attentive, as she knew what Louisa had been through, but of course, could never divulge any of it, not even to the doctor. The doctor had made his examination.

'You are an extremely lucky young woman to be alive, Louisa,' he said. 'You have a very serious infection of the womb. I shall give you something to help clear it up and each time you take a bath, please put these powders into the water, they will help you heal. Why an earth didn't you call me sooner, Louisa, when you knew you were losing your baby?'

Louisa nearly choked in shock at the doctor's remark.

'Doctor!'

Louisa put her fingers to her lips to stop the doctor talking of her lost baby. She knew that just because she could not hear the doctor it didn't mean that prying ears wouldn't hear.

'Don't worry my child,' the doctor said 'your parents are downstairs waiting on news of your health so they cannot hear us.'

The doctor covered Louisa with her blankets and made her lie down.

'I shall call again in a week to see you, but should you become feverish again, or feel ill, please, Louisa, send for me. Good day to you and don't

The Visitor

worry, your secret is safe with me. Your parents shall never hear about the baby from me.'

The doctor smiled as he left Louisa's bedroom, closing the door behind him.

CHAPTER XIII

Love Blossoms

Jacqueline and Bertie had returned from their honeymoon in Montreal. Louisa knew she couldn't tell them about the loss of her baby and the night with Peter in the summerhouse. Peter and Miriam's death had come as a great enough shock to Jacqueline and Bertie and anyway, they were now engrossed in setting up home in Solihull, so how could Louisa tell them about her lost baby? It was best forgotten.

Jacqueline was busying herself with the furnishings of her new house and had precious little time for her friend and her girlish ways. Bertie worked very hard in the city and his company received more recognition every day.

Louisa's deafness had not improved; she had seen many specialists but none could help her. She found their diagnoses unacceptable and frustrating and often cried for long periods after examinations. She found people did not want to be bothered mouthing their words so that she could understand them, or gaining her attention before they spoke to her. She was so relieved she had some good friends, namely, Sarah, John and Mavis.

Her mother's mouthed words kept echoing over and over in her head.

'You will have to find an occupation, Louisa! No man is going to want a deaf woman for a bride, that is, no one with any breeding.'

How cruel my mother's words were, Louisa thought.

Louisa found herself walking in the garden once more towards the summerhouse and her lost baby's grave. She often talked to her dead baby when she knew no one else was around to hear her.

She stood over the rose bush now in full bloom with beautiful, red roses glistening in the sunlight. She prayed quietly to herself, wishing her baby well and for him to be with Peter.

Someone tapped Louisa on the shoulder.

'Penny for 'em, Bab.'

John smiled at Louisa.

'You startled me, John. What are you doing? Can I watch?'

Louisa followed John to the vegetable patch where John had been working.

'Corse yow can watch, Bab. Nothing much to see though, only me digging. Eah yow are Bab! Nibble this carrot, I'll brush it clean, it's so good for yow and makes yow see in the dark!'

The Visitor

John laughed loudly with Louisa doing the same. She felt so at peace when with John and was not afraid of anything or anyone when he was around.

'It's good to see yow smile again Miss Louisa. Yow 'ave such a pretty one! Shame to 'ide it away all the time.'

Louisa glanced back at the rose bush on top of her baby's grave.

'Come on, Miss, don't keep looking back on life, yow 'ave to go forwards now, don't yow agree? I know yow are upset about the bab, so am I and Sarah, but it will get better. Yow will see.'

She nodded in agreement with John. He was right but she had so much wanted her baby to live.

'Shall I take these carrots to Sarah for you, John? I would like to be of some use.'

'What, Miss, no fear! Yow mustn't do that, I will get shot by the mistress if she found out yow 'ad 'elped me. Dirtying those beautiful, piano fingers? I 'eard yow play once when the winders were left open and it was so beautiful. I thought I was in 'Eaven listening to yow play.'

John took the carrots from Louisa's hands. As he did so, he squeezed her hands and drew her close to him.

Louisa did not object.

'Eah, yow 'ave some soil on yower hands, let me brush it off for yow.'

John brushed away the soil from her hands and she could only wonder at his gentleness and he lifted her hand to his lips, kissing it with such tenderness. John knew no one from the house would see them for the summerhouse blocked the view.

'There, all gone now.'

Louisa studied John's tall, muscular frame; she had never really noticed his physique. He looked strong and tanned because of working outside all the time. His eyes were almost as blue as she had remembered Peter's eyes. A real contrast to her own colouring. Her heart pounded with excitement; she felt it was going to burst out of her chest as it beat faster and faster the nearer John came to her.

'Sorry, Miss, that was very wrong of me, kissing yower 'and like that, please forgive me.'

John brushed the side of his trousers with his hand in embarrassment. He hadn't noticed Louisa's eyes studying him, filled with warmth.

'I 'ad no right, Bab! I realised the day yow were taken bad and I kissed yow, I 'ad no right. It was wrong of me'

Punching the side of the summerhouse wall with his fist in frustration, John turned around to face Louisa and mouthed his words very carefully so that she would not misunderstand him.

'God, yow fill any man with such passion, yower so beautiful, it would be stupid of me to turn away from yow. Can't yow see, I am so in love with

The Visitor

yow? There! I've said it now. I'll get meself sacked but I don't care any more. I 'ad to say it to yow Bab.'

John looked down, studying the ground and not daring to see what the reaction from Louisa would be. What would she think, what would she do? She could, if she wanted to, get him sacked for what he had just said, but he no longer cared for he could no longer keep his feelings for her to himself.

Louisa slowly walked towards him, turning him around to face her.

'John, please don't upset yourself. I didn't mind you kissing me, really I didn't, it was a very beautiful experience. You looked after me so well and I would never have you dismissed, not for any reason. You are so very kind, my knight in shining armour and ...'

John stared back at her, hardly daring to believe that she might even care for him, even a little bit.

'Bab, yow are wonderful, everyone loves yow, how could they not and ... er ... me, too!'

John thought it best to start working and proceeded to dig and weed the garden, as if he didn't, he wouldn't be accountable for his actions of love towards Louisa. Louisa followed him. She felt she wanted to flirt with him, although she knew it was wrong. She stood over him watching his strong arched back as he pulled each weed from the ground. The breeze blew Louisa's skirt across John's face as he looked up from the ground into her beautiful, smiling face and he could no longer control his urges. Taking Louisa's hand he pulled her along with him towards the summerhouse.

Louisa didn't care for she was willing to go with John and felt pangs of excitement in her heart as to what was about to happen. She knew she would allow him to kiss her; in fact, she wanted it now more than anything in the world. John securely closed the door of the summerhouse behind them, still tightly holding Louisa's hand. Taking her in his strong arms, he lowered his face slowly down to hers, gently meeting her lips and kissing her fully on the mouth with a passion so great that Louisa thought she would surely faint. As John drew himself away from Louisa's face, her eyes were still tightly closed and her lips still pouted for yet another kiss, with which John followed swiftly.

'Bab, oh, Bab.' John continued to smother Louisa with his kisses. 'Bab, we had better stop! Would yow agree to meet me later tonight? Say, yes, please, it would make me so proud and 'appy if yow would.'

Louisa had to hesitation in agreeing and nodding back a 'yes' hardly daring to think too deeply about what she was doing with a mere servant. How could she? Whatever was she thinking of? Louisa May couldn't help herself. She once more nodded 'yes' and told John it must be midnight when they met. He could hardly believe it.

'Yow will come, won't yow, Bab? I shall see yow at midnight then.'

The Visitor

John watched Louisa walk back towards the house.

All through dinner that evening, Louisa could hardly contain herself until she saw John again. How could she have been so blind to the fact that she actually felt love for him? Was it possible to love a servant, or was it just loneliness driving her to his side? No, she felt not. She had unbelievable passion inside her for John and could only be sure it was real love by meeting him later that night.

Sometime Later in the Kitchen of Sycamore House

Mavis busied herself washing up the family dinner plates.

'Look at this plate; I should think it is Miss Louisa's. She's hardly touched any of her dinner tonight. Chicken an' all! If yow ask me she must be in love or somert.'

Mavis chuckled as she looked across at John eating his supper heartily. John always enjoyed Sarah's home cooking.

Sarah gathered up John's empty plate, handing it to Mavis to wash up.

'Don't yow be so cheeky, Mavis, no one is asking yow, ducks and don't be so rude about our miss.'

Sarah would not have a bad word said against Louisa or John, or for that matter, anyone in the household.

'How many times do I 'ave to say this to yow, John, there's napkins each for yow to wipe yower mouth. Not on the tablecloth or yower sleeve please, lad.'

Sarah passed John a clean napkin.

'All right! All right! Worse than me mam, Sarah is, I tell yow, Mavis! It's bad enough 'aving yower mam telling yow, but with two women now nagging me, what chance 'ave I?'

The two women laughed.

'Any road, I think I shall 'ave me bath tonight. I'll get the bath down from the back wall.'

John lifted the tin bath from the hooks on the wall, placing it in front of the fire to warm.'

'Can yow put some water on for me Sarah, or can I tek the water from the dolly tub, if yow finished with it?'

John felt the water in the dolly tub, but it had gone cold.

'But John, lad,' Sarah said, 'Yow 'ad a bath last Sunday, and it is only Tuesday.'

'So, what of it, I feel I need to be cleaner these days.'

John flushed and the two women laughed.

'If yow ask me, there must be a woman involved here somewhere, don't yow think, Sarah?'

The Visitor

Mavis giggled away as she continued to wash up.

'As I've said before, Mavis Riley, no one asked yow, so mind yower business.'

With that, John jumped up from his seat and started to tickle Mavis furiously, sending her into fits of hysterics.

''Eah, yow two, less of that,' Sarah said. 'I'll boil yow some fresh water, John; yes, now I'm looking at yow, yow do look a bit grubby!'

Sarah filled her saucepans, placing them on the lighted gas rings to boil up the water.

'Course, Mavis, I shall need someone to scrub me back, the other young maids here used to, didn't they Sarah?'

Mavis blushed.

'No, they didn't, did they Sarah?'

'Tek no notice of 'im Mavis. He is just a tease, but I wouldn't be around 'im if I were yow, when he is 'aving 'is bath, like a whale 'e is! Water everywhere! We shall probably tek all night mopping up all the water after 'im!'

Sarah laughed and laughed.

''Ave yow got any of that special powder stuff, Sarah? Yow know, the one that makes yow smell like fresh flowers.'

John started to unbutton his shirt.

'This yow mean?'

Sarah threw talcum powder all over John.

'There yow are lad, yow don't need yower bath now!'

Sarah continued to chastise John with Mavis holding her sides as they ached from laughing; she hadn't laughed so much in a very long time. John took off his shirt placing it on the laundry pile, much to Mavis's disgust. He tried not to show any sign of love in his face, for no one, not even Sarah, must know of his liaison with Louisa in the summerhouse. Mavis took John's shirt placing it ready for the next day's washing.

'Yow always make me more work than I should 'ave, John Garton. Feel sorry for the woman who gets yow.'

John slapped Mavis's bottom as she yelped out.

'Get off, yow are stupid. Fancy 'aving two baths in one week! Any road, I am sure yow 'ave a girl. Where did yow meet yower young lady then, John, around 'eah was it? Yow 'ave precious little time to go walking out.'

Mavis was inquisitive of John, as she had taken a shine to him herself and thought perhaps one day …

Tapping Mavis's nose gently, John said:

'Mind it, Mavis, as I said, none of yower business.'

Mavis felt slightly annoyed for she wanted to know what her competition looked like, as she was not bad looking herself. She felt sure, with a little encouragement, she could win John Garton over one day.

John started to fill his bath tub with the hot water from the saucepans. He only wished he could confide in Sarah or Mavis, he would love to but dare not. He knew he could never tell, not even his best friend, Sarah.

'I expect yower need me shampoo for yow hair an all, John? Eah, tek it. She must be sumert really special for yow to go to all this trouble, lad.'

Sarah handed a large bottle of green-coloured shampoo to John.

'Thank yow, Sarah, yow really are me own best mate.'

John started to unbuckle the belt holding up his baggy garden trousers, ready to step into his bath of hot water.

'Come on, Mavis, unless yow want to see sumert really terrible, come on, girl.'

Sarah took Mavis's arm leading her out in to the large hallway so they could retire to their rooms. John was left to soak in his bath dreaming of later that night when he would meet Louisa May in the summerhouse.

Later The Same Night at Midnight

Everyone in the household was in bed, when Louisa cautiously crept down the stairs carrying her shoes in her hands and taking care to miss the top stair that always creaked. She was sure everyone would be fast asleep by this time. Louisa's heart pounded and her stomach swirled with excitement at the prospect of seeing John Garton.

On reaching the kitchen, she stood motionless, hardly daring to breathe and wanting to see John so much that she was sure her heart would explode. Even the family cat didn't awake as she turned the key to unlock the kitchen door. Outside in the yard, she paused for a moment to gather herself together and to see if she could see John making his way towards the summerhouse. She couldn't, so she nervously took her first steps towards it. The longing inside her was almost too much for her to bear. Common sense was not an issue at all, she just knew she must keep her appointment with her beloved, John.

The night air was rather chilly; the breeze shook overhanging branches on the trees as she passed and tousled her hair around her face. Her hair hung over her shoulders for she was sure John preferred it loose and free. Peering through the open doorway of the summerhouse, there was no sign of John. Louisa stepped inside. She sat down on the rattan sofa, feeling a little afraid sitting there alone. She re-groomed her hair, arranging it to fall around her shoulders perfectly. She pinched the sides of her cheeks with her fingers to give herself more colour, although it wouldn't matter as it was dark, but she did it nevertheless. She sat for some minutes fidgeting and grooming herself, wondering if John would come. Was she making a mistake,

The Visitor

a complete fool of herself and reading far too much into their love talk together in the garden? What if John had thought better of it and decided not to meet her after all? Oh, no! He must come, surely he would never leave her waiting alone?

Louisa's mind drifted back to those far-off days with Peter Dupont making love in the very same summerhouse. Was she insane? What an earth could she be thinking of? Louisa felt panic; was this all a huge mistake? Should she leave now, while she had the chance and pretend that she felt nothing for John? Their meeting could only lead to trouble! It would be the sensible thing to do. But the pangs of excited love in Louisa's heart became stronger every time she thought of him; she had to stay and meet him. God! if only mother knew. John would be sacked, her mother would see to that. It will all be my fault for encouraging him and I will never see him again! Oh, God! A thought not worth considering.

Suddenly the summerhouse door creaked open and John made his way towards Louisa. She rushed towards him throwing her arms about his neck, with John's kisses smothering her face and lips. The wind outside howled, blowing the branches of the trees to and fro as John kissed Louisa even more passionately. His kisses were soft and gentle, not like Peter's had been. Hours passed and the couple found themselves lying beside each other on the summerhouse floor, not caring or knowing how they got there. The night air had become chilly and Louisa May shivered. John gallantly took off his jacket, placing it around her shoulders.

At this point, I wondered if I should be discreet and leave the couple to whatever … it was clear, they were definitely in love with one another. I found myself pinned to the spot though, unable to leave once more. I was obviously meant to witness *all* Louisa's story and she certainly did not want to leave anything out of it for me, but I couldn't help feeling that I was invading the lovers' privacy.

'There, that's better, Bab.'

Once more, taking Louisa in his arms, John kissed and caressed her, not caring where his kisses landed on her face and body, or the consequences of them. Louisa thought that she was no longer alone in the world as she had felt for such a long time and knew that she would follow John to the ends of the earth if needed.

Over the next few months, John and Louisa May frequently met for nights of passion in the summer house. Louisa had still not spoken of the affair to Jacqueline or Bertie and John had not confided in his dearest friend, Sarah!

Lack of sleep was beginning to tell on John's face. He yawned constantly. His work began to suffer and he was all but falling asleep at mealtimes in the kitchen. There were no such pressures for Louisa May for she had no job to do, nowhere to go and could sleep as long as she liked during the

The Visitor

day time and sometimes did so.

One night at around eleven thirty, John waited in the summerhouse for Louisa as usual. She was late. Not like Louisa! John made his way down the crazy paving pathway back towards the kitchen to see if he could find her. He was sure she would never forget to meet him. He waited outside the house, leaning against the wall near the kitchen door. He could have fallen asleep easily as he was so tired. But nothing was going to prevent him from meeting his Louisa, even if he was only sleeping for four or five hours a night! He would suffer it for her. He would surprise Louisa when she did come out and they could walk together to the summerhouse.

Sure enough, Louisa stepped outside the kitchen door, closing it quietly behind her and started to tiptoe down the path. John caught up with her, spun her around to face him and before she could scream out, embraced her with a loving, passionate kiss. The couple kissed madly. They knew they were taking a great risk so close to the house, but caution, it seemed, had been 'blown to the wind'. They loved each other so much that they just didn't care any more if they were caught embracing.

Sarah yawned, taking her lamp to her bedroom window to close her bedroom curtains for the night. It had been a very busy day, with all the cooking for the visitors, and she was glad to be going to bed at last. She was not prepared for the sight that greeted her outside on the pathway below.

'For God sakes! Who is that down there with our John? What a tart! Fancy, at this time of night! Should be ashamed of 'erself and for that matter, so should John at this 'our.'

Sarah dimmed her lamp so that she could see the couple more clearly.

For God sakes! It looks like, it can't be! It is! For goodness sake! What on earth do the youngerns think they are doing? Miss Louisa and me very own John! Whatever has possessed them? So that is why the lad wouldn't tell me who the young lady was 'e was courting? No wonder! Sarah watched the couple go towards the summerhouse.

Sarah peered out of her bedroom window for as long as she could, but couldn't see what was happening inside the summerhouse, although she had a pretty good idea! The stupid little fools! she thought. So that is why young John has been so pale and tired lately. I wonder 'ow long this 'as been going on? Long time it seems. I shall talk to 'im tomorrow. Staying up 'alf the night. Stupid lad!

Sarah drew back her curtains and climbed into bed. She was exhausted, but found she could not sleep properly for the rest of the night, cursing Louisa for her beauty and John for his stupidity.

The sunlight pushed its way through Louisa's bedroom curtains. Stretching her arms out and wriggling inside her cocooned bedclothes, she felt warm and very much loved. She couldn't wait until midnight again. John's gentleness

The Visitor

and his beautiful blue eyes penetrated her every thought. Peter was gradually fading away more and more from her mind, but never her tiny lost baby. How will it all end, she thought. What can I do? John could never be with her in the married sense, so yes, she felt she was right to take her happiness where and when she could. She was convinced there would be no one in her mother's social circle of friends whose son would be prepared to marry a deaf, but beautiful, woman. Anyway, she did love John, but where would it all end? Louisa's deafness was never a problem for John; in fact, they enjoyed each other's company so much that it never seemed to come between them. Louisa gave a little chuckle to herself, but was really quite frightened should they be discovered. What if Sarah ever found out? She was like a mother to her so how could she deceive her so? Surely John would be sacked if she ever did find out. Fiddle-de-dee, how could she ever find out? Louisa felt John and herself had been more than discreet!

Later That Day in the Kitchen

'Oh God, yow 'ave done me some sausages, my very favourite. When did yow make them, Sarah?'

John hung his peaked cap on the nail on the wall and sat astride his chair waiting for his meal.

'John, yow 'ad better wash yower hands first lad, yow know 'ow I hate serving any food when yow 'ave dirty hands.'

Sarah was in a bad temper slamming every saucepan and utensil down with a great thud.

'All right, yower in a bad mood today! What's up then, Sarah? Who upset yow? Tell me and I'll sort 'em out for yow!'

John scrubbed his hands at the sink with the large scrubbing brush.

Sarah grunted.

'I can't tell yow, Mavis is 'eah. When she's out, upstairs, or wherever, I want a word with yow.'

Sarah continued to bang everything around and John got up from his chair.

'Come on Sarah, what's up, ducks? I always know when yow are mad, yow give me that 'urt look. What is it?'

John swirled Sarah around and around trying to make her laugh, but she pushed him away.

'Is it somert I've done, but I can't think what?'

'Get off me, lad! Enough of yower nonsense. I need to speak with yow alone, serious like, but after yower eaten yower sausage and mash.'

Sarah sat opposite John watching him devour his food; the hurt and worry inside her was overwhelming.

The Visitor

'What's wrong Sarah? Yow never told me about anything that could be wrong. Are yow bad, or 'as the mistress said somert? She is a cow she is, I wouldn't be surprised if it was 'er upset yow Sarah,' said Mavis.

Mavis took John's plate away to wash it up.

'No, Mavis, it ain't 'er. As I told yow before, yow do not speak about the mistress or anyone in this 'ousehold. But thank yow anyway, for being concerned Mavis. Now get on with yower duties. When yow finished, yow can 'ang out all the washing, so I can talk to John in confidence.'

'Oh, can't I stay and listen? I promise I won't snitch on yow.'

'No, Mavis yow can't. Do as yow are told.'

'Oh, blimey.' Mavis shrugged her shoulders and continued to wash up.

Sarah kept giving Mavis glaring looks and wished she would hurry up and just go outside to hang out the washing.

'I know when I'm not wanted. Why can't yow let me into yower secrets? I wouldn't tell, honest I wouldn't.'

Mavis took the basket of wet washing outside, ready to hang on the washing line, closing the kitchen door behind her.

'Now Mavis 'as gone, well Sarah, yow 'ave my undivided attention, what's up?'

John leaned back on the kitchen chair waiting for Sarah to speak.

Sarah found it difficult to start her story of seeing Louisa and John together.

'This is going to come out all wrong, John, but I 'ave to tell it like I saw it. What the bloody 'ell are yow playing at with Miss Louisa? I saw yow two from me bedroom window last night, kissing and cuddling, plain for all to see from the 'ouse. Good job the mistress or master weren't looking out from their windows, like me! What do yow think yow are playing at, eh? I thought somert was going on when yow kissed Louisa's cheek that day when she was took bad, I 'ad my suspicions then.'

John's face reddened with embarrassment.

'It weren't going on then, Sarah, in fact, it happened sudden like. Neither of us planned anything.'

John shuffled about on his chair. 'Well, Sarah, now yow know. Louisa and me, we love each other. There is nothing anyone can do about it, Sarah, I mean we *really* love each other, She loves me and I 'er. I would gladly die for 'er, Sarah.'

Sarah put her arms around John.

'Yes, lad, yow may 'ave to if the mistress finds out. Yow ... yow are really stupid lad, but you 'aven't done anything yet, 'ave yow? Yow know what I mean?'

She hugged him again. 'Lad, oh, lad, be very careful, Louisa is so vulnerable, after everything she's been through lately. God forbid there would be another bab!'

The Visitor

'Sarah, I meant to tell yow all about it, but I knew yow would be mad and would never approve, so that is why I didn't tell yow. Not that I didn't want yow to know about it. I suppose, yow will sack me now then. Yow would 'ave the right to being the housekeeper 'eah.'

John looked down at the floor, praying, wishing and hoping that Sarah would not sack him. How could he bear to leave Sycamore House without Louisa and not see her again? But if he was forced to go, he would devise a plan to see her, he would make sure of that.

'Sack yow, lad? Why, I wouldn't ever do that, I couldn't. Yow are like me own son, a stupid one, but nevertheless, like me own. I just want yow to be very, very careful lad, don't be silly. After all as I've said before, what can yow, a mere servant, ever give Miss Louisa? Nothing! Why lad, I would 'ave no one to tend to the 'orses, or do the garden and help me at big parties. No, lad, yow are more precious to me than anything. All I am saying is, be very, very careful. Yow could get us all sacked if ever the master and mistress, or even young Mr Bertie found out!'

Sarah playfully punched John's chin.

'Sarah, I 'ave to confide in yow. Well, er … we love each other so much, we did, er …'

John looked away from Sarah's amazed gaze; his eyes filled with tears but with love for his Louisa May.

'Yow stupid fool. My God! Let's all hope and pray no bab comes along, John, that's all.'

The Next Morning at Breakfast

Louisa looked particularly beautiful as any woman does who is in love. Abraham kissed his daughter's forehead.

'My, I am the most fortunate of men, having the two most beautiful women in Birmingham sitting at my breakfast table; and you, Louisa, look very much better lately, particularly glowing, doesn't she, mother?'

Louisa flushed.

'Father, you are embarrassing me.'

Agnes's eyes flashed with jealousy.

'He can say all he likes, it is very flattering to be told you are beautiful, Louisa, especially by your own father, and to be told that when you are my age, well … but when I was your age my girl, my beauty was second to none and I think I had slightly better skin than you, dear, at your age!'

Agnes smoothed out her serviette.

'Some more eggs, Miss Louisa?'

Sarah nudged Louisa as she passed. She did not like Agnes's remarks directed so unkindly at Louisa.

The Visitor

'No thank you, Sarah.'

Louisa dabbed her mouth with her serviette, then picked at her breakfast, moving food from one side of her plate to the other; she was not at all hungry. She could not wait for eleven thirty that night so that she could be with John. She could see him through the dining room French windows, busying himself in the garden. After breakfast, Louisa was asked by her mother and father to accompany them to the city shops.

'Can't believe you are turning us down, Louisa, an opportunity to buy a new hat! Well, never mind, perhaps next time. I keep forgetting that our little girl is no child any more and makes her own decisions these days, quite the young lady.'

Agnes pinned on her huge, flamboyant feathered hat and took Abraham's arm to go out to the waiting automobile in the driveway. Abraham had decided that he liked to drive the automobile himself rather than being driven by John Garton and drove Agnes out down the long driveway of Sycamore House and towards the city.

Louisa was free at last to rush out to the garden and talk to John. She wanted to ask about Sarah, for she was sure that she had her suspicions about their romance.

'John! John!'

Louisa beckoned to John to come over to her with Sarah looking on the scene in a most disapproving way.

'What is it, Bab?'

John got up from his gardening and walked across to Louisa.

'Come into the house! Come up to my room! My parents have gone out now for hours, come on, don't be afraid, John!'

Louisa tugged at John's sleeve, something I had become very accustomed to.

'Bab, I mean, Miss Louisa, sweetheart,' John twirled her around to face him so that she would understand his lips.

'Sweetheart, this is very dangerous for yow and for me! What if yower parents should come back unexpectedly and catch us? We really shouldn't.'

John hesitated, looking down at his muddy boots. 'Where shall I put me boots, anyway?'

Louisa continued to tug at John's sleeve, watching Sarah and Mavis busily hanging yet more washing on the line. They both had their backs to the lovers and would not see if John went into the house or not! John took off his boots on the patio, leaving them just outside the French windows and followed Louisa through the house and upstairs to her bedroom.

Sarah finished pegging out the last of the washing, carrying her wicker basket towards the kitchen. She noticed John's muddy boots outside the French windows and shrugging her shoulders, went into the kitchen. None of my concern, she thought. Stupid little fools.

The Visitor

'Come on, John, this way.'

Louisa kept tugging him by the sleeve to follow her and soon the lovers found themselves in a passionate embrace.

'Bab, please! We 'ave to be careful. It is so dangerous, we ought not to make ...'

John mouthed his words very carefully to Louisa, but she did not care for all she could think of were John's passionate kisses and embraces.

Shutting the bedroom door behind her she said:

'We are completely alone now John, don't be so frightened. There is no possibility whatever of my parents or anyone else disturbing us. We have the ideal opportunity to make love here, on the bed, in comfort.'

John looked into Louisa's face, could not resist her any longer and kissing her intensely they fell onto Louisa's bed, making wild and passionate love. John had never known such happiness and he didn't want their lovemaking to end; neither did Louisa. With each kiss he tried to speak to her, mouthing his words, but always ending with a kiss from her with each word.

John made Louisa stop for a moment.

'Louisa, my bab, my sweetheart. How can we continue to live apart? I do love yow so much, it 'urts me inside to be apart from yow, even for one minute.' John spoke very clearly so that Louisa would understand.

'I know of rooms in the city, in Tower Street. They are vacant at the moment and not expensive. Let's get married and go ...'

Louisa sat bolt upright in the bed; she certainly understood John's lips.

'Married! Oh, John, how wonderful, how romantic, but John, how could we? I mean ... I don't want to hurt you, my dearest sweetheart, but you are just the gardener and servant here and me, well, how could you support me properly? I need so many things which I know you could not afford. My gowns, my hats and everything.'

John jumped from the bed, leaving Louisa gazing at him shocked by his sudden movement. John was hurt, his heart sank; how could his beloved Louisa be so hurtful? Wouldn't she give up all those things for his love and to get married?

Louisa quickly spoke:

'That does not mean to say that I would not marry you, John, or that I don't love you. You know that I do, terribly, you know that I do with all my heart?'

John nodded at her. She was right. How could he support her? It would be an impossibility and after all, she was being sensible about their affair. He would never be able to give her the things she was used to, so why couldn't he just accept the love she offered him? He wanted to own her!

'Come on, Bab, I think we 'ad better go downstairs now, don't yow? Yower parents could come back or Mr Bertie. Time is ticking on!'

The Visitor

John helped Louisa to get up from the bed, once more kissing her lips.

Days had gone by since Louisa and John had made love in her bedroom and they were still meeting each other late at night in the summerhouse whenever they could. No one had time to notice the lovers or had any clue; that is, no one except Sarah!

Jacqueline and Bertie were frequent visitors to Sycamore House, returning each time for a few days, allowing the builders at their new home to carry out their specified alterations without hindrance. There was so much to be done at the new house, with Jacqueline and Bertie hardly knowing where to begin, and they were involving Agnes and Abraham more and more in their daily shopping sprees for their new home.

'So, you are off shopping again, darling?' Bertie kissed Jacqueline's cheek.

'What for this time, need I guess? Buy yourself something pretty, not just for the house.'

Bertie once more kissed Jacqueline as she straightened his bow tie.

'You will come later if you can, darling, won't you? Mother and I shall choose some fabrics for curtaining and cushions and I would so dearly love your opinion on them.'

Jacqueline pinned on her neat hat that completely contrasted with Agnes's hat, festooned with flamboyant, red feathers, making Louisa May smile in amusement at its ridiculous shape and size.

'Bye, Louisa, we shall see you later on no doubt, at dinner time? Bye, Bertie, see you later dearest.'

Jacqueline left with Agnes and Abraham to go to the city shops once more.

Louisa was so very glad she was not going with them, her heart dancing at the thought of getting ready to see John later. Nothing in the world and nothing anyone could say or do was of the slightest importance to her now, only her love for John. It had not gone unnoticed by Bertie that Louisa was preoccupied about something; he knew his sister too well!

'So, my little sister, what have you been up to whilst we have been away? Made lots of new friends and conquests no doubt? I should think all the young men for miles around are lining up ready to escort you wherever my lady wishes to go. Am I right?'

Bertie bowed down, kissing Louisa's forehead, making her giggle and think him mad.

'Oh, Bertie, you are so funny. Nothing has happened at all! I just mope around as usual and go shopping with mother, but that is nothing new! No young men – who would have me now that I am deaf? Mother does not even try to match me with any young men now that I am ... Not that I like any of her choices anyway. I really am not interested in young men.'

The Visitor

Louisa bowed her head.

Bertie laughed.

'Not interested! That's not like you Louey.'

Louisa flushed. She dearly wanted to confide in Bertie about John, but how could she? He would go raving mad and would definitely not understand her love for John, a mere servant.

'Bertie, er ... um ...'

'What is it, Louey? It isn't like you, my dear sister, to be lost for words! Come on, out with it. You want to tell me something, I knew that ages ago, and I've also noticed you have been somewhat preoccupied.'

'No, Bertie, it isn't anything, really it isn't.'

Louisa tried to hide her reddened face from her brother, but he knew his sister better than she knew herself! He knew she was hiding something from him.

'Look, Louey, I know something is bothering you and I demand to know what it is. I shall not divulge any of your secrets, you can trust me, surely you know that by now?'

'Well, Bertie, you must swear never to tell, please?' Louisa begged Bertie.

'I knew it, I just knew it! You do have a secret.'

Bertie sat Louisa opposite him so that she could see his lips and understand his replies to her.

'Bertie, well ... er ... I am in love, wonderfully in love.'

Louisa started to fidget. How would she explain to Bertie about John?

'The young man, I take it, is in love you with Louey?'

'Yes, he is.'

Bertie threw back his head and gave one of his bellowing, loud, laughs.

'How wonderful, at last. But why couldn't you tell me and why haven't you told Jacqueline and mother and father, eh?'

Bertie took a huge cigar from the silver cigar case on the round coffee table, lighting it and puffing smoke everywhere in the room.

'This calls for a celebration and we shall arrange a party to welcome this fortunate young man into our family.'

Bertie continued to puff on his cigar.

'No, you must not tell the rest of the family Bertie. The young man in question is not from our station in life, well ... I mean ... I've just got to tell you, Bertie, or I shall explode. You must promise me you will never tell mother, father or even Jacqueline.'

Bertie looked at Louisa with amazement.

'Not Jacqueline, but why, for goodness sake? Surely the fellow can't be that bad? Anyway, Jacqueline is your very best friend.'

'I know, I know all that Bertie. Please promise me you will never tell anyone? Bertie, it is all such a mess, but I do love my young man and he me. However, there is one other thing to add to the worry of our relationship. Well ... I think ... I am pregnant by him, Bertie!'

Louisa fell into Bertie's arms, sobbing with relief at telling her dearest brother her secret.

'Pregnant! For God's sake! There, there, Louey. Are you sure, how do you know you are pregnant? Does your young man know? Who is this scoundrel? I shall have his guts for garters.'

'Bertie, he is not a scoundrel, it is really my fault. I led him on, but I love him so much, neither of us could help ourselves. Please don't be cross, please. I am sure, yes quite sure I am pregnant and well ... no, my young man does not know about the baby coming.'

'My God! Now, first of all, Louey, you are not to worry yourself about anything. I shall look after you. We shall sort this mess out, leave it to me, Louey. Of course, you will have to tell me who this young man is. Of course I shall have to speak with him and see what he intends to do about it. He will marry you, no doubt about that, but we shall not tell mother and father until we have talked to him. Now, Louey, tell me, who is this young man?'

'Oh, Bertie, I have been so frightened these past few days, he does love me and he does want to marry me, he says so.'

Bertie was pleased to hear the news.

'Well, that's all right then, next time you see your young man, tell him I need to speak with him. There is nothing to fear, Louisa, really.' Bertie sighed. 'Please do try and stop crying, Louey. This is something to be happy about and your young man will be overjoyed from what you say, to discover you're pregnant. You shall have a very quick and wonderful wedding.'

Bertie threw his head back and laughed out loudly, with Louisa's face breaking out into a wide smile.

'I know you have had a very difficult time Louey, especially after Peter and no one is blaming you for anything that has happened; I am just happy that you have at last found real love. Never thought you would, my dear, after, well, your accident.'

Bertie mouthed his words very carefully for Louisa.

'Now, tell me, who is this lucky man? Where and when did you meet? I am intrigued.'

Bertie took Louisa's outstretched hands.

I could not help wondering what his reaction would be to her news about John being the father of her unborn child. Here goes, I thought, she will just have to tell now.

Louisa told her story to Bertie with such tenderness, that he couldn't help but feel sorry yet at the same time an uneasy feeling crept over him about what the future would hold for Louisa and John.

'Louey, dearest, I have to think. Not that I am not pleased for you both,

The Visitor

but how can you marry John? He can't support you, sweetheart. A servant! Love does not pay the bills, dear.' Bertie looked at Louisa's frightened face. 'We must speak to John, but first of all, you must tell him your news and then my dear, we have to face mother and father, who will be, to say the least, not pleased, as you can imagine.'

Louisa just nodded, knowing that Bertie was right, but could only dream of her John and did not care what the consequences would be as long as she could be with him. Bertie pulled the servants cord at the side of the fireplace.

'What are you doing, Bertie?'

Louisa dashed over to him. 'Why are you sending for Sarah?'

'Louey, my sweet, there is no time like the present and no time to waste; an ideal opportunity to speak to John, whilst the family are out.'

Louisa bit her lip in anguish, pacing to and fro in front of the fireplace.

'Ah, Sarah,' Bertie said. 'Please ask John Garton to come in here, would you? Do it as quickly as you can please.'

'Yes, Master Bertie, straight away.'

Sarah hurried from the sitting room down the long hallway and out to the kitchen.

'Blimey, oh, very blimey! There's going to be trouble now! I think Master Bertie knows about John and Louisa, he's going to sack 'im, I just know it.'

She found John cleaning his gardening tools and her face told him that there was something wrong.

'What's up, Sarah? Yow look as if yower 'ad a shock.'

'Yow could say that, John. Master Bertie wants to see yow in the 'ouse. Miss Louisa is there! John, I am so worried for yow, lad. I should think they 'ave found out about yow and her.'

Sarah smoothed John's blond hair out of his eyes, wiping the mud away from his cheek.

'Better get it over with, lad, Miss Louisa looks so pale and worried: hope it isn't as bad as we think, lad, go on with yow, they are waiting.'

Sarah watched John brush the dust from his trousers and take off his boots at the kitchen door, looking back at her as he walked along the long hallway.

John knocked on the sitting room door.

'Come in,' a voice said.

He entered the room, his heart pounding.

'Ah, John! Do take a seat, please. I would like to talk to you.'

Bertie held out his hand to shake John's. John was very confused, giving Louisa a questioning look.

Bertie continued:

'I need to talk to you and of course, Louisa on a matter that is extremely delicate, and I wish to do it before my parents get back from the city. I want no interruptions and want you both just to listen to me.'

The Visitor

Bertie positioned Louisa in front of him so that she could read his lips.

'Louisa tells me that you have both been meeting with each other and how you helped her, John to get over the loss of Peter Dupont. I commend you, lad and am glad you have given my sister comfort. However, now she tells me, well … she is pregnant with *your* child, John, so I have to say …'

John turned around to face Louisa, drawing her into his arms.

'Bab! Why didn't yow tell me, this is the most wonderful news!'

John was about to kiss Louisa, when Bertie patted her shoulder to gain her attention away from John.

'Just one minute; it is wonderful news, but can I please continue with what I want to say?'

Bertie was clearly agitated.

'We have to think about what we are going to do about all this. How are you going to support my sister and more importantly, a coming child? I will not see her degraded or demoralized for any reason, not any, John.'

John nodded.

'Of course not, Master Bertie. I love 'er very much and will work 'ard to support 'er and our baby, I shall protect and marry 'er and do me best of 'er always, Master Bertie.'

John looked towards Louisa when he was speaking.

Bertie patted John on the back.

'I am sure you will do, but we have to be realistic John. We have to broach the matter with my parents and I suggest for the moment, you let myself and Louisa handle it. You should come into it all later when everything has calmed down. You can imagine how my parents will take the news. Not well.'

Bertie once more blew smoke from his cigar.

'Master Bertie, I would appreciate a few moments alone with Louisa before I go back to work, with the baby coming and everything?'

John drew Louisa close to him.

Bertie nodded in agreement.

'Of course, how remiss of me, I shall give you ten minutes. By that time my parents will be back I should think, so make it as quick as you can. I shall come back at say, four o'clock.'

'Thank you, Master Bertie.'

John watched Bertie leave the room then drew Louisa closer to him and passionately kissed her.

'Why didn't yow tell me, Bab, why? Yow weren't frightened of me, were yow?'

Louisa stroked his face.

'I didn't know how to tell you, John. I was afraid of what your reaction would be and I didn't want you to feel trapped by a baby coming and that

The Visitor

you might have me for the rest of your life.'

'But, Bab, I want yow for the rest of my life, this is what I am saying to yow. I want to marry yow.'

John once more kissed Louisa and could not believe that his dreams of making her his very own would now be coming true.

'I know of rooms, as yow know, in Tower Street and will put a deposit on them for us. Whenever yow feel yow want to make the break Louisa.'

All the two lovers could do was to hold each other and marvel at the expectation of married life together with no thought of the consequences, just of their love for one another.

Bertie rushed back into the sitting room.

'That is it you two. Time is up. We shall have another meeting together very soon and decide on the best course of action to take. Until then, John, off you go, until I send for you.'

Bertie showed John out of the room with Louisa craning her neck to catch a last glimpse of him before he went back to work.

Several days had passed with Bertie patting Louisa's arm every time he saw her in reassurance that everything would be all right, but neither dared to tell Jacqueline, Agnes or Abraham of the coming baby just yet. When would be the right moment? What day? Everyone seemed so busy with Jacqueline and Bertie's new house and all the shopping expeditions for new furniture, curtains, carpets and kitchen equipment, they didn't have time to notice Louisa's swelling stomach. Bertie knew that once mother found out about Louisa and John, there would be no way on earth that they would be allowed to stay at Sycamore House. Mother would surely disinherit Louisa and possibly disown her for that was the Jewish way. If only John had been Jewish, he might have been more accepted into the family.

Each family mealtime became more and more uncomfortable for Louisa to bear. She refused the food she most liked to eat, feeling revulsion and nausea welling up from her stomach at Sarah's tasty food suggestions.

CHAPTER XIV

Cast Out

*L*ouisa was positive that Sarah had noticed her stomach swelling and if *she* noticed, surely it would not be too long before her parents did? None of her gowns fitted her properly now so how could she keep her pregnancy a secret from the rest of the family any longer?

Five Days Later

'Sarah dear, do fetch some more logs for the fire, it's cold in here.'

Agnes huddled herself nearer to the open log fire, fanning out her newspaper to read it, with the flames of the fire fiercely licking at the logs and making the occasional spitting sound. Louisa looked into the flames dreamily imagining faces and figures prancing around. Perhaps she should tell mother now, whilst father was out? Perhaps now was a good time …

'Oh, there you are, Mavis, about time girl, I did ask Sarah to bring some logs, but you've brought them. Build up the fire, dear, stoke it up a bit, let's get some warmth into this room for goodness sake!'

Mavis cleared her throat and gave a quiet cough.

'Excuse, madam! I'll just stoke up the fire and put the logs on then.'

Agnes put her paper down and looked at Mavis in amazement. Was this servant being cheeky! Mavis smiled across at Louisa weakly. Louisa was sure Sarah and Mavis knew about her pregnancy and were showing her as much kindness as they could, without making it obvious and drawing too much attention to her predicament.

'Well, I never did?' said Agnes. 'A servant daring to speak without being spoken to! Then again, girl, you show more initiative than most and have made up the fire quite quickly. Good girl.'

Agnes carried on reading her newspaper, fingering the pages with the ends of her fingers and making a rustling sound that broke the silence in the room, not that Louisa heard anything at all.

The Visitor

In the Kitchen

'Mavis! where 'ave yow been, girl? I needed yow in 'eah to 'elp me.'

Sarah was clearly agitated.

'I stoked up the fire for madam and put some more logs on it.'

Mavis shrugged her shoulders.

'Stoked up the fire, girl? That's my job. I was just about to go and do that.'

'I've done it now anyway.' Mavis shrugged her shoulders.

'Don't yow shrug yower shoulders at me, girl! Why, the very idea.'

Sarah pushed Mavis towards the dolly tub once more. Yes, it was wash day again – Monday!

It always seemed to be Monday to Mavis, who hated wash days and her duties at the dolly tub.

'Anyway, Sarah, I think there is somert up with Miss Louisa, I really do,' Mavis said.

'What do yow mean, girl?'

Sarah frowned disapprovingly at Mavis.

'Well, if yow ask me, she's getting a little too fat for her own good, don't yow think? She's always crouched over like, bent double, well I think she is ...' Mavis was stopped in mid-sentence.

'Yow ain't paid to think, girl, so shut up and get on with yower duties, before I get really mad!'

Sarah piled even more dirty washing on the side of the drainer, which made Mavis give out a daunting sigh. She left Mavis to her daily chores and made her way along the long hallway to the sitting room where she observed Louisa staring into the log fire and Agnes reading her daily newspaper.

'Madam, excuse me!' she said.

'What is it, Sarah? The fire's been made up already. What a considerate girl that Mavis is. A credit to the household. At least she came and stoked up the fire for us. We could have frozen to death in here, if it weren't for her.'

Agnes fanned out her newspaper once more. The frown mark on her forehead became more prominent with each of her displays of bad temper, Sarah thought. She felt deeply wounded, as there was no one who cared for the madam and the rest of the family like she did, but then, she was used to the madam's cruel outbursts.

'Would yow like the curtains drawn now, madam?'

Sarah started to pull the velvet curtains closed as Agnes nodded.

'Is there anything else you require, madam?'

Sarah looked across at Louisa, studying her closely. Surely there is nothing wrong as she doesn't look fat to me! she thought.

The Visitor

'No,' said Agnes. 'That will be all Sarah, we shall have our usual cocoa and teacakes at around nine o'clock.'

Agnes carried on reading her newspaper and gave her command without even looking up at Sarah, or for that matter, Louisa. Louisa shuffled about in her chair. She felt sick and ill and feared that her mother would surely guess soon about her pregnancy.

'Mother ... I ...'

'What is it, Louisa, stop muttering girl. Every time I start to read my newspaper, someone interrupts. I am so sick and tired of interruptions!'

Agnes fanned out the newspaper once more.

'But, mother, I feel so sick and I think I am about to ...'

Louisa felt that she would surely faint and could not get to the bathroom in time before she heaved and was sick into her lap, covering her velvet dress with vomit. Agnes rushed over to her, taking out her handkerchief to give to Louisa.

'Go and clean yourself up, girl, I never did. Why didn't you tell me you were ill and why leave it to the last minute to go to the bathroom? Look at your beautiful dress!'

Agnes helped Louisa upstairs to the bathroom so that she could change her dress and clean herself up.

Louisa felt sure that her mother would have guessed now. How could she miss all the clues? Louisa May knew she would have to tell her about the pregnancy. There was nothing for it but to tell the truth. She still felt ill, but managed to wash her face and hands and change her dress before her mother's questions.

'For goodness sake, girl, whatever is wrong with you? You have looked so peaky these past few weeks and if I didn't know better, I would think you were pregnant!'

Agnes giggled as she knew her Louisa would never be that.

'Now, mother, this will absolutely shock you, I know it will, but I have to speak with you.' Louisa dabbed her face with a towel.

'Nevertheless mother, I am not ashamed of my state and feel that now is the appropriate time to tell you.'

Louisa folded the towel and neatly placed it back on its towel rail.

'Tell me what, girl, what?'

Agnes studied Louisa's pale face.

'Well, mother, Bertie was going to help me tell you, along with John Garton, but I can't wait any longer, so mother I ...'

Louisa had absolutely gained Agnes's full attention.

'Well, go on girl!' Agnes stiffened.

'Mother, I am very much in love with ...'

'In love! In love! With whom?' Agnes snarled. 'How have you had time

The Visitor

to be in love with anyone? Have you no shame girl, it isn't even a year since poor Peter died and here you are, in love!'

Agnes was standing facing Louisa by this time.

'Mother, please listen to me. Yes, I am in love with ... John Garton, the gardener and he with me.'

'Don't be so stupid girl.' Agnes shrieked with laughter. 'Is that all? You just have a crush on the lad, many girls at your age do on the servants. It's not love though girl, not with him, a mere gardener. No, you are not in love with him, we shall find you a very nice young man, someone with position and money, you mark my words. Don't become infatuated with a mere servant, girl, please. Give yourself more credit dear.'

'Mother, will you please listen? Will you stop for one moment and listen to me?'

Louisa raised her voice.

'Thank you mother, as I was saying, John Garton and I, well ... we are very much in love. John has asked me to marry him and I have accepted.'

Louisa's eyes were lowered for she hardly dared to look at her mother as she knew what fury was to follow. Agnes's face filled with rage as she lifted Louisa's chin so that her daughter's eyes could study her mouth.

'What! Are you mad? Have you lost your senses? We shall see about that! I shall ring for John Garton now and he shall be dismissed this instant! Why, I have never heard such rubbish. A Hirons marrying a mere servant? Never! Over my dead body, girl.'

'Mother, mother, please!'

Louisa knew that she had to complete her story and admit to her pregnancy so she grabbed her mother's arm, stopping her from ringing the servants cord.

'Mother, please! There is something else.' Louisa lowered her head. 'I am to have John's child. I am five months pregnant!'

The two women just stared at each other and Agnes could not believe what she was hearing. She could not comprehend the fact that her only daughter could be pregnant by a servant of the household and one she didn't particularly care for. She slumped herself down in the chair. The shock of what Louisa had said was almost too much for her to bear. What would all her friends say? They must never know anything about it: as far as Louisa was concerned, she had gone away to finishing school abroad, or something of that nature. Perhaps the doctor could help? Perhaps he could abort the baby before it was too late? No one must ever know that her only girl was pregnant out of wedlock. Agnes's mind filled with schemes of how to conceal the shame. Looking over at Louisa May she knew that her daughter would not be persuaded into leaving John Garton, she could tell that by the look of love in her eyes, or to having her baby aborted or adopted. There was

The Visitor

nothing for it as far as Agnes was concerned, Louisa must be evicted for ever from Sycamore House and her life!

Agnes arose to her feet, her face red with fury. Louisa had never seen such rage in her before and she wished now that her John and Bertie were with her. Louisa began to feel afraid of Agnes as she lurched towards her.

'Get out of my house now, you slut, you harlot! Take your bastard child and get out of my sight right now!'

'But, mother, you can't mean that, can't we wait for father and Bertie to come home? Surely we can all discuss the best thing to do in a civilised manner. Mother, please!'

Louisa felt terror like never before, as tears filled her eyes.

'Don't try and get round me Louisa with your tears, that won't work. Why wait for your father or Bertie, you slut? Go to your man, let him look after you! Him a Gentile too! How could you do this to me, Louisa? How? You, of all people. Haven't I always given you everything you want? And now, this is how you repay me, with a bastard child, a Gentile's child. No, you are only fit for the gutter, girl, and that is where I am sending you. Get out!'

By now Agnes was screaming at the top of her voice, bringing Sarah and Mavis rushing from the kitchen into the hallway looking up towards the landing as Agnes rained blows into Louisa's small frame.

'Mother! Stop, please, I don't want to fight with you, mother please stop hitting me!'

Louisa's cries brought Sarah between the two women.

'Madam, please control yowerself. Please, madam.'

Sarah managed to stop Agnes for the time being, sending Louisa rushing to her bedroom.

'That is better, madam, calm yowerself. Whatever is wrong? Surely it isn't that bad, whatever it is?'

Sarah guided Agnes to the sofa on the landing, sitting her down. She burst into floods of tears.

'There, there, madam, shall I fetch the doctor to you?'

Sarah looked so concerned, but she was more concerned about Louisa and what had caused the two women to fight. She knew it wasn't at all like Louisa to fight for she was usually so gentle.

Mavis could only gape at Sarah as she comforted madam.

'Do yow want me to fetch the doctor for madam, Sarah?'

Mavis straightened her moll cap.

'No, Mavis, thank yow, Bab. Go into the kitchen, carry on with the washing and stay there till I send for yow.'

Mavis shrugged her shoulders and dutifully went back to the dreaded washing.

'Now, madam, that's better. Can I get yow anything, what can I do to 'elp yow?'

The Visitor

Sarah put her arms around Agnes and knew she could console her, knowing she must be diplomatic to save the day for Louisa. If she could restrain Agnes, perhaps whatever was wrong between them would be resolved as the evening went on.

'Oh, Sarah, do you know what my stupid, stupid, daughter has done?'

Agnes started to weep into her handkerchief.

'No, madam, but surely whatever it is can't be that bad, can it?'

'Bad! Bad!' Agnes's temper once more erupted and her face flushed red with temper.

'Well, Sarah, she is a slut, no more than a common prostitute, that is what she is. She has only gone and got herself pregnant, yes, pregnant, by that … that … excuse for a man, that, John, John Garton.'

Agnes burst into angry tears as Sarah's thoughts rushed to the night she had observed Louisa and John kissing passionately in the courtyard below her bedroom window; things now began to make sense to her about Louisa's behaviour over the past few weeks. She couldn't believe what she was hearing and knew she would have to warn John quickly. Agnes's fury would certainly vent itself on him and he would surely be sacked! But what of her lovely bab, Louisa, what would become of her? Surely madam would not throw her out of the house in her condition? Oh, God! Sarah didn't dare to think about the consequences of it all.

Meanwhile, Louisa knew what her fate would be; she would surely be asked to leave Sycamore House.

Oh, where are Bertie and father? They are not home yet? They must come home soon, they must. Why did I tell mother now? Louisa felt alone and afraid and wanted John by her side now that their secret was discovered. She packed a few belongings and Peter's sapphire ring in her crocodile skin bag.

Louisa knew her time at Sycamore House was coming to an end. Where is John, Louisa wondered: I must get word to him in case mother throws me out, which is now very likely. Louisa peered out of her bedroom window down onto the courtyard and the garden below. John was nowhere to be seen.

Agnes was still ranting with temper downstairs and Sarah was trying to console her.

'That's it, Sarah! She is going! I will throw her out of the house. She is not staying here, or setting foot in my home ever again. Daughter! What daughter? I have no daughter.'

Agnes started to rush upstairs towards Louisa's bedroom. Sarah chased after her.

'Madam, please, nothing is to be gained by another fight. Please wait until the Master and Mister Bertie get home. Don't do something now yow will

The Visitor

regret forever.'

It was no good, Sarah's pleas went unheeded. Louisa's bedroom door flew open, displaying Agnes in the doorway looking like a spitting dragon.

'I told you to get out of my house. Why are you still here, girl? Get out! Out!'

Agnes grabbed Louisa by her beautiful hair, dragging her to the top of the stairs. Louisa had managed to pick up her crocodile skin bag as she was forced out onto the landing. Sarah rushed to Louisa, trying to release her from Agnes's grip.

'Madam, please, consider the baby.'

Sarah tried to unclasp Agnes's fingers from Louisa's hair. The three women struggled and screamed. Louisa's cries could be heard all over the house.

Agnes still held onto Louisa's hair, pushing Sarah out of the way as she went.

'Get down those stairs you slut! Out! Out!'

Agnes dragged Louisa down each step at a time with Louisa begging her mother to let her go. The pain of pulling her hair was making her feel faint.

'Mother, stop! I shall go of my own accord. Just let me go!'

Agnes let Louisa go and she made her way to the front door.

'No, girl! Not that door. That is for respectable people. You use the back door, the kitchen door. A servant's door. That is what you are now, a slut, a servant. Let them all see what a slut you are, go on, let them all see.'

Agnes pushed Louisa towards the back of the house and the kitchen door.

'Get out!' Agnes said once more.

Mavis looked shocked, and opened the kitchen door for Louisa. She glanced over at Sarah, who had her hands to each side of her face in horror.

'Madam, please! If only you would reconsider and wait for Master Bertie and the master to come home.'

Sarah positioned herself between Agnes and Louisa to shield Louisa from any more of her mother's blows.

'Get out of my way Sarah, how dare you interfere!'

Agnes pushed Louisa out through the back door, ordering Mavis to lock the door and bolt it behind her.

'Under no circumstances admit Louisa back into my house at any time! Sycamore House is out of bounds to Louisa and also John Garton, whom I have yet to sack. Believe me he will be sacked and good riddance to them both!'

Bristling and still ranting and raving Agnes made her way down the hall to the front door, bolting and locking it. Sarah and Mavis quickly followed madam down the hall, not knowing what to expect next. Agnes turned to her servants.

'I want no one to speak to my daughter again and if they do, it will be instant dismissal. From this day forward, I do not wish my daughter's name

The Visitor

to be spoken in this house again. I now have no daughter! Do you both understand me?'

Agnes looked from Sarah to Mavis, both women nodded.

'I shall now go to my bedroom and when the master and Mister Bertie come in, you will not discuss what has happened here this evening. If asked and if they want to know where Louisa is, you will refer them both to me. Do you understand?'

The two women nodded once more.

'I want Louisa and John Garton off my property in ten minutes and if they are not, I shall send for the police and get them removed by force!'

The two women gasped in horror, but nodded.

Louisa May stood motionless outside the kitchen door, in the courtyard where she had spend so many happy times. She felt numb and vulnerable. Whatever will become of me and where is John, she wondered. He was nowhere to be seen. Louisa slid down the door, reaching the ground with a thud. The baby inside her kicked and moved and she felt sick and ill. It was getting dark and the hour late. I shall go around to the front of the house, she thought. Perhaps John will be there waiting for me.

Louisa May wondered if she should wait on the main road to see if she could catch Bertie and her father as they arrived home and tell them what had happened. They would know what to do. She picked up her crocodile skin bag and walked to the front of Sycamore House.

John Garton had been waiting patiently outside the grounds of the house. He knew Louisa would not be long as madam, whilst sacking him instantly on the news of their coming baby, had told him that Louisa May would have to leave too. He didn't dare to make an appearance anywhere in the grounds of the house or near the stables. He felt upset that he could not say goodbye to his mates, his beloved horses, or to Sarah and Mavis. He didn't have time as madam's fury was so great. How could he get his things back from his room above the stables? I don't possess much, but I would have liked to get my shaving mirror and buckle belt. Never mind, at least now I do have my Louisa, he thought.

Seeing Louisa walking down the long driveway from the front of the house, John ran to meet her.

He lifted up her chin so that she could read his lips.

'My Bab, Louisa. Everything will be all right now! This is the first day of our new life together. It will be wonderful sweetheart, yow will see. Don't yow worry, I am with yow now.'

He kissed her gently on her lips and took the bag from her hand to carry it for her.

'What yow got in 'eah, the kitchen sink?'

John tried to make Louisa laugh, but he knew it was useless as she was

The Visitor

so distressed. She glanced back at the house once more and knew it would be pointless waiting for her father and Bertie to return. She would miss them and Jacqueline terribly and for that matter, Sarah and Mavis, Sarah most of all. What could father and Bertie do against mother's wrath, especially when her mind was made up about something? Louisa knew her father was terrified of Agnes's temper and would never lift a finger to help Louisa against her. She knew he would have great sympathy for her, but that would be all.

Bertie was a different proposition. He would, she was sure, fight Agnes, but what would be the point of upsetting his relationship with mother and father? It was not Bertie's house so he would be powerless to insist that Louisa and John stayed at Sycamore House. Even if they could stay, what sort of a life would it be with Agnes? No, Louisa was convinced this was the best way, just to leave. Perhaps when they were settled into the rooms in Tower Street, she would send word to Bertie and Jacqueline that she and John were all right.

Sarah sobbed bitterly into her white, starched apron.

'Oh, Mavis, she was like a daughter to me, poor Louisa! What a terrible thing to 'ave 'appened to 'er and in 'er state too. What with poor Peter, the dead baby and all. 'Ow can she cope? She needs 'er mother more than anyone else at the moment, but look what's 'appened.'

Sarah sobbed bitterly as Mavis put her arms around her.

'She'll be all right, yow will see Sarah. John, well, 'e is strong and will tek care of 'er. We shall get word from them, yow will see, and we can visit on our days off. Don't get upset Sarah. I know about 'is bad lung, but 'e will find work and look after 'er.'

Mavis wanted to ask many questions, but she thought it best to leave the questions for the time being.

Agnes's screams of temper could be still heard all over the house, even in the kitchen. Mavis wondered if the household would ever be the same again; would it ever return to any sort of normality?

Outside the grounds of Sycamore House, John comforted Louisa as best he could. It was dark and late and he knew he would have to ask Louisa to walk many miles to his rooms in Tower Street.

'Bab, I know what yow are thinking. It ain't a good idea to wait for Master Bertie or yower father. Best for us to go. I shall go back to the 'ouse later and get word to Sarah where we will be. Bertie and Jacqueline will know, so come on, let's get out of 'eah. Me rooms in Tower Street ain't the Savoy, but it's a roof over us 'eads.'

John put his strong arms around Louisa's shoulders as they walked away from Sycamore House on the road from Edgbaston into the City of Birmingham.

In my ghostly state and following the couple on their long walk to Tower

The Visitor

Street, I still could not help wondering what it was that Louisa needed me to know. I had documented her story to this stage but there was nothing that struck me as valuable information on anything or anyone. Well, I had better just keep following the couple and observing, that was all I could do. Something would turn up, I had no doubt.

'All right, Bab?' John asked on the long walk to Tower Street.

'Yes, thank you John. I am getting a little tired, are we nearly there?'

Louisa clasped John's hand even tighter and knew that he would look after her for the rest of her life.

"Eah, yow do look tired. Oh, look! There's a tram, come on! Can yow run, Bab?'

Louisa and John ran, just managing to catch the last night tram into the city. Louisa had never travelled by tram before and felt quite excited at the prospect. The couple sat on the long seats nearest the doorway with the ticket collector asking for their fare and clicking his ticket machine for two pennies each, then giving John his change. John held Louisa's hand tightly, squeezing it in reassurance. Small, neat houses flashed by, with parade upon parade of suburban shops on the way into the city. Louisa knew she had to forget everything in her past, except of course, Jacqueline, Bertie and Sarah. She must now be positive about her new life with John, which she was sure was not going to be easy.

"Eah we are, Bab. We 'ave to get off now, only a short walk from eah.'

As John helped Louisa off the tram, the baby inside her kicked and moved like never before. She felt she could not walk another step.

'I shall have to rest, John. Let's sit down here on this bench.'

The bench was comforting and Louisa insisted that she would have to sit for quite a time as the baby was restless. The couple watched the city traffic going by. The lights from the carriages and trams twinkled in the darkness.

Back at Sycamore House

Abraham and Bertie had arrived home, unaware that Louisa and John Garton had gone for good.

'Mother, are you there? Where is everyone? Louey where are you?'

Bertie took off his top hat and scarf, handing them to Sarah to put on the hallstand. Abraham went into the sitting room and sat in front of the log fire warming his hands.

'By golly, it's a chilly night tonight.'

Bertie followed his father into the sitting room, pulling up the back of his jacket to warm his rear end in front of the roaring fire.

'Did you notice anything peculiar about Sarah tonight, father? She looked decidedly pale and a bit, well ... distant and nervous. Not like her. Maybe it's my imagination, but I feel something is not quite right around here.'

Bertie lowered his backside even more towards the flames of the fire.

'Feel sorry for any poor devil out on this cold night. I'm taking a time to warm up. I'll ring for some hot drinks. We shall eat in here I think tonight father, what do you say?'

Bertie rang the servants cord.

Abraham poured two whiskies from the cut glass decanter.

'Wonder where your mother is. Not like her to be missing when we get in. Took us a long time tonight though, didn't it son, getting through the traffic. It always seems worst at seven, don't know why. Glad we got those contracts completed though. It was worth the extra hour at the office.'

'Perhaps she has gone to bed early,' Bertie said.

Abraham handed Bertie his drink.

'What's that peculiar noise? Listen, father, like a groan. Can you hear it?'

Bertie and Abraham listened.

'Yes, I do hear it.'

Abraham went into the hall.

'It's coming from upstairs I think.'

The two men went upstairs; as they came closer to Agnes's bedroom, Abraham said:

'My word, it sounds like your mother. I'll go in and see what is wrong. You go downstairs son and call me when the supper arrives. I can't think it is anything serious, your mother having another of her tantrums I would think.'

Abraham opened the bedroom door and saw Agnes sprawled across the bed, her hair loose about her shoulders, her false curls strewn over the bed. She was looking thoroughly miserable, not at all like the usual Agnes, who at any moment of the day or night was impeccable.

'Whatever is wrong, dearest? Please tell me, why all the tears?'

Abraham sat on the edge of the bed and his wife buried her tearful face in his chest.

'Well, my dearest, you will never believe what has happened and I hardly know where to start to tell you. It's Louisa,' Agnes said.

'Louisa! She is not ill ... or dead ...? Not had an accident? Where is she, what has happened?'

Abraham pushed Agnes away from his chest, taking her by the shoulders.

'Well, Abraham dearest, I had no choice, just no choice at all, I had to do it,' Agnes sobbed.

'Do what, dearest?' Abraham became even more worried.

'I threw her out of the house! She's gone off with that rat, that excuse for a man, that John Garton. They are to have a child, Abraham. Our Louisa! Can you imagine that? Our Louisa with a Gentile's baby. She is five months pregnant and we didn't even notice it. Abraham, I never knew I could be so angry with anyone.'

Agnes burst into floods of tears once more, ranting and raving about Louisa and John.

'We must go and find them, Agnes. We can't throw our only daughter out of our home because she is pregnant! Whatever were you thinking about to do such a thing? Where have they gone? I'll get the automobile out and we shall go and search for them right now! I can't believe you did that, Agnes.'

Abraham got up from the bed to leave.

'If you go after them, Abraham, I shall divorce you believe me! I mean it! I shall leave you, be sure of that. Louisa has disgraced our family name and has bedded a Gentile so, she is, in my estimation, worse than dirt. Abraham, don't you dare to go after them!'

Agnes's screams were so loud and ranting that Bertie could not help overhearing.

Abraham once more sat down on the bed, devastated at the loss of his daughter, but knowing Agnes was right. How could they entertain Louisa at Sycamore House ever again? She had betrayed them and was probably best left to John and the life before her. Agnes and Abraham agreed that from that day forward, their daughter would be considered dead and that this would be the message to whomever asked after her.

'Mother, father, did I hear right?'

Bertie had run into the bedroom on hearing Agnes's wailing and screams.

'What do you mean, Louisa has gone with John Garton? Gone where and for how long? Of course she must come back home. This *is* her home! Whatever can you both be thinking of?'

Bertie was on the verge of tears for he couldn't believe the cruelty of his beloved parents.

Abraham stood up.

'Bertie, son, there is nothing more to be said about the subject, nothing! Be told, go home to Jacqueline, be content and happy. You must forget about your sister for she no longer exists. She is to have a child by John Garton and that is the end of it. She has made her bed, now she must lie on it. She is not Jewish any more so she doesn't belong to this family. Just forget her.'

Abraham spoke with a stony coldness Bertie had never known before.

'Forget her? Never! You two might be able to, but I cannot. Never! Jacqueline and I will search for her and we shall find her! She will be in this city somewhere and I intend to find her! I can't believe you two; how could you do this to your own flesh and blood? She and John can live with us if needs be, but I can't erase her from my mind and wonder how you two can think this way.'

The Visitor

Bertie slammed the door as he left the bedroom, vowing that he would find his sister if it took the rest of his life to do it. He had friends in the city, status, he wasn't without money; but his relationship with his parents would never be the same, ever again, he realised that. He would branch out on his own in his business. Start a new business abroad somewhere. He knew he could do it.

'Master Bertie!'

Sarah ran along the hallway seeing Bertie making towards the front door. She hugged him and they both comforted each other in their sorrow.

'Master Bertie, if it's any consolation, John 'as rooms somewhere in the city, but I don't know where. He didn't talk about them much and said sometimes he would tek a girlfriend there, yow know. Perhaps I should not talk of 'im that way, for 'e is like a son to me and Louisa, like a daughter.'

CHAPTER XV

The Reunion

Once more I found myself being dragged through time itself, being pushed faster and faster along my time tunnel. I could hardly breathe. I had been granted my wish; yes here I was in Tower Street in my ghostly form, watching the Garton family reunion. Dora, Gwen, Hilda and Connie were back from the orphanage. John was joyfully hugging his girls with Bert in his arms. Bertie laughed with happiness at the happy reunion. Louisa had obviously given birth to another baby boy in between my comings and goings. This must have been the baby boy she was pregnant with when I last was at Tower Street waiting with her for the girls to return home. I wondered what the boy's name was, but no doubt I would find out soon. Poor Louisa, I thought, she now had six children!

'Me very own girls. Me very own babs.'

John hugged each daughter one by one and kissed the baby, who was somewhat restless in Louisa's arms.

The girls were pleased to be home again and rushed from room to room admiring everything their Uncle Bertie had brought for them; new beds, bed linen, it was like being in Heaven to them. No longer would they have to search the mattress for bedbugs before going to bed. In the bad old days it had been Dora's job to find and kill them, then everyone could go to bed. What a relief to get into clean beds without the bedbug routine.

Dora and her sisters were so impressed, especially admiring the new writing bureau that Uncle Bertie had given their mother. The girls in turn caressed the wood as it shone with rich, inlaid, mahogany luxury. Louisa May clapped her hands to gain everyone's attention.

'Gather around, everyone, I have yet another surprise for you all. Your Uncle Bertie has acquired a wonderful three-bedroomed house for us all, with its very own garden and your own bedrooms! Now what do you all think about that?'

Louisa hugged Connie who looked up into her mother's happy face in utter disbelief. The girls jumped around in excitement at the prospect of their own rooms, smothering their Uncle Bertie's face with kisses of appreciation. Excitement was everywhere, the girls chattering incessantly about their Uncle Bertie and their new home and hardly daring to believe that they

The Visitor

could once more be a complete family in a new house at last! Young Bert started to jump and shout with happiness, copying the girls, simply because they were doing it. He didn't understand what was happening, but he was happy.

'Mother,' Dora said. 'At least we are all here together now and we shall never be parted again. At least baby Alfred will never know the heartache we have all had to face over the past two years, will he?'

'My dearest Dora, you are so caring. No, he won't, thank God.'

Louisa smiled at Dora, then at Bertie and John.

I now knew the baby's name was Alfred.

Bertie also clapped his hands together to gain everyone's attention.

'Girls, girls, Bert, listen! That is not all! Your mother, my dear sister, shall have a real gas cooker, linoleum on all the floors and even proper curtains at all the windows. Your father, well, he shall have plants and vegetables to put in the garden; no good having a garden if you've nothing to put in it!'

Bertie once more threw back his head and laughed loudly with the girls, Bert and John rushing to him hugging him, John shaking his hand vigorously.

'Master Bertie, how can we ever repay yow or thank yow enough, I ...' John wiped a tear of relief from his eyes.

'Now then, why would I need thanks? Less of the Master Bertie, call me Bertie. Anyway, I have the means to help you all, so why shouldn't I put my money to good use and to my family who need it? I Love you all, especially Bert and baby Alfred. He is walking so well now, isn't he Louisa? Having no children of my own, well not yet, how could I let my beautiful nieces and my nephews go without the necessities of life, eh?'

Bertie once more hugged all the girls, for he loved them all dearly. He had got to know them very well and wished he could have his own family. Perhaps one day, he thought.

'The only thing I ask of you girls and your mother,' Bertie drew Louisa's face around to his for her to read his lips, 'is that you must write to me; there is no excuse, now that you have the bureau, there is absolutely no excuse!'

Bertie handed Louisa his card with his new home address printed on it and gave her a wink.

She smiled back gratefully, knowing that Bertie was signalling to her to use the secret drawer in the bureau if she was ever desperate for money. It was such a relief; a security she had not known for a very long time. She would keep the tiny key around her neck on the gold neck chain Jacqueline had given her and make sure she kept it on her person at all times, even when bathing.

A month had passed by and Bertie had arranged for a removal firm to take the Garton family from Tower Street to their new home in Redstone

The Visitor

Farm Road in Hall Green, a suburb of Birmingham.

The day of the house move was so exciting for the girls, as they had only once left Tower Street to be taken away to the orphanage and they watched as all the household furniture was loaded onto the removal lorry. The neighbours watched with great curiosity as the family ran in and out of the small terraced house helping the men to load the lorry. Each neighbour in turn came to say their goodbyes with Louisa hugging each one, especially Margaret Thompson.

'Hope yow get on all right ducks, keep in touch with me won't yow? I hope I can visit yow sometime and yow must visit me.'

Margaret hugged Louisa close to her, as she was a very dear friend.

'Of course,' Louisa said. 'I shall miss you terribly Margaret, but we are not on the other side of the world, so of course we can visit each other, and it's not "goodbye" is it? Alfred is getting a little fractious; I had better get him into the lorry now Margaret. Bye, my dear friend.'

The two women hugged each other for some time.

Louisa May climbed onto the front seat of the lorry sitting baby Alfred on her lap with Bert standing by her side. The girls chatted amongst themselves in the back of the lorry as it was their job to make sure none of the furniture moved when the lorry started up and pulled away. The lorry drove out of Tower Street, with all the neighbours running after it shouting 'good luck' and 'goodbye'. The lorry carefully turned the corner onto the main street leading out of the city towards Hall Green. Louisa thought about all the things that had happened to her and the family when living in Tower Street and, in some respects, was saddened to leave.

A few months had passed by and the Garton family were settling into their new home in Redstone Farm Road, which seemed very spacious after their cramped accommodation in Tower Street. John had managed to secure an outdoor job with Bertie's help, as a street gas lamp maintenance man which gave him a small weekly wage.

Louisa, John, Bert, Alfred and the girls had been to visit Jacqueline and Bertie frequently in Solihull, promising to keep in touch with them after they had emigrated to Montreal. Bertie felt at ease, knowing that Louisa and her family were safe and felt he could continue his business ventures abroad without worrying about his sister. Louisa was very saddened by the news that Jacqueline and Bertie would be thousands of miles away on the other side of the world and possibly she would never see them again. Yes, she would certainly write, every week; she had enough money to post the letters and could use the bureau's secret money to do it. She was sure her brother would be more than successful with his business ventures in Montreal as he had always wanted to go back there after enjoying his honeymoon so much.

The Visitor

Louisa was saddened that her mother and father had not seen her since that fateful day when she left Sycamore House with John, and that they had never seen their grandchildren. She often wondered how they were and how Sarah and Mavis were getting on, but did not dare to contact the servants at the house. Her mother's fury at finding out if she did would get them all into a lot of trouble or even the sack! Bertie gave her snippets of information but nothing very substantial. But never mind, she had her own family now, whom she dearly loved.

Some months later, with the family happily going about their daily routines, Louisa had had no occasion to use any of the cash from the bureau's secret drawer. Bertie and Jacqueline had emigrated to Montreal and Louisa had already written several letters to them, receiving replies to them all. Montreal sounded so wonderful and Bertie and Jacqueline were settling down very well and were very happy. Jacqueline had written with the good news that she was, at last, pregnant herself!

Connie was her usual theatrical self; Louisa and John were convinced that she would be an actress or singer on the stage when she grew up. Hilda was her very independent self, not allowing anyone to help her, and Dora, the sensible one, hard-working and very dependable, guided her sisters wisely. Gwen was confident and defiant, not afraid of anything or anyone. Louisa was only sorry that the secret drawer couldn't fund an art scholarship for Gwen as she was so very clever with colours and any painting. Louisa knew she could not fund the scholarship for Gwen from the secret drawer as John would wonder where the money came from to do this. So the secret drawer would be used as intended, for food and survival.

Louisa smiled to herself as her rosy-faced Bert hugged his reluctant brother, Alfred.

John came in from work very tired that day, much more so than usual.

"Ello my babs! Yow all look very well today.'

John ruffled Connie's black hair, kissed baby Alfred and picked up Bert giving him yet another kiss, which he did not like at all. He dearly loved all his children, but most of all, his Louisa May. He kissed her tenderly on the forehead.

John looked worried and said:

'Bab, I need to talk with yow... um ... can the girls go out to play somewhere and take Bert with them? Something 'as 'appened at work!'

Louisa looked dismayed.

'Girls, can you go and play outside please and take Bert with you. Only for a while. I will call you when your tea is ready. Watch Bert please, don't let him out of your sight girls.'

'Oh, Mum, must we?' Connie was fed up as she wanted to stay and play with baby Alfred.

The Visitor

'Yes, I'm afraid you do have to. Please, off you go. Daddy and I want to discuss something.'

Louisa ushered the girls outside and closed the door behind them, then sat opposite John, still with baby Alfred on her lap.

'Bab, I 'ardly know what to say or where to start. Well, through no fault of me own, well ... I've lost me job!'

'What! Darling, how terrible, but why?'

Louisa could hardly believe it and hugged John close to her as he buried his face in his hands.

'I 'ardly know where to begin to tell yow, Bab! What about the boys and our girls? 'Ow are we to manage now?'

Louisa brushed back John's blond hair and stroked his face.

'We'll manage John. Please try not to worry.'

'Don't worry? I am frantic, Bab.'

'You'll get something else John. Everyone does. There are jobs about. You will see.'

'Yes, yower right. Don't tell the girls yet though. I don't want them worrying about me. I'll tell 'em in good time.'

John took baby Alfred from Louisa's arms as she went into the kitchen to make the tea for the family. He wondered why she didn't cry or curse him but then, perhaps she had learned to be tolerant of his failings after all these years. Louisa knew she was more than safe for she had the secret drawer to turn to. She could take small amounts of money out of the drawer, so as not to alert John's suspicions, which would pay for some food. John had no idea that there was a great deal of money in the bureau's secret drawer. Louisa felt deceitful because she had not involved John in the bureau's secret. But how could she tell him, knowing that he might use the money for alcohol to deaden his pain?

CHAPTER XVI

The Bureau

As John rocked baby Alfred to and fro in his arms, Louisa peeled the potatoes in the kitchen and started to chop the onions into small pieces. She was only thankful that John had grown all their vegetables for the family meals in the garden. She felt loath to use the secret drawer just yet, as things were not that desperate and perhaps John would soon get another job.

The stew she had prepared look appetising. She called the girls and Bert in from playing to eat their meal.

'Girls, Bert, teatime!'

The children came scurrying in to the house, eagerly awaiting their meal as they were always hungry. Louisa May knew she would please Connie with her home-made stew as she always loved to dip her bread into the gravy even though this, as always, was frowned upon by Louisa.

Perhaps tomorrow would bring luck for John in his search for another job. Louisa was determined that the secret drawer of the bureau would not be opened until it was absolutely necessary. She fingered the gold chain around her neck, making sure that the small, gold key was still attached to it. It was! Louisa felt sad when she thought of how deceitful she was towards John, not telling him about the secret drawer. How could she tell him? John had such a drinking problem and if he knew about the money hidden in the bureau he would be bound to take some of it to pay for his dreaded beer! Louisa understood completely; he was in pain most of the time and he needed the beer. However, he was being so good lately and was managing to keep off it and sober. He didn't have the funds to buy beer for he had six children now depending on him. Louisa thought to herself, if only he could keep clear of drinking for a while at least, it would possibly break him of the habit and they could find some other way of controlling his pain. Maybe she could fund a doctor, who would help John, with the proceeds of the secret drawer?

The days and weeks had drifted by with the girls trying to economise as much as possible to help their mother, knowing that their father was out of work. Louisa made more and more stews, as they were so economical for her large family, sometimes making dumplings with them and towards the end of the week, a piecrust over the top of the stew. The stew lasted the

The Visitor

family several days sometimes.

John would walk for miles, queuing for non-existent jobs in the city, being turned down time and time again and becoming very despondent. Louisa was pleased that her girls understood how their father felt, but often wished they could have experienced the life she had known at Sycamore House when a young girl; shopping in large stores in the city and eating at elegant restaurants. Even if she explained about those times to them, she doubted if they would believe her! How my girls would love the experience, she thought.

John could only marvel at Louisa's thrift. How did she manage to feed the family on just a few shillings a week.

One wet afternoon, John returned home after his long job search in the city and passed by the window of a second-hand furniture shop, not far from his house in Redstone Farm Road. The shop was always crowded with people who had an eye for bargains and money to buy them. His thoughts raced. He could sell that stupid bureau Bertie had given Louisa and was sure she wouldn't mind at all when he acquired money for it. After all, it would buy some very good food and nice presents for the girls, Bert and Alfred and perhaps a new hat for Louisa or the vase she really liked. Louisa would probably not notice the missing bureau for days anyway! It was always kept in the sitting room and hardly ever used so yes, he would sell it, but not tell Louisa until he had the money for it; he would surprise her. He would go into the shop and ask the valuer to call when Louisa was out taking the girls to school.

John opened the shop door and went inside. A smartly suited shop assistant came over to him.

'Yes, sir, can we help you?'

John was a little nervous about what he was about to ask and do.

'Well, er ... yow see ... I 'ave this writing bureau. Very nice it is too, inlaid engraving and everything and good wood. A present it was from me missus's brother, who is rich.'

John stumbled on his words for he was not used to negotiating.

'Really, sir?' said the assistant, not really wanting to believe John's story as he looked very poor and he was sure his bureau would be worthless.

'Yes, it would fetch a very good price I am sure. Wondered if yow would come and value it, perhaps buy it of us like? Yow could come round eight thirty tomorrow morning.' John rubbed his hands together in anticipation.

The assistant called over the shop manager to talk to John. He became very interested in the description of the writing bureau and agreed to view it at eight thirty the following morning. John knew Louisa would be out at that time and would not be back from taking the girls to school until well after nine o'clock, so he would have ample time to negotiate the bureau's

The Visitor

worth. Louisa would probably not even notice the bureau had gone! She hardly ever went into the sitting room anyway, as it was reserved for visitors only and kept for very special occasions.

When the bureau is sold, I could go into the city, he thought, buy some presents and the vase Louisa likes, look for a job and go to the pub at the same time. Yes, John was convinced this was the right thing to do.

The following day, Louisa took her girls, Bert and baby Alfred tucked up in his pram, to school as usual, leaving the house promptly at eight thirty. Louisa was never late for anything and always very particular about time keeping, which she passed on to her girls.

At eight thirty-five, the furniture van pulled up outside 99 Redstone Farm Road. Louisa had barely turned the corner of the road. John showed the shop manager into the sitting room to see the bureau.

'So this is it? If I may say so sir, a very fine piece of furniture indeed. You were so right sir! It is a particularly quality piece of furniture and I shall give you a good price, well ...' The shop manager stroked his chin.

John rubbed his hands together in anticipation of an agreed price.

'The bureau woz the wife's brother's, 'e gave it to us. Gone to Montreal now he 'as, so we 'ave no need of it yow see.'

John studied the shop manager's face.

'Yes, it is a good piece? So I shall offer you, say, five guineas for it.'

'Five guineas! It's worth more than that, twice that I would say!'

John was clearly agitated.

'Well, it is second-hand sir? People will say to me, well, it is second-hand! Tell you what, sir, I shall offer you seven guineas and that is my final offer. Take it or leave it sir.'

'I'll tek it.'

John knew the bureau was worth much more, but agreed on the price. Spitting on his hands John offered his hand to the shop manager in agreement but he declined from shaking it. He counted out the money into John's waiting hands and it felt more than good to him. Excitement raced through his whole body at the expectation of spending the money, especially on some beer.

Shouting through the open front door, the shop manager ordered his men who were waiting in the van outside to collect the bureau. They carefully took it out to the waiting van and then drove away. John took his coat from the hook on the wall in the hallway and carefully closed the door behind him, checking each way up and down the road for any sign of Louisa. He could afford the tram fare into the city and would treat all his mates to a drink in the pub. They had often bought him a drink and he had never been able to return the compliment, so now he could with the money he had made from the bureau. John caught the nine fifteen tram into the city.

The Visitor

It was nine thirty in the morning when Louisa returned home with Bert and baby Alfred who was sleeping peacefully in his pram. Louisa hung her hat and shawl on the hook in the hallway, noticing that John's cap and coat had gone. He must have gone out to find work, she thought.

Louisa filled the kettle with water from the kitchen tap and put it on the gas hob to boil. It was such a joy to do that after Tower Street and thank God she no longer had to pump every bit of water from the communal pump in the yard! It was real luxury here with running water inside the house from a tap at the sink and with a real gas cooker to cook on.

What shall we have to eat this afternoon, Louisa thought.

I tried to will Louisa to go into the sitting room for she would surely notice the missing bureau! But no, I suppose there was no good reason for her to go there; after all, she hadn't got visitors and the family did not use the room unless for special occasions. It was always kept spotlessly clean and the best items of furniture and pottery were kept in there. No one was allowed to go in there without permission from either Louisa or John.

I did wish Louisa would go in there! Was my clue something to do with the bureau? Should I have followed the bureau to wherever it was taken by whoever bought it at the store? I just did not know what I was supposed to be learning from Louisa's story.

I watched Louisa drink her tea and peel yet more potatoes and vegetables. The two boys were sleeping peacefully and a few hours had passed by.

Louisa had managed to catch a few minutes' sleep on the sofa during the afternoon whilst the boys slept. She only hoped John had been successful in acquiring a new job. She assumed that was where he had gone.

'Is that you, John? You've been a long time, where have you been?'

John looked red in the face and smiled in an all-too familiar, alcoholic grin. His breath stank of beer.

'John! Whatever have you been doing? Where did you get the money from to get in this state? Tell me! Really, John, I am so very disappointed in you! You promised me and the children, you promised.'

Louisa was extremely angry but John hugged her to him, singing at the top of his voice and waltzing her around and around the room.

'Yower me lady love, yow are me love, me lady love!'

John sang louder and louder, swirling Louisa around until she found herself actually laughing along with him.

'John! Please! Don't be so silly. Why, anyone would think you had found a new job, or better still, come into lots and lots of money or something.'

'I 'ave, I 'ave Bab.' John said, belching loudly.

'Really, John? A new job, money! How wonderful. Where? With whom?'

'Not exactly a new job, Bab, but lots and lots of money! Look!'

John rummaged through his pockets throwing all his remaining money

The Visitor

from the bureau sale up in the air, sending it cascading down to the floor. There were bank notes and coins everywhere.

'Well, Bab, it's a long story, but I 'ave somert else to show yow. Look!'

John took out of his pocket the beautiful cut glass vase Louisa had always admired in a shop window every time they went walking along the local shopping parade, thrusting it into her hands.

'Oh, John, it is so very beautiful. It's the one I always wanted so much and ...'

'I know, Bab. What do yow think of yower John now, eh?'

John leaned over to kiss Louisa's lips, his breath very pungent from the beer, but nevertheless, she kissed him back.

'John, it is so beautiful, I really don't know what to say. Thank you.'

Louisa's long fingers glided over the cut glass patterns; she had always loved cut glass. She continued to question John for she was worried as to where he had acquired so much money.

'Well, Bab, yow won't believe this, but then again, I thought to meself, well, what is that stupid bureau for? What does it do? We can't eat it. No one sits at it. So I sold it.'

John continued to waltz around the room singing the song, 'Lily of Laguna'. Louisa could not believe her ears and sat down on the sofa utterly dismayed at what John had done!

'John! Oh, no! How could you have sold the bureau, how could you? Bertie's bureau, the only link I have with him. You stupid, stupid fool!'

Louisa wept bitterly, covering her face with her hands.

'Bab! What's up? I thought yow would be pleased. Yow hardly used it anyway, did yow and I thought ... well ... we needed things and money so I ...'

'Oh, John, your intentions were good I've no doubt, but you drank again, you promised us you would never do that again! John you promised me and the children you would never ever drink and worse than that ...'

Louisa felt that she should tell John about the secret drawer in the bureau with all the money, jewellery and bonds hidden in it. How did John think they had lived so well for the past few months? Certainly not from his pitiful few shillings a week, but sometimes from the money from the secret drawer. She decided to really shock John and told him about the secret drawer.

'John, I have been less than honest with you, but exactly what I dreaded all these months has now happened.'

'Bloody 'ell Bab, why didn't yow tell me before?'

John found it difficult to stand.

'Well, Bertie made me promise I would keep what was in the bureau a secret, to secure financial stability for the rest of our stupid lives and for the children's sake. He gave us, well me, a considerable amount of money,

The Visitor

bonds and jewellery that were hidden in the secret drawer, to which I have the key around my neck, look! Only I know the combination of the drawer and it wouldn't be apparent to anyone who was just looking at the bureau that there *was* a secret drawer!'

John could only stare at Louisa in disbelief.

''Ow much money was in the drawer Bab?'

'Oh, John, don't ask me, I just don't know. There was at least four to five thousand pounds I should think, plus the bonds and jewellery, but I was to use them only in a real emergency and of course, there was Peter's diamond and sapphire ring. I could have sold the ring, Bertie said. Oh, John what have you done?'

Louisa May sobbed once more.

The girls and Bert rushed into the house laughing and chattering but soon realised that something was very wrong when they saw their mother crying.

'What is it mother, father?'

Gwen put her arms around Louisa.

'Nothing for you to worry about my dears. You can't do anything about it Gwen, but thank you.'

John took Louisa's hand.

'That's where yow wrong Bab. I think there is somert we can do? Girls, look after Bert and Alfred. Yow mother and me 'ave to go out! Won't be too long.'

John took Louisa by the hand and dragged her out of the front door. She just had time to snatch her shawl from the hook on the wall in the hallway as John pulled her outside into the street.

'John, where are you taking me? Where are we going?'

Louisa could hardly keep up with John as he was running so fast. The couple came to the second hand furniture shop, but the bureau was nowhere to be seen in the shop window.

John flung open the shop door.

'There's the bloke who I sold the bureau to. Maybe 'e'll let us 'ave it back. I 'ave some of the money left and we could repay the rest out of the secret drawer, Louisa, but don't say nothing about that to 'im.'

Louisa nodded for she had read John's lips well.

'Yes, sir! Oh! You are the gentleman from Redstone Farm Road! This must be your lovely wife?'

'Never mind that now, mate, 'ave yow still got the bureau I sold yow, the one yow bought from me yesterday? We would like it back please, we will pay for it.'

John impatiently looked around the shop at all the furniture, but the bureau was nowhere there. The shop manager quietly spoke to John, not wanting the rest of his customers upset.

The Visitor

'But, sir, a gentleman came into the shop not long after I had put the bureau on display, he really liked it and bought it! Took it away there and then himself in his own cart, sir!'

Louisa's heart sank for she understood all that the shop manager had said.

'Cheer up Bab. It don't mean that we still can't get it back. We'll get the bloke's name and address who bought it and go and see 'im.'

John smiled at the shop manager whose face flushed.

'I'm afraid, sir, we don't have an address. You see, there was no need to take one, as the gentleman paid in cash and had his own transport to take the bureau away. I am very sorry!'

John's face reddened with temper.

'For God sakes! Well then, which way did this bloke go, did yow notice that?'

The shop manager scratched his head.

'Well, as I remember, he went towards Sparkhill down the Stratford Road way. Well he went left out of here anyway, sir.'

The shop manager pointed along the road.

John once more took Louisa's hand, dragging her out of the shop and across the road to a waiting tram. They both jumped onto it. John gave the ticket collector some money and attentively looked at every house and driveway along the route towards Sparkhill, with Louisa doing the same to see if they could spot the cart as described by the shop manager.

'Come on, Bab! I am so very sorry. I've lost it for yow, ain't I? We are nearly into Stoney Lane, Bab and it's no use now. We shall 'ave to go 'ome. Perhaps we can put an advertisement in the paper or somert for it, but I think it's gone Bab!'

John tried to comfort Louisa as best he could and knew he was in her bad books, perhaps forever. Louisa could only nod for her beloved bureau and only link with Jacqueline and Bertie had gone, she knew, forever, together with her financial security.

Years Later

Surprisingly, Louisa and John's marriage had survived, despite John's recurrent illness and drinking bouts to deaden his pain and of course, the missing bureau, which the family never found. Louisa May went on to bear John three more children, Reginald John (Reg), Edward Joseph (Ted) and Teresa Esther (Tess).

Louisa had become frail and ill in her old age, after years of childbearing. John had drifted more and more towards his painkiller, beer, to deaden the pain from the tuberculosis in his one remaining lung. Louisa had taken small cleaning jobs in big houses to help support the family as John had become

The Visitor

too ill to work, spending many months in sanatoriums. Louisa did the best she could, often sending the eldest daughters out to grand houses to clean, so that their wages would help support the family. The girls did not mind at all and were only too willing to help their mother. Maybe whilst cleaning at the grand houses, it would give them the opportunity to search for the missing bureau? It could be anywhere, even in one of the grand houses.

John often thought about his life. It had been hard and cruel, except for his love for Louisa May. He had little chance of a successful career as he was always ill and there were no drugs to help him. He now only had the strength to do light work; after all, he would get the lamp lighting job back if he swallowed his pride and asked for it. He had noticed his beloved Louisa looking paler and more tired as each day passed by. He couldn't bear to see her like that and he felt it was all his fault.

My ghostly form was being once more catapulted towards Tower Street, which I thought I had left behind forever, and then to 99 Redstone Farm Road, as if something was pushing me from one place to the other. Was there yet still something I needed to know? I certainly hadn't discovered what it was. Why had I been chosen to observe these things and this woman, Louisa May Garton, née Hirons? I still did not understand her story, why she had chosen me to tell it, or the disjointed way in which she had collected me to observe her life. I just hadn't found any clue about what it was she wanted me to know, if there was a clue.

Strangely, here I was in my ghostly form suspended in mid-air, would you believe, in a hospital ward? I guessed that I was in Birmingham, judging by the accent around me. I looked about and saw signs on the walls of the hospital ward saying, Selly Oak Hospital.

My ghostly form was ushered towards a small group of people gathered around a hospital bed and studying them all closely, I recognised them as people I actually knew. They all looked so familiar, but I didn't recognise the old, white-haired woman lying so still in the bed. Who was she? As I studied her more closely, she suddenly opened her eyes and looked straight at me! Those heavy-lidded black eyes were unforgettable. Yes, it was ... it was Louisa May. She was white-haired now and old and looked so ill.

It took me some time to realise that the people around her bed were her children, now adults! The old white-haired man sitting by her bedside holding her hand was John Garton. Horror-struck, I thought, she couldn't be dying, could she? Oh, no! Not yet, please Louisa! I don't know what it is you want me to find out or know about you. You haven't shown me. I tried to shout out to her, but she was slipping away fast into death's clutches.

What year was this? It must be the early 1950s by the style of clothing. What did it matter anyway? Poor Louisa May was dying and I hadn't helped her at all by discovering her secret. She had gone through all this for me and I was not clever enough to help her. I felt so angry with myself.

Suddenly, Louisa sat bolt upright in her bed looking straight at me and pointing her long slender finger towards me. Of course, everyone around her bed looked in the direction of her pointed finger, but could see nothing. Obviously, they could not see me for I was a mere ghost!

'What is mother smiling at, Hilda?'

Dora brushed back Louisa's thick white hair.

'To think mother had such beautifully long, thick, black hair when she was younger,' Dora said.

'I don't remember her having black hair, Dora.'

Connie took her mother's hand in hers for she knew she was near to death.

'Oh mummy,' she said.

Everyone looked down at her and wept as Louisa May took her last gasp of life with no fuss, no screaming or lurching about, just peacefully and calmly with dignity, as she had led her life. Louisa May had died.

As my ghostly self, I could only observe in complete disbelief. How would I get back to my own time now that she was dead? Who was going to take me back? She couldn't? Would I remain a ghost forever? I had failed her anyway for she had obviously depended on me to find something out and relay it to her family. I was sure of that. Yes, I had definitely failed to find out what it was and failed my mission. She was gone ... dead. I was so angry with myself for not trying harder to pick up her clues. Perhaps I had to follow the girls now or maybe, Ted, Alfred, Reg, Bert or Tess? Perhaps they would hold the clue for me?

I watched the family leave one by one and the nurses drew the curtains around Louisa's hospital bed. I was left suspended in mid-air, no one in the hospital ward aware of my ghostly presence. I sighed. I was completely bewildered.

Suddenly, I was aware of gardenia perfume filling the air all around me but I was so used to the scent that I paid little attention to it. As it became more and more pungent, I began to move, swirling about as I had done on so many occasions before. I just couldn't believe it. It couldn't possibly be my Louisa, for she was dead. But then, she had always been dead!

I heard Louisa's infectious, giggling laughter coming closer and as I looked all around the hospital ward for her, there she was, beckoning me to join her. She was young again, about seventeen years old, dressed in her Edwardian clothes and looking so very beautiful. At either side of her were two young men, holding each of her hands. Her hair was once more long, thick and black, cascading down over her shoulders. All three ghostly visitors were suspended in mid-air, just like myself, hovering over the hospital ward and they all looked so happy! I also felt happy that she had come back to me as I had grown very fond of her and still needed to pick up her clue and

The Visitor

to know her secret. Who were the two young men? I thought I recognised one as Peter Dupont, but I didn't know the other just for a moment.

Louisa May once more beckoned me to join her, but somehow I couldn't move. I was pinned to the spot. I could only observe her from one end of the hospital ward. Who was the other young man with her? As all three came closer I saw I was right for one was Peter, dashing and handsome and the other, yes, now I knew, it was Bertie, her brother. He must also be dead, I thought.

There was a strong breeze blowing my clothes and hair as all three came closer towards me. I felt myself being prodded and I knew it was Louisa May doing it and I found myself being swirled around and around. She did not want to leave me for she tried to pull me along with all three ghostly beings, but I was unable to move. Some force was keeping me firmly pinned down in the hospital ward. Louisa May obviously liked me as much as I had grown to like her and I only wished I could have been mortal and alive at the turn of the twentieth century to have known her in the flesh. We would have been such good friends, I am sure of that.

Louisa laughed and laughed. Her laughter became louder and louder, until I had to cover my ears as the sound of it penetrated my brain and was actually hurting my ears. I felt sick and dizzy, but yet very happy, as Louisa always made me feel happy when she visited me. I realised she had gone back to the happiest point in her life when she had loved Peter Dupont and that was how she wanted to stay for eternity.

Peter, Bertie and Louisa were joined in their ghostly forms by a small infant holding on to Louisa's hand and I realised that this must be her baby who died, the father being Peter Dupont. They were all together now, which made me feel very happy. Peter, Bertie and Louisa turned away from me and started to fade into the distance and as they did so, Louisa May turned once more and glanced back at me. I really did want to go with them, but I just couldn't move.

'Please stay, don't go!' I shouted.

Louisa waved and giggled, unfastening the gold chain around her neck and throwing it through the air towards me. It landed at my feet. Louisa laughed hysterically, louder and louder, pointing at the neck chain and myself and I knew she wanted me to pick it up and keep it. I did pick it up and noticed a tiny gold key at the end of the chain.

'Yes, I have it Louisa,' I shouted.

As I looked up, Louisa May was being led away by Peter and Bertie, blowing me kisses as she went, still pointing at the gold chain and key.

'Louisa!' I shouted. 'I know now what it is you want of me! This is the key to the …'

It was true, yes, this was the key to Bertie's bureau! I knew now what it

The Visitor

was she wanted me to do. She wanted me to find the bureau! I had the key to the secret drawer, but where would the bureau be after all these years? Where would I start to search for it?

'Louisa May! Come back! Please come back! Don't leave me now!'

It was no use for I knew she had gone, perhaps forever. Would I ever see her again? But I had the gold chain and the key ... it was entrusted to me to find the bureau and, surely I now knew the significance of Louisa's visitations and story, even though very disjointed. I was to locate the bureau, Bertie's bureau, find the secret drawer and give the contents of it to Louisa May's remaining family.

If any of my readers know of such a bureau, perhaps they would contact me. I doubt if they would find the secret drawer for only I know the secret combination of opening it, as I have the key!